OUT OF BOUNDS

Also by Mike Seabrook from The Gay Men's Press

UNNATURAL RELATIONS

CONDUCT UNBECOMING

OUT OF BOUNDS

Mike Seabrook

THE GAY MEN'S PRESS

First published 1992 by GMP Publishers Ltd,
P O Box 247, London N6 4BW, England
Reissued in The Gay Men's Press Collection 1996

A CIP catalogue record for this book
is available from the British Library

Distributed in North America by
Inbook/LPC Group,
1436 West Randolph Street, Chicago, IL 60607

Distributed in Australia by Bulldog Books,
P O Box 300, Beaconsfield, NSW 2014

Distributed in South Africa by Judith Wengrove Agencies,
P O Box 1080, Northcliff 2115

Printed and bound in the EU by The Cromwell Press,
Melksham, Wilts, England

AUTHOR'S NOTE

This story is true.

So is that statement; but it needs a little elaboration if it is not to mislead.

Most novels contain a statement by the author that all the characters and their activities are entirely fictitious, bearing no relation whatsoever to any real person, living or dead. Yet everybody knows, if they think about it, that this conventional disclaimer is an absurdity. Certainly, every author who prefaces his book with it knows it. The truth is, as R. F. Delderfield once wrote, that no-one ever *invented* anyone. One suspects strongly that it's usually a case of only the names being changed to protect the guilty (and occasionally, I suppose, the innocent — though one wonders why they should want *their* names changed).

Be that as it may, all the characters in this story are fictitious in their details — names, appearance, ways of behaving and, mainly, in the dialogue I have ascribed to them; but in essence, it all happened.

I have taken, for the usual reason of dramatic expediency, one very small liberty with current legal procedure. I mention it only for the benefit of purists.

I am very grateful to the Koninklijke Nederlandse Cricket Bond, and in particular to its administrator, Mr Alex de la Mar, for his kindness in taking time off from much more important duties to give me valuable information about Dutch cricket. And of course, I am more indebted than this note can express to my wife, Perviz, whose contribution was, as always, great.

The book is dedicated to the memory of my beloved friend, the late Barry Lucking, Club Captain of Sheringham CC, who loved the game as passionately as anyone I ever knew and understood it better than most. There are no words fit to be said of how I miss him; but he was a cricketer, and a man, I am glad I had the privilege of knowing. I hope they play cricket wherever he is.

BOOK ONE

PARTNERSHIPS

"...*la voiture franchissait un portail et Xavier reconnaissait l'amertume des vieux buis.* The carriage... er... *franchir*... yes, turned in at a gate, and Xavier recognized the, er... the smell, I suppose, sir, is it?"

"Carry on for the moment", said Graham Curtis. He nodded to the boy, who frowned in concentration.

"Xavier recognized the smell of old... old... *buis*... should that be *bois*, sir? the smell of old woods?"

"Not bad for a guess", said Graham, "but wrong. *Buis* is 'box' — the wood of that name. As in Box Hill, in Surrey. There are acres of them there. It's a kind of tree. Very tight, dense foliage. They used to be very popular as ornamental trees in country estates and suburban lawns. So, 'Xavier recognized the *amertume* of old box.' *Amertume*, anybody?" The form looked blankly at him. "Aroma?" suggested someone. "No, more than that", Graham went on. "No-one know? 'Bitterness'. Xavier recognized the bitterness — but here clearly he means 'the bitter scent' — of old box. But it would be better style to say 'ancient', wouldn't you agree? And I think we can do better than 'recognized' for *reconnaissait*, don't you? Any ideas?"

"More like 'detected', sir?" said a lanky, studious boy at the back. "'Picked up' the bitter scent?"

"Yes, good, Silvani", said Graham encouragingly. "But there is the 're' prefix, and you must do it justice. So there's the element of repeatedness, of 'again', as well as your idea of 'picking up'. Back to you, Stubbs."

"Yes, sir... Xavier picked up *anew* the bitter scent of ancient box-trees", translated Stubbs.

"Not bad. But a bit archaic. I'd tackle it differently, by importing a completely new word, not needed in the French. 'Xavier caught the familiar, bitter scent of ancient box-trees.' Still, not bad, Stubbs, not bad at all. That'll do from you. Go on from there, Hill." There was silence, broken by a faint titter as the class all looked over towards the open sash window at the back of the room. "Hill", repeated Graham, crescendo. The silence continued, and the titter spread among the boys.

Through the window came the echoing "crack!" of a cricket ball struck in the middle of a bat, followed by a distant but clearly audible cry of "Shot, Paul", drifting in on a swirl of summer breeze. It was followed by a discordant, jangling crash as a heavy bunch of keys landed on the desk by the window, and then by a yelp of surprise from the boy sitting there. "Wow!" Startled, the boy spun round to face Graham, and immediately went bright red as he glanced round and saw everyone looking at him and grinning.

"Oh! I... I, er... Sorry, sir", he stammered.

Graham sighed gently. "I suppose it's probably asking too much, Hill, but I wonder if we might have the pleasure of your company", he said in exaggeratedly long-suffering tones. "Not all the time — that would be asking the impossible — but perhaps just now and again...?" Seeing that the boy had no idea of what had been going on, he went on "I was wondering if you might care to favour us with a translation of the next passage. But I don't suppose you know where the next passage is?"

"I, er... no, sir", muttered Hill, the blush deepening.

Graham sighed again under his breath, stepped down off the dais and strolled towards the back of the room. Coming to rest beside Hill's desk, he looked sadly down at the copy of *Le Mystère Frontenac* where it lay unopened in front of the boy. Tut-tutting in mild exasperation, he found the page and thrust it at Hill. "*Deux pavillons, construits...*" he said, indicating the passage with a finger, and making a small private bet with himself. "Give us a version of this passage, if you will", he murmured in mock courtesy.

"Er... *deux pavillons, construits par l'arrière-grand-père...*" read the boy.

Graham allowed him to read to the end of the paragraph. "All right, Master Hill", he said gravely. "You read French very well.

Let's see how you construe it." He folded his arms and waited, turning as he did so to glance out of the window towards the match in progress on the First XI pitch across the wide quadrangle.

Hill translated fluently and confidently. "'Two pavilions, built by their great-grandfather, disfigured the eighteenth century monastery that had been home to so many generations of Frontenacs...'"

"Hmmm. Yes. Very good", commented Graham, surprised. "None the less, you've won my bet for me, Master Hill." The boy looked up at him, puzzled. "I had a bet with myself", elaborated Graham, "having seen where your attention was concentrated. I didn't think a mind so firmly billeted with the First XI would miss a chance of mistranslating *pavillons* as 'pavilions'. It's 'wings', you idiot child, *'wings'* — since when did monasteries in Bordeaux have pavilions? Oh, good shot!" he ejaculated, and brought his palms together in a single sharp clap. The titter of the class swelled to a full-throated gust of laughter. Graham, after a momentary flicker of annoyance, a little reluctantly but sportingly joined in. A second later the bell went.

"All right", said Graham. "Read on for prep. I'll expect you to be ready to translate to the end of Chapter 3 by next time. You can clear off now. Quietly!" he bellowed at the top of his voice as they began slamming desk-lids, scraping chair-legs and heading for the door in a thundering herd. He moved to the door himself. It was games afternoon, and he was keenly anticipating watching the School XI's match to its conclusion. Waiting for the knot of boys to untangle itself in the doorway, he found Hill beside him. "Going to watch the match, Stephen?" he asked amiably.

"Yes, sir", said the boy, his face alight with pleasure at the prospect. "It's the County Club and Ground side today. Should be a good match."

They walked together through the dusty, institutional corridors, past the chemistry laboratories and out into the sunlight. A blustery breeze was swirling the litter about in the quadrangle, and the sun was thin and without warmth. "You'll be in the First XI yourself before long judging by your form this term, I should think, Stephen", observed Graham as they strolled companionably towards the field.

"Hope so, sir", said Hill, his face lighting up at the prospect. "I'd certainly like to — there's nothing I'd like more than to get my colours. But it's a very strong side. They've got so many good batsmen it's like waiting for dead men's shoes, really. Still, they haven't got a regular off-spinner, sir, so I live in hope."

They came to the field. "Walk round?" suggested Graham, and they began their first circuit of the boundary. As they strolled, talking cricket shop, he saw that the boy's head never turned away from the game. "Cricket means a lot to you, doesn't it, Stephen?"

"Shot, Paul!", called Stephen before there was time for reply. Then he turned a bright face briefly to the master and said "Oh, yes, sir. I've been keen on the game ever since I was a little boy, but I really fell in love with it when I was thirteen — when our Under Fifteens went on tour, you remember, sir?" The boy's face clouded a little as he recalled the time.

"Yes, I remember", murmured Graham. "Wasn't there a bit of trouble over that tour?"

"There certainly was", said Stephen, with an edge of bitterness coming instantly into his voice.

***

"...But Dad", he had protested, "I've been picked for the Under-Fifteen XI. It's a... an honour. I mean, not everybody gets selected. There's a lot of competition for places in the side. A hell of a lot. *Everybody* wants to get into the side — it's representing the school. And it doesn't cost much. Only thirty pounds. And we get to play on some of the best school grounds in the country. Please, Dad", he said for the tenth time since the storm had broken. His ear unerringly picked up the note of pleading, almost desperation, which he had sworn to himself that he would not allow to creep into his voice, and he spared a moment for a fleeting but savage flash of rage and self-contempt. "I've *promised*, Dad. Surely you can see that."

"I see that you've seen fit to make arrangements on your own behalf, without doing us the elementary courtesy of even mentioning that it was in your mind", said his father in judicial tones. "Your mother and I wouldn't mind so much if you'd had the common manners to give us some sort of warning, so we could think about it. More to the point, we would then have had a chance to let you know what we were planning for the holiday. As it is, if you will keep secrets, make your own arrangements in this...this underhand fashion, you can't complain if you then find that we've made arrangements also. No, Stephen, you've got yourself into this mess, you'll have to get yourself out of it. In any case, I'm not throwing good money after bad by subsidizing this scheme of yours having already laid out a considerable sum on the holiday — the very luxurious and exciting holiday, I may say — that your mother and I have arranged."

"But Dad", he repeated yet again, "I wasn't keeping secrets. I didn't know I'd been selected until last week, and there was no point in saying anything then, because they didn't know if I could go on tour. I wouldn't be going now if Rutherford hadn't got injured. There's only room for fifteen players. Mr Page only told me officially this morning. *Please*, Dad, you *must* let me go. If it's only the money, I've got thirty pounds of my own that I was saving for that new bat..." He shot a furtive glance from under his eyelashes at his father's face, and saw immediately that it was hopeless; but he pressed on as best he could.

"Surely", he urged, "you're always telling me how glad you are to see me representing the school at things, taking part and all that. You should be glad I've been picked like this. It's an honour, like I said."

His father pursed his lips and looked gravely at him, with the expression on his face of one determined at all costs to be fair and do justice dispassionately. "I see that you think more of your cricketing chums than you do of the family that do their best to plan interesting and enjoyable holidays for you", he said eventually, in the same maddening, more-in-sorrow-than-in-anger tone. The more heated his son grew the calmer and more judicial his tone became, the more implacable his determination to proceed with his own plans. "However, let's see what your mother thinks", he added. Stephen suppressed a snort, knowing perfectly well that his mother would do what she always did when faced with a conflict of interests between her husband and her son. "Judith, what are your views?"

"I agree with you, Anthony, of course", she said in the gentle, ever-so-slightly hurt tone she reserved for occasions when her son dared to prefer his own ideas to those prepared for him by his parents. "You must be reasonable, Stephen, dear", she went on, turning to him and bestowing a gentle, indulgent smile. "After all, you know very well that when we plan things, it's you we're thinking of, first and foremost."

"Huh!" He was finally unable to suppress any longer the snort of contempt that he had been manfully keeping out of his voice up to then — as long as he thought there was any realistic possibility of persuading them to see his point of view. Giving that idea up, he let it out, curling his lip in an ugly sneer. He was almost in tears, born of frustration, anger, and a familiar feeling that he recognized all too well from past experience of trying to persuade his parents to see his point of view. He sought for the word that expressed this feeling, of being manipulated, of an argument permitted in the furtherance of an affected fairness, while the result was all the time a foregone conclusion. He found the word, and strove to keep his voice quiet and level. "Bullshit!" he said in a jeering tone.

"Stephen!" ejaculated his mother, affecting shocked surprise.

"There's no need whatever for that kind of language, please, Stephen", said his father. "Especially in front of your mother. And don't you think you're a little above trying to secure your own way by indulging in childish tantrums and the language of a spoilt little boy — a little too old for that kind of thing?"

"If I'm too old for that kind of thing, I'm too old to be treated as if I *was* a little boy", he snapped. "And it is bullshit, anyway — the whole of the way you treat me is bullshit. All this stuff about bending over backwards to be fair, and how you're always thinking of me first when you make plans... how come I'm never consulted when you're making them, then? I didn't even know you'd planned this holiday until tonight, and I wouldn't've known now if I hadn't dared to have a mind of my own, would I? As for me being anything to do with it, well, if I've told you once I've told you a thousand times what I think of that prison in the Algarve. If you don't know by now what I think of those flash holidays we have down there, you ought to. And you don't know. You haven't got a clue, and the reason is cos you're far too busy taking in all the flash restaurants and swimming pools and all your rich pals in that little England down there to have five minutes to even notice what I'm thinking of it all. You forget I'm there five minutes after we get off the plane."

"I see", said his father quietly. "Well, perhaps you'd better enlighten us, then. What do you think of our carefully planned holidays in Portugal?"

"They bore me stiff", snapped Stephen; and, deciding that he had gone so far that he no longer had anything left to lose, added "They bore me bloody brainless. That's what I think of them. Which is why I jumped at it when I got the chance of going on the cricket tour." And as he said at last what he had been minded to say many times before, his resolve stiffened, and he decided to go for broke. "It's why I'm going on the cricket tour", he said, his voice rising and almost cracking as apprehension rose sharply up his gorge. He let that sink in for a few moments. Then he gave them a defiant glare, swung round and stamped out of the room.

In morning break the next day he secured an urgent, whispered conference with the games master who was running the cricket tour. At lunchtime he slipped out of school and withdrew his entire balance of forty-seven pounds from the post office, and in the afternoon break he handed the lot to the games master, who promised to telephone his parents the same evening.

***

"And in the end I got it", he said, concluding his account of the affair to Graham. "I don't know what Jack — I mean, Mr Page — said to them, but they let me go. And I've never been on another family holiday in Portugal since. Or anywhere else for that matter. They take their flash snob-holidays in Switzerland, kidding themselves they can ski, and all over the place. I go on the school tour, and we don't even bore each other talking about what we've been up to."

"Did they ever say anything about what Jack Page said to them?" asked Graham interestedly.

"Only one thing", muttered Stephen. "They said I was an ungrateful little sod for not being suitably impressed by all the time everybody'd been spending on making plans for me. The fact that I'm not party to something isn't supposed to make any difference to that. Yes, they said that after all they'd done for me it was bloody ungrateful to treat their comfortable home like a doss-house. That was the word they majored on — ungrateful is what I am.

"Not that they used precisely those words, mind you. They're far too respectable to use language like that. But you could see that's what they'd have liked to say, if it wasn't letting themselves down in front of me. When the old man was giving me a dressing down for saying 'bullshit' he actually said 'there's no need *whatever* for language like that'. 'Whatever' — can you believe it? Prissy bastard."

"You're not very happy at home?" said Graham. He said it in a casual tone; but he watched closely as the boy pondered the question.

After some time Stephen spared a few moments from the cricket to glance at him. "Is anybody?" he said lightly. Graham looked sharply at him, but his expression was inscrutable. He let it go for the time being, and they continued ambling round the boundary.

A few minutes later, however, somewhat to his surprise, Stephen returned to the subject. He had obviously been thinking about it while they strolled. "It's not exactly that I'm unhappy", he said, sounding anything but happy as he spoke. Graham stopped, briefly applauded a cover drive and prepared to suspend interest in the match. If the boy needed someone to confide in he was willing to abandon his planned afternoon's spectating in a good cause. He gave attention.

"It's more that I feel as if..." Stephen trailed into silence as he strove to find words. "As if, somehow, I'm alien", he said at last. "That's it, really. Alien. I feel like some sort of cuckoo, as if I was the milkman's, and they both know it, but they're preserving a decent silence about it, for the sake of the family name, you know." He stared gloomily at the ground for a moment, but then, suddenly, he laughed. "Come to think of it", he said, in a much merrier tone, "that's just about what they would do if that was the way things were. Like I said, they're a pair of prissy bastards. A pair of Pooters", he said, laughing again. "I've just been reading that book, and I kept wondering why everybody else raved about it while I just found it horribly depressing. I was wondering what was wrong with me. Of course! Why didn't I realize?

"Does that tell you anything about how it is at home, sir?" he asked after a further pause.

Graham found himself considering the boy with more interest than he had shown in him before. He had always considered him an agreeable, bright member of his year, with a friendly manner and a pleasant look about him; but he had never paid him any special attention, other than marking him down as a cricketer of promise, and therefore to be watched closely as an investment for the House XI, which Graham ran. Now he perceived an unsuspected depth of articulacy, and even wit, in him which, he thought, would repay attention.

"To begin with, I really wish you'd drop the 'sir'", he opened. "It's a pretty formality in classes, a little tiresome but necessary in the main; but you're too old for it here – and I'm too young for it, I hope." He saw the boy acknowledge the small privilege with a brief smile, no more, and Graham's dawning respect for him took another small step forward. "I'm Graham to my friends", he went on. "As for what you say about your home, I know all too well what you're talking about. I'm constantly appalled by what I see and hear of people's families. I really do wonder if Plato's idea of state crèches wouldn't be a better bet sometimes. I've got a private theory that if we took a poll of the entire middle and upper school, somewhere round eighty per cent of the boys would vote for the idea..." He fell silent for twenty or thirty yards. "There aren't many who are desperately unhappy", he said quietly, as if he was thinking aloud more than addressing Stephen. "But the sense of alienation, of not belonging, is the commonest childhood ailment among the prosperous British middle class, I think..."

There was a further long silence, which they were both too occupied with their own thoughts to break. It was broken instead by a sudden howl from the middle, which made them both jump. "Hmm. Pity", commented Graham as the school's star opening bat began the walk to the changing room, swiping his bat against his pads in annoyance. "Still, forty-six for one, that's not bad. Shall we go on?" They continued their walk.

"I... er... I think there's something a bit more to it than just middle-class-itis with me, si... er, Graham", said Stephen, a little tentatively, after a few more paces. He halted and watched as the incoming batsman took guard, twiddled his bat nervously in the crease and prepared to receive his first delivery from the county side's rather fast, and very hostile opening bowler. "Well kept out", they said in chorus, as the batsman played a nasty rising short ball down into the gulley. "Nasty one to get first ball", said Graham, clapping the stroke as the batsman wrung his jarred bottom hand. They watched in silence as the boy played out the rest of the over without mishap.

"What's the extra problem, then?" Graham asked as the field changed.

Stephen half turned towards him and he just caught the tail end of a sharp, speculative look in the boy's large grey eyes. He deliberately turned his attention to the game to give the boy the chance to decide whether to confide or not. Eventually Stephen said "It's really just that they disapprove of everything I do, or even think, as far as I can see.

"For instance", he went on after a pause, "I joined the Labour Party about a year ago. I never said anything, just did. I wasn't particularly keeping it a secret, or anything silly like that. I didn't really think about it much... just joined, because I'd decided I wanted to, and — well, if I'd thought about it I suppose I'd have realized they wouldn't like it specially, but I really didn't think it would matter — you know, make any difference to anything. But the first time the party newspaper came through the letterbox, well, really, you'd have thought I'd... well, it was as if I'd signed up for the IRA, or stuck a poster of Colonel Gadaffi in the front window or something...

"Well, there was a proper bloody Spanish inquisition about it. You wouldn't believe it, sir — Graham. Really, you would not have believed the fuss it caused. It was like a Victorian melodrama..."

"I've got a private theory", said Graham softly, "that life doesn't imitate art. It imitates melodrama. I used to think, for many years, that Othello was one of the silliest plays Shakespeare wrote. All that catastrophe, and all caused by something as piddling as a handkerchief. Well, I've long since revised that opinion. I now think he was closer to reality with that one than most. Nearly all the really dramatic rows and crises in your life will be sparked off by something just as trivial and piddling as that, I think you'll find. And you seem to have started finding that out pretty early. Not a bad thing, I'd say, Stephen... Dear God in heaven, look at that!" he added in a groan as the new batsman played an atrocious cross-batted smear at a perfectly innocuous, but perfectly straight long-hop and was bowled neck and crop. He glanced at the distant scoreboard and grunted. "Humph! Fifty-eight for two. What in God's name did he think he was doing...?"

They strolled on, watching anxiously as the fourth batsman took guard and then as he negotiated the first two overs and began to look a little more confident, before Stephen resumed his confidences.

"Then there was another almighty bust-up when I refused to go to church any more", he said. Graham watched his face as a series of expressions chased each other across his fair, regular features. Anger followed dismay, and was followed by a baffled, puzzled frustration, and the lot were replaced by a strangely old and wise half-grin, suggesting to the increasingly admiring Graham that the boy possessed a strong and invaluable sense of the ridiculous. "I'd been going ever since I was a kid", he eventually continued, "and I'd carried on going mainly because I couldn't be bothered to stop — to break the habit, you know?" Graham nodded, understanding.

"Well, I hadn't actually believed any of it for years", he went on. "I'd decided by the time I was about ten that it was all a lot of superstitious nonsense. But I quite enjoyed the hymns..."

"I like the hymns myself", assented Graham. "They're bloody good tunes, and it's a good yell, as a very fine choral singer of my acquaintance would put it. Sorry. Go on."

"Well, I started to feel a couple of years ago that I simply couldn't sit there and listen to all that crap any more. I mean, in a way, I think I felt that I had too much respect for the church to carry on... you know what I mean? As if I was insulting decent, sincere people, who really believed in what they were doing, and meant what they said: it seemed — oh, I don't know, just somehow not right, that I should be sitting there silent, me, an atheist, and not — not saying anything. And yet there's no way I could do anything. I tried getting the vicar into conversation one Sunday after the service, and he obviously didn't mind discussing things. But my parents did. I got a royal bollocking for it when we got home. Not for trying to argue theology with him, but for..." He hesitated, searching for the word.

"Rocking the boat?" suggested Graham. "Introducing a wholly unwanted element of questioning and thought into a comfortable, reassuring Sunday ritual? Oh yes, you won't be forgiven lightly for that. You have to understand these rituals — for a start you have to understand that virtually the whole of English middle-class life is governed by such rituals. They don't mean much — most of them go so far back into the mists of antiquity that they lost whatever meaning they ever had — if any — several centuries ago. But disturb them, and God help you."

Stephen grinned, from the sheer pleasure of finding himself understood, and hearing his own incipient, barely formulated yet strongly felt convictions so clearly and precisely enunciated. "You've got it, s... Graham", he said excitedly. "That's *exactly* the feeling I had. And it's exactly what my parents didn't like me doing. So, of course, I said I wasn't going to church again, and honestly, you'd have thought I'd sprouted horns and a tail on the spot! And d'you know what hurt and irritated me the most of all?"

"I think I could have a shrewd guess."

"Go on then, sir. Graham."

"That it wasn't that you were no longer a believer that was important, or that you thought the entire apparatus of religion was absurd self-deceiving superstitious mumbo-jumbo, but that you weren't going to church. I imagine there was quite a lengthy part of the proceedings devoted to the text of 'What The Neighbours Were Going To Think?'"

"Spot on, sir", cried Stephen, laughing aloud in his delight at finding such understanding. "I suppose", he said, calming and looking shrewdly at Graham, "that we all think we're the first one this sort of thing's happened to... and then we're all ridiculously surprised when we find that someone else has been through it all before, and it's all old hat?"

This time it was Graham who felt a *frisson* of pleasure at the quick intelligence revealed. Without thinking about it at all, he gave Stephen a grin, expressing pure delight in his company; Stephen spontaneously gave an identical grin in return; and that was the moment when the first bond was formed. Until that moment they had been master and pupil, an ordinary, pleasant schoolboy, fair of face and able in class, but one who did little in general to stand out from the hundreds of others around him, and a master, sharp of wit, tongue and intelligence, who had no special favourites and no victims at all, who had marked the boy's presence and his attainments, but otherwise taken no special notice of him in the crowd. From the moment when they exchanged grins, acknowledging each other's intelligence and marking out the common areas of their experience, they were on the first steps towards becoming friends.

They walked on once more. As they made circuit after circuit of the field, commenting on the match as it progressed unevenly on its way, the talk became general. It was the experience that comes the way of many people when, often apparently by the merest chance, they strike up an unexpected friendship with an especially enlightened schoolteacher, or by some genetic accident chances to be on similar wavelengths. In that afternoon as they watched the cricket Stephen's horizons began for the first time in his life to broaden in distances large enough to be measurable. Graham talked of numerous things, never like a schoolmaster, and often descending to flippancy when he felt it judicious; but he managed to implant into Stephen's mind a series of suggestions for future reading that the boy declared happily would be regarded as positively subversive by his parents. When they parted at the end of the afternoon Stephen would please Graham by heading straight for the library in search of John Stuart Mill.

Meanwhile Graham felt certain that there was something else that Stephen had not yet felt confident enough to speak of which was at least a part of the underlying unhappiness at home. But he was far too wise to risk undermining the boy's new-found confidence by pressing him, and he let it lie, feeling fairly sure that it would come out when the boy was ready, and that it was almost certainly nothing to necessitate any anxiety in the meantime.

"...ah, it's tea", said Graham. "Come on, let's go and swipe a bun. I want words with that Roger Hillier. He ought to be disembowelled with a blunt pig-sticking device for that shot he got out to." They turned off the boundary and walked across the field to where the teams were milling about on the grass and taking their tea from trestle tables. "Who do you play for at weekends?" Graham asked as they arrived at the wicket and stooped simultaneously and automatically to press fingers into the strip, assessing the surface.

Stephen stared at him, momentarily taken by surprise by the question, and by its underlying assumption that he must play for someone in his leisure time. "Oh! Well, I, er... I don't play for anybody, actually", he said, causing Graham to stare back in his turn, in considerably greater surprise. "You don't?" he said, astonished. "Good lord. Don't you want to, then?"

"Er, well, no, it's not that", said the boy in mild confusion. "It's just that I've never really got to know a club. I suppose I've always had other things to do, and..." He hesitated, then blurted out "It's my parents, I'm afraid. They don't approve of cricket. I have thought about it, actually. A lot. But when I've mentioned it, well, it's always got such a frigid reception... They said cricket clubs were dens of iniquity where they'd try to get me drunk and... and... well, to be honest, si...Graham, I'm not sure quite what they're afraid of. All I do know is, they've never wanted me to join one, and I... well, I've just never found one, I suppose."

"They don't want to lose you, I'd suspect", murmured Graham. "That's the usual reason." He straightened up. "Ought to take spin in the second innings", he said, and began making for the tea-drinkers. "Look here", he said as they reached the boundary, "would you like to play for my club? It's local. You live in the town, I take it?" Stephen nodded. "Well, you must know of us — we're very strong: we play in the local league, and won it the season before last. I'd be glad to put you up for membership, and I reckon, from what I've seen of you in the last couple of House matches, you'd walk into our Twos. We're a friendly crowd, and you don't have to get drunk after the match. Most of them do, but it's not actually compulsory. I'll be quite happy to reassure your parents, if they make trouble for you. I'm sure you'd like us."

"Which club is it?" asked Stephen, his eyes alight as he thought about the proposition. "The Town?"

Graham snorted in derision. "Huh! That bunch of National Westminsters? Good God no, my dear child. We stuff them twice a year as regular as clockwork. No, I play for Elderton Park — we're far stronger than the town. You must know where we play. So why don't you give us a try? You're going to have to find a club

22

to play for some day soon, when you leave here if not before, and I'd hate to see a good off-spinner wasting himself on the Town or somebody like it. At least you'll get a bowl with us. We've got a club captain who values spin. Why don't you come along this weekend and at least have a look at us?"

Stephen thought it over for three tenths of a second before looking up at Graham, his eyes shining. "I'd love to", he said. Graham looked very pleased. "Good", he said. "That's settled, then. And now, by sheer chance, look over there — you see the man with the glasses and the MCC sweater? That's Don Parker. He opens for us, and for Hertfordshire — and he's as stylish a batsman as there is in Hertfordshire. He could play for a first-class county if he really wanted to, without any question. But he's too used to making serious money to be willing to play cricket for ten thousand a year, so we've got him instead. Come on, I'll introduce you."

**

By the simple act of accepting Graham's invitation to join the cricket club he added an entire new dimension to his life. He made friends outside school and his own age group for the first time, and that helped him in his determined attempts to extricate himself from the coils of his narrow family; but it also eased the tensions between him and his parents, whom he had been rapidly coming to see almost as enemies. Once he had an outlet for his exuberant energy, and other groups of people with whom he could share interests radically different from any he had encountered in his parents and their circle, he was able to take a more balanced view, and there was an instant drop in the temperature at home.

Even his parents were rather relieved to find him less prickly, less sulky and more ready to take some part in the life of the household. It was increasingly a minor part, but such part as he did take he took willingly and generally pleasantly. It took less time than either he or they had expected for them to become used to the idea that he was not going to return to the church. There were occasional grumbles when he took to coming home after midnight on match days, and more when he began to gravitate to the club on Friday nights as well, but they were half-hearted and didn't last long.

He was introduced to Elderton Park by Graham and Don Parker, who remembered him from their impromptu meeting at the school, and coming with their recommendation he was rapidly accepted into the social life of the club. He quickly got to know a group of half a dozen of the younger players, and being a friendly, naturally attractive yet unassuming boy he found no difficulty in making himself popular, in a quiet, unobtrusive way. He spent more time with Graham, however, than anyone else. They walked endless circuits of the boundary when neither of them was at the wicket, and their friendship deepened quickly.

He had felt very shy that Saturday morning when he had walked into the big, spacious bar and social room of the pavilion. There had only been half a dozen early arrivals there, sitting about on the edges of tables gloomily looking out at the light but persistent rain falling on the pitch.

Leading him up to the only one of the members present who was wearing a jacket and tie, Graham said "Ray, I'd like you to meet Stephen Hill, from the school. Good batsman and off-spinner. He's interested in playing for us. Stephen, this is Ray Fellows, our Hon Sec. Can you fix him up with an application form, Ray, please?"

"Sure can", said Fellows, shifting his large behind along the table he was sitting on. He squinted at Stephen through small, piggy eyes concealed in rolls of fat and magnified by thick glasses. "Glad to meetcha", he said, offering him a friendly grin. "You Steve or Stephen? Not that it matters, they'll call you Steve whatever your preference. I used to hate being called Ray, but it never did me any good complaining about it. Don't mind now — it's better than some of the things they call me." He chuckled, causing his double chin to ripple up and down over his collar. "Hang about", he went on, squirming his backside off the table. "I'll get you a form. You'll be proposing?" Graham nodded.

While the Hon Sec was waddling off through a door marked PRIVATE — COMMITTEE ONLY, Graham took him rapidly round introducing him to the others. Coming from a school where formal rules of conduct were the norm, and from a strict, rather narrow family, where "manners" and "standards" were the most frequently used words in the house, he didn't know quite what to expect, and so was rather surprised by the easy informality of the cricketers. Though they ranged in age from fourteen to seventy they all nodded or stuck out a hand, gave him a friendly grin, and went back to their chatting or staring out of the enormous picture windows that ran the length of the pitch side of the pavilion.

As he was being introduced a grey-haired, middle-aged man in a club blazer hurried in, waving his arms about in a preoccupied way, and hastened across to intercept Ray Fellows as he emerged from the committee room. "Ray", he yelled urgently. "Seen the availability book?"

"Nope", said Ray shortly. "Was there on that table five minutes ago. Why?"

"I'm one short", said the red-faced man in a bad-tempered voice. "That bloody Ashokh Patel hasn't turned up. It's not good enough. This is the umpteenth time this season already that somebody's been late or not turned up at all. But why the hell does it always have to be *my* bloody lot that do it?"

"Oh, yeah", said Ray in a contrite tone which did not correspond to the airy manner of delivery. "I've had a phone call. He's had to go to the quack with his asthma, so we shan't be seeing anything of him today. I meant to ring you earlier this morning, but something cropped up and I got sidetracked. Sorry, mate."

The newcomer snorted ferociously. "Gorr. It's all very well for you to say 'sorry, mate', but what am I supposed to do? We've got to leave in twenty-five minutes", he snapped. "I was scraping the bottom as it was. Come on, Ray, help me find the bloody book, will you. I'll have to ring round some of the colts."

The Secretary turned to go back into the room from which he had brought Stephen's membership form, but immediately turned back again. "Haven't got your kit with you, by any chance, I suppose?" he said, coming towards Stephen and Graham. They exchanged glances.

"No, I haven't", said Stephen, with a hopeful look dawning on his face. "But I could...I think I could..." He looked at Graham, who nodded. "I'll run you there, no problem... Pat", he said to the distracted newcomer, "this is Stephen Hill. We hope he'll be playing for us. He's a good bat and off-spinner — plays for the school. Want him? Better speak now or forever hold your peace — he'll be in the Twos next week." He turned to Stephen. "Stephen Hill, Pat Hayward, third XI skipper."

"How d'you do?" said Stephen. "Hi Steve", said Hayward, sticking out a hand and giving him a rapid scrutiny. "Welcome aboard. Would you like a game? You'd be helping me out no end, as you've just heard."

Stephen grinned joyously. "I'd love to play", he said, then added in a more sober tone, "but I wouldn't want to keep anybody else out of the..."

"Don't you worry yourself about that", he said briskly. "Very glad to have you. We've got a lot of people away this weekend for one reason or another. If you want to play, you're in."

"I'm in", said Stephen, delightedly. "Graham, would you mind...?"

"Come on", said Graham, fishing his car keys from his pocket as he headed for the door. "Just got to whizz him round to get his gear", he said over his shoulder as they went through the doors. "I'll have him back here in ten minutes, Pat. Okay?"

"Yeah, fine", called Hayward after them. "Thanks very much, Graham."

***

"How'd you get on?" asked Graham with interest when the third eleven came crowding into the pavilion at ten o'clock that night.

"All right!" crowed Hayward, shouldering through the pack at the bar and shouting for jugs. "Stuffed 'em by eight wickets."

"How did Stephen do?"

"Your boy?" Hayward shouted over several heads. "He was great! Christ, practically won it for us on his own. Got forty when we were in trouble, and took three for bugger all. *And* took a blinder in the gulley. He's a good boy, Graham. Where've you been hiding him all this time?" he went on, extricating himself from the mob round the bar and appearing beside Graham with a huge jug of beer in each hand. "Have a top up, Graham", he said in his normal voice, pouring lager into the glass that Graham obligingly emptied for him. "He's a damn good little cricketer, you know", he went on enthusiastically.

"I know", said Graham, feeling very proud of his protégé. "What have you done with him?" he added, looking round and craning his neck over the milling crowd.

"Oh, he went straight home", said Hayward. "I tried to get him to come and have a drink — told him new signings had to buy a jug if they got runs..."

"You bugger!" ejaculated Graham. "Impressionable kid like him, he probably believed you and hadn't got enough cash..."

"Don't be a silly arse", laughed Hayward. "He knew I was pulling his plonker. No", he said, suddenly looking thoughtful, "I got the feeling he'd got trouble coming. He muttered something about his parents not being too keen on his playing. I hope he hasn't got trouble coming from there. You know anything about that?" he asked, looking speculatively at Graham.

"Yes, I'm afraid all's not well there", said Graham thoughtfully. "His parents are rather strict, I believe. I know they're religious, and he's told me in the past that they're a bit stuffy about him having any sort of social life of his own. Still, he swore he'd square things with them."

"Poor little sod", said Hayward. "He's — what? How old is he? Eighteen?"

"Seventeen, I should think, maybe coming up for eighteen."

"Well he's old enough to make up his own mind, isn't he?" said Hayward brusquely.

"Well don't look at me", said Graham mildly. "I'm not keeping him in at nights. I only have the doubtful privilege of teaching him French. Trying to", he amended.

"It's ridiculous", said Hayward forcefully. "Kid of that age. Christ, we've got kids of twelve round here till bloody near midnight every week. If I was him I'd — why, here he is! Hey, Steve, over here. Get yourself a glass", he said, throwing a heavy arm round Stephen's slim shoulders as the boy slipped through a break in the mob and came up to the two of them.

"Pat's just been telling me you had to go straight home", said Graham, looking closely at Stephen. He thought the boy's face had a slightly flushed appearance. "Tell you afterwards", Stephen mouthed at him as Hayward came thrusting his way through with a pint glass. "Here y'are, get your laughing gear round this", he said, sloshing a pint of lager into the glass and shoving it into Stephen's hand. "Glad you could make it, son", he went on gravely. "This lager jug's almost empty..."

"I..." was as far as Stephen got. Graham, laughing, seized the jug from Hayward's hand, and Hayward winked at Stephen. "Only jokin, kid", he grinned. "Only way of gettin that tight bugger to shell out for a jug."

Hayward stayed chatting for a few minutes more, then set off with the two jugs, now refilled, to top up his team's glasses. Graham and Stephen gravitated to a corner of the room where it was a little quieter and the drifting blue haze of smoke was a little thinner. "Something happened at home?" Graham said. It was more a statement than a question.

Stephen nodded, and a grim frown flitted briefly across his face. "They were up waiting for me. It was roughly what you might have expected: 'we graciously allowed you to go and play cricket — as if they'd licensed me to go on a guided tour of the bloody red light district — and now you abuse our great trust by rolling in at ten o'clock at night. Ten o'clock, Graham! As if I'd come in with the milk in the morning and a dose of the clap!" Graham raised his eyebrows in surprise at the vehemence, and rather more at the choice of language. He also registered that it was the first time that Stephen had used his christian name naturally and without awkwardness. For no reason that he could have defined, he suffered a momentary, fleeting feeling of light-headedness.

"So what happened, then? How come you're back here?"

"I did something I should have bloody well done years ago", declared Stephen. Graham suppressed a chuckle. "I laid down the law a bit. I said I was nearly eighteen, and old enough to decide for myself what time I got home and went to bed. Ordering me around like a little bloody child! I said I'd agreed to meet you after the match and have a drink with you." He stopped abruptly and stared at Graham as the implications of what he had said struck him for the first time. "I say, I hope I haven't..."

"Don't worry about it, Stephen", Graham said, releasing the chuckle now. "You're quite right, you're quite old enough to stay out if you want to. I'm afraid your parents are a bit old-fashioned. Still, I imagine the concern underneath is genuine enough. They're just being a little over-protective. Don't upset them for the sake of upsetting them, Stephen: they're on your side, really,

I'm sure. Try to understand their point of view — even if it sometimes seems a little restricted. Don't set out to antagonize them..."

He broke off, and then impulsively reached up and ruffled Stephen's hair. "All the same", he said, "I'm glad you could make it back for a drink. I gather from Pat that congratulations are in order."

Stephen blushed, but looked very pleased with himself, and Graham had no trouble in coaxing an account of his game out of him.

"You've made a very good start with the club, then, Stephen", he said when the ball-by-ball replay was complete. "Let me get you a drink." He waved Stephen's protests down and went to the bar. "One for the road", he said when he came back with fresh pints. "Cheers. How did you get here just now?" he added as a thought struck him.

"Walked", said Stephen. "Well, jogged, actually. Only takes fifteen minutes."

"I'll give you a lift home when we've drunk these, if you like."

"Really? Oh, well, thanks. If it's really no trouble..."

"None whatsoever."

They drank their beer, talking mostly of school affairs and gossip, and set off for the door. As they made their way through the still crowded room towards the door several members of the Third XI called goodnights to Stephen, and Hayward and Fellows, the Hon Sec, converged on them from opposite directions. "Don't forget to sign the book", said Hayward, thrusting a battered ledger book into Stephen's hands. Seeing Stephen's blank look he elaborated, "availability book. So the selection committee know who's available for next weekend's matches. Teams are picked for tomorrow, but we'll see you next week, I hope?"

Stephen flushed with pleasure at the man's obvious sincerity, borrowed a pen from Graham and marked himself as available for both days of the following weekend. "Both days?" Graham, looking over his shoulder, murmured very softly in his ear. Stephen glanced briefly over his shoulder at him and flashed him a grin. "Not half", he said. "I've never enjoyed myself like this in my life." The poignancy with which he said it touched Graham, and he left it at that.

"My turn now", said Fellows when Stephen handed the fat book back to Hayward. "Your application for membership. Still got it with you?" Stephen took the folded form from his back pocket and handed it to him. "Be approved at the next committee meeting", said Fellows. "Won't be any problem. Consider yourself elected. Nets every Tuesday and Thursday, six-thirty. See you there, I hope?" Stephen nodded. "Try and keep me away", he said happily.

The Hon Sec bustled away. As they started once more for the door Graham put a hand on Stephen's arm to steer him through the gap in the crowd. Stephen could not place exactly what he had seen, or in whose face he had seen it, but he experienced a very brief sensation of something unpleasant and curdling; a split second later the feeling was gone, but he was aware of its having existed and of its passing.

When Graham drew up outside Stephen's house it was in darkness. "You can feel the atmosphere even out here in your car", observed Stephen. He shivered suddenly. "Christ, the place even looks like an accusation, doesn't it? I wish I had somewhere else to go", he added feelingly, and it was Graham's turn to shiver. He ruthlessly shut off the thoughts that had begun to sparkle in his mind like a cascade of bright fireworks and turned the conversation to neutral topics. They sat in the darkened car, talking of all manner of things, for almost an hour before Stephen reluctantly got out. Graham sat silently, watching while Stephen walked to his front door and let himself in. Then he drove quietly into the night.

***

"All right, Graham", said Doctor Reginald Westwood. "What's the trouble?"

"I'm afraid I've upset Andrew Tyldesley", murmured Graham.

Westwood stared at him. "Are you sitting there, drinking my whisky at two o'clock in the morning, and telling me that you've kept me up to announce that you've upset that air-headed ninny?" he asked. His tone sounded acid, but it did not fool Graham, who knew that Westwood was very fond of him indeed.

"No, Reggie, of course I'm not", he said, laughing. "Upsetting him was an effect, not a cause. I was dreadful company, he informed me earlier this evening, because I stood propping the bar up in his ghastly pub not saying a word to anyone..."

"I should have thought that would have positively endeared you to Tyldesley", rumbled Westwood grumpily. "I had the impression he liked his conversation partners in the passive voice, rather than the active."

"Quite", agreed Graham. "That's what upset him. I wasn't listening to anything anyone said, either. Especially him. As a matter of fact, he came in rather useful, for once in a way. His voice and that frightful cacophony they insist on perforating your eardrums with in that pub made it quite easy simply to lie back and think. Which is what I was doing, Reggie."

"Thinking about something you now want a second opinion on, eh, Graham?" said the old man, and the forbidding expression he had been wearing since Graham had mentioned Andrew Tyldesley softened. His eyes were very bright in the subdued lighting of his vast St John's Wood flat.

"Yes, please, Reggie", said Graham, looking at him across the space between the two huge club armchairs with great affection. Westwood had been his first lover, when Graham had been a nineteen-year-old virgin, confused, racked by guilt, disgust and fear of the opinion of other people and, most of all, utterly terrified of what he had divined about himself. As Graham had gained in experience and wisdom himself he had gradually realized how immensely fortunate he had been to fall in the way of a gentle man who regarded the exchange of kindness as the highest refinement of sexual accomplishment.

Though they had not been lovers for many years they were still very close friends, and when he was troubled Graham sought counsel and comfort from the old man in much the same way as the boys came to Graham himself. The wisdom he received was sometimes not at all what he wanted to hear; but the stern objectivity of the old man's judgment was bearable because of the unconditional love that both inspired and accompanied it.

Westwood was seventy-one now, and occasionally accompanied Graham on tours of London gay pubs and clubs, "partly because I've got an enquiring mind, my dear", he had said the first time he had asked Graham to give him the conducted tour, "and partly because the finest way of confirming how civilized one's own way of life is is seeing how thoroughly beastly other people's are." He had met Andrew Tyldesley, with whom Graham had been dallying at the time, once, and dismissed him in fifteen seconds when Graham saw him home. "Saw through him like a small square of flyblown transparent plastic, my dear. I've seen thousands of his type in my time. Vain, flashy, and treacherous. Avoid him, Graham, or you'll end up paying him like you pay a blackmailer — which, emotionally, is what he is. Have nothing to do with him."

Graham had stayed away from London for three months from that day, and Tyldesley had moved on to lusher pastures. When they met in pubs from time to time he often caught Tyldesley watching him with a curiously speculative look, as if he still puzzled over why the passionate sexual partner of the past few weeks — they had both been too honest, and had too much respect for the language, to think of themselves as lovers — had dropped like a stone out of sight overnight.

"Come on, then, Graham. Out with it. What's troubling you? I could make a fair guess, mind you, but best to get it from the horse's mouth."

"What would you guess, Reggie?"

"It's happened, would be my guess", said the old man, looking at him with his usual disconcerting intelligence. He waited, but Graham sat silent, waiting for him to elaborate. "You've finally met the boy, haven't you? The boy who has started feelings you couldn't sublimate, or bury under work. You've fallen in love with one of your pimply, unwashed little charges, haven't you?"

"He's not pimply or unwashed", Graham burst out in a sudden rush of passion. He was aware, in a detached sort of way, even as he was blurting it out, of how absurd he sounded; but he was as powerless to halt the flow as Canute with the tide. "He's the most fastidious boy in the school", he heard himself saying, and he heard his voice rising with every word, yet still he rushed on. "I've never met a boy as clean, and I shouldn't think he's ever nourished a pimple in his..."

He broke off, suddenly feeling ridiculous, as the old man leaned back in his armchair and laughed until he choked. "My, my, Graham, you've got it badly, my boy. By God, how the mighty have fallen..." He coughed, an old man's cough, racking himself back and forwards in the chair until the paroxysm had soothed itself away. Then he spoke again. "Graham, Graham, you mustn't mind me making fun of you, in my mild way", he said gently. "It was the thing we liked best about each other once — or had you forgotten?"

Graham stared at him in silence for some seconds, thinking of the old man's unnumbered kindnesses, and suddenly felt small and mean, as well as ridiculous. He smiled, a little sheepishly. "Reggie, I'm sorry. I don't know what came over me. I know it's trite to say such a thing, especially to a cliche-hound like you, but really, I..." And he found that for a moment he had nothing intelligent to say, so he relapsed into silence.

"I do understand, you know", said Westwood, still gentle. "It was bound to happen sooner or later, Graham, my dear. The only problem is how to deal with it. Tell me all about it. And fetch some more whisky before you start", he added, picking up the empty decanter from beside his chair and thrusting it at Graham.

Graham left the room silently, returning with a bottle of Tullamore Dew. He decanted all forty ounces into Westwood's enormous Waterford decanter, and replaced it beside the old man's chair after pouring for them both. "I'll start with this evening, and work backwards", he began, sitting down again.

***

"Cheer up, Graham, for lord's sake", Andrew Tyldesley had said. "You look as if you've tossed for your breakfast and lost." Graham smiled at him, and found it hard work. He tried to pull himself together and take some sort of interest in the conversation that had been eddying about him as he stood at the bar, and that was harder still. Five seconds after making the effort he had slipped into a brown study once more. He leaned against the bar, sipping absently at his pint of lager from time to time, not noticing the puzzled, suspicious glances that his friends were shooting his way every now and then. He normally loathed the deafening disco music that thundered unceasingly in the bar they met in every week or so; but this evening he simply allowed it to flow over him in tidal waves of meaningless sound, and found it, in a perverse way, rather soothing. It made it very easy for him to recreate his pleasant daydream.

Like a great many homosexual schoolmasters, Graham kept his professional and private lives rigorously separate. It was not in his nature to indulge in self-deception, and he had long ago accepted candidly that one of the dominant reasons for his choice of profession had been that he was fond of boys. He accepted that, and regarded it as a qualification for his work rather than an impediment to it. As a very young trainee teacher he had subjected himself to a self-examination that verged on the ruthless, to establish whether or not he was entering the profession in order to gratify sexual hungerings for young boys, and had satisfied himself that that had nothing to do with it. He was not attracted to young children, or even very fond of them, preferring the company of older boys, on the point of maturing into young men; and his liking for them, he felt reasonably sure, was predominantly a matter of liking to watch growing minds maturing and putting on their strength.

The corollary of this, he had recognized equally early and with equal candour, was that he *was* attracted to young men, and attracted powerfully at that. He had expected that to be a serious problem, and had made his tentative entry into teaching with an unbreakable resolution already forged in his mind, that the day he saw that he would not be able to resist the older boys in his charge, that day would also be his last as a teacher. From that resolution he had never seen it necessary to deviate. But, oddly, the problem it was intended to forestall had never arisen. He had been teaching for seven years, and throughout that time he had seen many boys every working day whom he found attractive. Some of them were beautiful, some plain, most in between. He acknowledged privately a particular weakness for shy, vulnerable boys, the ones who blushed and were given to seeking solace in their own company. He was also, as he had once put it to himself in one of his self-analytical moods, a sucker for intelligence. There had, inevitably, been occasional opportunities.

But Graham had been lucky, in one way in particular: he was a born teacher, and had revealed himself as such, to his superiors and more importantly to himself, from his first tremulous step into a classroom. Where others more confident as well as less endured torment as they laboured in the black arts of commanding obedience and inspiring respect, Graham had his first unruly class of guinea pigs quelled and silent within one minute of that first step into the room; in five they were eating out of his hand, and in ten they were hanging on his words, eager for more of whatever he had within him to give them. It had gone on from there.

Among the results of this, apart from a rapid, almost meteoric rise to better and better posts, came blessed reassurance for his inner, worried self: he discovered early that he was going to have no trouble controlling his feelings for the boys. He responded to them as they did to whatever it was in him; they came to him readily in times of trouble, knowing by some sure instinct that they could trust him to take them and their troubles seriously, that he would not laugh at them or lie to them. A few — a very few — of the ones with the most sensitive antennae of all saw deep into him and knew him for what he was, and the first few times he was confronted by such a boy he trembled; but they responded as readily as the majority, and that reassured him more than anything else, he thought. But in the main, it was the relentless demands of the work that saw him through the pain of attraction. The demands on his time, his emotions and his resource were endless, and he was freer than most to let them flow out. The boys became a huge, diffused family, with wounds that needed his special gifts to be healed, crises and panics to be smoothed over, and a thousand small problems to be negotiated round every day. In the simplest terms, he realized after a few months, he could keep too busy to have time for perilous emotional attachments. He acknowledged the truth gratefully, and hurled himself into work with a strongly reinforced will.

And so, having served his apprenticeship as a teacher, he thought he could properly feel comfortable and reassured about the wisdom of a man of his sexuality entering work that left him surrounded by attractive boys in all stages of sexual maturity.

And yet he knew, all the time, that one day the supreme test would come.

Falling in love with one of the boys he dismissed as not hazardous at all — it had happened once or twice, and control came so easily and automatically that he hardly even felt its application. The crunch would come one day, he knew, when he fell in love with a boy and the boy was of a sexual make-up to match, and returned the feeling. He had rarely, in all his years of teaching, been able to contemplate that vertiginous prospect for long at a stretch, and the reason was quite simply that he had no idea at all how he would deal with it. It had, of course, entered his mind at times; but when it had he had dismissed it as fast as he could; and the only method of dealing with such a situation that had occurred to him so far had been to hope for the best.

And now, he reflected, as he ignored his offended friends in the gay pub in London, now it's happened. And that's what I'm doing, isn't it? Hoping for the best. But am I? Or is what I'm hoping for the worst? What do "best" and "worst" mean in a situation like this? The questions milled around in his mind as Tyldesley jogged his elbow in vain to ask him what he was drinking; and no answers came in their wake, only more questions.

"For Christ's sake, Graham, what the hell's the matter with you?" came Tyldesley's voice, getting through at last. Graham had no idea what he had said, but the querulous tone suggested that he had committed some social gaffe, and he came reluctantly back to the surface of his consciousness, dismissing the daydream to the back of his mind with regret. "Eh?" he said.

"I've been talking to you for the last five minutes", said Tyldesley crossly. "What's the matter with you? Are you in love or something asinine like that?" His expression changed to a leer. "Have you been eating of the tree that beareth the fruit which is forbidden, Graham? Is that it? Come on, now, you can tell me. Have you found a succulent little botty in the lower fourth dorm, my dear? Or been playing with a nice smooth little pee-pee behind the bike sheds? Lucky Graham — all those opportunities for real vice. Yum-yum. Come on, now, dear, don't keep it all to yourself, that would be wickedly selfish. It's all for one and one for all, isn't it? Among friends, I mean."

He burbled on in the same vein for some time longer, taking a visible pleasure from Graham's increasingly uncomfortable protests and rising anger.

***

"He never really forgave me for ditching him like that, you see, Reggie", said Graham, pouring more of the Tullamore Dew for them both. "And in a way, I suppose I can't really blame him. I think maybe that's one reason why I still drop in and say hi to him when I come up to town. I mean, I never offered the slightest explanation, did I? Just dropped out of existence for months on end, after — well, we were an affair, weren't we, more or less? I know you were right about him. I'd pretty well seen him for what he was myself by the time you did your character assassination number on him. But to be fair to him, he'd never actually done me any harm, had he?".

"Yes, he had", grunted Westwood, "and the fact that you're still talking like that about him is the clearest possible proof that he had. I told you, boy, that's how people like him operate. He's as weak as watered-down piss, and he'll need emotional crutches to walk with as long as he breathes. Human crutches — strong, reliable people, with consciences and integrity. People like you, in short. He needs someone strong and honourable to prop him up. If I hadn't warned you off the course he'd have had you snared in five more minutes, and you'd have spent the next five years making his decisions for him, acting as his conscience, picking up the pieces after his irresponsibilities and weaknesses, like the man with the bucket and shovel who walks behind the elephant. After the Lord Mayor's Show... In his case, it could have been you. Think yourself lucky you had me to administer the necessary clip round the ear. He'd have sucked the strength and integrity out of you, spending it as profligately as if it were his own. After five years you'd have been a worn-out husk, and he'd have walked away from you like fleas off a dying rat, because parasites have a use for you only while you're still full of blood."

Graham pondered this for a moment. Then he nodded, and muttered "Ye-es. I see all that. But I still can't help feeling I treated him a bit roughly — before he'd actually done any of those things..."

"Do you know the trouble with decent people like you, Graham", said Westwood. Graham looked at him expectantly.

"In some ways decency is a get-out", Westwood continued, not unkindly. "It's sometimes a bloody good cover-up for indecision, or rather, for wriggling your way out of taking hard decisions. Because you're decent, you shrink from inflicting hurt — even on parasites and reprobates, such as your friend Tyldesley. So you wrap yourself in your shining white robes of purity and avert your head, saying, "No, I cannot stain my hands with brutal acts. I cannot deal with this cur as he requires to be dealt with. And you go whining and cringing off telling everybody how pure and saintly you are. And there, slinking along a hundred yards in your wake, unseen behind the radiant clouds of glory you're trailing, safely out of the glorious effulgence left by your passing, creeps a thug with a hatchet, on which the blood still gleams fresh and red. After the Lord Mayor's Show... comes the shitcart, and after the serene departure of the virtuous... comes the assassin, who makes the world safe for the virtuous to continue to appear in public."

He leant forward, examining Graham's face to see what effect his words were having. Seeing the distress clearly imprinted there, he leaned over and patted him gently on the knee. "There, there, Graham, I don't mean all this personally, against you. All I'm trying to say is that decent, honourable, high-principled folk like you, who acknowledge their responsibilities and shoulder them, ought not to disdain to do unpleasant things. Every benevolent despot needs his thugs and his hatchet men. In your case, you're a thoroughly principled young man, but you're a little bit lacking in something. I don't know whether it's just worldly savvy, which will come in time, or whether it's a real weakness in the fabric, which won't heal. But you've got to dredge deep, and find the stomach to take nasty, harsh decisions — like, for instance, the one you ought to have taken for yourself with Tyldesley."

"What exactly do you think I ought to have done, Reggie?"

"Well, you say you'd seen him for what he was yourself. If so, then what you ought to have done was to tell him what you saw him for, and that you were going to ditch him accordingly. Then you should have ditched him. As it was, you needed me to tell you what you already knew, and then you needed me to tell you what to do about it. Well, I did so, because I have the advantage of being at least half a thug myself — no, don't protest. I know what you think of me, and I'm flattered. But flattery is by definition untruthful, and I never was so pure as you thought me. So I have little difficulty in telling parasites, for example, that they're parasites. And when I'd done so, you did the easy bit — ditching him. But even that you did the easy, painless way, under an anaesthetic, by simply dropping out of sight — thereby, perforce, depriving us who love you of your pleasant company also. But, Graham, this is all a digression. You were telling me about being in that appalling hole of a pub…"

"Yes", said Graham, licking his wounds and feeling rather hurt. "Well, as I said, he's never really forgiven me for breaking it off with him, even though it was three years ago. He's never really found anyone else, you know, since then. No-one to look after him, you know, as I might have done…"

"Proves what I've been saying", said Westwood in a more amiable tone. "Go on."

"Well, to be honest, Reggie, I've always had a nagging feeling that he's never really liked me much since then, either. In fact, I've had a feeling that he hates me, sometimes. No, that's too strong. But *something*, you know? A feeling that he'd…" He groped for the words. "A feeling that he'd like to be avenged on me, I suppose is the best way to describe it. It's bloody difficult to describe, but that comes as close as I can get to analyzing it. And all the time he was going through that mock-leering and simpering act over the boy I was supposed to be seeing back at school, I had this feeling very strongly — that he was somehow taking his revenge on me. You know what I'm talking about?"

"Of course I do my boy", said the old man, "and I think your senses were right, just as right as your intellect was wrong about him when you first got friendly with him."

"And of course, there was another thing", continued Graham. "He was getting pretty perilously near to the truth, as well, wasn't he? I started feeling pretty nervy. I don't think I see him in quite as hard a light as you do, but even I admit he's not someone I'd want to know too much about my business, and the idea of his knowing I was besotted with one of the kids in my own sixth form is a pretty scary one, I can tell you…

"Anyway, the upshot of it was that I made some feeble excuse, and got out. I was getting a headache by then, anyway", he concluded lamely.

"And thereby demonstrated my point", said Westwood. "You didn't have the headache at the time, any more than you needed to invent it for my benefit, or your own more likely, just now. You hadn't quite got the stomach to tell him he's a howling shit and walk out leaving it at that, no, you had to invent a headache to allow you to flounce out on him with a stainless conscience. Didn't you?" he added, speaking gently once more, to Graham's relief. "And now", he went on, "tell me about the boy."

***

"Very well", Westwood said when Graham had completed a thumbnail panegyric of Stephen Hill. "Now tell me the answer to the big question. Is he one of us? Is he of the fraternity? *Is he gay?*"

"I don't know", said Graham. "Not for absolutely sure. But I think so. I'm almost sure. That time when I first took any real notice of him, the time I told you about, when we were walking round the boundary and I asked him to come to play for my club, I had this strong feeling that there was something else he wanted to talk about. But he didn't at the time, and I didn't press the matter."

"Very wise", commented the old man.

"Quite. But there have been other times since, when I've felt almost sure he was going to unburden himself. But each time something's happened to destroy the moment, to destroy the intimacy. Some ass blundering in wanting to talk about the game or something, or buying us drinks, or what-have-you. There's something there, something that's making him deeply unhappy, especially at home. Something he can't, or at any rate doesn't want to talk about to his parents — not that he can talk to them about anything that matters, but this is something pretty fundamental. I'm sure of that much. And, well, you know better than I do, Reggie...oh, it's just something about him... you can tell, can't you? I can tell."

He sat back, relaxing from the forward crouch into which he had unconsciously stooped in the intensity of his concentration. "That's as far as I could say", he finished. "I think he's gay, though I doubt if he knows it himself for certain. I think he probably suspects, and would like to find out, from someone he trusts. And I think I'm the person he trusts most right now. We've become very close, you know, Reggie", he said, a little wanly, and yet with a depth of happiness lying clearly visible to the older man, close beneath the rather sad, pinched smile, like the outline of a fish just beneath the surface of deep water.

"He knows nothing about you?" asked Westwood.

"Not as far as I know", Graham nodded. "And as far as I know there's no-one to tell him, either at the school or at the cricket club." He hesitated. "There are a few who suspect, I think. That's about as far as I can say for sure. I've heard one or two things at the cricket club. Just small things, you know...odd times when I've walked into the dressing room or the bar, and it's suddenly gone quiet — you know how it is. And once in a while you hear the odd ribald remark, or more likely catch the tail-end of one, and maybe some mention of queers or poofs — well, again, you know the sort of thing. So I suppose it's just possible that he may have heard something there. Come to that I suppose he may have heard something at the school. You know what schools are like, or anywhere where it's all males — anyone who's still unmarried at thirty, and so forth..."

"But all in all you don't think he's got any clear idea of what you are?"

"All I can say for certain is that I don't think so. I've got no reason to think so. What I want to know is what I should do if he does ask me for advice. I mean, Reggie, suppose that *is* the problem he's got at home, or rather, suppose that's his problem, and the one of all his problems that he can least talk about at home. If he goes to anyone I'm certain it'll be to me. What do I tell him? Do I advise him and say 'I happen to be something of an expert on this, because...'? Or do I tell him and then say, 'oh, and by the way, I'm in love with you, so while we're at it you can check it out — you've had the theory, now bend over and prepare for the practical'?"

Westwood laughed at the extravagance, but quickly sobered. "You must advise him as you would advise any boy who came for guidance in such a difficult area", he said with certainty. "And that's all. Leave it at that. You know all this already, of course. I know you well enough to know I don't need to be telling you all this. You don't need me to point out what an unmitigated catastrophe it would be if you embarked on an affair with one of your pupils. You can supply the headlines in the *News of the World* for yourself. Quite apart from which, you're in a fiduciary position, and it would be utterly improper for you to do any such thing. That's something else you don't need telling.

Graham sighed. "No, Reggie", he said, "I don't."

"Then have a last tot of this magnificent popish poison, and then go and have a peaceful night's rest. I keep a room made up for you."

Graham offered him a smile full of gratitude and affection, and hefted the half a hundredweight decanter off the floor for a last time. "Good God, we've drunk half a bottle", he said, eyeing the level of the amber liquid, refracted through thousands of prismatic cuts in the glass. He swirled it, and the vessel flashed and sparkled amber, orange from the glow of the fire on the old mahogany furniture and the dim lights flowing from concealed sconces in the walls, and a rich indigo blue that seemed to emanate from some mysterious depth within the lead-weighted crystal itself.

"I think about him all the time, you know, Reggie", he said inconsequentially as he handed his old friend his refilled glass. "I dream about him, too. I was daydreaming about him all the way up to town on the train, and all the time I was propping the bar up in Andrew's ridiculous pub. That's why I got alarmed when he started getting perilously close to the truth — I suddenly had this notion that he was looking into my mind. Silly, I know, but it made me shiver for a moment — you know, somebody walking over your grave?"

"There's no harm in thinking about him, or dreaming about him", murmured Westwood, smiling fondly at him in the near-darkness of the great high-ceilinged room. "Though I'd suggest that it's likely to bring you more pain in the form of frustration than joy from the sight of his face. And as long as it doesn't interfere with important things: your work, your relationship with the boy himself — he's become dependent on you in a sense, Graham, as I'm sure you're aware. So you've got a responsibility to him. Don't let lust come between you and that responsibility."

"It's not lust, Reggie, my dear", Graham said sadly. "it's love."

Westwood stroked his chin before answering. "Yes", he said eventually. "I suppose, you being you, it probably is. Infinitely worse. Just keep it platonic, that's all."

***

"Christ, Colin", groaned the captain of the Elderton Park First XI. He briefly covered his eyes as his no. 6 batsman flashed airily at a fast leg-cutter well outside the off stump. "How many times have we told him to leave those alone?" he muttered, exchanging a grim glance with his vice-captain in the next deckchair.

"Shall the leopard change his Ethiopian?" murmured the vice-captain as the bowler tramped back to his mark. "There he goes again", he added. The next ball was identical, and so was the stroke. This time he got a thin top edge, and they could hear the close fielders' strangled yelps of anguish as it flew an inch above second slip's convulsive salmon-leap and shot to the boundary. "Four more, anyway", said the vice-captain. He craned his neck to see the face of the scorebox. "One-eighty-nine", he announced. "Fifty-seven wanted. We should do it, Bill. We've got thirteen overs after this one."

"We've also got a tail long enough for the *Guinness Book of Records*", his captain reminded him. "I still don't know which way to play it. What do you think, Alan? Do I shut the shop, or do we still go for it?"

"See how many Colin can put together", suggested Alan. "Oh", he added in dismay. No. 6 tried the same flashy stroke yet again to another fast ball drifting away outside the off stump. This time his luck was out, and so was no. 6, caught by the wicket-keeper, who, seeing that it would not carry to first slip, had hurled himself to his right and taken the ball one-handed, at full stretch, three inches above the ground. "Great catch", said the captain, clapping despite himself. "Good luck, Simon", he called as no. 7 got out of his deckchair and set off for the crease, pulling on his gloves. "He'll bloody need it", he added, aside to Alan, but he considerately waited until the batsman was out of earshot before he said it.

"Made up your mind yet?" asked Alan.

"I'm making it right now", muttered Bill, craning to look at the score, which had not changed. "Yeah, I'm going to give it one more wicket. What's that new kid's name? The one Graham Curtis brought from his school?"

"Steve, isn't it? Yes, Steve Hill", supplied Alan.

"Yeah, that's right. He's been getting a lot of runs for the Threes, so they tell me. Only been with us about three weeks, and I heard he got his first fifty last week. Sydney or the Bush", he said after musing for a few moments. "Hey, Steve", he called, looking about and spotting Stephen leaning in at the hatch at the scorebox. Stephen looked up and hurried over.

"Get padded up, will you, Steve, please. I'm putting you in earlier than I'd expected. Next wicket down, okay?"

"Yes, fine. Great. Thank you very much", said Stephen, beaming as he hurried into the dressing room. "Well, he's keen", said Alan, looking for a bright side.

It was fortunate that he got his pads on quickly. No. 7, having got nicely off the mark by thrashing the dealer in leg-cutters handsomely through backward point for four, then squirted the last ball of the over through the slips for a streaky single. He now had to face a straight-up-and-down man, who, however, had been rested and was extremely fast. He slashed the first ball of the over uppishly, but wide of gulley's clutch, for four more. The second ball was short of a length and pitched on middle stump. It reared ferociously, moved a fraction of an inch to the off, and flew with hardly a deviation off the shoulder of no. 7's bat into the wicket-keeper's welcoming hands. He trailed disconsolately back to the pavilion, shaking his head sadly at the captain and vice-captain. "Sorry, Bill", he said. "Too good for me, that last one."

"Hard luck, Simon", commiserated the captain. "See from here what a peach it was. Okay, young Steve", he said as Stephen passed in front of him on his way to the exit from the enclosure. "Take it steady, now. Let Graham do the scoring. You just stay there. Occupy the crease, and the runs'll come. How many do we want, Alan?"

"Forty-eight."

"Good luck, then", they chorused, and Stephen was alone.

Graham met him halfway to the wicket. He was looking serious and preoccupied. "I take it they told you to take it steady?" he said. Stephen nodded. "They're worried about the long tail."

"Well, take my advice, and just play your natural game", said Graham. "Temper it, be careful, certainly don't take any risks — the bowling's far too good to take risks with. The man you're going to face is pretty quick, but he's straight up and down most of the time. The one he got poor Simon with was a freak. He won't bowl another one like it if he lives to be a hundred. Just play straight, and take any singles there are going." Stephen nodded, and they went to their ends.

Stephen took guard, twiddled his bat as he stared round the field, then settled into his stance and waited for the first delivery, hoping the slight trembling he could distinctly feel under the white shirt was not visible to any of the field.

The bowler retreated an improbable distance towards the sight-screen, turned and raced in. Stephen patted the toe of his bat in the crease, and could hardly believe his good fortune when the first ball turned out to be an amiable long-hop a clear eighteen inches outside his off stump. It lolloped along and sat up like a rather dim but amiable old dog, asking, begging and praying to be hit. His captain's and Graham's admonitions were still in his ears; but batsman's instinct was too imperious to be denied. He stepped carefully onto the back foot, and fairly flogged the soppy, lolloping ball on the up, through extra cover for what felt like the finest four of his life.

"SHO-O-O-T!" came a stentorian roar from the crowd gathered in the enclosure in front of the pavilion. He cantered a few paces down the pitch, feeling the after-shocks of that glorious contact tingling through his body, and knowing in every sinew that there was no need to run for it. He pulled up as he saw it rocket over the rope, and met Graham halfway.

Graham's eyes were shining. "That was as good a shot as I've seen all season", he exclaimed, dropping an arm round Stephen's shoulders. For an instant Stephen felt a kind of electric current pass through him, similar to the physical tingle induced by the perfect contact of the ball in the middle of his bat. Then it was gone, leaving him with some vague feeling of *déjà vu*, some faint after-image of memory which he couldn't place but knew was recent. It had come and gone before Graham's next word.

"Great shot, Stephen, as I say, but take it steady. Nothing rash. We've got tons of time. You all right?" Stephen nodded, feeling as happy as he could remember ever feeling. "I'm fine", he said, and as he said it he felt a bolt of elation shoot through him. "Let's blow these buggers out of the water", he said.

Graham grinned at him, and they went back to their ends.

Six overs later, the game was finished. Stephen had not been able to hit another boundary, but he had gone for his strokes and made a highly creditable fifteen, and Graham had polished off the remainder, finishing with a capable, carefully compiled sixty-two. Stephen's main contribution, as Graham was telling him as they walked into the enclosure to receive the rapturous acclamation of the others, was the psychological effect of his first scoring stroke. "You'll never forget that shot, Stephen" he said, and Stephen felt inclined to agree. It was only as they walked up the steps and into the dressing room that he became conscious of the fact that Graham's arm had been round his shoulders all the way from the crease. He turned his head to look at Graham, and his eyes were glittering strangely.

***

Stephen showered with quick and economical movements and with his back turned to the others, erecting an invisible but almost tangible wall of privacy in a corner of the large shower bath. He wrapped a towel round his waist and flitted back to his peg, where he dressed with the same slightly fussy quickness. He accepted the congratulations of the others modestly, with a shy smile, but wasn't very communicative, and the moment he was dressed he slipped out into the bar. No-one noticed the sudden dissipation of his elated mood except Graham; but he noticed it with the anguished poignance of a lover, and had an appalled suspicion that he could ascribe a reason. He had to swallow hard before leaving the security of the dressing room. Then he squared his shoulders, almost in the manner of a soldier preparing to walk into the room in which he is to be court-martialled, and stepped through into the bar.

"Have a noggin" he said, schooling his voice to normality as he walked to the bar and stood beside Stephen. "Have two. That cover drive was worth one on its own."

Stephen gave him a thin smile, drained his pint glass quickly and allowed Graham to refill it. They chatted idly for a while, breaking off for digressions as other players drifted in from the dressing rooms, joined them while they got drinks and drifted away again. After half an hour Graham took a calculated gamble. He peered closely at Stephen and said in a low voice "Is there anything the matter with you, Stephen? You don't have the air of the conquering hero." He was careful to disguise the

said anything today to...upset you in any way? In particular, have I said something wrong? If I have, I'd like to know."

He could see Stephen's eyes in the darkness as the boy looked steadily at him. There was a long pause, during which Graham suddenly became conscious that he was holding his breath. When Stephen spoke it came as a bigger relief than he had expected. "No!" he said, so emphatically that it sounded like a protest. "No, Graham, you haven't said anything. You're the last person who'd upset me." There was a silence. Then, "I've been a bit quiet, haven't I?"

"Well, yes, you have, and it seemed to start when we were batting together. I wondered what I must have done. I couldn't see who else could have caused it..."

"No, no", Stephen repeated, and there was something almost desperate in his anxiety to reassure. "Please don't think you did anything — nothing to...to upset or offend me. No, it was just something I wanted to ask, something I wasn't sure about. I was thinking about it, that's all. That's why I went a bit quiet. Honestly", he added, after another pause. For a moment he sounded like a little boy.

"Something you wanted to ask me?" said Graham softly.

"Yes."

"Ask away", he said. "You know you can come to me with anything that's worrying you. I hope you know that, anyway."

"Oh, yes, of course, sir — I mean, Graham", the boy said, sounding a little more like his normal confident self once more. Graham noticed the unconscious reversion to their old master-pupil form of address. "Would you mind if I — er — if I left it for a little bit?" Stephen said quietly, after a time.

"Of course not. You're not bound to ask me anything. But if there is something and you think I might be able to offer anything sensible, or helpful, well you know you can talk to me any time you like. But you want to leave it for the moment?"

"Yes, I think so, please, Graham."

"Well there's an end of it, then. You're playing tomorrow, aren't you? Want picking up? We're away tomorrow. Eleven-thirty start. I'll pick you up here at ten o'clock. Okay?"

He could just see Stephen's grateful smile. "Right, Graham. And... thanks. Maybe I'll be ready to talk about it tomorrow", he said, opening the car door.

"Any time." With the release from the worry that had gripped him since he had surmised what he might have done to upset the boy, Graham felt buoyant again, and answered easily. "If so, fine, if not, well, still fine, by me. See you at ten", he repeated as Stephen got out and opened the back door to take his kit. "Good night."

"Night, Graham", said Stephen. His head appeared in the open window of the passenger door. "Thanks", he murmured quickly, and was gone. He left Graham feeling glad that he hadn't offended the boy, but also more sure than ever that his assessment of the boy as he had explained it to Reginald Westwood had been accurate. He drove home, aching with the first pains of a fast-blossoming love that he was sure would never be requited. That night they both slept badly.

***

"Who's got the club comb?" asked Bill in the dressing room the following Saturday. He glanced about hopefully, and Stephen shyly offered his comb.

"Thanks, Steve. You played well again", Bill said, busily raking it through his wiry red curls. Stephen had been promoted in the order to no. 5, and scored a bright thirty-nine in even time. "I think we'll be wanting you regularly for the rest of the season", Bill added, almost as if it was an afterthought. Stephen flushed with pleasure. "Another thing", went on his captain. "How're you placed for the tour?"

"Tour?" queried Stephen. "I didn't know about a tour."

"Oh, yeah", said several players at once. "You must come on tour if you can make it", said Alan, taking it up. "We go to Yorkshire every year."

"The nice part", put in someone else. "North Yorkshire, in the Dales. We stay at a very decent boozer in Malton, where they never close before five in the morning. Cricket's good as well — course, you'd expect that in Yorkshire. Reckon you can make it?"

"I... well, I'd love to come if I can", said Stephen, gazing into space as he thought about the idea.

"Ever been on a tour before?" asked one of the others.

"I've been on school tours", he said diffidently. "With the

50

Under Fifteens. Twice. Playing Winchester, Marlborough and Clifton."

"Got some high-grade cricket, I should think?" commented Alan, and Stephen nodded. "Not quite the same sort of thing, I'd suspect", said Bill, with what to Stephen's eye looked like a meaning glance round the others. "Early to bed with a cold shower and a run in the morning under Graham Curtis's watchful eye, eh?" He glanced round, and Stephen was sure this time that he saw him glare fleetingly but fiercely at someone behind him.

"Graham wasn't there, actually", he said. A strange, queasy, sickish feeling had lodged suddenly in his stomach, and he had to fight off a moment of panic when he thought he was going to be sick. "The head of games runs the school tours. Anyway, I'd really like to come. When is it?"

"Twenty-third of July", said someone. "We leave on the Friday evening — get into the hotel about midnight in time for a drink, play through the week, and come back the following Sunday."

"Eight games, back to back", said Alan happily. "We... oh! So that's where my towel got to. What do you think you're doing with it?" he demanded, advancing on Bill with his eyes fixed on the bath towel wrapped like a loincloth round his captain's lower body. "I've hunted everywhere for that. What's the game?"

Bill unwound the towel from his hips and threw it over his deputy's head, grinning without any of the contrition that was clearly expected. Stephen suspended his dressing operations to see what his captain could possibly have wished to wrap a stolen towel round his loins for. Bill saw his expression and laughed, meanwhile capturing Alan's head in its suffocating coils of towelling and massaging his hair vigorously. Muffled howls issued from within. "I always use a towel to bat in", he told Stephen. "Far better than a thigh pad — much more cushioning effect."

"Helps to soak up the shit when the fast bowlers are on, too", cried someone from across the room, and there was a general cackle.

"Gah! Ach! You shitbag, Bill!" cried Alan, finally managing to escape from the voluminous towel. "Do you expect me to use this after it's been round your dirty arse? I gotta dry my face on this, you bastard!"

"Well of course, why not?" grinned Bill. "Your face, my arse — cricket's a team game, as I shouldn't have to remind you."

"Fuck it", moaned Alan. "I'll bath when I get home. Deodorant can do the job of soap for now."

"No it bloody well can't", cried Bill. "It's June, remember? Bath month. In with him, lads!"

Stephen looked on, grinning shyly as the team hurled themselves on the vice-captain and manhandled him, yelling and struggling, towards the showers. "Turn it on, Steve", panted Bill, roaring as one of Alan's flailing hands caught a generous fistful of his hair and yanked it fiercely. "No, no, the other one!" he yelled, freeing his mop with a wrench. Stephen obediently turned the shower full on cold, and leapt out of the path of a tidal wave that washed over the dressing room floor as the hapless Alan was forcibly bathed.

"Al always has a bath in June, whether he needs one or not", explained Bill, sticking the comb in the breast pocket of Stephen's shirt. "Have to have him nice and clean for the tour, see." He grinned at Stephen's uncertain expression, and ruffled his hair briefly. "Don't get worried, kid. He doesn't mind, really. Now, then. Tour", he said, with an abrupt change of tone. "If you'd like to come, there's plenty of space. It won't cost you too much, either, in case you were worried about... hey, hey, HEY, careful, you buggers. I felt water on my neck. I'm getting moist."

"Well, this is an exciting bath", came a breathless shout from the scrum in the shower.

"That's not in the script", returned Bill, retreating towards the door. There he turned back to Stephen. "Come on, son, I'll let you buy me a drink while I give you the rest of the griff."

He propelled Stephen through into the bar, laughing at the boy's bewildered expression as he looked back at the continuing horseplay in the shower. Half the side now appeared to be taking additional baths, some still in whites, some stark naked and others in various stages in between.

"As I was saying", he resumed, refusing to allow Stephen to buy a drink and sticking a pint into his hand instead, "it won't cost you too much, because we run a subsidy scheme here. Not many clubs do, but we think the youngsters are important, so the club pays for their hotel and coach. All you've got to find is your beer money — and you won't find you buy much of your own beer, come to that. We get a lot of innocent fun out of watching you kids getting mildly pissed, so we pay for a good deal of it. It's in your school holidays, so provided your folks haven't got anything fixed up in Bognor Regis for you, you're laughin sandbags.

"We play eight fixtures, as I said, and we normally take a party of about twenty-five. That means everybody's guaranteed at least three games — probably more if you want 'em, because a lot of 'em like to have a day or so off to do other things. You might like to pop into York — that's about twenty-five miles, and there's the Jorvik Centre — sorta smellerama museum affair; and there's a steam engine museum. Then there's Scarborough — sort of up-market Blackpool, or Torremolinos but cold, and there's some lovely countryside round there too." He stopped his catalogue and drank half his pint in a draught. "Fancy it?" he ended, wiping his moustache.

Stephen fancied it immensely, and said as much. "How much d'you think I ought to bring?" he asked.

"Oh, I dunno", said Bill. "Long time since I was your age. Can't really remember how much I used to drink in those days. But certainly fifty quid oughta be far more than enough."

"Oh", said Stephen, his face brightening. "Good. I've got more than that. I was thinking it'd be...well, more than I've got, anyway. Yes, I'll come", he concluded. He grinned as he thought of the horror his parents would presumably feel at the idea of his spending ten days at a pub with a cricket team of whom they disapproved in principle already.

"Good", said Bill, pleased. "I'll bung you down. One other thing: most of us share rooms at the hotel. A few have rooms of their own — Alan, because he's a world class snorer, and I do, because I'm captain — though the others'll tell you a lot a lies about me farting when I drink beer. Start thinking about who you'd like to share with. List's on the notice board." And he started towards it himself, taking a ballpoint from his pocket.

"Will Graham be coming?" asked Stephen, trotting after him to investigate the notice board. "I imagine I'd share with him, if he comes on tour."

Bill glanced down over his shoulder at him, with, he thought, a slightly quizzical expression. "Oh, yes, Graham never misses the tour", he said, nodding. "Hasn't got anyone nagging him not to go, for a start, bein a bachelor. And he loves his cricket, too. He'll be glad to have you." He hesitated, and Stephen thought he was going to say something more; but in the end he only looked at Stephen for a second more, with a curious expression, then shut his mouth without saying any more, and turned to add Stephen's name to the list on the board, and then to another copy of it in his own wallet. "Come on, son", he said, slipping pen and wallet back into his pocket. "I'll get you a pint." Ignoring Stephen's protests that he had bought him one already, he barged up to the bar and began buying an enormous and complicated round of drinks for himself and Stephen, the rest of the team and the opposition, who were now coming into the bar in ones and twos from the dressing rooms, rubbing their hands in anticipation of the first drink of the evening.

Stephen sat sipping his pint and exchanging the occasional word here and there with other players and hoping Graham would get back soon. Graham had scored a rapid twenty at his customary no. 3 before holing out at long-off trying to hit a six, and had changed and left immediately to attend a meeting at the school. Stephen had got to know a good many people at the club in his few weeks there, but Graham was still his staple conversation partner; and he realized how much so as he sat there, glancing at the door every time it opened. After a while he took his pint across to join a group conducting the usual annotated re-run of the game; and at half-past ten he collected his bag from the dressing room and, feeling a little forsaken, said his farewells and went out under the last lemon-and-indigo remnants of the sunset, and set off on the short walk home. He walked more or less on automatic pilot, enjoying a series of pleasant mental pictures of what a real cricket tour might be like. He was hardly aware of feeling vaguely that his evening had been somehow incomplete.

***

In different ways they both led double lives over the few weeks that remained of the school term. It was less of a strain for Stephen, and he was much the less unhappy of the two. Having grown up a largely solitary only child, he had found joining the cricket club and suddenly throwing off the shackles of his increasingly uneasy relationship with his parents enormously liberating experiences. He had become very close to Graham in the process, and he was aware that they were forming a friendship of a kind that he had never previously known. But he was also making other friends among the cricketers, each of them with something to teach or show him about an outside life that he had previously only dimly suspected.

Thus Stephen found it far less irksome than Graham to have to go through the formality of conventional forms of address in classes, and correspondingly easier to slip into the intimacy of friendship when they were at leisure. He was becoming strongly aware that there was a further dimension of their relationship that lay as yet unexplored, and that it would have to be confronted sometime soon; but he hadn't yet identified it clearly, so he wasn't vulnerable to it. He knew he was very fond of Graham, and becoming fonder as the days passed. But he had in full measure a boy's ability to take things as they came on a day-to-day basis, to accept things without undue questioning, which had been wholly lost in the man.

Graham, by contrast, had had no difficulty in identifying the increasingly powerful feeling for the boy that moved him. His problem was to keep his feelings within bounds. He knew only too clearly that he had a passionate nature, and that if his feelings for the boy once broke free from his iron self-control they were more than likely to become an obsession, with disastrous results in prospect. The form his control took was to make him more severe with Stephen, rather than less, in classes; then, as soon as they were released and able to stroll round the cricket field, or left free to enjoy their weekends together, he would offer unnecessary explanations for his new, brittle manner in class. When they were together thus he yearned to touch him, and faced every day the sickening necessity to keep his hands to himself, his words of passion unspoken and his affection masked beneath a cloak of cricket-club joviality. Often as they strolled together the conversation would turn to more serious matters, and then, just occasionally, he rested his hand lightly on Stephen's arm. Stephen smiled, accepting the small gesture as unremarkable, and apparently thought nothing of it, while Graham boiled and churned with an agonizing cocktail of physical lust and spiritual yearning for possession.

Meanwhile Stephen too had a problem. Because it was wholly unfamiliar to him, he had nothing to compare it with, and this lightened the burden; and because the whole habit of his family life up to then had been to suppress emotion, he had grown up without the expectation of being able to confide in anyone when he was troubled. This had left him with self-control as the pattern of normality, and he bore it lightly. Somewhere beneath the surface he knew that he would confide in Graham soon, but he was content — as Graham would not have been — to let the moment pick itself. Besides, although he was only a boy, and although his growing up had been a smothered affair, thanks to his parents' inhibited vision of life, there was nothing wrong with his eyes or ears, or with his wits; he had a fair idea how things were between them, and he was beginning to realize that the relationship was in his, rather than Graham's command. So Graham lay in bed at nights and tormented himself with speculations about what the boy had come to the brink of confiding, while Stephen himself thought about it little.

Not surprisingly, it was a relief to both of them when term ended. They met every Saturday and Sunday, and on Tuesday and Thursday evenings for nets. In addition Graham was much in demand as a guest player for other clubs in the area, and played a fair amount of midweek cricket. Whenever possible he got Stephen a place in one of the teams, and occasionally he rang the boy and asked him along to score, or simply to watch. He had to be careful in this, to avoid arousing Stephen's parents suspicions; but they managed to see a lot of each other over the first month of the holidays.

One of Stephen's special pleasures was sitting outside his house in Graham's car when Graham dropped him off after matches. It was his first experience of the delight of conversation with a worldly, knowledgeable but sympathetic adult, and it acted on him like some magical drug on a willing new addict. He sometimes found it especially hard to credit his good fortune in having it so easily and freely available, on tap. Sometimes they sat there in the cocoon of darkness until two and three in the morning, the conversation putting out runners and sports until it seemed to Stephen that they must cover the whole of human knowledge in a single night.

It was the most golden of all golden days in the sun, and Stephen wanted one run for his hundred. Graham ran up to bowl to him, and Stephen knew before the ball left his hand that he would give him a nice, easy long hop outside the off stump, and so it turned out. Graham stood back and offered him a warm, conspiratorial smile as the ball sat up and asked to be hit. The ball was actually his father, shrunken to the size of the armadillos used in the croquet match in *Alice in Wonderland*, and his bat was the stiffened form of his mother. He and Graham had carefully dipped her in starch before the match, then laid her, glowering furiously but impotently through the glistening coat of varnish they had applied when she had dried out, on the back seat of the car when they set off for the match.

He connected with the ball sweetly, right on the point of his mother's chin, and his father sped like a rocket to the extra-cover boundary. The father-ball cannoned with a report like a thunder-clap against an advertising board beyond the boundary rope, and rebounded back into the field. Then things began to go horribly awry. Instead of rolling to a halt, the ball uncoiled itself like smoke, and his father, reconstituted and growing at terrible pace back to his proper size, began to race towards Stephen. At the same time the varnish peeled off his mother, and she began to unstiffen and curl up towards him in his hands. Her legs, compressed to form the handle of the bat, came unglued. She flailed in his hands, and fell, writhing, on the pitch. Both of them started growing to vast size, and towered above him, blotting out the sun. He heard Graham's voice, grown thin and toneless, crying out to him to do something. He knew that if he could only do whatever it was he would be safe, but he couldn't quite hear what it was that he had to do. The monstrous shapes of his parents coalesced to form one enormous black shadow, and the light vanished. His last conscious memory was Graham's voice, calling, "Stephen... Stephen... Steve..."

"STEVE!" roared Bill. "Wake up! We're here. Come on, you little sod, WAKE UP!" He took Stephen by the shoulders and shook him hard. Stephen gave a convulsive shiver and opened his eyes. For a second he gazed wildly about him, wondering where he was, still in a cold, clammy sweat from the nightmare. Then he came to his senses, and dragged a deep breath down as the relief washed over him. "Ooogh!" he said, as he flexed cramped, stiffened limbs. "How long have I been asleep?"

"Couple of hours, I should think", said Bill. "You and most of 'em. Lucky I stayed awake. Driver got himself lost twice. Still, we're there now. Look lively."

"Whassa time?" asked Stephen, rubbing his eyes and stretching.

"Ten past midnight. Don't worry. Bar'll still be goin strong. John here never closes." He hastened on towards the back of the big forty-seater coach, shaking and bawling at sleeping players.

Stephen did some more luxuriant stretching, stood up and looked about him. Graham's head appeared over the head-rest in front of him. He gave Stephen a sleep-drugged grin, and shook his head to clear it. "You were snoring well", he said. Stephen blushed in the ghostly light from the few little reading lights above the seats here and there along the bus. The back was in complete darkness, with cricketers festooned about the seats in a variety of uncomfortable-looking postures, still asleep or groaning into semi-wakefulness under Bill's less than gentle ministrations.

Eventually they all tottered blearily off the coach, most of them still trying to shake themselves properly awake, and stood around in a bunch in a dark, steeply sloping yard. Stephen could see that they were at the back of a large building, in which he could make out a glass door by the faint light coming from behind it. "Down there", came Bill's voice. "That's the back entrance of the pub."

"Do they know we're late?" came a voice which Stephen thought he recognized as Don Parker's.

"Yeah", came Bill's voice again. "I phoned from a call-box by the side of the road, twenty miles back, while you lot were all gonkin."

"Gonking?" muttered Stephen, turning to the dark shape of Graham beside him. "What's gonking?"

"I don't know, for sure", said Graham. "Bill's always coming out with words I've never heard of, but I imagine from the context it probably means sleeping."

"Marinespeak", said a voice. "Bill was an officer in the

Marines", it continued, and they recognized it as belonging to Colin Preston, the airy square-cutter. "Either that or he plays the trivia machine in the Rat's Castle. There's dozens of questions on Marinespeak on it." There was a general chuckle. The club captain's addiction to trivial pursuit games on pub machines was well-known. The crowd began to drift towards the dimly illuminated rectangle in the looming cliff of the building.

They went in single file along a narrow corridor towards another door, outlined above, below and down one side by narrow lines of bright light. Stephen was temporarily dazzled as the door was opened, and a few moments later they were all standing in a small reception area, blinking like owls in the sudden glare of lights.

"Leave the bags here", said Bill, dumping his own bulky holdall and his cricket bag beside the reception counter. "Bar's through there", he said to Stephen, gesturing and immediately leading the way. The others all deposited bags, holdalls and cases about the reception area and followed him into the bar. There were three or four late drinkers leaning on the bar, and a wiry, thin-faced man behind it, holding a glass up to one of a vast array of optics as they piled into the room. The drinkers glanced round, and all broke into simultaneous smiles of recognition. "Eh, howdo, lads", came a chorus of welcome. The landlord wiped the bottom of the glass he was holding carefully along the bottom of the optic and turned towards them.

"Hullo, lads", he cried. "Good to see you again." The warmth in his voice was unmistakably genuine.

"He seems very pleased to see us", murmured Stephen to Graham.

Graham grinned. "He is. He takes two months' money off us in the week we're here, the way we spend", he said in a low voice, for Stephen's ears only. "I must say, it's good to be back", he went on in a normal voice.

The landlord opened the hatch and came through to the customers' side of his bar, and was immediately engulfed by a swarm of cricketers, competing to shake his hand, slap him on the back and generally make a fuss of him. "He's popular", murmured Stephen more or less to himself.

"He's a bloody good bloke, is John", someone said, and Stephen looked up to find Alan beside him. "He always looks after us right royally", Alan went on. "Never closes the bar, always buys his round, and never complains about the singing. Hi, John, how you doing, you old bugger?" he said, pumping the landlord's hand. "This is Steve Hill, new member this season. His first cricket tour, this is."

"Eh, well, you'll do a'reet wi this lot", said the man, grabbing Stephen's hand and shaking it long and vigorously. "They're a good crowd a lads, are these. You'll find us a'reet, an all. Always look after 'em, we do — don't we Fred?" he called. A short, fat man of indeterminate age had appeared in the bar from beyond a partition and, on seeing who had arrived to fill the room to overflowing, had followed the landlord round and was being fallen upon with great affection by the cricketers.

"Owd Fred, my barman", said the landlord, turning back to Stephen, still clutching his hand in a vice-like grip. "Been ere over fifty year, has Fred, though you'd never know it look at im. Now then, I'm John Tozer, I'm t'guvnor ere, an very pleased to meetcha. Lemme say howdo to't rest of em, an we'll ave a drink." He released Stephen's hand as if he was parting from a beloved friend, and moved on to greet the remainder of the party. Fred meanwhile had gone back behind the bar, and was already filling glasses.

Stephen felt very happy. "Nice to feel you belong, isn't it?" said Graham, materialising beside him out of the crowd with a pint of lager in each hand. "Cheers, Stephen. Good tour." They drank.

Half an hour later the orgy of reunions and greetings had come to an end, and the party had resolved itself into groups of three and four. The landlord was sitting on a barstool talking animatedly with Bill and Don Parker. ("...an ow many toons've you ad this season, Don?" Stephen heard in broad north Yorkshire brogue.) Fred, the barman, who was, Stephen had heard incredulously, eighty years old, was bustling about behind the bar, serving continuously while he listened, with his head cocked on one side and his eyes bright with intelligence, to an account from Alan and Colin of the events of the year since he had seen them last. The few local after-hours drinkers were laughing and chatting with other groups.

Stephen, as new boy, took a back seat, sipping his lager at nothing like the rate the others seemed to be drinking at, and listening to the conversations going on all round him. A deep, glowing feeling of contentment enveloped him. He felt almost as if he was properly, fully alive for the first time. After a while Graham separated from one of the groups and came to sit with him, and he felt a wave of affection sweep over him, mingled with gratitude — it was Graham who had initiated him into all this, who had, in a sense, freed him from the prisoning confines of his life up to then. He smiled softly at Graham. "Happy?" asked Graham. "Happy", he said, and his eyes were shining.

By half-past two everyone was thinking about bed. Several of the party were already dozing where they sat, and virtually everyone's eyelids were drooping heavily. "Can we sort out the rooms, John?" asked Bill, and the two of them headed for the door. There Bill turned and called "anybody wanting to turn in?" There was a murmur. "Well, if you do want to we're going up to sort out rooms and dish out keys now. Come with us if you want to." He followed John out into the passage to reception. Graham glanced enquiringly at Stephen, and Stephen nodded. They got up and went, with several of the others, after the skipper and the landlord, finding them with their heads together over a sheet of paper on the reception counter.

"Right", said Bill, surveying the group gathered round him. "Don and Simon, twenty-one. Here y'are." He handed Don Parker a key on a huge plastic fob. "Colin, who you sharing with? Pete Staples, yeah? Right, you're in nineteen." Colin took his key and joined Don and Simon rummaging among the mountain of baggage. "Graham? You and Steve, isn't it? Yeah", he mumbled to himself, ticking names on the sheet of paper, "fourteen. Here, Graham." Graham took the key and turned to find that Stephen had salvaged their bags. He relieved him of his own, and led the way up a flight of stairs to their room. "Same room as I had last year", he said over his shoulder as they entered a long corridor.

"Who were you with last year?" asked Stephen, unable to suppress a slight tremor in his stomach as he asked.

"I was with Bill last year", replied Graham. "He wasn't club captain then — this is his first year — so he didn't have skipper's privilege."

"Does he really fart a lot?" asked Stephen with interest, remembering what Bill had said.

Graham chuckled. "Not as much as some of them'll tell you",

he said. "And a lot more than he'd admit. Ah. Here we are." He halted beside one of the uniform cream-painted doors along the corridor, with a bright brass number 14, and unlocked it.

The room was not very big, but the twin beds were big, old-fashioned and, as Stephen discovered by immediately plumping himself down on one, comfortable. "That one suit you?" asked Graham, sitting on the far one, under the window."

"Yes, fine", said Stephen, bouncing up and down on the bed.

"Do you mind having a window open?" asked Graham. "I like to, but I don't mind if you'd rather not."

"No, carry on", said Stephen. "I like a bit of air." He watched Graham covertly as he threw the heavy sash window wide open. I think, he told himself, the time has come. But not tonight... He felt oddly placid, and not impatient at all. "Ought to have a shower", said Graham, turning back from the window, "but I don't think I can be bothered. Have it in the morning. Don't mind me if you want one, though."

"No, I'm too tired", murmured Stephen, yawning. "Morning'll do for me too."

They started to undress. Stephen saw in a single rapid glance Graham's neat, prominent genitals. He felt a brief, hot flush pass over him, and could not help taking a second covert look. As he did so he saw Graham doing exactly the same, and laughed to himself.

"What's funny?" asked Graham, falling into bed.

"Nothing." As Stephen slid beneath the counterpane he looked up, and their eyes met. He gave him a friendly, sleepy smile. "Good night, Graham", he said softly, already curling up comfortably in the cool sheets.

"Good night, my dear... chap" said Graham, turning off the light at the switch by his bed. Stephen's mind registered the hasty addition of the final word. He just had time to formulate a last thought. Tomorrow night, I think... He was asleep.

***

The tourists got off to the best possible start the following day. When they arrived at Collingham Bridge's beautiful ground at ten-thirty the tough, springy turf of the immaculately mown outfield was still silver with dew, and very wet. The sun was a watery phantom, barely visible behind a high blanket of bright white cloud.

Bill won the toss and batted, and against a very good bowling side, expertly handled and led by the Collingham captain, they made 286 for seven — a highly respectable total, but far from unbeatable on a small ground. Don Parker scored an immaculate ninety, Graham a fine fifty-three, and Stephen a lively eighteen in a frantic run-chase towards the declaration. Then they bowled the powerful Yorkshire side out for 261. Stephen took two wickets with his airy, flighted off-spin, and rounded off a thoroughly happy day by catching the last man on the long-on boundary to end the game. His pleasure in a good catch was magnified by the fact that it was off Graham's neat, unostentatious seam-up trundlers.

The applause was tumultuous, and sporting, coming as much from the Collingham Bridge players on the balcony of their honey-coloured stone pavilion as from the tourists. Stephen and Graham were surrounded by the rest of the team, slapped on the back until their shoulders ached, and had their hair ruffled until it felt as if it was coming out in tufts. Then heads were lowered in the charge for the dressing room and the drinking to come.

By the time their coach deposited them back at the hotel in Malton a good many of the side were already happily drunk. Graham was sober, but he was highly elated, since his bowling rarely brought him tangible results. Stephen too was in an exalted state, partly because he had had a fine game and thought he had rarely been happier, partly because he had drunk four pints on a capacity of rather less, and partly because he had made his decision.

When the team were snugly ensconced in John Tozer's back bar — which they had made their own — and the serious drinking was in full swing, the two of them joined in, but both kept a careful watch on themselves, and poured a quantity of beer into various plant pots, umbrella stands and other people's glasses when the owners weren't watching. At half-past ten Stephen looked round to see who was sober enough to be worth saying goodnight to, and found that this by now meant half a dozen of the hardest-headed. He pleaded tiredness, and quietly slipped out, followed by a ragged chorus of "Why was he born so beautiful?" He was followed fifteen minutes later by Graham, bowling imaginary top-spinners along the corridors and replaying in his mind the ball that had brought him his wicket that evening.

***

Stephen waited for a few minutes after they had said good-night, then called softly across the room. "Graham."

There was a rustling of bedclothes. "Whassup?" Graham said sleepily.

"You still awake?"

"No, you young ass, I'm talking in my sleep", came the reply, but there was a kindness in the voice that robbed it of offence.

"Can I ask you something?"

There was a pause, with more rustling, and Stephen could make out Graham's dim shape as he sat up slightly in bed. "What's the matter?" Graham's voice now sounded awake and alert, with just the faintest muzziness from beer.

"Nothing's the matter. I just want to ask you something. If it's okay", said Stephen.

"Well, yes, of course you can. I hope it doesn't require me to think much", said Graham, taking his cue from Stephen and speaking very quietly. "Go ahead."

A moment later he woke up properly, as he heard Stephen slip out of bed and pad barefooted across the room to his own. A hand felt along the bedclothes seeking an empty part. Then he felt Stephen perch himself on the edge of the bed beside his chest. He could smell a faint scent of the soap Stephen had used in the shower. His senses were all alert now, and he could feel his pulse go on to rapid fire. For a moment he had nothing to say.

"Graham", said Stephen after a long pause. "Do you know what they think about you in the club?"

Graham felt a bead of sweat ooze from his forehead and trickle maddeningly down his face, but he dared not free a hand to brush it away for fear of upsetting the equilibrium of the moment. He was not absolutely certain what was to come, but he had a fair idea, and with it a strong intuition that it must be allowed to take its course. He waited, with further beads following the first. At last he said, forcing himself to keep his voice even, "I...er...I think I could probably make some sort of a guess..." He let it hang in the thickening darkness of the room, waiting for Stephen to speak again.

"They — some of them — think you're gay", said Stephen, in almost a matter of fact tone.

Graham went cold. His mind had been running on overtime in the last few moments, and he had been virtually certain that this was what Stephen was going to say. But hearing it stated outright like that, cold and unequivocally, he felt a momentary tremor of fright, almost panic, shoot through him. Again he took refuge in silence and waiting.

"They don't actually *know* anything", went on Stephen, in the same calm, quiet tone. "But some of them think so."

"I..." began Graham. But he felt a hand placed firmly on the curve of his hip beneath the quilt, and rest there, firmly, and moving slowly in small circles. He interpreted this, correctly, as a soothing message to be silent, and obeyed.

"You know I've told you a lot about my home and my parents, and so on", Stephen went on after a further pause. This time Graham permitted himself a murmur of acknowledgement. "And I *think* you've known there was something else, too", he continued. "Something else I wanted to ask you about, but didn't...wasn't ready to yet. I've had the impression you were aware of that...?" He made it a question.

"Yes, I thought there was something else", he assented.

"Did you ever have any idea what it might be?"

This time Stephen left it hanging in mid-air, content to wait for a reply.

Graham lay propped on one elbow in bed and gave the question some concentrated thought, then said carefully "I... think I could have had a guess at what it might have been. I think... I think I knew it was probably something big, something important. I think I was pretty sure it was something you couldn't, or at least didn't want to talk about to your parents. And — well, if you want me to be absolutely honest, which I take it you do, well, yes, frankly, Stephen, yes, I think I had a pretty good idea what the problem might be. I'm sorry to sound so hesitant", he said, his voice more confident as his bodily reactions began to slow back to normal. "But I'd hate to draw conclusions about you and find they were the wrong ones. I don't think it's my place to judge other people, or to speculate about them, except in private. Everyone forms impressions, opinions, about other people. But unless they concern oneself, well, I think they're to be kept strictly inside the mind of the person making them. But, since you ask me point blank like this, well, you've had my answer. May I ask if it's what you expected to hear?"

"Yes, of course", came Stephen's voice. "But can I ask you some more things first, please?"

"Yes, of course."

"Well, you haven't said anything about what I've just told you about what the club think about you. I'd have thought you'd be pretty shocked. But you didn't react at all."

"I did, Stephen. Just not audibly. But I wasn't very surprised to hear they thought that about me. I've had my suspicions from time to time. You know — or, well, perhaps you don't — but you get the odd impression here and there, overhear the odd word when somebody didn't know you were in earshot — that sort of thing. No, I wasn't surprised. And apart from being surprised, what other reaction is there open to me? I can't do anything about it, can I? I can't stop them thinking I may be gay. I can't stop their tongues wagging about it, if that's the way they want it. I've got my own ideas which particular members of the club may have been doing the talking. But what would you suggest I do about it?"

"They haven't actually said anything", said Stephen. "Not in so many words. Not to me, anyway. And I wouldn't suggest you do anything about it. I wouldn't have a clue how to react if people were saying that sort of thing about me." He paused, then there came a faint titter. "I expect they are, actually, don't you?" he said. "With me being such a close friend of yours, and sharing this room like this, and you bringing me from the school and introducing me, and so on...Now can I ask you the main thing? Please?"

There was a tone of soft pleading in the soft voice which stirred Graham's pulse in a turmoil of mingled love, fondness, protectiveness and yearning; but it was a pleading of a kind unattended by any sense of indignity: rather it was the tone of one who politely but without abasement asks something from one equal to another; the tone of one who asks only for that which he is owed by right. Graham wriggled one of his hands from under the bedclothes and laid it gently on Stephen's own hand, where it still rested on his hip. "Ask me anything you like", he said calmly, authoritatively. The twelve years between their ages vanished, and it was one mature man addressing another.

There was another pause, the longest yet. Then Stephen spoke again, still in the same level voice. "It's quite simple. How do you know if you're gay, Graham?"

"I can answer that quite easily", he said. "You have to ask yourself one question. And give yourself an honest answer, that goes without saying."

"Yes?"

"Which sex do you fancy?"

Graham could hear him breathing as he thought about it, almost hear him thinking. "Suppose I say 'men'?"

"Then you're gay."

"It's as simple as that?"

"Yes. I'm afraid it's as simple as that. I say 'I'm afraid', because it's not something everybody is very happy to accept. Some people are so unhappy they quite simply refuse to accept it. Others ask the question, answer it, and off they go, quite satisfied. They're the fortunate ones. All they've been needing is to have the question answered. They're not too bothered what the answer is, so long as they have it answered. But others... well..."

"Suppose I said 'I don't know'? What then?"

"I could go on, ask you a few further questions. I'd be able to get to the answer quickly enough, without much trouble, if you really wanted to know it. That would be the real difficulty — finding out whether you really wanted to know or not. Can I ask you something now?"

"Yes, of course."

"Do you want to know this? I mean, I'm taking it that this isn't just an abstraction, for the pleasure of abstract thought. Do you, really, want to know this about yourself?"

"Yes, please. Yes, I do."

"All right, then, Stephen. You tell me: which sex do you fancy?"

"I don't know. I think I do, but I don't know for sure."

"Which do you think?"

"Men."

"Then I think you're gay. Do you want me to go on — ask you the other questions?"

"Will you answer another one from me first?"

"Yes."

"Which sex do *you* fancy?"

"Men."

"Then will you show me which I am?"

Graham caught his breath. He had, he supposed, known all along that this was where it was leading, where it was all intended to end up. Yet when the boy came out with it, for the second time that night it had the effect of making the foreknowledge of it singularly unhelpful against the shock wave it set up. He lay back against his pillow to gather his thoughts. When he spoke at last his voice was sober, carefully schooled to neutrality, the better to conceal the sudden racing of his blood and the feeling of light-headedness that was making him feel sick and faint and threatened to lay him gasping and speechless on the hotel bed, like a freshly beached fish. "You want me to..."

"Yes, I do", cried Stephen, driven beyond his power to control his sudden, urgent need. Desire, lust, yearning flared within the boy as the careful facade of rationality cracked and burst, and he became what he was: a young, healthy animal suffering from years of sexual repression, ignorance and distortion when he was at the peak of his potency. The whole of it boiled up and broke the surface in three monosyllables, bursting from his lips like machine-gun bullets. As suddenly as they burst from him he subsided, and his next words were spoken quietly once more. "Yes, dear Graham, I do want you to. I want you to show me. Show me what I am. Now."

"It's breaking the law", said Graham, pushing back the quilt and the sheet as he spoke, and making room in the bed beside him. "We'd both be in the most frightful trouble with the police if it ever came out. Especially me. I dare say you know that, and I don't suppose you care."

"No", whispered Stephen, sliding into bed beside him.

"Nor do I", said Graham, and it sounded like a sigh.

***

"Mmmmmmm." Graham awoke with an erection, which was common enough, and with fingers running up and down it, which wasn't. He circled quickly back to consciousness to find himself entwined in Stephen's hard, vibrant embrace, and Stephen's lips and tongue busy about his own. "Mmmm", he repeated, easing himself slightly to one side in order to speak. "What are you up to?" he muttered as Stephen followed his movement and sealed his lips once more.

It was several minutes before he got free again. When he did it was to nibble Stephen's ear as his own passion rose rapidly. The boy's hands were everywhere, and he could feel a very erect penis pressing urgently into his lower abdomen. "You sexy little bugger", he muttered into Stephen's hair. "We shouldn't be..."

"Shhh!" murmured Stephen, exploring with tongue and fingertips. Graham stopped resisting, and gave himself up to being caressed, wondering how the boy could have discovered such expertise in the space of a few hours.

"Have you noticed", said Stephen conversationally, flicking the tip of his tongue round the convolutions of Graham's ear, "you get a sort of electric shock when your cock touches mine? I can feel it every time they touch."

Graham had noticed. "What are you trying to do to me?" he muttered as passion ached and throbbed through him.

"It's quarter to seven", said Stephen softly. "They won't be going in to breakfast till about eight. We'll have time for a shower before we go down." He closed Graham's mouth with his own, and resumed exploring.

"What do you want to do?" whispered Graham as his arms went tight round Stephen's waist and neck.

"You know bloody well what I want", hissed Stephen, taking Graham's penis and guiding it as he turned lazily onto his stomach. "I want to be screwed again, just like last night. Then I want to do it to you. Then we'll have a shower, and go down to breakfast looking as if butter wouldn't melt in our mouths, and then you're going to get a hundred against Driffield, and I'm going to get fifty, and take five for thirty. Then we're going to come back here and have a drink, and then I shall want to be screwed again, and so on, ad infinitum..." And since Graham was by now already halfway inside him, there was little point in resistance, even if he had been capable of it.

They showered together, giggling and splashing each other as they fondled and caressed under the heavy jets. Stephen, with the inexhaustible potency of his years, became seriously aroused in the little perspex cubicle, and Graham mischievously turned the jet to the coldest point on the dial as he pulled away, effectually quelling the boy's ardour for the moment. But even after they had dried each other, romping together on Graham's bed, Stephen was suddenly twined round him with renewed vigour, erect and urgent and locking his arms powerfully round the older man. Graham leaned back in his arms and gazed contemplatively at him. "You're going to wear me out before this week's out", he said, amicably. "I'm an old man, you know." Stephen tweaked him playfully, then began stroking him with a slow, confident rhythm.

"All right", sighed Graham in mock resignation as his desire rose to meet Stephen's. "I suppose I'll have to quieten you down. As I haven't got a bucket of water I'll show you something else. But then it's breakfast, okay?"

Stephen smiled lazily into his face, then impulsively leant forward and licked the tip of his nose. "Okay", he said softly, his eyes bright with arousal. Graham breathed another mock sigh, slid down through the boy's pinioning arms onto his knees, and ran the tip of his tongue up the exposed underside of Stephen's erect and quivering penis. Stephen moaned softly. "Oh, God", he breathed as Graham got to work, "you don't know how much I love you, do you?" Graham trembled, and got on with what he was doing.

***

"You don't need me to tell you we've got to keep this a total, deadly secret", said Graham very quietly as they went down to breakfast just after eight o'clock. Even though they were walking along a corridor less than four feet wide, with no-one in sight, he could not help casting a furtive glance round and behind.

"Of course I don't", said Stephen cheerfully. "I know we're breaking the law, and I don't give a shit about the law. Nor do you, do you? You and I are the only people who know what happened, and we're not going to talk, are we? The others may suspect something — you said yourself last night that they might. Well, let 'em suspect, I say. They can't possibly know anything, and they wouldn't have a chance of proving anything even if they suspected. Please, Graham, stop worrying", he pleaded, looking much younger and more vulnerable than he had at any time in the past twenty-four hours. Graham summoned up such strength as remained to him, and gave him an uncertain smile as they turned into the breakfast room.

They were among the last downstairs, and had to sit at separate tables. Stephen sat with some of the younger members of the party who had formed their own noisy clique in a corner of the room, and Graham dropped into a chair between Don Parker and Bill Stanley, a middle-aged beanpole of a man with a deeply-lined face and a Hitler moustache.

Graham sat silently toying with his breakfast, to the chagrin of the fat, motherly waitress, who clucked over him until he was driven to pleading a poor night's sleep. Stephen, by contrast, was in high spirits.

"They're hyperactive in children's corner this morning", observed Stanley as Stephen's voice floated across. "This roll would turn a yard", he was saying. "Give it a try", someone urged him. He jumped up, took a short run and bowled his perfectly spherical bread roll towards Graham's table. It leapt high to one side and struck Don Parker smartly on the back of the head. Don, who was not at his best at breakfast, clutched at his head so quickly that he crushed the roll into his hair. He directed an outraged glare in the direction from which the roll had come. "Ere y'are son, on me ead", cried one of the youngsters as Don hurled the remains of the roll back at them. "I said it would turn", cried Stephen triumphantly.

"Hey, hey", called Bill. "Let's have a bit of decorum, you kids."

"You get like that when you get old and miserable", said a youthful voice, and there was a chorus of geriatric sound effects.

The horseplay went on, only slightly subdued, and this set the tone for the day, with Graham moody and uncommunicative while Stephen was high-spirited and playful. At Driffield Graham amassed a grinding thirty-three runs in a manner reminiscent of Geoffrey Boycott in an especially entrenched frame of mind, while Stephen flashed and glanced blithely to forty-nine, only to get out square-cutting airily at a ball pitched well up on middle stump. So far from being depressed or annoyed at himself he almost danced off the field, swinging his bat cheerfully.

"That grin'd go right round your head if it wasn't for your ears", remarked Bill Stanley. Stephen put his tongue out at him as he skipped up the steps to the dressing room.

"He's chipper this morning", observed Bill. He jabbed Graham in the ribs with his elbow. "You bin putting certain substances in his tea, or somethin, Graham?" Graham gave him a brief, unconvincing grin and said nothing. Bill stared hard at him. "You all right?" he asked, narrowing his eyes.

Graham realized with a mental start that his depressed manner was attracting attention. He affected a wan smile. "Yes, I'm okay", he said, making a concerted effort to pull himself together. "I had a lousy night, and I've got a blinder of a headache, that's all."

"I've got some paracetamol", volunteered somebody. "Want a couple, Graham?" He nodded gratefully, noticing for the first time that he really had developed a headache over the morning. The tablets were produced and he went into the pavilion for a drink. The others exchanged glances briefly and then forgot him as they turned back to the game.

When Graham came out after taking his tablets he bumped into Stephen, emerging from the dressing room after taking off his pads. "Walk round?" asked that youth, brightly. Graham stood for a long moment, contemplating his friendly young face, and his mood lightened as abruptly as the depression had descended when they woke. "Yes. All right, come on", he said, in a brighter tone than he had used all day. They strolled off.

"You've been pretty grim all day", said Stephen as soon as they were out of earshot of the others. "Shot!" he added, as Alan Hood, the vice-captain, whipped the ball off his legs. He ran to field the ball as it came skimming fast across the billiard-table outfield and over the boundary. Then he returned to Graham's side, and the concerned expression returned to his face. "Is something the matter? I mean, you're not sorry about last night, are you? Please don't say you're sorry it happened, Graham..."

Graham looked at him with the faintest glint of a smile playing round the corners of his mouth and eyes. "No, I'm not

72

sorry", he eventually said, a shade reluctantly. "Not really. It's just..." He fell silent.

"Yes,", prompted Stephen, anxiously. "Just what?"

"Oh, I don't know", said Graham vaguely. "I just felt it was... I suppose I felt it wasn't right", he faltered.

"Oh, come *on*, Graham", protested Stephen. "How can you say it wasn't right? I wanted you to do everything you did, didn't I? I *asked* you to, didn't I, for Christ's sake? So what can possibly be not right about the whole thing? You tell me that." His voice had risen slightly in exasperation, but his expression was affectionate and concerned, and he put an arm gently about Graham's shoulders as they walked slowly on.

Graham looked fearfully round. Then he caught himself doing so, and his face set. "I'm sorry, Stephen", he said. "I'm brooding and worrying like a moulting owl. I'll do my best to pull myself together. Take no notice of me. It's probably just a reaction from last night. I was very worried — about breaking the law, you know. I mean, you can imagine the newspapers yourself, I dare say: 'Teacher in gay sex romps with boy, seventeen. Schoolmaster Graham Curtis, twenty-nine, of...' And so on."

"But no-one's ever going to know", protested Stephen, his voice rising in perplexity. "I mean, how's anyone going to know, ever? Unless we tell them, that is? And I'm certainly not intending to sell my story to the *News of the World* — are you?"

It was so absurd a suggestion that Graham laughed for the first time that day. "As I said, Stephen, take no notice of me", he said. "I'll get over it. It's just a reaction. You don't know how I've wanted you, since we started getting to know each other. You remember that day", he went on, in a happier tone than he had used all day, "when we walked round the ground and I introduced you to Don?"

Stephen nodded, looking fondly at him. "How could I forget it?" he asked lightly.

"Well, I think I fell a little bit in love with you that day", said Graham. He halted, and his eyes slipped out of focus as he cast his mind back and remembered. "It was something you said. I'm damned if I can remember what it was now, but I remember suddenly thinking 'this boy's got a sharp wit' — I remember that quite distinctly, using the word to myself. Wit — it's a very rare quality, perhaps the rarest of all, and certainly not a word you expect to find yourself using about one of the boys every day. But I thought it to myself, and that's when I really started to take notice of you. Up to then you'd just been..."

"A face in the crowd?" suggested Stephen. "Just one school-boy out of hundreds, I suppose?"

Graham nodded. "Yes. But never again, not after that day. So, as I say, my dear, you don't know how I've wanted you, or how badly. So this morning, having attained what I'd been yearning for, well..." He left it at that, glanced at the boy to see that he had understood, and started walking once more.

They turned the conversation to the game as they completed their circuit of the boundary and set off on another. As they were coming home to the pavilion after the second, Stephen said quietly, "You really aren't regretting last night, are you Graham? Please tell me you're not."

Graham gave him a slow, tentative smile. "No, I'm not regretting it", he said. "I couldn't regret it. Don't worry about me, Stephen. I enjoyed every moment of it, of course. And I'm not having secret second thoughts or anything like that."

"I hope not", said Stephen, suddenly mischievous now that his anxiety was allayed. "You're fucking me tonight, don't forget."

Graham jerked his head round, shocked into a wide-eyed stare of surprise. Then, abruptly, he laughed. "Hah! You're a boy, aren't you?" he said.

"Well, I'm not just a silly girl", said Stephen, in a remarkable imitation of Bill Stanley's lugubrious voice — it was one of Bill's favourite catch-phrases. Graham laughed, and got hiccups for his pains, which cracked both of them up. "That's better", said Stephen in satisfaction.

"Who's running this show?" asked Graham when he recovered.

"I am", said Stephen cockily. "Until tonight", he added in a soberer tone.

"Come on, you little bugger", said Graham. "The bar'll be open. I could do with a drink."

***

Driffield resisted vigorously before succumbing, but eventually lost by fifty-odd. The drinking was hearty, and Stephen allowed himself to get a little tight after they got back to Malton. It was after midnight when he slipped out. The surviving drinkers were all too preoccupied with singing rugby songs, led by Bill, who had an inexhaustible repertoire of them, even to notice his going. Graham, whose earlier depression had been replaced by a pendulum swing into a bright, confident cheerfulness, stayed on for another half hour, then yawned and left the hard core to continue with John Tozer until long after dawn.

The room was silent and in darkness as he stepped in. He shut the door and turned the key that Stephen had left in the lock, and cat-footed across to his bed, knowing it was occupied. He stripped off and slid easily down beside Stephen. The touch of the boy's cool naked body was a long bliss, which he took his time to savour. Then arms came round him, and a murmur. "Still feel the same about me?"

A cool current of air came cheekily into the room from the window. He let out a long, shuddering breath, then began to stroke Stephen's body. "Just the same", he said. "Or stronger."

***

At the selection meeting in the bar after breakfast the next morning Bill announced that they were both rested for that day's game, to give some of the others a place. They saw the players off on the coach, then wandered about the little town for a couple of hours. There was a livestock market in full swing, and they stood for a while listening with townsmen's fascination to the incomprehensible proceedings at various auctions going on. They watched some prize pigs being sold for sums that made their eyes widen in astonishment, and admired the dimensions of the testicles on the boars. They had a couple of pints in the Spotted Cow, a dingy little pub of nooks and narrow passages, full of farmers in identical tweeds who appeared to be selling each other things. Then they went back to the hotel for lunch, after which they went to their room and fell on each other.

In the afternoon they hired a car and went to York, where they ambled round the railway museum gazing at steam engines, which Graham just about remembered seeing once or twice as a small boy. Stephen had only seen them on television, and fell unreservedly in love with the gleaming monsters. When they got back to Malton they made love again, and had just got down to the bar when the team got back from their game. They exchanged accounts of their day with the players and the other small groups of people who had been rested and drifted off to one point of the compass or another. The drinking was beginning to tell, and by some communal instinct most of the party drifted off quite soon for a restorative early night.

This set the pattern for the remainder of the tour. They played cricket enthusiastically, and when they made way in the side they wandered about the Dales, stopping for drinks in quiet country pubs and eating meat and potato pie and faggots and mushy peas. ("Does this count as cannibalism, do you think?" Stephen said, taking a large bite out of a faggot.)

One day they drove out to Harry Ramsden's fish and chip shop and tested the claim on the sign there that "If it swims, we sell it". Stephen had swordfish and chaffed Graham for conservatism when he stuck soberly to haddock. They rambled in the wild and beautiful hills, and at one point, high and carried away by elation and a general feeling of well-being, looked quickly about, saw no-one, and plunged into some bushes to appease a sudden sexual craving that struck them both powerless at the same moment and would not be denied. Once or twice Graham became moody and quiet again, worrying about what they were doing, but the attacks were short-lived, and Stephen's consistently high spirits as he continued enthusiastically on his journey of discovery into his newfound delights rallied him rapidly. And all too quickly, almost before they knew it, the week was over and it was time to go home.

***

"You want fuckin with a rusty ragman's trumpet, the lot of you", said Jack Page furiously, tramping into the midst of fifteen naked eighteen-year-olds in the visitors' changing room. "What the hell was the matter with you?" he demanded. "They were all over you." He stared angrily round his team of hopefuls. "I mean, I really had hopes for some of you miserable specimens. What went wrong? You had enough ball to've stuffed 'em out of sight, and you played like a bunch a women. I might as well've had fifteen from the girls' school out there." He blew out his cheeks in ill-controlled temper as he threw off his referee's strip and stepped into the shower. There he found Stephen Hill, who had changed in a hurry and been first under the jets. "You, for instance, Master Hill", he snapped, slapping Stephen's backside hard enough to extract a "Wow!" of pain from him. "I had you down as certain for loose-head, and what did you do? Eh? What did you do to repay my confidence? Played like a pregnant duck, is what you did. My seven-year-old would've played more of a game. My seven-year-old daughter. I mean, honestly, someone tell me, what went wrong?"

The first rugby occasion of the Michaelmas term was the traditional trial for the School XV between the whites — the Fifteen Elect, comprising those of the previous year's team who were still at school and the pick of last year's reserves and Second XV, against the colours, who represented the brightest hopes from the rest. Jack Page, a small, lean, ferret-like Welshman of forty who kept himself fanatically fit and active and, besides teaching German to the lower forms, was head of games at the school, made a point each year of forsaking his beloved First XV and taking personal charge of the colours team, and rivalry among the boys for promotion into Page's elite was ferocious and, often, unscrupulous. Stephen had been among the most hotly favoured for elevation; but he had played half-heartedly, almost as if he was uninterested in the game or its momentous consequences. Accordingly he came in for an especially bitter measure of angry disappointment from Page, who regarded a less-than-enthusiastic attitude on the rugby field as something akin to felony, if not crime against humanity.

Mr Page was dressed well before any of the team, and leaned on the the dressing room wall while they got into their clothes. Stephen finished first, and was halfway through the door when Page's voice halted him in mid-step. "Not so fast, my lad. I haven't finished with you yet." Stephen looked enquiringly over his shoulder. "Sir?"

"Back here, boy." Page crooked a finger, twinkling ominously. Stephen sidled back, looking apprehensive. The others looked likewise as they completed their dressing and wondered what was to come.

"Got a staff meeting tonight, lads" he said when they were all gathered- apprehensively round him. "Otherwise it would've been my pleasure to arrange a little work-out to express my appreciation of your efforts out there today." They glanced at each other, and a faint grin appeared here and there, like a watery sun trying to show through cloud. They failed utterly to escape his eye. "Aye, you may smirk at each other", he said cheerfully. "You'll be smiling the other side of your horrible little faces tomorrow, I reckon." The grins vanished instantly.

"Yes, my boyos. I've been wondering how to reward your labours for me out there today", he went on. "If you want to humiliate yourselves to Graham Curtis's shower, that's your own affair. But when you humiliate me as well, it becomes my affair too, don't you agree?" He waited, in a profound and fearful silence. "Well, well, I'm glad to see you've got enough sense of shame that you don't want to argue about it. Fortunately for you, I haven't got a staff meeting, or any sort of meeting, tomorrow", he continued, still twinkling mercilessly. "So, my friends, I've been thinking while you've been cleansing your bodies — which I shouldn't't've thought you needed to do, considering the amount of honest sweat you *didn't* work up out there today — what should I offer you as a consolation prize for failing to get into the School Fifteen, which should've been your rightful reward? Well, I've decided to be kind, lads. Tomorrow you run ten miles for me."

There was a general groan. "Oh, NO!"

"Oh, YES", he said. "I'll see you all here at nine o'clock tomorrow. I shall be feeling especially ready for a nice trot, having missed my little work-out tonight, you know. Ta-ta, lads."

"Sir", called one of the team urgently. Page turned back. "Yes, White?" he said, raising an eyebrow.

"Tomorrow's Saturday, sir."

Page stared at him. After a few moments a smile spread slowly over his face. "It is, isn't it?" he said, and strolled out of the room, whistling.

They looked at each other in dismay. "The old bastard!" said someone feelingly. "Let's give him a send-off", cried another.

As Page reached the outer doors of the gymnasium block he

heard a chorus, to the tune of "Clementine", ringing out from the changing room he had come from. "Who's your father, who's your father, who's your father, Jacko Page? You ain't got one, you're a bastard, you're a bastard, Jacko Page..." He smiled satanically to himself as he pushed the door open. Then, on a second thought, he turned and walked silently on his crepe soles back to the dressing room, pushed the door open and peeped round it at the crowd of disgruntled and indignant boys picking their gear up and preparing to leave. There was a sudden silence as they saw him. They looked at him angrily, almost mutinously, but apprehensively.

"I saw a film once, with Jack Palance in", he said, smiling affectionately at them. "You won't have heard of him, you being a bunch of philistine, uncultured little ragamuffins, but never mind that. Anyway, someone in this film calls Jack Palance a very rude word, suggestin that he was born the wrong side of the blanket. And Jack Palance says 'In my case an accident of birth; but you're a self-made man!' Well, lads, I don't suppose you're self-made men. More like hand-reared women, I'd say. Or breech-born spastics, maybe." His smile grew broader. "I reckon you need toughening up. We'll make it fifteen miles tomorrow, shall we?" He disappeared, leaving fifteen young men in such a depth of dismay that they had not a word to say between them.

**

Of the subdued little throng who eventually trudged dismally out of the gymnasium, wishing from the bottom of their hearts that they hadn't decided to give tongue to their little impromptu valediction, Stephen alone went with a light heart. He was as disgusted with the imposition looming horribly over them as the others, but nothing could really depress him that evening.

When the Elderton Park party had got home from Yorkshire he had settled more or less cheerfully back into the routine of home, revision of A-level work and the casual job in a supermarket by which he earned himself pocket money. He found it all more and more unsatisfying having tasted a bit of independence. But he had his weekends to look forward to, and the first week after their return opened up a whole new horizon for him.

He passed the week as best he could, measuring its passing by the high spots — Monday and Tuesday he spent looking forward to four hours' net practice on Tuesday evening, followed by a drink in the pavilion that kept him out until bedtime. Wednesday and Thursday were a simple repeat, waiting for nets on Thursday night. Friday he spent watching the clock until he could set out for the pre-weekend booze-up in the pavilion. And he had boldly decided to see if he could secure for himself a bonus.

"Cheerio, Mum", he had said as he set off. He was carrying his cricket bag, which he had packed extra carefully to cram in an extra set of daytime clothes and two cricket shirts and flannels instead of the usual one. "I may not be back tonight", he added casually as he gave her the expected peck on her cheek.

"Oh?" she said. "Why not?"

"One of the lads at the club has invited a few of us round to see some videos", he lied, crossing his fingers in his trouser pocket. She was instantly suspicious. "Oh, really?" she said, compressing her lips into a thin line of disapproval. "What kind of videos?"

"Honestly, Mum", he said, laughing. "They're not *blue* films, or anything. He's got the complete *Fawlty Towers* and some Clint Eastwood films, that's all." He laughed again, a real laugh this time, as he reflected privately that the kind of pornography she had in mind quite genuinely wouldn't interest him. "Don't worry about me, Mum. I'm a big boy now", he said lightly, and was gone before she could think of an objection to make, or ask him which player's house he was going to be at. She watched him out of sight, then made a small, faintly comic gesture of defeat to herself. "Oh well", she muttered. "I suppose he's old enough..." She left the thought unfinished, and went back into the house.

That evening he waited for Graham's arrival with suppressed impatience and excitement. Graham greeted him with the affected casualness they had agreed on as the best camouflage for their real relationship, which they had discussed at length in private moments on the tour. After a couple of drinks and an exchange of the small news of the week between the two of them and some of the others Stephen managed to catch Graham on the quiet, and murmured urgently to him. They rummaged in the kit lockers in the dressing room, took an old bat and a ball out to the outfield, and began knocking up skied catches to each other. In the intervals between catches Stephen was able to tell Graham of his neat little deception. "So you see, I can stop out tonight", he said eagerly, "and it'll be okay, because they'll think I'm watching videos. They'll probably assume I'm watching porn", he giggled, "but it doesn't matter what they think, as long as they don't know what I'm *really* doing. So we've got the whole night clear", he finished excitedly.

"Hmmm. It's a bit risky", Graham said, pursing his lips. "But I must admit, I've been missing you badly this week."

"Have you?" said Stephen, halfway between mere happiness and bliss. "Have you really missed me?"

"Of course I have", said Graham seriously, and then he smiled. "Didn't you expect me to miss you?"

"Well, I..." began Stephen. "I missed you terribly", he said. "But I thought you'd... well, I suppose I didn't dare to hope that you'd..."

"I know what you mean", said Graham kindly. "Well, of course I missed you. And since you've fixed things so we can spend the night, well... Not that I altogether approve of your methods", he broke in on himself. "I don't much like being a party to your deceiving your parents, however shaky your relations with them may be. Still, it's done now, and I can't say I wouldn't hate to waste the chance now it's there to be taken." He smiled, rather uncertainly, at Stephen. "I can't help feeling, you know", he said with a grunt, whacking the ball into a vast parabola. "Chase that one..."

Stephen hared after it, head thrown back and hair streaming, and took a perfect deep catch dropping over his head. "Well held", called Graham. They converged once again. "What can't you help feeling?" asked Stephen, seizing the ancient, tape-swaddled bat from him.

"I was going to say, I can't help feeling that this is all wrong", said Graham. "I'm a schoolmaster, put in a position of trust over you — *in loco parentis*..."

"Like I told my mother this afternoon, I'm a big boy now", interrupted Stephen. "I'm old enough to know what I want, aren't I?"

"You're old enough physically. Maybe — probably — you're old enough emotionally", conceded Graham. "What you certainly aren't is old enough by law, and even more certainly you aren't according to conventional morality in this country."

"Fuck morality", said Stephen cheerfully. "And this country. Are other countries more relaxed about this sort of thing?"

"I don't really know", said Graham. "I know most countries have lower ages of consent. Whether they'd be any more likely to condone a relationship between a schoolmaster and one of his own pupils I don't know at all, but I very much doubt it. Put one up for me."

Stephen hit the ball as hard as he could, and Graham ran for the catch. When they met again he continued. "I can't help thinking our luck can't last. I mean, we were all right on tour, sharing a room — it was only natural for us to share, because you knew me far better than anyone else. They'd have been surprised if we hadn't shared. But if we carry it on now, well, we're going to get caught one of these days, if we're not very careful indeed."

"Well we will be", grunted Stephen, whacking another high one into the air.

They carried on with their catching practice, and some new arrivals came out to join them. "Slip cradle?" Graham suggested. "Good idea", chorused several newcomers. Graham handed over their old bat and ball to some of the others, and he, Stephen and four others dragged the heavy, fifty-year-old cradle out and settled down to hard close-catching practice until the light began to fail. Then they went back inside to join the drinkers in the now crowded bar.

At ten-thirty, following a plan they had worked out while they were out on the field alone, Stephen said "cheerio" to the group of youngsters he was drinking with and left. Graham carried on drinking for a further half-hour, leaning negligently on the bar and entertaining Bill and some of the other seniors with anecdotes picked up in the masters' common room. He left when the bar closed at eleven, and strengthened his alibi by volunteering when Bill asked if anyone could give him a lift home. He declined Bill's offer of a nightcap when they got there, and it was barely half-past eleven when he parked his car outside his flat. As he walked from the street to his front door a shadow detached itself from a clump of bushes on the front lawn. Casting a hurried glance round, Graham hustled Stephen into the flat, followed him in and was very glad to get the door closed behind them.

They spent a blissful night together, with a leisurely morning to follow before they set off for the day's game, and with a precedent nicely set, Stephen felt confident enough to make a regular practice of staying away from home on Friday nights. At the same time they worked a series of variations on their routine for blinding their tracks at the cricket club. Some Fridays Stephen would not turn up for drinks at all, once or twice Graham stayed at home, and on one occasion they both stayed away, and revelled in the luxury of a whole stolen evening as well as the night. Once or twice, with his parents getting used to the idea that he was becoming independent and growing rapidly away from them, Stephen stayed out on the Saturday night as well.

Stephen's eighteenth birthday fell on the last Saturday of the school summer holidays. He gave himself the very satisfactory birthday present of four cheap wickets; but afterwards he was put out when Graham insisted that he should go home and spend the evening with his parents, who took him out to an expensive restaurant and bored him witless with their notions of conversation. However, when the drinks with which the cricketers had plied him after the game had worn off a little he was glad he had given way to Graham's gentle insistence, and he had the grace to admit as much when he went to Graham's flat the next evening.

Waiting for him there were three presents. There was an early, beautiful leather-bound edition of the works of Mill, which he had read immediately after the County Club and Ground game when he had first got to know Graham, and an expensive hardback of *Le Mystère Frontenac*, which his form had been reading in class earlier that same day. Graham sat watching him fondly as he excitedly tore the wrappings off them, like a small boy. "I thought we ought to have something to remember that day by", he said, very pleased indeed when Stephen remembered and remarked on the significance of the books. "There's one other little thing I got you", he said, and went out of the room, returning with a heavily wrapped item which could only be one thing. Stephen took it and looked up at Graham with an expression he could not read for the moment. "Go on, have a look", he said. Stephen stripped it of its paper, disclosing a beautiful Gunn and Moore cricket bat. Stephen gazed down at it, and did not raise his head for a very long interval, stroking the silky-textured, creamy blade like a woman with her child. When he finally did look up his eyes were glistening. "Oh, Graham", he whispered. He stood up, laying the beautiful bat carefully on the sofa, and came into Graham's arms. There was no more to be said.

And so for the remainder of the school summer holidays and for the first couple of weeks of the Michaelmas term, they were able to spend enough time together to keep their hunger for each other reasonably well in check; and they took such intricate pains to preserve secrecy, paying infinite attention to the smallest details of alibis, reconnoitring obsessively before meeting and keeping constantly alert to behave with master-and-pupil formality in school hours, that they began to feel very settled with each other. Their relationship gradually acquired a more subtle and rounded shape, as their simple physical desire began to put on flesh and fill out. They learned more about each other, and with the knowledge came deepening affection and regard. A sexual affair gradually became a love affair. Graham had a front-door key cut and presented it to Stephen, and he started spending more and more of his evenings at the flat, and occasionally stayed the night.

Then, out of nowhere, disaster struck, and it seemed as if they were doomed.

***

Graham had to attend the same staff meeting as Jack Page on the Friday of the mass sentencing of the colours XV, so he hung around at school, getting odd bits of paperwork out of the way.

Stephen went home. He stayed long enough to appease his conscience, which was beginning, just occasionally, to prick him over the negligible amount of time he spent there; this proved long enough also for the atmosphere to begin to get on his nerves, so he decided to go and have the customary Friday-night drink at the club. He took part in a desultory practice knockabout with some of the other youngsters, but the evenings were beginning to draw in, and they quickly decided to pack up and go inside. Stephen was left alone out on the field, because he had been the last with the bat, and had to hunt for a ball he had hit into some undergrowth beside the pavilion. He was poking about for it, swearing luridly to himself after being stung by some great coarse nettles, when he heard voices.

He straightened up to see where they were coming from, and realized after a moment that he was hearing people talking inside the pavilion. His ears pricked up immediately as he heard Graham's name mentioned. He edged closer and saw that he was directly behind the home dressing room. Taking great care to make no sound, he pressed himself against the wall of the building, straining his ears to catch what was said, and immediately identified the voices as belonging to Bill, the club captain, and Alan Hood, his deputy.

"I'm only telling you because I don't know what to do about it myself", he heard Alan saying. "I wouldn't even have paid it this much attention if I hadn't got it from where I did."

"But for Christ's sake, Al", came Bill's deep boom in exasperated tones, "you've said yourself it's none of our business. Jesus, I overheard you squashing that twat Colin flat not long ago when he was coming out with some of his imbecile gossip. Leave well alone is my motto."

"Yes, yes, mine too, if you come to that", said Alan. "Except for the kid. What about Steve? I don't know if there's anything in it, any more than you or anybody else. But they did share a room on the tour, and... well, you said yourself there was a pretty dramatic change in the kid over that week. Oughtn't we to do *something*? Have a word with his parents, maybe? Or..."

"Christ, no!" said Bill sharply. "That's the last thing we do, talk to the poor kid's parents. I've heard some of the other kids talking about them. They're some sort of religious freaks apparently. He doesn't get on with them. I'm not stirring up that kind of mare's nest, thanks very much, and nor will you if you've got any sense. I tell you, it's none of our business. Christ, suppose — just suppose — he is sleeping with Graham. Well, so bloody what? We've all known about Graham for years — well, pretty well known, haven't we? Suspected, and been pretty sure. All right. Well, Steve's eighteen, isn't he? He's old enough to ride a motor bike and join the fucking army, he's old enough to give Graham one, if you ask me. If the poor kid's queer, that's his look-out. That strikes me as bad luck enough, without us poking our bloody oar in and getting him in the *scheissen* with his people.

"In any case", he went on after a brief pause for thought, "how do you know this bloody man — what was his name — Page is right? We all know schoolteachers are the bitchiest bastards on earth. How do we know this isn't just some staffroom feud, or that the bloody bloke's put two and two together and made five and a half of it? No, Al, for Christ's sake do yourself a favour and mind your own business. Do me a favour, and the club too, for that matter. And most of all, do Graham and the boy a favour. It's none of your business, or mine, or anybody else's, and that's the end of it. Just don't breathe a word of this to any of the others. Not anybody, Al, please. I'll have a word with fucking Colin, and make sure he keeps his trap shut. I've got enough on Colin to guarantee he doesn't tattle. So you just keep your face closed, and forget all about it."

"Suits me down to the ground", said Alan, sounding, Stephen thought, rather relieved. "That's what I told Colin when he first told me — he was crowing as if he'd got a scoop for the papers, silly-born prick that he is. If you think it's something we can forget about, and if you can make sure Colin keeps his lip buttoned, that's fine. Unless you think we ought to talk to Graham, maybe."

"Oh, yeah?" jeered Bill. "And what do we tell him? That one of his colleagues thinks he's bent, and can't keep it to himself? And that he's suspected of knocking off one of his own school-boys? Oh, fuckin yeah, I can see me taking Graham aside and telling him that little lot. No, Al, I keep telling you, it's none of our business. Steve's old enough to look after himself and make his own decisions — if he's up to anything with Graham, which he might not be, for all we know. And Graham's more than old enough. He's a good friend of ours, too. So let's just forget it, as I'm sick of hearing myself say."

"Okay", said Alan peaceably. "Just what I hoped you'd say."

"Right, then", said Bill. "Now for Christ's sake let's get out of this and have a dri..." His voice faded, and Stephen heard a door slam. He leaned against the wall of the pavilion, trembling from head to foot. He dragged the sleeve of his shirt across his forehead to mop the cascading sweat off it. His legs felt as if they had suddenly dissolved, and he tottered a few paces away into the bushy undergrowth and sat down. His shirt was sticking clammily to him, and he noticed that he could smell his sweat, a rank, foul smell, reminiscent of unwashed groins, utterly unlike the clean, neutral-smelling sweat of exertion.

He sat for some minutes, allowing the night breeze to cool him down a little, and shortly felt a little better. He thought fast, trying to decide how to play the new circumstances. To begin with, he knew he was in a few moments going to have to walk back into the pavilion and act as if he had heard nothing. His next step would have to be to get away and tell Graham. Beyond that his mind refused to produce any ideas. He physically shook himself, angrily, striving to clear his head, and found to his immense relief that his limbs were steadier and he was sweating less. After a minute or two more he found that he could stand and walk steadily. He bit his lip, steeled himself, and walked round to the front door of the pavilion.

***

Quite how he got through the ordeal of the next few minutes he could not have said afterwards. He knew only that he came through it better than he could have imagined possible. He walked in, rubbing nettle stings on his legs, and for the first time in his life drank a pint of lager down in a single draught. Then he rejoined the gang of younger members and chattered and laughed about nothing much for a fair time, until he judged that he could leave without provoking any comment. Then, amid a chorus of goodbyes, he slipped off. The only clear memory he took away with him of that awful half-hour was catching Bill's eye and waving to him and Alan and calling "See you tomorrow" as he was going through the doors into the soft summer darkness outside. Less than half an hour later he was letting himself into Graham's flat. He could smell the rank odour of that peculiar kind of sweat once more.

Graham was sitting on his sofa putting in a stint of knocking in Stephen's new bat with a mallet with half a cricket ball for a head when Stephen silently opened the door and crept in. He looked up in surprise to see who his visitor was at such a late hour. "Why, Stephen", he exclaimed "what are you..." He saw the expression on Stephen's face, and immediately put down the odd-looking tool and rose swiftly to his feet. "What's the matter?" he asked quickly, taking charge like any schoolmaster faced with a pupil in extreme distress.

Stephen, just about at the end of his tether, was so relieved to be able to transfer the insoluble problem into capable adult hands that he simply rushed across the room and flew into Graham's arms, almost bowling him over, bursting into tears of mingled rage, helplessness and fright.

Graham sat him firmly down on the sofa. "Stay there", he said, and went out of the room. He came back a moment later with a glass. "Here, drink this", he commanded. Stephen, glad to let someone else be in command, drank it, choking and spluttering. However, it rallied him. "What — groogh — what is it?" he asked.

"Only a small brandy", said Graham, sitting beside him and smoothing his ruffled hair gently. "Now calm yourself down and tell me what's brought you charging in here at this time of night looking like the wreck of the *Hesperus*. Something's upset you, or shaken you badly, I can see that. What's happened?"

Stephen told him, fighting to keep calm and tell exactly what he had heard without omitting any detail.

Graham listened without saying a word. He had determined not to show any reaction, so as not to upset Stephen any further, but his face was set grimly and his eyes were gleaming by the time Stephen finished his account.

He sat for a long time, pondering what he had heard. "This is nothing too serious, love", he said eventually, not certain whether what he said was true, but feeling the need to say something to reassure the boy, who half sat, half lay, cradled in his arms, quivering slightly from strain, anxiety and an assortment of unformulated fears. Stephen sat up, snuffling slightly, and looked searchingly into his eyes. "Are...are you sure, Graham?" he asked, a little tremulously. "Will we be able to put it right?"

"Yes", Graham said after a further pause for thought. "I don't know how Jack Page reckons he knows about me. I can't see how he can possibly know anything. Second, if he does know anything about me, he certainly can't know anything about us. And third, if he knows about me, and if he does even suspect anything about us — which, as I say, I don't see that he can — he's no damn right to say anything about it. I don't know how he knows Colin Preston, although I've got a fair idea, but in any case it's outrageous of him to say anything like this about me, let alone about you. To mention you in such a context, on the basis of mere suspicion, or empty-headed gossip, is the most deplorable, disgraceful piece of unprofessional conduct I've ever heard of. He could be dismissed for such a thing.

"In any case", he went on, becoming red with indignation as another aspect of the matter struck him, "quite apart from the ethics of the thing, pure common sense ought to have told him he shouldn't mention something like this to Colin Preston, of all people. If there was ever a competition for the world's most blithering, blathering, dunderheaded idiot who did all his thinking below the belt, Colin would win the gold, silver and bronze medals all on his own. Jesus Christ! Whoever said nature won't tolerate a vacuum would only've had to have a look inside his skull to see what balls he was talking. Colin bloody Preston. Jesus!"

"What will you do?" asked Stephen, calming down greatly as he saw how smoothly and capably Graham had received what he thought must have come as a devastating shock. "And how do you think he might have told Colin? You said you had a good idea."

"Oh, that's easy enough. I reckon they belong to the same rugby club. Jack doesn't get enough rugby at school — he only runs three teams, plays for two and referees several matches a week — so he plays for the town side whenever he can find the time, and goes along after matches to sing their half-witted songs with them. As for what I'm going to do, I don't know exactly, not yet. I'll sleep on it."

"How about sleeping on me?" asked Stephen, feeling much better.

"You ought to go home, sweetheart", said Graham, reluctantly. But Stephen began caressing him, and he relented, and less than an hour later Stephen was sleeping peacefully in his arms. It was very late into the small hours before Graham himself was able to drift into an uneasy and fitful sleep.

Stephen woke up with a jolt at six-thirty, wondering what it was that he had to remember to do that day. Then he remembered Jack Page's punishment run, and shot out of bed in a hurry. Graham had finally fallen into a deep sleep, induced by exhaustion, the long hours of worrying at the problem that had been dropped so unexpectedly in his lap, and the physical strain of remaining still enough not to disturb Stephen while he lay there thinking his way round and round in circles wondering how best to deal with the matter. Stephen made himself tea, crept back to the bedroom and kissed him lightly enough not to wake him, then left a note for him by the kettle in the kitchen.

He went home first, hoping desperately that no-one would be up yet. His luck was in, and he was able to sneak in, grab his gym kit and leave without a sound. Then he walked slowly to school, turning various ideas over in his mind and finding himself able to reach no definite conclusion from any of them.

He was still undecided what to do, if anything, when he and the fourteen other luckless rugby defaulters had changed and assembled in a shivering, grousing line in front of the gymnasium. At one minute to nine Jack Page marched up, inspected them and, to everyone's surprise, nodded appreciatively. "You're all yer, then? Good. Very good, lads. I'm pleased. Not that it'll make me make you run any less ragged, but I'm glad to see you all had the sense to get off in the right spirit. Right, then. You can walk to the startin line, then you're off. I'll be ten minutes behind you now, an woe betide anyone I catch up with. Right? Okay, off with you." He went round to the doors to the changing rooms. The fifteen boys, muttering darkly but secretly rather gratified by his welcome, set off for the starting line of the cross country course, in a nearby park which abutted onto the wild tract of countryside through which the course ran for most of its way. Somewhere in the quarter of a mile walk, Stephen suddenly knew what he was going to do.

"What about getting as far as the woods, then cutting across to Bewick's Hill and just sitting there till we've been out the right time?" suggested one of them when they approached the starting line.

"No good", said another without hesitation. "Jacko'd know the moment he saw us. We'll get plastered in mud going through Bugger's Bend", he went on, referring to a notorious tract of woodland where the course was low-lying and the ground was never completely dry. "If we turn up looking like new pins he'll smell a rat a mile away."

"Besides", contributed another boy, "Jacko often runs round the other way, trying to catch someone skiving off."

"Huh! Hoping to, more likely", put in another. "He enjoys catching people out and shitting on them."

"Anyone got a fag?" somebody asked.

"Jesus!" said someone else. "You're running against Jacko and you ask for a weed? You'll cough your lungs up, and get Jacko's boot up your arse into the bargain." However, he produced a crushed packet from the pocket of his running shorts, extracted an equally crumpled, stubbed-out half of a cigarette from it, and handed it over.

"I still think we could lie in wait and save ourselves most of this sweat", said the first speaker. "After all, we could find some mud and daub it on our socks, couldn't we? And we could post look-outs either side of where we lurk. Then if he comes round the wrong way we can cut back and be running to meet him, and if he just comes round after us we get warning and start off as if we're just running normally."

"Jolly boring, wouldn't it be, just sitting round for half an hour", said someone. "What'd we do?"

"Better than tanking round knackering ourselves for nothing", said someone else hopefully.

"I know what Geoff wants", leered another, jabbing the advocate of short-cuts in the ribs. "Running always gives him a hard-on, doesn't it, Geoff? One off the wrist is called for. Just what the doctor ordered." There were grins all round. Then someone said "What do you think, Stevie? You're quiet." Stephen came out of a brown study with a small start. He was the only one of them to have taken no part at all in the chattering so far.

"Eh?" he said, looking at them blankly. "Sorry, I was thinking about something else. What do I think about what?"

Someone explained the proposed run-dodging plan. Stephen gave a faint grin. "You won't have to worry about Jacko", he said. "I'm going to run round the ordinary way. At least, I'm going to start. And I'm going to be caught — within the first quarter of a mile. By the time he's finished with me he'll have forgotten the rest of you're out there at all, let alone worrying about whether you're finishing his stupid run. I should do as you like."

There was a sudden flood of interested questions. "I've got a bone to pick with him, and I'm going to pick it this morning", he said. "That's why I'm going to make sure he catches me." They clustered round, the run all but forgotten, pressing him for details, but he clammed up and resolutely refused to say any more. At length somebody looked at his watch, and they dismissed Stephen and whatever he was being mysterious about and set off at a fast trot along the prescribed course. Stephen jogged sedately after them, and before he had gone a hundred yards they were out of sight. He slowed to a walk, and after ambling for another couple of hundred yards he stopped altogether, sat on a conveniently situated fallen tree, and waited for Mr Page.

The master appeared in sight within a minute of his seating himself on the tree trunk. He rose and waited, feeling his heart beating unpleasantly quickly. He was feeling a little sick, because he was genuinely a little frightened. He had spent his entire schooldays as a quiet, biddable boy, normally mischievous and in all the sorts of trouble that any boy gets into. But he had never set himself up as a rebel or a defier of authority; and certainly he had never in his most outlandish daydreams imagined himself deliberately setting out, in cold blood as it were, on a collision course with a master — with any grown-up for that matter. He gulped several times in an effort to swallow the sizable lump that was forming in his throat and attempting to swim up his gorge and stifle his speech. He could feel the fear forming itself into a cold knot in his stomach, pulsating regularly in time with the rapid dance of his heartbeat. But he never for a moment contemplated tamely changing his mind and accepting Page's withering sarcasm, or any punishment for slacking, because there was another emotion, far stronger than the fear. He was in the grip of a blazing, passionate anger, for himself but stronger by far on behalf of his friend, and his resolve was helped by a feeling of deep conviction that he was within his rights to be angry. He gulped again, swallowed hard, and squared himself for whatever might be coming his way.

"Hah-hah!" cried Jack Page, smiling demonically as he came up and saw who was waiting for him. "My first victim of the morning, and I didn't expect one this early. Poor lad. A stitch, maybe. But no, not this distance out, surely? Well, well, Stephen Hill. And what could be the trouble? Come on, boy, I don't want to have to start puttin the boot in this early. I'll be indulgent, my lad, shut my eyes if you like. You can start again, and no hard feelings."

"I'm not starting again, sir" said Stephen, quietly, with a tremor in his voice, but with a cold feeling of resolution settling over him like a mantle. "Not till we've sorted something out, anyway."

Up until that moment, Page had been running gently on the spot to keep his rhythm going. At this utterly unexpected defiance he stopped dead in his tracks. "What?" he said, dropping his affectation of merry banter. "What did you say, boy?" His voice had turned cold. But then he looked more closely at the youthful figure hopping up and down before him. When he spoke again his voice was still quiet, but there was concern coming into it. He could see, though he couldn't analyze, the fear possessing the boy, and he could see from the chalky face, wide eyes and jittery demeanour that either something was seriously amiss or that at any rate this was no trifling matter to be joked away with sarcasm or banter. "What's the trouble, Hill?" he asked. And giving Stephen another hard, cool look of appraisal he sat down on the fallen tree, patting it to invite Stephen to join him.

"I've got a bone to pick with you, sir", said Stephen, "and I'm not taking any further part in this run until it's resolved. If you won't make me the promise I want, it goes to the headmaster. And if you won't sort it out with me, I'll never pick up a rugby ball as long as I'm at this school", he finished, making what he hoped Page would regard as the most serious threat that could be issued.

Page felt an almost irrepressible urge to grin as he divined that intention behind the last words, but he straightaway composed his features into owl-like gravity, recognizing clearly that the boy genuinely thought he had some grievance of a serious nature. He would never, Page thought, have invoked the headmaster's name unless he had been in quite deadly earnest. He sat and waited for Stephen to go on, racking his brains to think what he could possibly have done to upset the boy so. "Tell me, Hill", he said eventually, "this isn't anything to do with this run, is it? Dammit, I always hand out runs and work-outs if I think a team hasn't tried. But surely you wouldn't get so het-up about a fatigue run? Most of the lads take it in the same spirit..."

"It's nothing to do with the rugby, or the run", said Stephen, and his voice had such a hard, cold edge that Page sat back silent, becoming quite seriously worried.

"It's these horrible rumours you've been spreading about me", Stephen suddenly burst out. All the curdled emotional poisons that had been swirling through his mind over the preceding twelve hours spurted out, like pus from a lanced abscess. He forgot his fear, forgot that he was a pupil speaking to a master, and a senior master, on the staff of his school, in a burst of passionate, righteous fury, fury of the special kind that only the young know when they feel the injustice of adults. "These sickening, filthy stories you've been telling every Tom, Dick and Harry all over the town", went on Stephen. "It's wicked, and disgusting, and you ought to be ashamed of yourself. I wouldn't have thought my worst enemy would...would stoop to such a thing, and here you are doing it. It's not even as if I ever did anything to upset you. Why, I... I liked you..." He broke off, in great distress, and the master could see that he was very close to tears, at the same time as he himself sat on the log wondering if he was dreaming.

"I'd never get upset about your silly punishments. Nobody does", Stephen went on, still pouring it out in a torrent. "We all think it's funny, and I thought you did it to be funny. I never thought you'd ever do anything really frightful, like this. You must hate me, to do such a thing..." Stephen ran suddenly, completely out of steam. He sat there staring at Page for a moment longer, his eyes distended and his lip quivering, and then he started to cry.

"But Stephen, my poor child", said Page after a moment, in utter consternation. "What am I supposed to have been doing? Please tell me. You must tell me. What in the world have I done?"

Stephen, having once lost his tenuous hold on his self-control, had dipped perilously close to hysteria, and for all that Page was a very experienced schoolmaster indeed, and one who was well-known to be exceptionally good with boys at that, it took him a long time to calm Stephen down. At first he tried to put an arm round Stephen's shoulders, but the boy thrust it away as if it burnt him. However, at last he managed to persuade him to quieten and listen, and by and by he had Stephen half-convinced that he was genuinely unaware of his supposed misdeeds.

"I tell you, Stephen", he said, almost pleadingly, "I've never knowingly started rumours, not about *anyone*; and about a pupil? Why, God help me, I'd have my tongue cut out before I'd think of doing such a thing. For God's sake, boy, tell me what rumours these are, and why you think I set them."

And, at last, it came out. Stephen, half-tearful, half defiantly angry, began to talk. "You...you p-p-play rugger for the town club", he said, sniffing.

"I do", admitted Page, still at a loss.

"You know a man called Preston there", went on Stephen.

"Yes, I know Colin Preston", agreed Page, none the wiser. "Though how you know I know him I can't imagine. What of it, though?"

"It w-w-was him you t-told the rumour to", said Stephen, feeling another paroxysm forcing its way up and out. "Y-you told him you thought Graham Curtis was gig-gig-gay." He got it out at last.

Page sat and looked at him in utter mystification. "Well, my boy, I haven't the foggiest how you come to know such a thing, but, since you obviously have heard, yes, I repeated a rather silly, rather scurrilous story that'd been going round the common room. I don't feel very proud of it, now I see it's got back to the school, and I'm very distressed to find it's upset you. But it's a rumour that's gone round common room more than once, and schoolmasters are only human like everybody else, you know — we gossip, talk about the latest bit of scandal, just the same as other people. Not that I said it maliciously, in any case. There's lots of schoolmasters that way inclined, and no-one says they don't make fine masters, too. Often being that way actually helps them in their vocation, see — if they're genuinely fond of boys, they're likely to look after the ones in their care, aren't they? You see the logic of what I'm sayin?"

"Yes", snapped Stephen, his anger rising rapidly once again just in time to head off the incipient tears. "And if you can sit there and calmly say all that, that makes it even harder for me to understand how you could have said what you did. You must have hated me to say such a thing..."

Page sat looking at him, and if Stephen had been less consumed with warring emotions he could not have failed to recognize the blank incomprehension on his face. As it was, he simply carried on from where he had left off. "Whatever you think about Graham Curtis, and whatever they may say about him behind his back in your stinking common room, you had no right to say that about me" he stormed. "You don't know a thing about me. Even if you had known anything, and it had been true, you would have had no right to say it, especially to someone like Colin bloody Preston, who you knew would go and blab it all over the place."

A little light dawned in Page's mind, but he had no real idea what he was supposed to have said. "Stephen", he said, very gently. "I've never said anything about you, not at the rugby club or anywhere else, not to Colin Preston or to any*body* else. I give you my word of honour, lad, I have never, once, uttered a single word to your discredit. Not ever, you hear me? Now please tell me, what do you *think* I said about you, and why do you think so? I must know, boy, so I can try to put it right if I can."

"I...I thought you told Colin that Graham was gay, and that I was his... his... that I was his boyfriend. Just because we're friends, and he introduced me to the cricket club, and gives me lifts to the matches and home after them and so on, and we shared a room on the tour, but that was only because he was the only one there I knew, and now it's all over the club that I'm, that he and I are..." The rush of words ended in a gulp, and he left it at that.

"Oh, my God", said Jack Page after a while. At first he had just sat looking at the boy, aghast and stunned into silence. "Oh, my dear God", he repeated. "You poor, poor lad. What in God's name have I done?" He had a sudden inspiration, and jumped up off the tree trunk. "Here, up with you now", he said in something closer to his normal voice. "Come on, run with me for a while. Just a gentle jog, so we can talk comfortably."

Somewhat to his own surprise, Stephen found himself getting up and trotting along beside Page and, more surprising still, he found that the physical effort made him feel considerably better within moments. "Now", said Page, glancing shrewdly at him out of the corner of his eye and seeing the improvement. "Tell me, how did you find out about this?"

Stephen told him. "I see", Page said, thoughtfully. "Well, let me try to clear one thing up with you. I never said a word about you to Colin Preston. Not a word. I'll be having words with

Master Preston, by the way, next time I bump into that bugger, and you can take my word for that. It's clear enough what's happened, now. I told him enough, and he's embellished it and passed it on with his own bit of interest tacked on the end. He's seen how close you and Graham are, and drawn his own conclusions, hasn't he?

"But don't get me wrong, boy, it doesn't make my part in it any more honourable, and I'm deeply ashamed of myself, believe me. I can't do much, but I can do my best to cancel some of the damage, starting in the place where I did the damage to begin with. I can start scotching this talk at the rugby club, at least. It's little enough, but I must do whatever I can. And if it's any consolation to you, which I don't suppose it is, I'll never pass on gossip again as long as I live. My God, this is the worst thing that's ever happened to me in all my time as a schoolmaster. It's the worst thing I've ever done in my time, I should say. I'm not asking you to forgive me, lad. Not yet. I will, one day, soon, but I can't ask you now. I'll just make you one promise. I'll see Graham Curtis, right away — I'm turning back now, and I'll go round and see him the moment I'm changed, and do what I can to set things right with him. Will you trust me to do that, please?"

He turned off the course and began jogging through a ride in the light woodland they had reached, heading back in the direction of the starting line and the school. Without thinking, Stephen followed and continued jogging beside him. "You don't have to ask me to forgive you, sir", he said quietly, seeming to be back in possession of himself now. "You never did anything against me, so there's nothing to forgive. I'm glad you're going to square it with Graham, though, sir. As for me, well, don't worry about me. I couldn't care less what people think of me. If the cricketers think I'm gay, well they can think what they like. Nobody gives a damn about somebody being gay these days. But Graham could lose his job if people thought he was, sir, couldn't he? If the wrong people thought so, anyway."

Page looked steadily at him for a few strides as they ran. "You're letting me down mighty lightly, lad", he observed. "I shan't forget it. And you're half right, but I'm glad to say you're half wrong too. I said, there's a lot of schoolmasters are gay, and it generally does no harm. You get the odd one that does a lot of damage — monkeying with little boys and so on — but most of 'em are as honourable and decent as anybody else. Graham Curtis is a friend of mine, and a damn good friend. You can take it from me, I'll do my utmost to set things straight with him." He slowed to a halt in the middle of the sunny woodland ride and turned to face Stephen, who obediently stopped beside him.

"It's damned lucky, you know", he said, and paused awkwardly.

"What is, sir?" prompted Stephen after a wait.

"Several things", said Page. "First that we had this silly fatigue fixed up. I'm glad you lot played like dummies yesterday, on that account, at least. Lucky too that you're the lad you are, and decided to waylay me there and have it out with me. There's not many would've had the pluck to do that, and there's fewer still would've had enough decency to think about what this would do to Graham first, and of themselves second. He's lucky in his friend, and I'll tell him so when I go and throw myself on his mercy. That's it, really, Stephen, except that I'd like to count myself a friend of someone who makes as good a friend as you do. If I may?" And, somewhat to Stephen's surprise, he put out his hand. Stephen shook it willingly enough, feeling faintly embarrassed but on the whole very pleased with the way the day had started.

"And now, if you'll allow me to, I'd like to leave you", said Page. "I've got a lot to think about, and I'd... I'd like to be alone while I think about it, if it's okay by you."

"Of course, sir", Stephen said, nodding.

"You know your way back from here all right, do you?"

"Oh, yes, sir, I think so. If I go straight on through this lot of woods I come to the main path just the school side of Bewick's Hill, don't I?"

"That's right. Well, Stephen, I'm glad you had what it takes to face me out like that, as I said. And thanks for letting me off as lightly as you have." He turned away and set off, but after a few paces he stopped and came back. "You know what? I'd clean forgotten about the others, poor little sods. If you see 'em before I do, tell 'em the punishment's cancelled. That'll please 'em no end, I should imagine", he added with a wry grin, "after they've done fifteen for me."

"Maybe you could owe them a punishment, sir", suggested Stephen, beginning to feel happy for the first time since the dread moments behind the pavilion the previous evening. "You know, the next time you think they ought to run fifteen for you, you could let this one count against it."

Page looked quizzically at him. "Owing a punishment? Never heard of such a thing. But since I owe you, young Master Stephen, I'll do it. Okay, lad. I'll see you later, and we'll see you in the First Fifteen, too. Courage — first quality you look for in a rugby player. You've got it." He turned and ran off again at a hard, relentless pace, chuckling. This time he didn't turn back. As he came to a bend in the ride several hundred yards ahead of Stephen, jogging easily along behind him, he turned briefly and waved a hand, and passed out of sight.

***

"So that's how it all happened", Jack Page explained, sitting on Graham's sofa and playing a little nervously with the cricket bat mallet. "And I'd never have realized what a frightful thing I was doing if that boy hadn't had the pluck to come and face me down with it. A damn good boy, that one. Strong sense of honour, too — I could see a mile off it was you he was thinking of first, and himself only second. Worried about you losing your job, he was."

"Well, I'm only too glad to have got it sorted out", said Graham. "I'll have a word in Colin bloody Preston's ear, when I see him, but I'll have him collapsed like a deflated gas-bag without any trouble."

"I was thinking I'd have a word or so with him myself", said Page, draining the beer Graham had offered him and getting up to go. "Won't do any harm at all, that I can see, if he gets an earful from the villain of the piece and the victim, don't you think?"

Graham nodded. "He needs it, and richly deserves it", he said, getting up to show his visitor out.

"Can't get over that kid", muttered Page, shaking his head. "Didn't mince his words, not for a moment. Came right out point-blank, he did. If I couldn't resolve it, he was going straight to the headmaster with it, and if I wouldn't resolve it, he'd never set foot on a rugby field again as long as he was here. Good kid." Graham saw him out, and he walked briskly away, shaking his head and absorbing the lesson he had learnt from his punishment run. Graham watched him out of sight, then went in to put in another stint on Stephen's bat, feeling very proud of its owner, very relieved at the unexpectedly easy resolution of a potentially horrendous problem, and most of all feeling that he was blessed in the love that fate had sent his way. He looked at the clock, and saw with pleasure that it was already time to set out for the day's cricket match.

***

As usual, when Alan Hood, the Elderton park vice-captain, had arrived home the night before, he had sat up for a while with his wife, sharing a last can of beer with her and exchanging local news, gossip and anything interesting that had befallen either of them during the day. It was inevitable that Alan would mention to her the incident with Bill, in which they had found confirmation of their long-held suspicion that Graham Curtis was gay.

"Well, now you've had confirmation", said his wife, "what are you intending to do about it?"

"Nothing", said Alan. "Forget it, I suppose."

His wife didn't forget it. She never actually set out with the intention of passing it on; but she found that it was one of those most maddening little items of news: impossible to forget, and even more impossible to keep to herself. A few days later she was under the dryer at the local hairdresser, trying to think of something to say. In the end she told her friend, in total confidence, what her husband had told her.

That night the best friend told her husband. The next morning her husband telephoned and told Graham's headmaster at school. "I don't want to seem like a busybody", he said ("I can hear the insincerity radiating from you in a nimbus", thought the headmaster bitterly) "But I've got a young son of my own who'll be attending your school one day, and I think I have a duty to pass on the information to you..." The headmaster sighed, and felt a headache coming on as he put the receiver down.

***

"I suppose I'll have to resign", Colin Preston said. He was sitting in the corner of the locked dressing room, trembling slightly and feeling utterly humiliated. He could not meet the eyes of his accusers, who were both standing. Bill, oddly, considering that he was not the injured party, was much the wrathier of the two. His eyes were hot and angry, and he had been the chief prosecutor. Graham merely looked cold and bitter. Now he made an effort, and found some pity for the wretched young man huddled almost tearfully in the corner.

"No, Colin, we don't want that — or at least, I don't, speaking as the bloke on the receiving end of your bloody idiocy. I don't say malice, because if I thought you'd done what you did maliciously I'd be going for your blood. I just think you ought to grow up, that's all. For God's sake, think what damage you might have done. Not to me, especially: I'm old enough and big enough to take care of myself — although you've already made life difficult for me, and you might have done more damage than you'd have dreamed of. But mainly you want to think about poor young Stephen. The boy's eighteen years old — just — and still at school. He's got A-levels to come at the end of this year. Can't you imagine what a scandal would have done to him, if things hadn't worked out so luckily? If he hadn't had the courage to do what he did, I ought to say — can you imagine the effect it would have had on his life?"

Colin did look up then, and now there were tears glinting. "Yes", he muttered miserably. "I can imagine. I can only say I never meant it. I just didn't think..." He trailed dismally into silence, overwhelmed by the yawning pit that had opened up, utterly unexpectedly, in front of him. When Bill had called him into the dressing room after the game, later in the day of Jack Page's visit to Graham's flat, he had not had the remotest idea what was to come. But when he had found Graham waiting for them he had suddenly felt himself turning an interesting shade of green and his legs had announced an unwillingness to support him.

Now, it seemed, he was to be let off lightly. Graham turned to Bill. "I don't think this needs to go any further, does it, Bill?" he said. "He's apologized, there's no lasting damage, he's sworn he'll never tattle again, and he's going to make amends at the rugby club. I'm ready to leave it at that, if you are."

Bill assented. "Okay, Graham, if that's the way you want it. I think he ought to have a word in person with Steve, though, don't you?" Graham nodded. "Yes, I certainly do. Do you agree to that, Colin? You'll take Stephen Hill aside, and apologize to him, as you have to me? And I mean, really apologize — no letting yourself down lightly with some perfunctory 'sorry about that, no hard feelings?', just because he's only a kid, you understand? He's more important in this than I am, simply because he's a kid, and there's no 'only' about it, see. You okay with all that?"

Colin nodded, looking a little happier. "I've got nothing against the kid", he snuffled. "I just can't help myself with gossip. I like telling stories, and I sort of get carried away. But I've got nothing at all against the kid, and I want to tell him I'm sorry. I'll do the job properly, you can trust me for that much."

"Okay", said Bill. "I think we can consider the matter closed, if you're willing to make a proper apology to Steve. You make sure it is a proper one, though, Colin. We're trusting you, but not quite all the way. I'll be seeing the kid, to make sure he's satisfied with what he gets from you, all right?" Colin nodded.

"Okay then, Col. Now I want to finish this off with Graham. You go back in, and as far as I'm concerned it's over, and nothing more needs to be said. Okay, Graham?" Graham nodded.

"Th-thanks, Bill, and you, Graham, for taking it so well. I'll never forget it", quavered Colin. Bill unlocked the door and let him out. He went, plumbing depths of shame, contrition and humiliation that only a young man can plumb. Bill shut the door.

"You're letting him off bloody lightly, Graham", he said. He was acutely conscious that his own conduct in the matter under discussion had not been wholly stainless. "I hope you'll be able to be as kind to me."

Graham looked at him in surprise. "You? What have I got to let you off about, then?"

"Well, I'm afraid my own handling of this...this miserable affair hasn't been what you might call masterly", Bill said unhappily. "I mean, when we first heard about these rumours, when that kid was earwigging outside, all I was bothered about was hushing it up. If I said 'it's none of our business' once to Hoody I must've said it a dozen times. I ought to've been interested in snuffing it out, oughtn't I? I ought to have been at pains to kill off a foul slander. I ought..."

"Bill, Bill", said Graham, laughing, much to Bill's surprise. "Stop cataloguing all the things you ought to have done. If I'd always done all the things I ought to have done I'd never have had any time to do the things I wanted to do. If everybody had followed your rule and minded their own business none of this unpleasantness would have happened. It's not a bad rule, you know."

"Yes, I know that. But this isn't the first time a rumour of this kind has gone round about you", said Bill, getting the habit of confession. "And in the past I've joined in the speculation. I've even privately marked you down as qu... er, gay. I should have stopped it on all those other occasions, shouldn't I?"

"Give yourself a break, Bill", said Graham, a little wearily. "Don't you think I've known about these occasional speculations? You get used to them, believe me. Every man who's still single when he's getting towards thirty has to put up with it some time or other. And in schools — well, masters' common rooms..." He left the thought unfinished. "I was more concerned about Stephen in this case. I mean, obviously I was a bit worried about my job — rumours like this can't do a master in a boys' school much good, you understand — but mostly my concern was for the boy. I'm very glad it's been closed so painlessly, and you've played your part in that. I've got no real complaint against you or the club. I'm not specially pleased to have my personal life made a talking point; but there's nothing much I can do about it, so there's no point in making an issue of it."

"Well, it's good of you to take it that way", said Bill, eyeing him curiously. "Graham", he went on after a long pause. Graham was aware of the scrutiny, and waited patiently, having a good idea what was coming. "Can I ask you something? It's only being nosy, and you're completely free to tell me to mind my own bloody business if you want to, but I'm curious about one thing — but it's quite a big thing..."

"Am I?" said Graham with a faint smile.

"Sorry?"

"You want to ask, but aren't quite sure if I'll be offended or not, isn't that it? You want to ask 'Am I really gay, after all?' don't you?"

"I, er... well, actually..."

Graham laughed. "There's no need to be **embarrassed**, you

know. It's not something I'm bothered about. Yes, I'm gay. Homosexual, if you prefer it. Not queer or bent, thank you, and never a poof or a poofter, if you value my friendship. But yes, I'm gay. I don't advertise it, partly because why the hell should I? Who else advertises his personal attributes? It's also partly, I admit, because doing the job I do it would be foolish to advertise it — there are so many silly asses about that if I advertised it I'd spend my entire life explaining that I'm not a potential child-molester, and it would get almighty bloody boring to have to keep on going over the same old ground over and over again. But I don't make any particular secret of it either, among my friends or among decent people. Satisfied?"

"Thanks, Graham", said Bill. "You didn't have to tell me any of that. I'm honoured", he went on, looking a little self-conscious as he uttered the word.

The silence swirled round the dressing room. It had started to rain, and it could be heard drumming above them, slightly amplified and distorted by the attic space between the pitched roof and the high ceiling of the dressing room. There was a sudden flurry of drops against the window behind where Graham was standing. He turned and peered out into the dark. He went up to Bill and patted him gently in the small of his back. "Come on, let's go and have a drink."

"Sure", said Bill. "Fine. And thanks for telling me. It'll make it easier to handle if anything like this crops up again in the future. Funny, you know. This isn't the first time something like this has circulated about someone or other; and yet I've never pursued it to the end and actually resolved it, you know? Actually sorted it out, properly. Never thought enough about it, I suppose."

"Few people ever do think about us, Bill", said Graham. "And that's entirely as it should be. People generally don't go round thinking about other people's sex lives. They're too busy going round thinking about their own. But people like you, who don't think about us, are all right, until the odd occasion crops up when you're used, mobilized and used as cannon-fodder, often unknown to yourselves, or even positively against your actual wishes, by the occasional people who go around thinking altogether too much about other people's sex lives — and they usually seem to have an awful lot of time to devote especially to thinking about ours. Now, come on, I'm dying of thirst."

He led the way out into the main body of the pavilion, and Bill followed him, with a new look of respect on his battered face.

***

"So there it is, Graham", said the headmaster, with a mixture of anger, embarrassment, distaste and worry sketched like grafitti all over his face. "That's the complaint. Now there's the matter of what we do about it."

"May I speak, Headmaster?" said Graham formally. He had kept his face expressionless with an effort, while seething underneath.

"Of course. I'd very much like to hear your side of the thing."

Graham had opened his mouth to speak, and he was taken so much by surprise by this response that for a moment he sat there with it open, deprived of speech. He found it again quickly. "My side! You want to hear my side of this? Well, you surprise me, Headmaster."

"Oh", said the headmaster, surprised himself by the fury that he could hear quite clearly in Graham's voice despite his efforts to suppress it. "What have I said to surprise you?"

"Well, to begin with, I'm surprised to see you paying this kind of muck the compliment of pursuing it at all", said Graham. "I'd have thought the proper course to follow with an anonymous letter was to put a peg on your nose and drop it in the waste paper basket, and then wash your hands carefully in disinfectant."

"It was a telephone call", said the headmaster mildly.

"What the devil does it matter whether it came in an envelope or over a wire?" snapped Graham. "It's still a piece of poison raked up by some dirty-minded shit-stirrer who hasn't got the guts to put his name to it, and I'm very disappointed to hear that you didn't tell him what you thought of him and put the phone down. It's what I'd have done, I can promise you."

The headmaster sighed. "Well, you're not headmaster, and I am", he said, "and I took — I take — the view that much though it's to be deplored that, as you say, the man lacked the moral fibre to give his name, the allegation is serious, and demands some investigation. If we were to do nothing at all, well, he could take his complaint to the newspapers next, and think what that could do to the school's name."

"I'm wondering what it would do to the school's precious name if I talked to the local rag and told them that I was being investigated on the strength of this anonymous piece of garbage."

"Steady on, Graham", soothed the headmaster. "I didn't say you were being investigated. As far as the anonymity is concerned, I urged the caller most emphatically to give me his name. He refused. I couldn't do any more than that, now could I?"

"You could have done a bit less, though", said Graham savagely. "Like, for instance, you could have told him if he couldn't pluck up the grain of moral courage needed to provide his name he could go to hell, and then you could have treated it with the contempt and indifference it deserved, instead of raking me in here and giving every indication of taking the thing seriously."

"Graham", said the headmaster, doing his best to pacify him. "I haven't said for a moment that I'm taking what's been alleged seriously. I'm going through the motions, man, can't you see that? I don't put an ounce of faith in this slur, and I'd have hoped you'd have sufficient faith in me to take that for granted. I received the complaint, and I felt bound to follow it up. But it's a formality, nothing more. I put the allegation to you, as a matter of form, and I hope, and expect, to hear you tell me it's lies. That's all. Then I can say with a clear conscience that I've made all appropriate enquiries, found nothing to support the allegation, which, I can honestly say, is in my opinion a calumny of the foulest kind, and the matter is closed. That's what I mean when I say it needs investigation. I don't actually believe this...this piece of poison, not for a moment."

He watched anxiously as Graham sat thinking about it. "Well, I don't feel inclined to co-operate", Graham said at length. "That sort of sophistry may let you wriggle off the hook and comfort yourself that your duty's done and your conscience clear, but I'm disinclined to collaborate in sweeping it out of sight under the carpet. No. I'll take you at your word instead. You said you wanted my side of this affair. Well, you can have it.

"The specific complaint this piece of dirt has raked up came in two parts, I think? One, I'm homosexual, and two, I'm up to mischief with a boy. Right?" He sat upright on his chair, staring angrily at his chief, who slowly and reluctantly nodded his head.

"Well, here's my side of the matter, as you asked. Part one is true. Part two is false. Satisfied?" He sat back and glared truculently across the desk.

The headmaster's face sagged a little, and he said nothing for some time while he collected his thoughts and sought for the best way to respond to this unexpected frankness. The rumours and gossip that formed the staple conversational diet of the common room always penetrated to his study sooner or later, either on the ordinary grapevine or via the sycophants forming a minority of any staff, so he was well aware of the suggestions that flew about from time to time that this or that master was an active homosexual. He was aware that Graham had been the object of such tittle-tattle in the past, and he knew, of course, that his staff was bound, in the nature of things, to include a number of homosexuals, many of them repressing or sublimating their sexuality but some of them continuing to enjoy an active sexual life. But he was used to the subject being treated with a decent decorum. Plain speaking such as Graham's blunt statement was not customary. Nor was it welcome. However, he was stuck with it, and now he had to respond to Graham's forcing play.

"Just so there can be no possible mistake", he said at last, "I'd like you to spell it out for me, please, Graham. Tell me exactly what is true and what is false. I don't want there to be any possibility of the slightest misunderstanding about this if it should ever, ah, surface later."

"Happy to oblige", said Graham, still fuming with sternly controlled rage. "Part one of your smutty little complaint is true. I am homosexual. Part two is false. I'm not engaged in a sexual affair with a boy." He went on to give a rapid resume of the incident at the cricket club, and his answer to the unsubstantiated reports there. "That's the lot", he concluded. "I don't know how it got out: I suppose someone blabbed — to his wife maybe, or some friend. But you've heard the lot. I am what I say I am, and I wouldn't dream of getting involved with boys, any more than ninety-nine per cent of heterosexual masters would get involved with schoolgirls. Whether the boys came from this school or anywhere else is quite beside the point."

As he said it he was hardly conscious that he was lying. He no longer thought of Stephen as a boy; he no longer thought of him as a pupil, but as his friend, companion, solace in time of trouble and, with increasing certainty, as his lover. The truthful part of his mind did persist, annoyingly, in jeering "You're lying!" at him, but it was a faint voice, and more or less submerged under louder and more strident inner voices, haranguing his conscience like a couple of menacing dock orators looming over his shoulders at an old-style strike meeting.

There was a galloping sense of injustice, that a man of eighteen years, in every other sense an adult, with the right to join the armed forces and kill people, should be denied the right to spend a night in the bed of his own choice. The constant awareness of this gathered strength by the moment until it threatened to stifle him under its choking shrouds of outraged feelings. In the face of an injustice so monstrous his conscience had no difficulty in absolving him from any residual compunction about lying. Then there was a powerful realization that however little he liked having to lie, the consequences of the truth's coming out would be a catastrophe of the most shattering kind, for himself and for his young lover. Thus principle coalesced with necessity, and he lied without shame or regret.

"Well?" he demanded belligerently, breaking the painful silence. "You've had the awful truth. Yes, I'm homosexual. No, I'm not interfering with little boys, or any other sort of boys. Now what?"

The headmaster still sat in thought. Eventually his face cleared. "To tell you the truth, Graham, I'm rather relieved that you had the courage to come clean. I wasn't really surprised to hear you admit your homosexuality. You know as well as I do what the grapevine in this place is like. As for your denial of involvement with boys, of course I'm very glad to hear it, and I accept it without question or reservation. I never had the slightest fear that you could be engaged in anything so improper — not to mention dangerous to yourself."

"I don't accept the term 'admit', Headmaster", said Graham, somewhat disarmed by the headmaster's conciliatory words and tone. "You admit to wrongdoing, to fault or to error. As far as I'm concerned my sexual orientation is none of those. But I repeat, what now?"

"Well, your sexual preference is, of course, your own affair", said the headmaster, mildly. "We're not *quite* barbarians here, as I should rather have liked to hope you would know without my needing to tell you so. Since I've accepted your word as to your involvement — I beg your pardon", he corrected himself hastily, seeing storm warnings being hoisted fast in Graham's face, "I mean, of course, your non-involvement — with boys from this school, that's an end of the matter. As far as I'm concerned the matter ends here. I see no reason to bother the school governors with it, and I give you my personal word that I shall not mention it again. Satisfied?" He was unable to resist a mild-and-bitter imitation of Graham's sarcastic little jibe earlier on.

Graham sat and cogitated, feeling a little as if he had trodden where the last stair ought to be and found it wasn't there. He decided that the headmaster's reaction was sufficiently hand-some to deserve payment in kind. "Er, yes, Headmaster", he said slowly. "Yes, I am satisfied. Rather surprised, to be honest, but satisfied. I had the feeling from the way we started that this was going to be a witch-hunt. I'm sorry I was so aggressive. But I suppose you can imagine how it feels to be the victim of anonymous trouble-makers like this."

The headmaster spent several more minutes soothing him and assuring him that his position was secure, and that Stephen would not be dragged into the matter. "If you assure me that no boy of this school is involved in anything of the kind our anonymous friend alleges", he said, "your word is quite enough. The last thing the boy needs in his A-level year is to have his concentration wrecked by becoming embroiled in squalid and baseless accusations. No, let's let the matter rest between us here. I'm only sorry, more sorry than I can say, that I was forced to take it this far. Will you have a glass of sherry and agree to forget all about it?" He said it so graciously that Graham's anger and resentment evaporated. He gave the headmaster a faintly apologetic smile and accepted. Then he went away and tried to concentrate on inspiring thirteen-year-olds with a love of the French language as the worrying began.

***

That day was a Friday, but he had decided to give the club a miss, and Stephen arrived at the flat fairly early, soon after nine-thirty, playful, affectionate and randy as usual. Graham hadn't the heart to deflate him by imparting the decision he had come to, with a reluctance beyond description, during the course of the day. He had cast about for any excuse by which he might escape the necessity to reach the conclusion he had, but there was none. He took Stephen off to the bedroom almost before he had got through the door, and was especially attentive and gentle with him, spinning out every small act of love and desire to the utmost and savouring it like a last meal before a fast. His own desire was running high, with the desperation of last things, and they made love several times before he summoned up all his nerve and prepared to tell the boy the news.

He propped himself up on one elbow, pushed the covers down and looked appreciatively, and sadly, along Stephen's slim, firm body. He had become familiar with every muscle and how it moved under the silky skin. He ran a fingernail down the boy's broad, hairless chest, down the pale-gold stomach, and traced patterns along the inside of his thigh. For a moment he toyed with the smooth, heavy penis, with its glistening tip peeping through the red creases of the foreskin. Then he pulled himself together and concentrated on looking closely at Stephen's regular, triangular face, with its fair skin, its shaggy mop of dusty-blond hair and the two large grey eyes, which were at the moment looking up at him, placid and faintly creased with humour at the corners. He stroked the soft, downy cheek — Stephen could still go three days without shaving and feel as smooth as a child — and the wide, expressive mouth. The knowledge that he would in all probability never see that body naked again, or see the relaxed expression of lust sated in those eyes, made him ache with sorrow and self-pity, and he groaned involuntarily.

"What's up?" asked Stephen, instantly alert as he always was to any change in Graham's mood. His grey eyes focussed and gazed steadily up into Graham's blue ones, and concern etched its way across his face.

"I... I've got some bad news for you, Stephen", he said very slowly and quietly, awash with misery. "Bad for both of us. The worst news I could have, I suppose, really, health apart." He closed his eyes as the despair rose blackly up in his throat and temporarily sealed it shut. Stephen went rigid. "You'd better tell me", he said, also speaking quietly but with a hard edge in it that brought Graham out of his wallowing. Stephen's voice had sounded so utterly un-boyish, so controlled and adult, that he made an instant decision and acted on it.

He told the boy plainly, without any preamble or attempt to soften it, of the interview with the headmaster that morning, and what had precipitated it. It took very few minutes.

"Okay", said Stephen. "What decision did you make?"

His directness demanded the same in response, so once more Graham gave it to him without frills. "We can't see each other any more like... like this", he said. "At school, at the cricket — I'll still be able to pick you up and drive you to and from the games. But no more meetings here; and most of all, no more of *this*. No more sex. It's simply too risky. You can bet your life they'll keep watch after this, for a while, at least. Besides, I don't much like the fear of breaking my word to the headmaster. It was all right lying to him about what had gone before, but I don't like the idea of going back on what I told him today."

Stephen's first reaction was one of bewilderment, mixed with terrible hurt. He thought at first that he was in some way to blame for the sudden, overwhelming collapse of his new world. He argued and pleaded, begged and cajoled, to no avail. After a long period of non-stop argument, he fell silent from mere exhaustion. When he had recovered they were both too over-wrought to be capable of further toing and froing, and by some shared instinct they found respite in caresses, ending in a hard, almost brutal love-making. Then it began again. Stephen's hurt, puzzled inability to understand why risks that had been accept-able up to then were unacceptable from that night could not be easily explained, and the effort of trying to explain it left Graham drained and defeated.

Stephen meanwhile went from hurt to incomprehension to bitter, savage anger, when he said many things that might have been unforgivable if Graham had not known the love that spawned them, and then back through self-loathing and contri-tion to simple hurt again. At last, understanding Graham's point of view and hating it, and, for the moment, hating Graham and himself for allowing themselves to be put upon, he cried out from his pain, "But *why*, Graham? *Why* do we have to just put up with it? I don't give a fuck about my A-levels. Not *now*. Christ, I only wanted them so badly because I had a fancy to go into the RAF. Well, that idea went out of the bloody window the moment I met you — well, you know what I mean — when I started going with you, like this. Could you see me joining something that would have had me getting carted off to fucking Borneo or somewhere and not seeing you from one year's end to the next? I gave up the idea of the RAF months ago. To *hell* with my bloody, fucking, God-damned A-levels..."

Graham thought he had never heard swearing less superfluous, more meant, each profanity precisely enunciated and heartfelt; a desperate attempt to make mere words express the inexpressible. He tried to deploy once more the careful arguments he had prepared, rehearsed and marshalled against this moment, and found them vain and pitifully inadequate. Not that Stephen listened to them anyway. He simply flew from one impassioned argument to another, and Graham was reduced to stone-walling, saying the same things over and over again. They were worldly arguments, and he put them as gently, kindly and regretfully as he was able. He tried to make Stephen see that his education mattered. Stephen dismissed it in a single brief obscenity. He strove desperately to point out that Stephen would be free in a short while, and could then go where he wanted, do as he pleased. Stephen snorted furiously and cried that present satisfaction was worth double measure later, or quadruple or octuple.

Graham decided to let him have his head, and he railed against the hypocrisy of the people who had brought their world crashing about them, not forgetting to point out that it was worldly people, who could go where they wanted and do as they pleased, who had done it. At last, wearied to exhaustion by his outbursts and emotional catastrophe, Stephen produced his highest card, the one Graham found nearest to impossible to defend against, by simply dropping his head on Graham's chest, weeping piteously and pleading to be allowed to defy the world and the human automata that created conventions. When Stephen begged him not to turn him away he found him hardest to resist. He had half-expected much of what took place, but he had not begun to imagine how hard it would be, and when

Stephen begged, so far from finding it contemptible, as he had hoped, he found it unbearably moving, and almost broke down himself.

He pointed out that he had, in effect, given his word to the headmaster that he would not do what he had been doing with Stephen for months. This amounted, he argued, to a promise that he would cease to do it now. "Fuck him", howled Stephen, hysterical with grief and loss. "He extorted that from you. He got it by coercion — blackmail. A promise like that doesn't count, for Christ's sake, Graham. It's not worth the air you used to make it. We could go away together", he said, rallying and sitting up in bed, eyes gleaming as hope was reborn. You could get another job somewhere, and I could find something..." He trailed into silence as he saw clearly in Graham's face that it was another non-starter, and curled up on Graham again, burrowing down into the bed like a little boy determined not to see what he didn't want to see.

In the end, Graham compromised. He saw that if he offered the boy nothing to hope for they would not resolve anything that night, and he remembered, if Stephen did not, that they both had a life to live, starting on the following day — or rather, he reminded himself after a glance at the clock, later that day. They were both playing for the First XI in the penultimate match of the season, and he shuddered at the prospect of trying to explain a washed-out, tear-stained, semi-hysterical wreck of a boy to the cricket club. If that happened, after what had been happening recently, he thought, he might as well apply to join the French Foreign Legion and be done with it.

So he offered Stephen something to hope for. It was the slenderest reed he could extend, and he privately writhed under a lash of his own making, despising and hating himself for seeking to mislead and deceive the person he loved more than anyone in his life before.

"Look, Stephen", he said, almost prostrate with weariness. "Will you make a bargain with me? A pact, if you prefer?" Stephen uncurled, scenting concessions, and took notice. Graham saw enviously how instantaneously the vitality flooded back into his young face, for after all the difference in their ages was a mere twelve years. For a moment he felt like an old man. He pulled himself together and pressed on: "you're due to sit your

A-levels in... what?" — he frowned in concentration for a moment, doing sums in his head — "about nine and a half months, right?" Stephen nodded, looking as bright and attentive as if none of the preceding two hours' emotional switchback-riding had happened, and Graham found himself smiling fondly into his eyes in response, as if it was the most natural thing in the world.

"Right, then", he said, directing himself sternly to his argument, "the moment you've taken them, you're free. Once you've sat those pestilential papers, you've taken your A- levels, and no-one this side of the last trump can take the fact away from you. Right?" Stephen nodded again, becoming, Graham noted a trifle gloomily, brighter-eyed by the second. "All right. As soon as you've sat them, we'll consider our position, and our feelings, and if we both still feel then as we both feel now, then we'll have a look round at the possibilities. If you agree. Now, how does that sound?"

Stephen sat cross-legged, wiggling his toes and looking levelly at Graham. He could see quite clearly the grainy tracks of the tears that had zig-zagged their erratic way down his cheeks leaving tiny flecks of salt behind them. After a long wait Stephen asked very softly "Is that a promise, Graham?"

"Yes, of course it's a promise. If you want it to be. If we both feel the same way then as now, and if you want to rethink after you've sat your A-levels, we'll rethink."

"All right", the boy said, seriously. "I shall hold you to it. You know that already, I think." As on many occasions before since they had become lovers, Graham thought how curiously adult Stephen sounded when he spoke of anything that mattered, especially anything to do with the two of them. He looked into the grey eyes, and heard the words, uttered in Stephen's deep, nicely modulated voice, so different from the hysterical howling he had had to put up with for so much of the preceding couple of hours, and shivered. He didn't bother to try to deceive himself that he would not be honouring the promise in just under nine months' time. He experienced a sudden, sharp moment's intuition, like the after-image of a thousand-megawatt lightning flash, and knew for certain that this boy would be waiting on the appointed platform of the appointed station on the appointed day, precisely on the appointed time.

"All right, my darling", said Graham, huskily. He hesitated, wondering whether to risk anything emotional, but thought immediately that he owed the boy that much, at least. "I love you. Try not to forget that, if it's...when it's hard to be apart. You're not bound to wait for me. I don't deserve it, and I'm not asking you to wait for me, don't think that for a moment. I'm taking you at your word, and telling you that I'll be ready to try again if our circumstances are the same in nine months. I wish to God it didn't have to be this way — I suppose for some other people it might not have to be. For me, it does. Try to understand. Try not to hate me..."

"I shan't hate you", said Stephen, sounding more self-possessed than he had for a long time. "How could I hate you? I love you, and I'll be there in nine months. As I said, I'll hold you to it. In between I shall try and get you back. I'm not taking tonight as the last word, I warn you. But if I have to wait this ridiculous nine months, I'll wait. And as for forgetting you love me — well, I love you, and I don't think you'll forget that, will you?" Graham felt the same electric sensation of being talked to by someone far older than himself in the body of someone far younger. He shivered. Stephen slithered down into the bed, pulling the sheet and quilt up. "Come down here", he commanded. "We've got about nine hours before we have to go to the cricket. One hour a month. We'd better not waste any of it, had we?"

***

The Michaelmas term was a miserable period for both of them — but not as bad as they had feared.

Coming as it did after the emotional turmoil of the events of the day and the scene in Graham's bed that night, their lovemaking had a desperate, frantic quality which left them exhausted yet unsatisfied, physically drained but aching with unfulfilled need. They heard the birds strike up their morning uproar and leaned naked together in the bedroom window to watch the dawn flushing colours through the diluted blue ink of the morning sky. It soothed them a little, and in the end they slept for a while, waking stiff and unrefreshed but, at least, a little more resigned to their self-imposed exile of each other.

When they were ready to set off for the match Stephen took Graham by the shoulders, looked him levelly in the eyes and said "Are you still going through with it?" Graham returned the gaze. "I'm no happier about it than you are", he said. "But I don't think it's safe — for either of us, but the damage to you would be more serious in the long run. So yes, I'm going through with it."

Stephen's eyes fell. "All right, then", he said, speaking so quietly that Graham had to put his ear close to his mouth to hear the words. "I'm sorry for kicking up such a fuss about it last night. It was ridiculous. Like a little boy who can't have his own way. I'm sorry." He clung to Graham in a long, close embrace, burying his head on his shoulder and stroking his hair. Graham, feeling equally wretched, caressed him in return, rocking him gently to and fro in his arms and kissing his face and throat and tickling his neck with the tips of his fingers. "We'll still be able to see each other as often as...as possible, Graham?" asked Stephen, in a small, hopeless voice.

"Of course we shall, love", said Graham. "All the time. Until you feel it's making it worse. You must tell me as soon as you feel that, and I'll disappear."

"It won't happen", said Stephen dully.

They broke from each other, and went to play cricket for the last time but one that season.

They missed each other terribly, and, especially in the first few weeks, it was aggravated by the casual contact they were still able to have, in class and occasionally out of school hours — they even managed the occasional stroll round the cricket field, now wearing its shaggy, worm-casty winter coat. Gradually the acute pain began to diminish as far as meetings at school went. But every time they met at the cricket club, which kept up its *esprit de corps*, and its finances, by maintaining a vigorous schedule of winter activities and drinking, all the dull ache of pain and loss flared up in them afresh.

One Saturday about midway through the school term the club organized a sponsored marathon. By that time they were both beginning to wonder if it would not spare them pain to see as little of each other as possible, but neither of them could bear it, so they jogged comfortably round the long course together, rekindling all their old feelings, and not quite sure whether to rejoice as they found that their love had actually managed somehow to put down deeper roots than ever, or to groan under the reactivated anguish that went with it.

Halfway round the course they found themselves alone in a deep tract of woodland, with no other runners within a mile of them. Almost without communication they slipped off the course and into the trees, and fell into each other's arms. They clung fiercely together for whole minutes on end, until they were forced to release each other to draw the breath that their frenzied bear-hug had been too tight to allow them. Both felt tenderly over their ribs for spots that had been bruised in the embrace, and broke into spontaneous laughter. But though they were only too acutely aware of what they both wanted and needed, they didn't dare to risk it, and the dank, dripping trees and the chill cutting edge on the wind that penetrated even deep into the wood completed the deterrent.

They both found their own ways of dealing with the parting, the loneliness and the missing of the other. Graham solved it by hurling himself into work, generating a cyclonic burst of energy week after week that left the classes he took stretched to their limits and himself so exhausted that the weekends had to be dedicated exclusively to mental and physical recovery, leaving him no time for brooding.

Stephen solved the same problem in a very different way. He found himself a lover. He suffered severe pangs of conscience at first; but the colossal urgency of a very young man's physical desire had been awakened just as it was ready to scale its loftiest peaks, and was not to be denied its fulfilment. He conducted lengthy arguments with himself, talking aloud on long walks into the countryside around the town. After all, he told himself, his real feelings were as devoted to Graham as ever, while what he felt for the boy he had begun to covet was physical and very little more. He could take his friend or leave him, and if the day came when Graham was available once more to satisfy his physical needs as well as his emotional ones, he went on, the friend could be ditched so fast he would never see Stephen go. So the easy insouciance of youth came to his aid, and he began to pay court assiduously to his casual friend and upper-sixth form colleague, Richard Fitzjohn.

He had been vaguely aware of Richard from the first stirrings of realization that he was capable of physical attraction only to members of his own sex. Richard was a shortish, compactly built boy a few months older than Stephen, with a pretty, cherubic face, a lot of long golden hair and, as Stephen had not been slow to notice, golden thighs as well. He wore the golden hair in a long, curling fringe that was forever dropping heavily over his eyes, and he had a fetching little mannerism of blowing upwards over his upper lip to blow it out of them, which Stephen, having once noticed him doing it, found indescribably sexy. He was popular, partly because of his looks, partly because he was a lively, witty boy, but most of all because he was, quite simply, nice. He was friendly without being clinging, always ready to talk and to help lesser intellects with academic problems, and was blessed with a sunny, easy-going disposition. He was also a virgin; and, as he admitted cheerfully and without a trace of embarrassment to Stephen when they found themselves paired for cross-country practice one Friday shortly after the end of Stephen's sexual relationship with Graham, he rather fancied the idea of ceasing to be one at the earliest opportunity.

It was such a shameless and unmistakable proposition that Stephen was too surprised to take the bait, with the result that he passed the weekend that followed haunted by images of the pretty face, the long golden hair and, mostly, the golden thighs, alternately masturbating voluptuously and cursing himself virulently for a purblind halfwit too slow on the uptake to seize the offer of the decade when it was thrust under his nose.

He wasted no time in remedying his dull-wittedness, however. In morning break on the Monday following, Richard Fitzjohn was mooching alone in the quadrangle when Stephen fell casually into step beside him. "Did you mean what you said on the run last Friday?" he asked.

"Eh?" said Richard. "What did I say? I don't remember saying anything special."

"You said you were a virgin, and wanted to do something about it."

"Oh", said Richard, turning to look at Stephen and giving him a naughty grin. "That."

"Yes", said Stephen, striving to maintain his air of airy self-assurance. "That."

"Oh yes", said Richard, smirking openly. "I meant it all right. And I'm still a virgin, though another weekend's passed with all its promise. Tom Cruise didn't turn up, so it was the box of Kleenex again, I'm afraid, and I'm still available for deflowering if required. And if the right deflowering consultant turns up. I've got ambitions to be a tart, you see. I think I'd make rather a good tart", he said thoughtfully, as if considering it with the careers master. "The trouble is, I'm a bit particular about who to go offering myself to — hence the excessive prolongation of my regrettable condition...

"I'd love to lose it to you, though", he added after a pause. "I'd marked you down as the ideal rescuer ages ago... But you never seemed very interested", he said after another pause. "I supposed you were already fixed up."

"How the hell did you know I was a... a... *candidate*?" asked Stephen, staring at him.

Richard laughed. "Come on, Stevie. I could see you were gay a mile off. I've seen the way you looked at some of the men here, in the changing rooms. More to the point, I've seen the way you looked at *me*. I used to hang about in the showers, giving you a chance to make a move on me. It was like being eaten alive — except that looking was all you ever did." He smiled dreamily to himself. "I've often imagined being eaten alive by you, Stevie. Guess which bit I'd want you to start with?"

Stephen deflowered him that evening, in Richard's bedroom, while his parents watched the nine o'clock news below.

***

The relationship blossomed as the term passed. Stephen progressed from enjoying Richard's nubile and freely, indeed wantonly given body to appreciating him as a clever and amusing friend; and in the wake of liking came a firm respect. Richard was admirably free from illusions, about himself in particular. He was good for Stephen, who sometimes exhibited a tendency to mild priggishness. If he was in one of his occasional consequential moments Richard would poke fun at him until he came back to life-size; but he would do it in such a gentle way, without any malice, that Stephen had to laugh at himself, and so the lesson was learned without any loss of face.

Richard was also possessed of a gift of clear-sightedness, a refusal, perhaps an inability, to indulge in self-deception, which would have been remarkable in the most perceptive of adults, and was extraordinary in a boy.

One Saturday about halfway through the term his parents had announced without a moment's warning that they were treating themselves to a weekend away, and intending to leave in the next hour. "You're sure you don't mind being left alone, Richard?" his mother had asked, without any anxiety, for they knew their son very well, and trusted him unreservedly. "Yes, yes", he had said graciously. "You go and have your break, it'll do you good. The old homestead'll still be here when you get back. Which will be when, by the way?"

He established beyond doubt that he had the run of the house until very late on the Sunday night. His father, who placed a high value on having a self-reliant and competent son, winked at him and slipped two twenty-pound notes into his hand as he pushed his wife out of the front door. "Thanks for being reliable, Dick, old fellow", he said. "Treat yourself to a meal out somewhere. Or get some of your mates in with some cans. Just make sure if anybody feels he's got to throw up, he does it over something washable, okay?" Richard had grinned at him and watched them out of sight. Twenty seconds later he was talking to Stephen's mother on the telephone; in less than half an hour they were in Richard's bed and Stephen had his head firmly lodged between the silky thighs at which he had once shot what he had thought were covert yearning looks.

They went to the nearest pub for an hour late on the Saturday night, and for two hours Sunday lunchtime. The rest of the weekend they spent in bed. At one point on Sunday afternoon they were lying side by side on their backs, exhausted. Stephen had an arm thrown across his eyes. Richard wriggled onto his side and propped himself on one elbow to look down at him. "You've got someone else, haven't you?" he said, in a matter-of-fact tone.

Stephen removed his arm from his eyes and looked up at him, a little startled. "Eh? Someone else?" he said, trying to collect his thoughts from where they had been straying, and marvelling at the other boy's perception, that he should have picked the precise moment that he had to make his remark.

"Don't get worried", said Richard reassuringly, playing idly with the fine golden hairs on Stephen's chest. "I shan't mind, not in the least. I'm not going to throw a jealous tantrum or anything. I only said it because, well, really, because I just happened to realize it just then, that's all."

"Well, you're wrong", said Stephen, feeling faintly annoyed for some reason he couldn't identify.

"Honestly, Stevie, there's no need to get upset, or anxious", said Richard placidly, and laughed as he saw Stephen's eyes widen slightly at these apparent feats of mind-reading. "I know you very well, old scout, and I'm very, very fond of you. Very fond indeed. I dare say I'm in love with you, if I wasn't too shallow and idle and too lacking in seriousness to know what being in love with someone felt like."

"I don't think..."

"Yes, you do", said Richard, still serene and slightly amused. "That's exactly what you think of me, Stevie, darling, because it's what everybody thinks of me. And the reason everybody thinks that of me is because it's quite true. Or rather, it's exactly what I want them to think of me, because it's what I want to be the truth about me at the moment.

"I'm as much in love with you as I could be capable of at the moment, which is not very much. That's beause I want it that way. You're not built that way at all, Stevie, my lovely. You're good fun, and you're lively, but you've got a serious side, and it's more than fifty per cent of you. You've got a dark side, too, and it scares me, just a little. I wouldn't want to be whoever this someone else is. I couldn't handle it. You'd ask too much, and it would most likely take the worst possible form...no, let me finish. I've got a feeling, I don't know why or where it's sprung from, that this could be something important.

"I think you'd ask more than someone like me could possibly give in a million years. Because you'd ask the one thing above all others that I couldn't give. You'd ask to be allowed to give too much. Or rather, you'd demand it. And that's something I couldn't deliver. Do you understand what I mean? No, I didn't think you did", he went on as Stephen shook his head.

"Let me put it this way", he said, running his neatly clipped nails up and down Stephen's side. "Whoever this someone else is, he must be absolutely immensely strong — stronger than I'd know how to understand, let alone be. Because whoever he is, he can obviously cope with you giving him your all. It would finish me off in two weeks. Please don't get me wrong, Stevie. It's as I said. I'm very, very fond of you. You're good company, you're good fun, and you're dreamy here" — he ran his hand over Stephen's limp, slightly sticky penis. "Screwing you's lovely, and being screwed by you's beyond belief. Also you're funny — you make me laugh. Your sense of humour's a bit hard to find, but for anyone who's got enough time for you to take the trouble to dig far enough down, it's very rewarding. You're a pretty super sort of chap, Steve. Just too..." He hesitated, groping for the word, for the first time since he had started speaking.

"You're just too... what do I mean? I've got it", he said, rolling over and kissing Stephen briefly but with affection on the mouth. "You're too powerful, Steve. You're too demanding — in the special way I've been saying. You're too forceful. Haven't you noticed, when we two are together, it's always what you want that we end up doing? Even in the sex — how often is it me who says 'I want to fuck you', or me who just goes down on you and sucks you cross-eyed? Never. Not even 'not often'. It's never. You control the relationship. And you have done right from the start. Remember when we first started? On that cross-country run together? I did everything short of dropping my shorts and begging you to take me there and then. Did you? Of course you didn't. You weren't ready. I practically offered you myself that day because I'd fancied you so hard for so long that I was getting desperate. I'd broken three pairs of pyjama bottoms thinking about you at night and getting nowhere. But it was you who came up, next day, and said, let's go. In your own time. You like to be — you've got to be in control.

"Don't take all this as criticism. Please don't take it the wrong way. I'm not complaining, not in the very least. It suits me down to the ground to have it this way. I'm lazy, easy-going to a fault, I'm as decisive as blancmange and as tough as a ball of wool. I was born to be precisely what I am: a pretty, fluffy, nice-natured, generous little tart, who does it for love. No, don't interrupt. Just this once let me talk myself right out. It's quite possibly the only time I'll ever feel energetic enough to be bothered.

"So, it suits me to leave all the decisions — even microscopic things like do I fuck you or you fuck me first require decisions to be made, and you make em. Good. Great. It saves me the awful task of thinking long enough to make them.

"Now you're very fond of me. I know that. And I'm glad. I like giving pleasure, especially to someone I like very much, and admire, which at this time means yourself. Also, you needed someone like me, because you were as horny as a herd of goats and as frustrated as a necrophile in a crematorium. But if we were living together, say, as a married couple, I'd give myself about six months before you got tired of me, and when that happened, you'd drop me like a used french letter. Not that you'd do it cruelly, or callously. Because you're made as you are, you'd make yourself and me miserable, because you'd have a terrible conscience about hurting me, even though you'd know you were going to let me go. Then, when it became unbearable, which would be when you realized how unhappy you were making me, you'd drop me, and we'd go back to being casual friends who said 'Hi' when we passed each other in the quad or in the street; but all this" — he stroked Stephen again — "would be as if it had never been, as if it had never happened.

"That would happen anyway. I know that, and I can live with it. I think it would happen with ninety-nine men out of any hundred who went with me. Don't look boiled, Stevie. I'll find the hundredth, and he'll look after me. Don't think because I know my weaknesses and my shortcomings that I don't know my good points equally well. I know what I've got to give the right one, and I'll know him when I find him, and keep him, at that. But you? Not a chance. You need stronger meat than me, Steve. I'm too milk-and-water by seven-eighths for you, love. And when this Mr someone else comes back, whoever he is and wherever he's gone, make no mistake, my life expectancy will be as long as it takes you to get from wherever you are to wherever he is, calling you.

"I know, you see. I haven't got a clue who he is, but I know that whoever he is, he's quite incredibly strong. He'd have to be, to handle you, and to secure his fifty per cent of the relationship. But he is, there's no doubt about that. And one day, soon, if I'm not mistaken, he'll be back, saying, 'Steve, I'm back, and this time, I'm here for keeps, if you want me.' He's the sort who'll say that, Stevie, because he's the very essence of fairness. He wouldn't do for you if he wasn't. Believe me, Steve, I've got a seeing eye for this sort of thing, and I know. You can prove it to yourself, if you want to."

He fell silent at last, with his face still cupped in his hand, looking down at Stephen's amazed expression. There was still the same mildly amused expression in his eyes, but also a still, serious affection, and something else, which Stephen, try as he might, could not identify. There was something yearning in it, some poignant sense of loss. Stephen gave it up. "How do you know all this, or think you know it?" he said, unaware that his voice had fallen to a whisper. "And how can I prove anything you say?"

Richard laughed, a soft, sexy gurgle of a laugh. "Prove it? Easy-peasy. Just ask yourself how close I've been so far." He watched as Stephen, despite a quickly-formed determination not to get enticed into any guessing game with him, thought about it. He laughed again as he saw the results in Stephen's eyes.

"Well", muttered Stephen as he focussed on Richard's face once more, "I don't know how you do it, but, well, yes, you're pretty close in a lot of what you say. You certainly described G..."

"Not his name, please, Steve. I don't want to know. I may be all the things I said, but I do bleed. I am capable of being hurt."

Stephen stared at him, and the last piece of the puzzle dropped silently into place. He knew what the final, enigmatic ingredient in Richard's expression had been, and his mind sheered away in protest, not wanting to acknowledge what he had seen, or what he had done. Richard saw that he knew, and smiled, blowing his fringe out of his eyes and looking heart-breakingly appealing. "He'll be back, Stevie", he said gently.

"How...how do you know?"

"Because he'll need you. People like you don't grow on trees, and he won't find another like you; and he knows he won't. And he'll know you need him — similar reasons — and he's as determined to shoulder his responsibilities as you are. He wouldn't have got to love you otherwise — you wouldn't've let him, and he wouldn't've needed you to stop him anyway. Oh yes, he'll be back. Sooner or later, most likely sooner, given that he must be at least as intelligent as you are, he'll accept that if he passes up the chance of having you he'll be throwing away what's almost certainly the only chance he's ever going to get of happiness. Like I said, people like you don't happen often. The chances of two of you meeting are about as remote as the last two blue whales in the entire Pacific happening to bump into each other to mate. So, for the seventh time, I say to you, he'll be back. And when that happens, well, your pretty little piece of blond ice-cream will shiver briefly and fade into nothingness before your eyes. If he walked into this room now, you wouldn't even be able to see me. I would be, quite literally, invisible.

"I don't resent that, Stevie. I might as well resent the winds that blow. I'm very happy to take you on your terms, for a little while, and be grateful for the time I have. When I become invisible, I shall accept it with my customary good grace. All I ask is, if you can spare a moment to remember me every now and then, when you're happy with him, just remember, we were the folks that told you first."

"I can't imagine ever forgetting this", said Stephen, meaning it. "I've never been psycho-analyzed before."

"I'm not psycho-analyzing you, my dear", said Richard gently. "It's nothing specially clever. Just street wisdom, you know. Or common sense, if you like."

"But how have you got it? How do you know all this? You're eighteen years old. Nobody can be that wise at our age. Nobody ought to be that wise at our age. How did you learn all this?"

Richard smiled, a strangely old smile. "My Dad, my dear chap, is a very wise man. He and I get on very well. We understand one another. My mother, who's got about as much brain as the silicon chip in a programmable washing-machine, still indulges in fond daydreams of what she'll wear at my wedding. I'm still waiting for the right moment to tell her. I'll know when I can do it most gently. So, you see, I get my wisdom, such as it is, from him. From my mother I get my easy-going nature and my air-head attitude; and most of all, my charm. Remember I said I knew my selling points as well as my faults? That's my biggest: I'm charming.

"How else do you think a man such as my father could spend twenty years with someone such as my mother, and be as bowled over by her, as blissfully happy and besottedly in love with her now as he was the day he married her? Or marry her in the first place? Answer: she's nice. She's the nicest person either of us has ever met. And she's a joy to look at — if you happen to go in for people of that peculiar anatomical construction — and when she walks into a room it's as if the sun's just risen, right there in the room. She could walk into a room full of dead bodies, and within thirty seconds they'd all be not only alive again but smiling and calling her by her first name, and feeling as if they'd known her all their lives. You don't need brains, or even much strength of character, if you were born with a nimbus of bright light shining round your head. That explains my father and my mother. It also explains you and me, for a little while. But my mother wouldn't have done for you, supposing you'd been made that way. You wouldn't have been happy with her for any length of time. And you won't with me. You've got this one mystical ingredient in your character which my father hasn't got — I'm very glad to say. As for me, I think if I'd had it I'd have gone screaming into a padded cell years ago. That or shot myself. But you've got it all right. That's why Mr someone else is on his way back right now, or will be very soon."

"What is this mysterious ingredient?" cried Stephen in alarm.

"Single-mindedness", said Richard, and began to fondle him in earnest before he could reply, or think about it much.

Stephen's body told him plainly that he had little time to fill in the last small gaps. He struggled free, and put his hands over his crotch. "Just one more question, Richard", he panted.

"Of course", said Richard obediently, ceasing to play with him. "Don't make it too long." He giggled suddenly and incongruously. "I'll make it long enough in a minute."

"You still haven't told me how you know all this. You went on about getting your wisdom from your father, but you haven't actually told me a single thing you've seen or heard, or...or picked up by intuition, which is what it sounds most like to me, that's told you all this."

"My wisdom is nothing very spectacular, Steve, my sweetheart", said Richard, almost playfully. "It's mostly a matter of conjuring tricks. Actually, that's rather what you're doing right now: asking the conjuror to show you how the trick works. You'll be very disappointed when you see that it's all done by a small and inexpensive gadgetry, or an accomplice in the audience, won't you?"

"I doubt it", said Stephen. "Whatever you may think of yourself, I'm pretty damn sure you're not cheap." Richard smiled. It was a grave, rather serious smile, a little sad, and very beautiful.

"All right, then, Stevie, I'll tell you a little of it. Not all. You must allow me to keep a little of my poor mystique. If I show you all the machinery and point out all my accomplices in the crowd you'll realize that I'm nothing but machinery and stooges. I'll be like a joke that's been explained, or a frog that's been dissected. You know how the frog works now, but you ain't got no frog. I'd sooner have a live frog that hops and think it a miracle to marvel at than have it spread and pinned out on a desk in front of me and know precisely why it will never hop again. Agreed?"

Stephen looked up at him, and nodded.

"You have dark moments", said Richard slowly. "They come at a rate of about two an hour, rising to peaks at certain times. I know when these moments are here. Do you know how I know?"

"I haven't got the slightest idea."

"In them, I become invisible", he said, and suddenly he looked terrifyingly old to Stephen, and infinitely sad. "That's how I know", he resumed, and the hallucination vanished. "I might as well not exist. For you, in fact, I don't. You go away, miles, miles and miles. It's not just like when we all do that, you know, going into a trance for a moment, or when you look at your watch and then realize a few moments later you haven't actually seen it, so you have to look again. In a way, *you* become invisible. You simply aren't there. And nothing I can do can bring you back. You're not just not here. You're with him, and I can't compete with him, Stephen. He's out of my league."

"Wh-when does this happen?" asked Stephen. He shivered, and registered the fact that he had done so a moment before, when Richard had, for the first time ever, called him "Stephen", instead of the easy, friendly, slightly flip "Steve" and "Stevie" that he liked to call him normally.

"When we're having sex", said Richard, shivering slightly himself. "When we're lying quietly after it. And every time certain things are mentioned. It doesn't have to be by us. On the television, a word in a newspaper, my parents, a man in a pub, anyone. I'm not going to tell you all of them. I don't think you'd like to know that I know all your signals. But I'll tell you this. Cricket's one of them. Not all cricket, or all cricketers. But certain things. I think there's a certain kind of cricket bat, though I don't know enough about cricket to be sure. And certain words. 'Box' is one. Cricket again, I suppose. Even I know what a cricketer's box is. I take it he's a cricketer, and — well, his box — you can work it out for yourself... There's a great black spider sitting on your belly-button", he said suddenly, loudly and distinctly.

"*L'amertume des vieux buis*..." heard Stephen...

"...You see, Stevie", Richard was saying. "You did it just then. Did you hear what I said just now?"

"I... er... I think so", said Stephen, feeling very awkward and uncomfortable.

"Did you hear what I said about the spider?"

"No", said Stephen dully.

"I said 'there's a great black spider sitting on your belly-button'. You weren't there, Steve. You were invisible."

"Do you know", said Stephen, slowly. "I think, if I had this... gift that you've got, it would frighten me, a lot."

"I'm only a conjuror", Richard laughed. "Just a fair power of observation, a heaven-sent lack of illusions, including, or especially, about myself; and the great blessing of an ability to put two and two together and always, always, make four of it, never three."

"Are you absolutely sure you're not God?" asked Stephen, with the same shiver. "Or somebody sent from him?"

For the first time Richard looked a little startled. It suddenly struck Stephen that he had never seen him lose his composure, even for the briefest moment.

"If I believed in God", said Richard, "I'm sure I'd say he was in all of us, wouldn't I? That's what all believers say. As it happens, I don't. Therefore I'm not. I don't think, therefore I'm not. Neat, eh? I'll tell you what I do believe, if you like, though."

"Go on."

"I believe I'd like to stop pretending to be a serious human being. One other thing."

"Yes?"

"Will you take your hands away from yourself, please? You look like a footballer in a defensive wall. And one other thing I believe. The last."

"Yes?"

"I believe I'd very much like to be fucked. Be gentle with me, Stevie. And stay with me this time, please. Please don't go away."

***

"That you, Steve?"

"Yes, speaking."

"It's Bill."

"Bill?"

"Bill McKechnie, from the cricket club. You know cricket? Game played by men with red leather balls. You start to play it, it rains. Casting a ball at three straight sticks and defending the same with a fourth. Breathless hush in the close tonight. You, me, and Hoody makes three. Don Parker makes four, and sundry other idiots make eleven, when I've rung em. We've just had the idea, and issued the challenge, which, you will be glad to hear, has been accepted in the spirit in which it was issued — namely Glenfiddich."

"What exactly do you mean, Bill — if you mean anything?"

"We're having a game, mate, and we want you to play in it."

"I suppose you're on the piss somewhere?"

"You must have been oiling your supposer, old chap. It's working quite well. But can you play? Boxing Day. Next Tuesday, to be precise. Here. To wit, here. At the club. Elderton Park CC, of the town which you grace immeasurably with your residence, outskirts of. Probable pitch conditions: permafrost. Unlikely to take spin, but should assist the fast bowlers. Projected weather conditions, your guess is as good as the Met. Office's. Real but unstated purpose of exercise, monumental piss-up afterwards, with bangers and mash in the club-house. That's it, I think. Oh, yes: opposition, negligible — or, to be precise, the Town Club. Having despaired of getting a worthwhile game out of them in the conventional summer setting, we've just challenged them to a winter variety. So, can you play?"

"Of course I will", cried Stephen. "What time?"

"Oh, didn't I say? Game starts at eleven o'clock. Thirty overs a side, or until the fielders' fingers start dropping off from frostbite, whichever shall be the shorter. Try to get there for nine o'clock, though: we're laying on a champagne breakfast. You'll enjoy it, if the Crimble cricket matches I've been to are anything to go by."

"I'll be there for nine", said Stephen excitedly. "Pity Graham

129

can't be there, isn't it? He'd jump at this."

"Why, what's the matter with him? He's next on my list of well-known local idiots to ring."

"He's gone to France", said Stephen. He felt a cold stab of pain in his lower abdomen at the thought of Graham. "He's in France", he said, striving to keep the sudden chill of loneliness out of his voice for Bill's benefit. "He always goes there in the Christmas holidays."

"Oh. That's a bit of a bugger", came Bill's voice. "I had him down as one of my dead certs. Thanks for telling me, Steve. See you Tuesday. Don't forget, nine o'clock, and tell your people not to wait up for you. There's enough booze here to keep us goin till next Christmas. See you, and have a dismal Crimble, son." He rang off.

Stephen put the receiver down and went back to his armchair feeling joyous relief at the thought of the cricket match, and at the same time missing Graham with a poignancy that was almost unbearable. The cricket match, he felt, was the solitary good thing that had happened so far this Christmas holiday, materializing as it had out of nowhere to rescue him from having to endure a deadly Boxing Day immediately after what he had little doubt was going to be a deadly Christmas Day. He watched seasonal inanities on the television with a jaundiced eye, and waited for his parents to return from one of their four trips to church that had characterized each day of the Christmas period for as long as he could remember. Christ, he thought to himself, I'd even have been better off going to church with them than sitting here moping about on my own. At least there'd be plenty of other people as miserable as me there for moral support.

In some ways he had been glad when the holidays had begun. They put an end to the pain of encountering Graham every day and having to pretend they were nothing more than a schoolmaster and a bright, personable pupil. He saw more and more of Richard Fitzjohn, and the better he knew him the fonder he became of him. Richard never again let his surface glitter drop from him as he had in the extraordinary conversation in his bed when Stephen had asked him, almost seriously, if he was God. On the other hand, for Stephen he never completely re-erected the curtain of superficiality which he was careful to keep in place for most people. For Stephen he was just clever, funny, sexy, permanently randy — in short, wonderful company, and the best possible thing to keep Stephen's mind off Graham, so far as such a thing was possible at all.

Richard himself loved Stephen deeply and simply. With the decidedly mixed blessing of his penetrating insight he knew that however much he gave of himself to Stephen he could never give enough to make up for Stephen's real love, for the good reason that he didn't have enough to give. Knowing this, he gave all he did have unconditionally. Stephen loved him for it, too, though with a love of a very different kind from his feelings for Graham; and it seemed to be enough for Richard, though Stephen suffered periodic torments of guilt for allowing Richard to shower him with more affection and devotion than he could return. When he tried to explain the feeling Richard simply laughed at him and then deliberately deflected the conversation by saying something sexy, flippant or, more often than not, both.

A character like Richard was, of course, as conspicuous as a peacock among his dowdy hens in the school, so there was no chance of their friendship not being noticed. But no-one appeared to suspect that there was more to them than two inseparable friends of the kind that flourish in boys' schools. If the sexual nature of their relationship had come to light Stephen knew very well that Richard could not have cared less, and a fair bit of this insouciance rubbed off on Stephen as they became closer and closer. Although Richard's flamboyant character took many forms they did not include parading his private life in public, and if it had he would have been too respectful of Stephen's more private nature to do so.

One result of this was that Graham never suspected how things stood with the two of them. He was very glad to see that Stephen had made one very close friendship, suspecting that it afforded him some relief from the unflagging sense of loss — which Graham could understand very well, suffering as he did from the identical feelings himself. But he had no idea that Stephen regularly shared Richard's bed. Nor would he have understood the significance of a map pinned to the inside of Richard's desk lid. It was a large, scale plan of the school buildings and grounds, which Richard, whose fertile talents included draughtsmanship, had drawn and inked in the school art room in his spare time. Marked on it in red ink were several neat little crosses like the crossed swords marking battlefields on Ordnance Survey maps. Each cross was accompanied by a date in tiny, neat figures, and from time to time Richard added another. The map was a mystery to all who saw it, and a source of much speculation among the boys and masters alike, but no-one ever came close to suspecting its real meaning.

It had been Richard's idea to see how many different places they could find in the school to achieve full sexual union; but Stephen, when he had managed to stop laughing in slightly scandalized delight at the idea, had gone along with it enthusiastically. By the end of term the map bore seventeen crosses.

On the last day of term the school was virtually deserted by eleven in the morning. Graham found Stephen as he was gathering books for holiday revision, and they walked round the boundary of the cricket field one last time. It was a melancholy stroll, with both of them too choked with frustration and yearning to take any real pleasure from the other's company, and they ended it by tacit agreement after a couple of circuits. When they parted — Graham to finish off loose ends, Stephen to go to Richard's house — they wished each other a happy Christmas formally, almost like strangers, each knowing privately that though the wishes were sincere they were so futile as to be meaningless. Graham told Stephen of his plan to spend the holiday in France as he always did, and Stephen's face fell. Though he had little expectation of restoring their relationship, the certain knowledge that it was now beyond his power depressed him more than he would have believed. When they finally turned away from each other to go in different directions Graham saw with a pang of pain as sharp as angina that Stephen's eyes were wet and glistening. He hurried out of sight with his head down, lest any other master should see the tears in his own. They both felt more thoroughly wretched than they had ever felt in their lives.

Richard, waiting by the school gates for Stephen to walk home with him, saw them part. When Stephen came up to him he saw the tears, too. His eyes widened in wonder. "So that's who it is", he said as Stephen came up. "Christ! I'd never have thought of him, if I'd guessed for a fortnight."

Stephen stared at him in horror. "You saw?" he said dully.

Richard glanced round and saw that there was no-one

in sight. He swung round into Stephen's path, put his arms round him and hugged him, his fingers stirring Stephen's thick dusty-blond hair. "It doesn't matter if I know, Stevie", he said softly, nibbling Stephen's ear. "I wouldn't say anything, you know that."

Stephen did, and allowed his friend to comfort him as they walked through the streets to Richard's house. Richard saw immediately that he didn't want to talk about it, and set himself to entertain him and distract his thoughts from his sorrows. By the time they reached the house Stephen had brightened up. "Come on up, Stevie", said Richard. "They're all out till tonight. I know how to take your mind off things." He bounded up the stairs, already stripping his pullover, tie and shirt off. By the time Stephen reached the bedroom, which was now as familiar as his own at home, Richard was already naked, and waiting with his arms open, and an expression on his face of pure love, softened by a deep pity. And Richard — pretty, randy and generous — seeing that Stephen was still in part unmanned by his misery, for once took the lead, and gave his body and all his ingenuity to comfort Stephen's troubled mind.

Richard too was going abroad for the holiday, leaving with his parents for Malta the following day, and so it was a depressed and lonely Stephen who trudged home to try to get on with his parents that evening. Even the recent memory of Richard's firm, muscular, sweet-smelling body faded rapidly from his mind.

He tried hard to make himself agreeable to his parents, whom he didn't want to hurt if he could avoid it. They too, having begun to reconcile themselves to his new spirit of independence and his striking out on paths they didn't especially like, were anxious to be on as friendly terms with their son as possible, so over the next few days he did cheer up somewhat, and they rubbed along reasonably well. But Christmas itself was the usual dismal affair, and he found himself almost counting the minutes to the cricket match on Boxing Day. His parents exchanged glances when he told them of the arrangements he had made; but they accepted it without any fuss, and his father even managed to hope, in a slightly chilly manner, that he would enjoy himself. He would have been a good deal chillier if he had known just how his son was destined to enjoy his midwinter match.

***

It was still half-dark when he arrived at the ground on Boxing morning, only twenty-five past eight, but he hadn't been able to wait, and had taken a chance that someone would be arriving early to get everything set up. All the lights were blazing out through the great picture windows along the front of the big pavilion, beaming a welcome through the gloom. His spirits had picked up the moment he had woken that morning, and now they positively soared. He trotted across the shaggy, muddy outfield, pausing out of unfailing cricketer's instinct to inspect the square, then hastened on towards the cheerful, homely lights.

"Hi, Stevie", bawled Bill as he slipped through the doors and closed them quickly against the bitter east wind. "Good boy. You're the first. Come and give me a hand with these shutters, will you?" Stephen joined him behind the long bar with its cage of heavy-mesh shuttering, and Bill's first act was to stick an opened bottle of Heineken into his hand. "Beer for breakfast, our kid", he said in his broadest Derbyshire brogue. Stephen felt oddly proud to find himself the first there, and to be asked to help and given beer at an unthinkable hour of the day as if it was the most natural thing in the world. He felt that it signified in some almost mystical way that he had really arrived.

They had got the bar ready by the time Alan Hood arrived at twenty to nine. Bill started rolling barrels around, attaching gas nozzles and making a fearsome din, while Stephen stocked the shelves with vast numbers of bottles of beers and minerals. Alan tossed his cricket bag into the dressing room and began laying out crockery, cutlery and glasses on the two long tables. As others arrived they busied themselves with all the little jobs to be done, and the place was noisy and cheerful with activity when the opposition rolled up at five to nine. They piled into the pavilion, loaded down with cricket gear and cases of booze, and immediately started opening the bottles and passing them to each other and the Elderton players.

The champagne breakfast was a happy, cheery business that did much to compensate for the glum time Stephen had had up to then. The supplies of champagne seemed endless; and when it finally did run out the president of the visiting side slipped unobtrusively out with a couple of his team, and returned a minute later with six cases of Mumm. There were cheers, and they had breakfast all over again.

Stephen had only drunk champagne two or three times before, and never more than one glass at a time. Bill's methods were uncompromising: he simply thrust pint mugs at everyone and told them to get stuck in. Every few moments someone would charge along the tables filling people's glasses, with the result that by the time players were peering into the last few bottles to make sure that the final drops had been consumed, Stephen had nine tenths of a pint of champagne still to drink in his glass, and he was already feeling more than a little tipsy. He thought it was perhaps the most wonderful feeling he had ever experienced.

He attempted to explain so to Bill, but found that for some strange reason he was having difficulty in finding the right words for what he wished to say. He also observed that he kept breaking into roars of laughter for no explainable reason. This would, he thought, have made him conspicuous, but for the fact that most of the others seemed to be afflicted in the same unaccountable way.

He guzzled some of his champagne. Then it struck him that it was very unfair for him to have lots of it to drink while some of the others round him had empty glasses, so in a warm, cotton-wool glow of generosity he offered the rest round. They fell on it like wolves, and in five seconds it was gone. Then they went out to start the cricket match.

It was a good match, because the first half was played in a warm alcoholic glow, while in the second innings they had sobered up from the champagne, but restored themselves with huge draughts of port contributed by the Elderton Park president, reciprocating the visitors' generosity at breakfast. Nobody scored many runs, but Stephen's team managed to amass 103 before they were all out in the nineteenth over, and the town scored the winning run in the twenty-eighth, with the last pair together. It was over by three in the afternoon, when it was practically dark, and they herded back into the pavilion feeling refreshed and bright from the unexpected exercise and fresh air, but chilled to the bone and more than ready for further supplies of drink.

Stephen trotted off the field feeling brighter and happier than he had for several days, skipped up the steps and through the pavilion doors, and ran straight into Graham Curtis. He was so surprised that for some moments he stood gazing at Graham with his mouth open. Graham smiled, a little tensely but with all the affection Stephen knew was there for him.

"Graham!" he eventually blurted out. "You're not supposed to be here. I mean, you were supposed to be in France. I told Bill, that's why he never phoned you. I thought..."

"Never mind, Stephen", Graham said. "I was in France, but I had to come back prematurely. I got a message saying that a very dear old friend of mine was seriously ill. They implied that it was really very serious indeed — you know, possibly the end, so I had to come back to London to see him. He wasn't as bad as they thought, it seems, so I didn't stay; but it wasn't worth going back to France for the rest of the break, so I came home. Got back this afternoon. Saw the game going on as I drove past, and here I am. You seemed glad to see me", he went on, glancing round and lowering his voice.

"Oh, God, Graham", said Stephen in a low, urgent whisper. "I've been having a dreadful time of it. I'm missing you so badly..." He broke off as other players appeared. "Hallo, Graham", said several of them. "Thought you were in France..."

Stephen went to the bar and got two pints while Graham was repeating his explanations. He carried one back to Graham, who thanked him pleasantly, but with all the conspiratorial intimacy gone while the others were about. They drifted over to a corner of the bar together, and Stephen gave a brief account of his holiday so far. Graham laughed at his description of the horrors of a family Christmas, but sobered when Stephen asked him "How have you been lately?"

"Well", he said, "about the same as you, I should think. No point in kidding myself about how much I miss you. I do, desperately. This is the first year when I haven't enjoyed going to France. I've loved the country and the people ever since I first went there as a boy younger than you are now, and I get withdrawal symptoms if I don't spend a month there at least once a year. That's despite having to teach the language to a lot of francophobic little Englanders. And Paris, which is where I was intending to spend this holiday, is a beautiful city. But my heart wasn't in it this year. I kept on thinking how wonderful it would be to take you there, and show you the real France, off the beaten track — all the little towns that the tourists never go near. I was actually glad to get the recall — apart from poor Reggie being ill, of course."

"Is he a very good friend of yours?" asked Stephen, meaning something else, and feeling a jagged bolt of jealousy skewering through him. It was so acute and unexpected that he physically flinched, bending as if he had been smitten with a sharp stomach pain.

"Are you all right?" asked Graham sharply, putting a hand on his shoulder.

"Yeah, yeah, I'm okay", gasped Stephen, feeling rather silly. "Just a twinge of indigestion or something."

"Yes, well, Reggie's a very dear friend indeed. He's a very wise old man, a doctor, retired now. He's a sort of guru for me. I ask his advice when I'm at a loss, and cry on his shoulder when I'm in trouble because I ignored the advice."

"Was he..." Stephen broke off in the middle of the question as he realized how impertinent it sounded, but Graham smiled.

"Yes", he said gently, "he was — my first. For a few years, when I was a year or so older than you are. He was a very kind, gentle initiator, who taught me most of what little wisdom I can claim. Don't be jealous", he added with a grin, reading Stephen's expression. Stephen looked sheepish, and they both laughed. Some of the tension ebbed out of them.

Various people came up and joined them at intervals, and in between Graham talked about Reggie Westwood, remembering anecdotes from years ago, and recalling some hilarious goings on in the gay pubs and clubs they had visited together. This rang a bell in Stephen's mind. "When you go to Paris", he asked, "do you go round the gay places ever?"

Graham raised an eyebrow at him. "Occasionally", he said. "Not a great deal. I'm not actually all that fond of pubbing and clubbing. Just once in a while, when I get lonely, and feel like a bit of company. When I don't want to pretend for a change."

"So you get lonely, too?" said Stephen, wistfully.

Graham stared at him. "Well, of course I do. What an odd thing to say. I'm human too, you know. I've been half out of my mind these last few months, missing you." He lowered his voice and shot a quick glance round. "I've had no love in my life, no affection, no sexual comfort, no nothing, you know. The nearest I've been to a thrill lately is tossing myself off thinking about that quick cuddle we had on the marathon, or what we used to have going for us. Lonely? Christ", he went on, with an edge of bitterness creeping into his voice, "I'm an internationally acknowledged expert on the subject. But I don't suppose I need to tell you that."

A brief pornographic production of himself and Richard Fitzjohn romping naked together in Richard's bed unreeled itself rapidly across Stephen's mind as Graham said it, leaving an acrid tang of guilty self-loathing. "Poor Graham", he said. His voice was very gentle. Graham detected the gentleness, and gave him a quick grateful look.

They continued chatting as they watched the cricketers gradually becoming more and more riotous. A sing-song started up in one corner, and everyone got roped in to sing rugby songs under Bill's lead. More beer went down, followed by spirits as people began to find themselves loaded up to the Plimsoll line, or, in numerous cases, above it. Sundry people ran to the lavatories or out onto the outfield to be sick; others fell asleep wherever they happened to be, and gradually the majority drifted away. No-one took any notice of Stephen and Graham.

At just after nine o'clock Graham shook his head muzzily and said "I think I've had enough, or rather, a bit more than enough. I feel a bit pissed. I think it's time I cleared off. Come outside and say cheerio, Steve." It was the first time Graham had ever abbreviated his name, and it gave Stephen a pleasurable tingle down his spine. It sounded so friendly and natural that for a second he experienced a kind of self-delusion that everything was well again, as if they could resume real life. It passed in a fraction of a second, leaving him feeling cheated and gloomy. But he followed Graham out of the pavilion obediently enough, and they strolled across the outfield together in the comforting, protective darkness. No-one noticed them go.

When they got to the other side of the field Graham turned to say good night. The night was so dark that he never saw the arms coming up until one locked itself round his neck and the other round his waist. He felt himself swept into a fierce, crushing hug. Before he had time to utter a word he felt Stephen's lips on his cheek, seeking his own mouth, and a second later a tongue slipped into his mouth and began flicking and playing. He felt passionate desire rising at record speed, and struggled to break Stephen's vice-like clasp. "No", he muttered. But Stephen would not let him go. "I want you", he gasped, gulping air. "I've been going out of my mind for months with missing you, and it's not bloody fair. I want you so badly", he said, and kissed him again.

He finally released Graham when a pair of headlights went on across the field beside the pavilion. "Come on", he said. "I'm coming home with you. My parents aren't expecting me home. I told 'em I'd probably sleep at the clubhouse tonight. They probably think I'm drunk... Knowing them they probably think it serves me right." He giggled. "I bet they'd rather I was lying pissed under a table than where I'm going to be tonight. Come on", he hissed as the headlights wove an unsteady path round the perimeter of the field.

Graham considered what to do as they set off in the direction of his flat. He had reached no firm conclusion by the time they got there, and there seemed no harm, he felt, in taking Stephen in for a mug of hot coffee. "Come on, then", he said, a bit gruffly, unlocking the door. Stephen scurried in, pulling Graham in after him and kicking the door closed. "Hey, mind my paint", said Graham, as Stephen pulled him hungrily into his arms.

They clung to each other for what seemed like a few seconds, but was in fact several minutes, in the darkened hallway. Then Graham broke loose and propelled Stephen on into the living room. He sat him down on the sofa, then went into the kitchen to make coffee. Stephen jumped up and followed him, unable to be out of sight of him now that, against all the odds, against Graham's own best judgment and against his own expectations, he had him to himself as of old. Both of them knew what was going to happen, and both knew that it would be futile to try to resist. Their mutual desire was so imperious that they drank the coffee too quickly, and both ended up with a badly-scalded tongue. Stephen got to his feet, and realized that he was trembling violently all over. He put out his arms to pull Graham off the sofa, and Graham came willingly up into his arms. They almost ran into the bedroom. There Graham said "Wait, love;

shan't be a moment", dashed into the bathroom, and came back with a small blue and white tube. Though he had been no more than seconds, when he returned he found Stephen reclining on the double bed. He was already naked and erect. Graham stood speechless for a moment, hardly able to believe that he had his young lover again, and hardly able to bear the poignancy and beauty of the smile that welcomed him into his own bed.

***

Graham Curtis was glad when it was time to return to work in readiness for the Lent term.

His frenzied, half-tipsy sexual reunion with Stephen after the Boxing Day cricket match had been followed by a harrowing scene when they awoke late the next morning. With the return of sobriety and clear judgment he had once again vetoed all sexual and most intimate contact. It had cost him almost more than he could bear, with Stephen's long, slim body naked and inviting beside him. Stephen had protested and pleaded, argued and demanded, flipping from clinging, occasionally tearful desperation to urgent, iron self-control. "But why, Graham?" he kept demanding. "For Christ's sake, why? If we could do it last night and get away with it, why shouldn't we do it tonight, or to-morrow, and get away with it then, as well? Christ, we did it for weeks before, and got away with it then, too. Why did it have to stop so suddenly?"

It was made all the harder for Graham to answer because in truth he hadn't got a ready answer, except the real one, which was simple prudence, or, in Stephen's view, simple cowardice. Knowing that he could hardly explain why he felt so adamant, at the same time as he knew that he still felt so, made Graham brusque and almost unkind with Stephen. Stephen responded by attacking Graham at his most vulnerable point, using his body and the remarkable range of sexual expertise he had garnered through his extensive experiments with Richard. Graham found himself wondering how the boy had acquired such blandish-ments, even in the moments when he had felt his resolve slipping from his grasp. Stephen smothered him with kisses, and he had almost yielded before wrenching himself quite brutally away.

They ended up standing in defensive attitudes on opposite sides of Graham's bed, glaring at each other almost with dislike, Stephen semi-hysterical, his face streaked with tears and his mouth set in an ugly pout, Graham torn agonizingly apart between certainty that what he was doing was right, essential and in Stephen's own interest, and grinding remorse and self-reproach at having to inflict such visible pain. He sat on the bed and begged Stephen to sit beside him. Stephen did so, warily. Graham put an arm round his shoulders, but he threw it violently off, glaring at him with a look of angry, bewildered hurt on his face that scored and burned Graham almost beyond bearing. He came very close to throwing in his resistance at that moment. But his dogged self-control prevailed, and he set about trying to reason with Stephen.

It wasn't very successful, and it all ended with Stephen stamping out of the flat in a boiling froth of fury, frustration at not getting the straight answers he felt himself entitled to, genuine puzzlement and badly hurt feelings. He hurled the door shut and stamped off in the direction of his home, glaring ferociously at a passing postman. Graham turned onto his stomach on the bed as he heard the tremendous slam and buried his face in the quilt, wondering what to do.

It might all have ended then, in unpleasant recriminations, with angry, almost contemptuous dislike on Stephen's side and guilty self-doubt on Graham's, but a cure was ready. It was triggered comically enough, when Stephen arrived at his front door. Groping in his pocket for his key he noticed for the first time consciously that he still had an immense erection. For a moment this amplified his rage to new record voltages; but a second later he suddenly saw the funny side of it, and started to laugh. It rose and swelled, and every new thought that entered his mind as he leaned against the doorpost, gasping and heaving with it, magnified and intensified it. Eventually he had to sit on the doorstep, doubling up in pain as fresh paroxysms hit him in waves.

So for the time being his sense of humour saved him. As the laughing fit eased and allowed him to think without starting him off again, he began to consider the heady cocktail of feelings he had been suffering when he had stormed out of Graham's flat. It took him very little time to see that his fury was little more than the tantrum of a child who can't have its own way; his feelings were still hurt, but in his calmer frame of mind he knew quite well that Graham would never have hurt them willingly; and he began to reason for himself why Graham had been so unable to explain himself, and to see the difficulties. He let himself in, called out a greeting and, finding that the house was empty, ran lightly up to his bedroom to do something about his erection.

***

Fortunately for both of them the slow ordeal of the vacation was almost over — a few days earlier for Graham, who was only too glad to return to school a day or so before the start of the new term to prepare for it. He hurled himself into the work with the furious energy of love and sexual yearning sublimated.

One evening two days before school started, while Graham was sorting out revision schedules for those of his French pupils who were due to take A-level that summer, Stephen was on his way out seeking consolation in a drink at the cricket club. As he was halfway out of the door the telephone rang. Swearing mildly, he went back, and was very glad he had when a distinctive voice came over the line. "Stevie? It's me. I'm back."

"Richard!" he cried, quivering with pleasure. He was more delighted than he could have imagined. "When did you get back?"

"Ten minutes ago", said Richard, sounding pleased. "Want to come round?"

"Are you on your own?" asked Stephen, lowering his voice.

"Er... no", said Richard. "But that doesn't matter — unless you've got somewhere else to suggest."

"I was just going for a pint at the cricket club", said Stephen. "You've never been there with me", he went on, suddenly feeling a desire to take Richard out and show him off, as it were. "Why don't you come with me for a drink?"

"Okay", said Richard. "How do I get there?"

"You know where I live, don't you? Well, it's on the way from your house to the club. I'll be waiting outside for you." Richard agreed, and Stephen put the phone down in spirits that had risen miraculously from the low that had, apart from the brief surge over Boxing Day and its aftermath, been the norm over the last three and a half weeks. He surprised his parents by yelling a cheerful "See you later", and let himself out of the front door with another immense erection making itself felt in his under-pants, and a firm intention of employing it altogether more inventively and pleasurably than he had been able to do with the last few he had had.

When Richard came up a few minutes later he was looking as pert and sultry as ever. There was no-one in sight. They ran a few hundred yards along the road and halted in the darkest place, midway between two streetlights, laced their arms round each other and fell into a record-breaking kiss. "What sort of a time have you had?" asked Stephen, coming up for air.

"All right", said Richard, nuzzling Stephen's cheek as he sought his mouth again. Stephen felt a twinge of irrational jealousy. "We had fun", Richard went on indistinctly, his voice muffled by their kiss. "Not doing much, just lazing, knocking round with Mum and Dad mostly. I spent a lot of time thinking about you, actually. Did you get my postcard?"

"Nope. Not yet."

"Oh, well, I only sent it a few days ago. I thought it would probably get back after me. It wasn't much, anyway. Just some-thing rude. I thought it might wake your people up if they found it before you did."

"What!" ejaculated Stephen, breaking the interminable kiss and letting out an explosive titter. "Maybe it has come, and they've burned it. Was it very rude?"

"It was just a bit naughty. Well, pretty naughty, actually. I got it in a gay bar."

"Christ!" yelped Stephen, goggling at his friend in a kind of appalled delight, and starting to laugh. "They'd go into orbit if they found anything like that on the mat. What was it?"

"Oh, it was nothing much", said Richard airily, having no conception of parents like Stephen's. "It was just two chaps walking on a beach — rear view, and holding hands. I picked it because they were both blonds, like us, you know. And because the taller one had a lovely peachy bum. Like you", he added, squeezing Stephen's in both hands as he said it. "I wrote something pretty banal on it. I did have enough sense not to give anything away on that side, and I didn't even put my name on it.

Just a sort of coded message, so you'd know I was missing you, and thinking of you."

They walked on a bit further, lingering in the darkest places. "How was your vac?" asked Richard.

"Bloody awful", groaned Stephen. "Couldn't have been worse. We had a cricket match on Boxing Day. That was all right, and I..." He broke off, deciding to follow a sudden impulse that it would not be sensible or kind to talk of what had followed the match.

But Richard was not to be deceived by sudden silences. "Yes?" he said, suddenly sounding tense. "You saw him, didn't you?" he pressed when Stephen didn't reply. Stephen nodded gloomily.

"Christ", breathed Richard. "What happened?"

"Nothing happened", snapped Stephen, as the same anger that he had felt on the morning after Boxing Day blazed momentarily in him. "Nothing. Just another bloody great blank. You've nothing to worry about", he said unkindly.

Richard looked away into the darkness. When he spoke next his voice was husky with sadness and pain. "I wasn't worrying about that, Steve. I told you once, I know how I stand with you." His voice dissolved into a choke, and he walked off ahead of Stephen, who halted and stood for a moment, hating himself for a graceless, ungrateful boor. He got moving, and hurried after Richard, catching him by the arm and swinging him round. "I'm sorry, Richard", he said, panting slightly. "Really, I'm sorry. I shouldn't have said anything of the kind. It was cheap and spiteful."

Richard looked up at him from beneath his eyelashes. "Forget it", he said in a low voice. "It was my fault. I shouldn't have asked. It's none of my business. Just forget it."

"It is your business", said Stephen. "I love you, too, you know that. And if we're the kind of friends I hope we are, anything I do's your business. I really am sorry, my sweet Richard. Forgive me?"

Richard looked sideways at him as they walked, and gave him a wobbly edition of his usual insouciant grin. "Forget it", he repeated, but the grin said more. They walked on to the club and had a drink, both wondering impatiently where they could go afterwards. They only had enough money for a pint apiece, but they pooled their last few pence and shared a third pint, taking alternate sips and making it last. "Sort of a loving cup", whispered Richard. "Better than getting separate halves." They were on the point of going out, broke but cheerful, when the kind-hearted Bill McKechnie noticed them sharing the glass and took pity on them. "Let me get you one each, lads", he said, getting the drinks anyway. He waved down their protests. "Naw, I was your age and skint once. Older blokes bought me enough beer to float the fleet then, and I can't pay them back, because they're all dead or moved on, or I've moved on. Puts it back into the game, see." He looked curiously at Richard. "New face", he commented, "Cricketer?" Richard made apologetic noises, but he smiled winningly at Bill, who promptly lost interest in him. "Oh well, it's not your fault, I don't suppose", he said, moving away. "Cheers, lads."

When they had finished their drinks they found Bill and thanked him, then strolled out into the night with the problem of where to celebrate their reunion still unaddressed. They discussed it on the way home, and found no answers. "Oh, well", said Richard, "we'll just have to use my room as usual. They never disturb me in there, and I can lock the door, anyway. I'll stick something noisy on the hi-fi, that'll keep 'em at bay." Stephen was deeply relieved to hear all the old bounce back in his voice again.

***

Graham was standing in the school hall, chatting for a few minutes with a younger master, who had joined the staff that term, and was known to be somewhat innocent, when Stephen chanced to walk past with Richard. Graham's and Stephen's eyes met as the boys squeezed by, and a small electric charge of common pain crackled briefly between them. The moment was over almost before it had started, however, and the boys were past the two men as the young master remarked in his already widely-imitated capital-letters voice "Of course, I'm sure there's no sexual hanky-panky in this school. None whatever, I'm sure..."

The two sixth-formers turned, simultaneously and involuntarily, to stare at the young man in astonishment. Stephen looked at Richard, Richard looked at Stephen, and the two of them hastened away. They had managed to put five yards between the masters and themselves before the pressure building up inside them became insupportable, and both let out a simultaneous explosive giggle. In a moment they had passed out of sight; but they were by no means out of earshot when the giggle swelled to a guffaw as they continued on their way. The two masters, left staring after them, looked at each other. The new man was becoming rapidly scarlet with embarrassment. Graham stood in almost a daze. His entire face felt as if it had been anaesthetised. He felt his hands trembling slightly, and thrust them, in an unconscious movement of self-concealment, deep into his pockets.

He lost all consciousness of time and place, as waves of conflicting, confused emotions swept over him, raking and scouring him. Bewilderment came first, followed by disbelief. A shredding feeling of self-reproach, almost self-loathing, seared through him as he wondered if he could possibly find such a depth of distrust of the person who meant more to him than anyone else alive. But the whole mess of feeling was ultimately swept aside, first by a blast of jealousy of such terrifying intensity that for a moment or two he felt that he could have killed — not Stephen or Richard Fitzjohn, but the puzzled, slightly silly, and now appalled and embarrassed young man beside him.

Another white-hot bolt of possessive jealousy seared its way through his guts, its intensity so great that he felt himself shudder momentarily under its passage. And then, out of nowhere a tremendous, unstoppable laugh, slightly hysterical and having nothing of humour in it whatsoever, forced its way remorselessly up his throat. He stood unable to move, trembling slightly. It came roaring up from his diaphragm and emerged in a stentorian bellow, echoing vastly round the great hall, that he could no more have held in than a sneeze or a hiccup.

"Whaaaa-hah!" he roared, and suddenly doubled up, helpless, where he stood, heaving and groaning in gusts of uncontrollable laughter. The other master stood rooted to the spot, with intense annoyance and bewilderment vying for precedence on his face. At last Graham managed to get himself under control, and rose unsteadily to his proper height. "C-c- come on", he said, fighting for control of his voice. "I'll buy you a coffee. But for C-Christ's sake don't say anything to me for a wh-wh-while, or I'll have another f-fuh-fit, and my ruh-ruh-ribs wouldn't stand the strain..." He plucked at his colleague's jacket and led him away to the masters' common room, still snorting occasionally, and walking bent forward, with his arms folded hard across his ribs.

***

It was a very different story that night, however, as Graham fidgeted, switched the light on and off and read the same passage half a dozen times before hurling his book into the waste-paper basket, and fought in vain to get to sleep. Tired though he was from his deliberate slogging over the last few days, the moment the room was darkened his mind turned ruthlessly and relentlessly to the simple addition of two and two; and however he went about it, the answer four clicked into place every time, like reels on a fruit machine, impersonal, inhuman, merciless, and bringing pain instantly in their wake. His imagination played reel after reel of succulent erotic dramas featuring Stephen's well-known, comely and much-loved body entwined in a hundred styles of embrace with Richard's — which Graham's fairly expert eye had taken in at a glance during the farce in hall that day, and accurately assessed as being every bit as desirable as Stephen's, if not more so.

Graham was a fit and virile man in his prime at just under thirty. In the end he gave way to the ever more red-hot fantasies that came piling in on his mind like white horses, and masturbated twice, angrily and in a record short period, in an attempt to stem his mind's tormenting ingenuity. At last, worn out and filmed with sweat, he dropped into an uneasy doze at five o'clock. What seemed like a few seconds passed, and the alarm was sounding its infuriating insect-like bleepings, and he was practically comatose. He dragged himself through the routine of shower, shave, breakfast and the short drive to school growling imprecations on Stephen's name, and in the worst temper ever.

As the morning crawled past, and he found it more and more difficult to keep his eyes open, his anger subsided from sheer lack of energy to sustain it. He had a free period straight after lunch, so he drove home and threw himself down on his bed for a couple of hours, which left him considerably refreshed. When the final period of the day ended he buttonholed Stephen and took him aside. "Time for a word, Stephen?" he asked politely.

"Of course", Stephen said, his heart accelerating a little.

"Good", said Graham. "Time for a stroll round the field, perhaps?" Stephen agreed, and followed him as he threaded his way through the milling crowds of boys pouring out of class-rooms to head for home. They had no chance to speak inside the building, Graham being kept busy curbing impatient spirits who couldn't wait until they were outside before breaking into a run. "WALK, Robertson, you uncouth youth", he roared at a small boy charging past them as they reached the main doors. "Oh!" gasped the child, pink to the ears. "Yes, sir, sorry, sir." He scuttled away, and the two of them followed him in some relief out into the comparative peace of the open air.

Graham led the way towards the cricket field at a fair pace, and Stephen had to trot to keep up with him; he still hadn't said a word as they reached the perimeter of the field. There he slowed to an amble, but still said nothing. Stephen followed, assuming Graham had something of a private nature to say.

They had reached a point halfway round the boundary when Graham finally stopped and turned to face him. His eyes were blazing. "You two-faced little bastard!" he said. His voice was not loud, but it was harsh, with a bitter, sardonic edge. It sounded almost like a sneer.

Stephen's eyes opened wide in astonishment. "I... what?..." He stammered, and broke off in confusion.

"Are you going to stand there and make sheep's eyes at me and tell me you don't know what I'm talking about, you little slut?" Graham said icily.

Stephen stood staring at him, while distress chased bewilderment across his face, followed by a dull red flush of anger. "I don't know what I've done to give you the right to call me that sort of name, anyway", he snapped, a glitter of anger kindling in his own eyes to match the white heat in Graham's.

"Oh you don't, eh?" said Graham, openly sarcastic. "So what's all this business about how desperately you've been missing me, then? Was that all just bullshit? Just a convenient cover, while all the time you were whoring round with that pretty little blond baggage? Well, congratulations on your taste. There's a candidate for School Tart, if ever I saw one." He swung round and started round the curve of the boundary at a fast walk, hands driven into his pockets, with rage radiating from the very set of his shoulders. Stephen stood rooted to the spot, overwhelmed for the moment by being turned on so utterly unexpectedly and violently from such an unlooked-for quarter.

Pulling himself together, he hurried after Graham, and put a hand on his shoulder to pull him back. Graham rounded on him, glaring straight into his eyes with such contempt and fury in his own that Stephen, despite himself, took half a pace backwards. Graham immediately turned again and walked on. Stephen rallied, feeling his own anger uncoiling smoothly within him like a deadly hunting animal.

"Wait!" he called sharply. Graham stopped, turned and looked back at him coldly as he approached.

"Look here", said Stephen, "you've no right to speak to me like that. If I'd been cheating on you you might have the right. But..."

"What do you call it then?" snapped Graham. "I've been going off my bloody head with missing you, and worrying about you, wondering how you were managing to cope. I've been lonely, as I remember telling you only the other day. I remember you seemed surprised at the time. Well I can see why now. You would be surprised, wouldn't you, knowing what was waiting for you when you got out of this place at the end of the day? I suppose you thought I'd get myself fixed up with some sexy little piece of tail to pass the time with, did you?" He blew out a long breath, and it formed a plume of white smoke before dissolving and fading slowly in the cold air. He looked bitterly at Stephen, and saw the look of blank incomprehension written all over his features. "Do you think I'm stupid?" he roared, his temper at last unleashing itself. "Do you think I can't put two and two together when the figures are stuck right under my fucking nose, you... you little bloody tramp?"

Stephen stared at him, his eyes huge with pain, bewilderment and alarm. He glanced wildly about them when Graham cursed, terrified lest anyone should be in earshot; but the field was deserted.

Graham's rage was still in full spate. "Good God!" he snorted, "you're not even content to whore yourself around with that little... but you've got to announce the fact to me in the middle of the bloody school hall. Christ almighty, man, you couldn't've made it plainer if you'd hired a bloody biplane to fly across the school and skywrite it."

And, at last, Stephen understood. His mind raced, and he came quickly to the only possible solution. He breathed deeply, gathering his resources. "I'm sorry you had to find out about Richard in the way you did", he said, forcing himself to speak calmly and holding Graham's eyes with his own. He went right up close to him, put his hands on Graham's shoulders, and looked earnestly into his eyes. "Look, will you at least listen?" he said urgently. "I can see why you're feeling pretty bitter, but surely you'll hear my side of things?"

Graham stared at him for a moment, his eyes still glinting. But some of the bitterness faded slowly from his expression. He glanced behind Stephen and gestured at a wooden bench twenty yards beyond the boundary line. "Let's go and sit down", he muttered. Stephen followed him, breathing a little more easily.

"To begin with, you're wrong about Richard Fitzjohn", he began when they had sat themselves down, awkwardly, at opposite ends of the bench. "He's not at all the kind of thing you said — though he said something of the kind about himself. But that was just his manner. He likes to say things like that. I think he enjoys shocking people. But he's as honourable and unselfish a person as you'd ever meet. He knows about you..."

"What!" roared Graham. "You mean you..."

"No, no, I never said a word", said Stephen hastily. "He saw us saying goodbye on the last day of last term, and put two and two together. He's fearsomely clever. He'd known all along that I'd got someone who had left me for the time being. He knew all that without a single word from me. He also said you'd — the someone else would — come back to me..." He gave Graham a quick summary of Richard's prophetic conversation. Graham listened, amazed, and more of the boiling, passionate anger and jealousy ebbed out of his system.

"He saw all that?" he said slowly. "He's bright all right. He's dangerous, if you ask me. I'll have to go into hiding."

"He's no danger to you", said Stephen seriously. "He's in love with me, but he knows you'll always come first. He's only waiting for the day when I have to tell him you've called me, and he knows that when that happens I'll have to leave him." He shrugged unhappily, and kicked idly at the tussocks of grass growing round the leg of the bench.

He went hurriedly on, speaking very fast to forestall any further interruptions or outbursts from Graham, trying to explain the other, deeper current of feeling that ran constantly in him beneath his uncomplicated regard for Richard, and Richard's strange, self-effacing understanding of it. Graham sat staring out over the cricket field. A light mist was beginning to drift across the table from the narrow strip of trees that bordered a stream on the far side. Stephen obeyed an instinct to remain silent for a while. At length Graham spoke, and to Stephen's immense relief it was in something nearer his normal, much-loved voice.

"I was bloody annoyed with you yesterday", he said. "And today, of course, but you've seen that for yourself. But when I started thinking about it yesterday, I could have strangled you — though I'd rather have strangled that bloody little temptress..."

Stephen suddenly remembered something. "But you were laughing your head off", he said, in genuine surprise. "I heard you. I didn't think much about it at the time. But I heard you. You did laugh, didn't you?"

"Yes, I did", admitted Graham, speaking more calmly than at any time since they started their walk. "It was funny, I admit that. At the time, anyway. It touched a nerve. All the same, it put me in a bloody awkward and embarrassing position, as I'd have thought you'd have seen for yourself. You might have thought of that before you played your little stunt. You might have thought about how I'd feel, too. I know you're only young, and I ought to know if anybody does how thoughtless people your age can be. I'm not so bloody ancient myself, apart from anything else. I can remember being your age. But I've still got feelings, and I'd have expected you of all people to recognize the fact. Christ, I know schoolkids think we're made in Birmingham — sorry, better make that Taiwan — and haven't got human feelings, but you're not a kid any more, and we haven't exactly got a normal schoolmaster-and-pupil relationship, have we?"

Stephen gazed at him, feeling a great surge of remorse flood over him, accompanied by an intense flaring-up of tenderness and affection. Without thinking about what he was doing he slid along the bench and put a hand on Graham's neck, stroking it lightly. Graham shot a swift glance round, but otherwise stayed still.

"It wasn't a stunt", said Stephen, looking at him anxiously to see if he believed him. "I didn't know Mr Mildmay was going to say what he said just as we happened to be passing. And I... we... I couldn't help laughing. I didn't mean to, and nor did Richard. I didn't even think...I mean, it would never have crossed my mind that you'd realize..."

"I'm not blind, Stephen, and I'm not so dumb that I can't add two and two, as I said just now."

"I know that", said Stephen desperately. "But really, I didn't mean to laugh when he said... what he said, and I know Richard didn't either. It just happened. I couldn't help it, honestly. I hadn't told you about Richard, because...because...well, because I suppose I knew it would hurt and upset you. But I would have told you, one day — and I mean soon, not in five years. It was just that everything's so complicated for us at the moment, I thought it would only be hurting you unnecessarily to come straight out with it now. I'd have told you when we're together. That I promise you. I'd have told you the moment we were in a position to come back to each other. I'd have had to tell you then, to give you the chance to...to...well, you know...

"But I really didn't think it was betraying you. I went with Richard first because I was...was frustrated. I mean sexually. I wanted it so badly. I mean, I'd never had it at all until you — you know, on tour. And then I found out, and, oh Christ, I wanted someone, and Richard...well, more or less chucked himself at me." He sat in silence for a while, thinking about it.

"It started as a sexual thing", he said when he resumed. "It was as simple as that, to start with. For me, at any rate. I'm not so sure about Richard. He says he fell in love with me after we started — er — doing it. But I'm not so sure. I've got a feeling he was in love with me, and then decided to have me. I don't know. He's a lot deeper than me. And cleverer. If he wanted something I'd bet on him getting it. But it started with sex for me. You don't know how badly I wanted..."

He broke off and looked at Graham with the same compassionate, gentle expression as before. "Of course, you do know, don't you?" he said softly. "You'd know only too well, wouldn't you. Poor Graham. I'm sorry. Really sorry. Can you believe that, when you think so badly of me?" He paused, then rushed on "if I'm to tell you the truth, I can't say I'm sorry, exactly, about going to bed with Richard. That was just a physical feeling, and I couldn't resist it. If he'd come to you, I don't think you'd have resisted him either, honestly Graham. Like I said, I'd back him to get anything he goes after.

"I can't even say I'm sorry for coming to love him, either. I couldn't help that. You can't help thinking, or feeling. You can only help what you do. But I can tell you this: I don't love him like I love you. It's nothing like that at all. It's deeper with you. It's not as much fun, but I expect that's only because we can't do anything together, at least if we're going to be seen. I learn when I'm with you, and I have fun as well, but it's... oh, I don't know, it's just different." He made a small, hopeless gesture with his hands at the impossibility of finding words to express what he wanted to say. Graham looked at him without speaking for some time. Then, quite unexpectedly, he put his arm lightly round Stephen's shoulders.

"All right, Stephen", he said, and his voice was gentle, as it usually was when he was with Stephen. "There's no point in inquests. Maybe I shouldn't have upbraided you like that. I certainly oughtn't to have called you those fancy names."

"Forget it", said Stephen. "I deserved them, didn't I? At least for not being straight with you. Maybe I should have been stronger and not gone to bed with Richard. I don't know. But I ought to have been honest with you."

"Well", said Graham, "It was me who put the relationship you really wanted out of bounds. If I hadn't done that, you'd have been settled with me, and, judging by the way you say he's spoken, this Richard wouldn't have made his approach. But I did put it out of bounds, as deliberately and as beyond doubt as I could — not once, but twice. Maybe I shouldn't scold you for finding yourself a consolation prize, in the circumstances."

He sat musing for a while, and then, surprisingly, smiled faintly. "What's funny?" asked Stephen.

"I was only thinking of my own body's response to your choice of consolation prize. Maybe he wasn't a consolation prize at all. More like a special gold award, maybe.

"Anyway", he said, more briskly, "it wasn't your actually being unfaithful that I felt so bitter and upset about, really. What really hurt was not so much your doing whatever you were doing with that little madam, but that you announced the fact to me, in about the most public manner possible, in the most public place in the entire school precincts, yet in such a way that I couldn't do a damn thing about it." And then, to Stephen's great relief, he laughed. It was little more than a brief bark, but it was a laugh.

"Anyway", he went on, "the long and the short of it is that I've been in an unspeakable temper all day today, tearing strips off people right, left and centre, all because I had an awful sleepless night last night. And as I felt worse and worse as the day went on, I started feeling more and more bitter, until I decided to come and dragoon you into this walk. The rest...the rest you know. Shall we go on a bit?" He stood up, shivering slightly, and looked down at Stephen, still sitting on the bench. He put out a hand, and when Stephen took it, pulled him to his feet.

"You're a strong man, aren't you, Graham?" Stephen said. "In both senses."

"You have to be, being gay in this job", said Graham quietly. They resumed ambling round the field, staying rigidly by crick-eter's instinct to the almost vanished, washed-out remnant of the old boundary line.

When they reached the far side they went and watched the little stream flowing in its gulley through the strip of trees from which the mist was flowing out across the field. After standing listening to the friendly chucklings and splashings of the water for a while, Graham said slowly, "I've spent the whole of last night and today in a thoroughly wretched state of frantic, desperate jealousy. And yet, when I came and dragged you out, I didn't really intend to let fly at you like that. I wanted... I just wanted...Oh, God, Steve, you know what I wanted — to talk to you, to be with you.

"In a way, I congratulate you on finding someone so...so worthy of your own sweet self. You'd better look after him, love. He's rare and precious. Take good care of him. And now I think, as we're more or less back, I'd rather like to go away and lick my wounds, if it's all right with you. Most of them self-inflicted, some of them probably deserved, but all painful. Friends?"

Stephen looked at him in great distress. "Of course we're friends", he said. "I think you must be the best friend anyone ever had. We'd be more than just friends, if I had anything to do with it. You've only got to say the word, you know that, and however good for me Richard is, and I know he's very good for me indeed, and to me — well... you know.

"We had an arrangement, if you remember", he went on after an awkward pause. "I told you I was going to try and get you back. Well, I am going to. But not until after I take my A-levels. Once I've taken those, there's nothing necessarily holding me to this place. It won't be a master-and-pupil relationship then, so we'll be in a position to do as we like. All I ask of you is that you wait for me that long, and then give me a chance to see if you still want me then. If you do, I shall hold you to it, and I shan't let you give me the elbow again. Agreed?"

"Agreed", said Graham, looking him directly in the eyes. But privately he was sure his goose would be cooked if he was found associating even with a former pupil of such recent vintage, and he took his leave of Stephen with a double feeling of depression and defeat.

Stephen, on the other hand, went off to Richard's house with a lightness in his step that had not been there earlier that day. He had a guilty feeling that he ought not to be heading for Richard feeling bucked about anything; but the relief of knowing that all his affairs were above board, and that he had Graham's blessing, even the realization that Graham was jealous, all pleased him in their own very different ways. He thought that his love for Graham had survived the painful moments when Graham had looked at him with contempt, almost with loathing, and emerged from the test greatly strengthened, and that was a cause for a profound, secret joy; and Richard was pure pleasure at any time.

***

Andrew Tyldesley was drowning in the grip of a profound personal crisis.

Unknowingly, Graham had diagnosed his state of mind quite correctly when he had spoken of him with Reggie Westwood. Revenge was indeed the mainspring driving Tyldesley since

Graham's utterly unexpected and not very principled disappearance from his life. Tyldesley was a man who needed not so much a life-partner as a life-support system; without such a partner it was highly likely that his lifestyle and his own volatile temperament would destroy him.

If this had been the only facet of Tyldesley's personality that was about to play a part in Graham Curtis's life, Graham might well have been safe. Unfortunately, there were two other aspects of Tyldesley that also came into the equation. First he was a man with a highly developed need for drama. Like many neurotics, he lived a secret life utterly different from the ordinary routine of his real everyday existence. This life was lived out within the unlimited world of his own imagination, and it was infinitely the more real to him of the two lives. And it constantly needed fuelling with dramas, real or imagined. Everything that happened had to be probed, tested and assessed for its dramatic properties, its potential as material for the stories which he recounted obsessively and interminably to his cronies in the endless circuit of gay bars in which he circulated in his "real" life. The cronies put up with him and the stories partly because he was open-handed with his plentiful money, partly because superficially he was amiable and amusing company, and partly because he was very good-looking indeed, not in any flashy way to match his character, but with real beauty of face and body, and many of the cronies lusted after him insatiably — though if they had known what kind of a personality lay beneath the beautiful exterior, most of them would have opted rather to go to bed with a well-dressed corpse.

One man who had seen through all the elaborate window-dressing without any difficulty was Reggie Westwood, who had demolished his character in Graham's interest, and done a thorough job. But even Westwood failed to understand the other aspect of Tyldesley, and the one which turned him from an averagely pathetic specimen of life's losers into a very dangerous adversary indeed.

Put simply, Tyldesley was a sociopath. Once activated by some grievance, real or imagined — there would be no difference in Tyldesley: it would simply be a matter of which of his twin lives it took place in — he would choose his course of action, and then pursue it. The whole affair might lie dormant. It might never emerge from that state. Or it might come out instantly, or after any kind of interval. But once he had made up his mind to pursue it, he would do so rigorously and with an utter disregard for any other lives on the periphery, however innocent, that he might damage. Provided he could strike at his intended target, he would be completely fulfilled and content.

***

The Lent term was well advanced. Graham and Stephen had resumed the edgy, unsatisfactory semi-acquaintanceship of the previous term, seeing little of each other but thinking about each other a great deal. Stephen was much the happier. His relationship with Richard continued to put down deeper and deeper roots, and Stephen sometimes lay in his bed, after a session in Richard's, wondering if he was ever going to be able to break it, even for Graham. But Richard never pressed it, hardly ever speculated about the future, seeming content to enjoy the present to its outer limit.

The cricket season was about to start, which was one source of consolation for Graham, and another for Stephen. Richard had declined, not very politely, to accompany Stephen to his games, remarking that if he wanted to bore himself to death he would be likely to choose a nine-millimetre bullet to bore himself with. Cricket, he said, suggested strongly to him that it had been invented by one of the more ingenious sadists employed by the Inquisition, and one who positively loved his work at that. But he said it with a friendly twinkle, and Stephen accepted it as a small blind spot in a character otherwise completely compatible with his own. "After all", as he remarked tolerantly when Richard had finished disparaging his beloved game, "everybody's a philistine in some small way or another." Richard had hit him once, hard, and then resumed efficiently pleasuring him.

Stephen had offered to drop out of the occasional Sunday game to be with Richard, and Richard had refused to hear of it, saying he had plenty of pursuits which he'd been neglecting since his life had revolved round Stephen, and therefore needed some of his own time. The only concession he made to what he insisted on calling, to Stephen's intense irritation, the life-cycle of the common, or garden cricket, was that he agreed to wait outside the ground after matches to walk back to his home with Stephen. "I won't come in and have a drink", he said firmly. Graham Curtis will be there, and it would hurt him awfully. It'd be rubbing his nose in it, wouldn't it? He must be in enough pain as it is." Stephen gazed at him in wonder. "You're always full of surprises, Richard", he said gratefully, "but sometimes you just take my breath away."

"We aim to please", said Richard, fondling him. "I'll just turn up and lurk discreetly outside, in that side road. If he wants to give you a lift home, go with him and ring me from home. No ring, no Richard. Ring me twenty minutes before you want me there. No need to waste money, though. Just let it ring three times, then put the phone down. I'll know it's you. That way when you've played away I'll know you've got back."

"What if you're out?" queried Stephen. "And won't your people think it's a bit odd if the phone keeps ringing like that?"

"Don't be a prat all your life", said Richard good-naturedly. "D'you think I'm likely to be out? And miss out on a bunk-up with you? I should coco. As for my people, well mother never wastes energy on thinking at all if she can help it, and I'll tell Dad that it's just a way of getting a message to me free."

"But then he'll know we're..." said Stephen, looking bothered.

"I told you, Steve, Dad knows me very well. Well enough to trust me. I don't know if he knows, exactly, what we get up to in my room, but if he did, he'd understand, and accept it, I know that." He laughed at the dumbfounded expression on Stephen's face. "But in any case, he's civilized enough to accept that I'm entitled to a private life of my own. He wouldn't dream of intruding—unless he thought I was doing something that put me in danger. Or you, for that matter. He thinks a lot of you." And Stephen, for once, had nothing to say.

They were both very happy, and Stephen only suffered when he saw or thought too much of Graham. Even Graham, who had not had Stephen's uncommon luck in finding a compatible companion to love, and hadn't even got Stephen's very active sex life to keep his mind off his loneliness, managed to dismiss his problems for much of the time and regain a little much-needed serenity. Work helped, cricket helped more, and Stephen, realizing that he was the luckier and happier, worked hard to make himself agreeable as far as Graham would allow it, and that helped more than anything.

And so they approached the Easter vacation, with, all in all, a fair degree of equanimity: three fat and contented fish who, having identified the single hook dangling in wait for them, were as yet unaware of the stick of dynamite about to be dropped into their small pond.

BOOK TWO

CLOSE OF PLAY

"Bugger!" muttered Graham cheerfully when the doorbell rang. He was sitting sideways on a kitchen chair in his flat, humming tunelessly to himself as he stroked whitener onto a cricket boot. Its partner and his pads were propped against the fridge, gleaming brilliantly as they dried.

He put the boot carefully down on an old newspaper on the kitchen table, put the cap back on the whitener, and went to the door, expecting the postman, or maybe the milkman after his money, and still savouring a mental vision of an extra-cover drive scorching its way to the boundary. He opened the door, and the vision of the glorious cover drive vanished instantly. On the doorstep, smiling genially, stood Andrew Tyldesley.

Had he been asked, he would have given his opinion that it was by any realistic criterion a human impossibility for anyone to discompose or depress him on the first morning of a new cricket season. Tyldesley managed both effortlessly.

"Aren't you going to ask me in?" he said, after Graham had stood staring at him for several seconds, too surprised to speak. "I can see you've been associating with too many rough boys, dear. Their manners are beginning to rub off on you."

"Yes. You'd better come in", said Graham, dully. He had woken early that morning, with a keen, expectant feeling of optimism like a pulse in his stomach. That bright, buoyant mood now vanished like a ship sliding beneath an oily, sluggish swell. He stepped aside to let Tyldesley past, and glanced about before he closed the door and followed his visitor through into the kitchen.

He found Tyldesley holding one of the freshly whitened pads

with a mocking expression on his handsome face. "*Very* butch, darling", he said, ogling Graham. "Really, I knew you were into these manly pursuits, but I'd never been able to see you urging the flying ball and all that. I can see I've been missing lots and lots of new experiences."

"Put that pad down", snapped Graham, his voice brittle and crackling with tension. "It's not dry yet."

"Mmmm. Wet paint?" he chuckled, and ran a finger along one of the snowy ribs of the pad. He inspected the tip of his finger, and grimaced comically as he saw the thick daub of white there.

"I said put it down", said Graham, beginning to recover from his initial dismayed surprise. This time his voice was steady, and a little menacing. Tyldesley showed, for the first time, a faint hint of uneasiness. "No need to get tough, Gray, dear", he said easily. "I'm very interested in these alien pastimes." He put the pad back beside its mate, carelessly, so that it slipped forward onto its face. Graham winced, and set it upright again, inspecting it and the floor for white smears.

"What do you want?" he demanded.

"I want a talk with you, dear", said Tyldesley. "But all in good time. First I think it would be common courtesy to offer me a nice cup of tea, don't you? And then we'll sit and have a talk, and then perhaps a drink somewhere?"

Graham compressed his lips, trying to keep his rapidly mounting anger under control. He glanced at his watch. "I don't know what you've got to say to me, but if you can say it in half an hour, go ahead", he said. "That's when I'm due to leave."

Tyldesley stared at him. "We aren't very friendly, are we?" he said softly.

"I said, I don't know what you can possibly think we've got to talk about", repeated Graham. "There's nothing to say, that I can think of. But since you've taken the trouble to come out here to see me, I take it there's something you think we've got to say. All right, say it, and go. Or, better, just go. I've got things to do. Re-whitening that pad, for one thing."

"Really, Graham, do you think this is good enough? Here I am, having to get up at a most ungodly hour, taking all this trouble to come to see you, and you're behaving like a bear. Anyone would think you're not pleased to see me." The rejoicing in Graham's discomfort was quite unconcealed now. "I don't think you understand quite how you're placed, my dear Graham", he said silkily. "I certainly don't think you realize that I'm not to be talked to like this, and lightly tossed aside any-old-how you like. Of course", he added, affecting an afterthought, "if it was a matter of lightly tossing me off, that would be very different. But it doesn't look as if that sort of thing's much in prospect, does it?" he said, as if addressing a third person. He leaned nonchalantly against the wall and surveyed Graham cheerfully down his nose.

Graham breathed very hard. "Listen", he said in a concentrated tone, "I don't know what the hell you're getting at, if anything, with all these supposedly subtle innuendos, and I don't care. It looks as if you've got something on your mind. Well, you've already wasted five of the thirty minutes you had. That leaves you twenty-five minutes. I suggest you spit it out, whatever it is, and then go. Whatever you decide, I'm leaving here at ten, and so are you — if I haven't thrown you out before."

"I don't think you'll want to do that, my love", said Tyldesley, silky again. "No, Graham, dear, I don't think there's going to be any of that kind of thing. Not unless you want trouble. But since you're so pressing, and since it doesn't look as if I'm going to be offered the elementary courtesy of a cup of tea, I'll do as you ask, and tell you what I want to talk about."

"Do that", snapped Graham.

"It's simplicity itself, my love. I want you back."

It took Graham several seconds to grasp what he had said, and several more as he tried to work out whether it was some elaborate joke and, if not, what it was. When it finally sank in that the man was in earnest, he laughed. He couldn't help it. He leaned on the nearest wall and rocked with laughter for some time, while Tyldesley, who had thought he might receive any reaction except this one, stared back at him, piqued and perplexed. For the first time, too, he showed signs of real nervousness.

"You're not serious?" asked Graham incredulously when he had regained control of himself.

But Tyldesley was very serious indeed, and he employed every artifice he knew to convince Graham of the fact. He tried alternately the man-to-man and the beguiling; he wheedled and demanded and he blustered and cajoled. Meanwhile Graham stood listening in growing astonishment, wondering what had driven Tyldesley, who started feeling homesick if he went outside the City of Westminster, into this desperate, and hopeless attempt to raise the dead. And why now, he asked himself, more and more puzzled. If he wanted to make this absurd and humiliating mission, why did he wait all this time? Why didn't he come out here with this embarrassing performance when he was first given the heave-ho? Why now?

In the end Tyldesley clearly saw that his attempt was doomed to failure. He stood upright, squared his shoulders as if preparing to box. His face cleared, and he looked squarely at Graham. "One last time of asking", he said, trying to sound straightforward, which given his nature was not easy. "Are you willing even to consider trying to make a fresh start with me?"

"No", said Graham. "Not even to consider it. We're through, as I told you a very long time ago. I can't think why you've decided to come all this way out of your natural habitat to ask me something you must have known quite certainly was out of the question. I'm even more surprised that you should have done it now, after so long. But I'm not really interested in those things, or in anything else to do with you. The answer is No, and that's the end of the matter. Now please go."

Tyldesley looked keenly at him, with doubt and uncertainty edging into his face. "Can it be..." he mused as if to himself, "can it be that I was given false information? Surely not."

"What information are you talking about?" Graham demanded. "Just before I kick your arse out of the door."

"Let's go and sit down", suggested Tyldesley. "Even if you have developed the manners of a Barbary ape there's no reason why we can't discuss the matter like gentlemen."

"There is", said Graham very sharply, as the last remaining vestiges of patience slipped from him. "There's only one gentleman here, for one. I'm not intending to sit down before I go out, for two. And you're not going to be here long enough to sit down, for three. Get on with it, do you understand me? Or else." He drew himself up, so visibly preparing to suit the action to the word that Tyldesley apparently realized for the first time that he was in real danger of being ejected.

"Well, the fact is, Graham", he said, levelly enough now, "I was given a little item of information about you, which I thought I might turn to account." He paused, organizing his thoughts.

"As you well knew, dear, I was very — *terribly* — upset when you walked out on me. You were the first lover who'd ever done that to me. It hurt my feelings badly, I can tell you."

"Hurt your *amour propre* more like it", said Graham in a hard voice. "I know you like to be the one who does the ditching and walking out yourself. Must've been a nasty blow in the vanity when I beat you to it."

"No need to be bitchy, dear. Well, I wanted you badly. Funny, I only realized how badly after you'd gone. But when you'd gone, well, I was as horny as a boatload of rhinos. But I needed you, too, Graham. You put some much-needed order into my life. I still need you, now. More than ever. We always got on well enough. I know you seem to have this need to put on these manly manners and this butch act that you're giving me today, but we were good for each other, and you know it." He waited, to give Graham the chance to comment, but Graham said nothing. Tyldesley shrugged theatrically, and went on.

"Well, I knew pretty clearly from what you said when we met up again after that three-month sabbatical you took — *most* uncalled-for, that — that there wasn't a lot of chance of it. But I always hoped you might see sense and come back and start enjoying life again, instead of rotting away here being a dowdy schoolmaster in your stuffy school. Well, there was nothing much I could do except ask you, and as I'm sure you remember, I asked often enough, love, and got precious little reward for my pains, as I don't need to remind you.

"Well now things are a little different. I still want you just as badly. You don't know how I've felt when you've come to town and treated me as if I wasn't there, or as just another of the crowd, while all the time I was remembering what we once had going. How humiliating it was for me. All the same, I still wanted you, just like now. I'm sitting here, wanting you just as I always wanted you. You do terrible things to me, Graham, and always did."

"I think you may be right about that, at least. I've got a feeling I may well be doing terrible things to you before you're much older", agreed Graham.

"Let me finish, and spare me the butch jokes, *please*. I still need you, too. That's the biggest thing of all. You were good for me. It was why I used to put up with all your sulks and moods, when you got these macho fits on you. That's something else you don't know about yourself, Miss Curtis, how bloody silly you used to look, treating me as if I was some powder-puff drag queen and you acting like Clint Eastwood. But I put up with all that, because I wanted you and needed you, and I'd put up with it all over again, too. But as I said, things are going to be different now..."

Graham looked pointedly at his watch. "You'd better get to your point, if you've got one to get to", he said, not troubling to conceal the rudeness of the interruption. "Four minutes."

Tyldesley looked at him as if he could have killed him. "Oh, well, if you must have it in the throat, have it then", he said in a heavy mock-sigh. "Well, dear Graham, I've been listening to a little birdie talking, and I've discovered that our plaster-saint in his dowdy schoolmaster's sports jacket — have you got leather elbow-patches, by the way? — isn't *quite* the stainless hero we've all been brought up to believe. Oh, no, not at all he isn't.

"Do you remember the last time you saw me and the crowd in the pub? Remember me asking you if you'd found some scrummy little piece of arse among the little boys here at your school? Or maybe, I remember saying, maybe you'd found a pretty little prick to play games of hot cockles with behind the bike sheds. So romantic, I thought at the time. I had quite a nice little fantasy going myself, later that night, imagining the two of you, at it, you and this scrubbed little cherub with his nice hairless face and his nice hairless willy and his little baby's bum.

"Well, of course I was only joking, as one does, you know. I never expected to hear that I was right on target. But that's what I've heard, Graham darling. I've heard that you and this peachy boy are a raving old affair, right in the middle of his A-levels. Well, I salute you, darling. Good for you, I say. I would never have dreamed that an old sobersides like you would have had it in him. But I think it's gone far enough, now. Yes, I really do think I must be ready to do my civic duty. And so there you have it, Graham my dear. *There's* my conclusion, if I have one, as you so rudely put it. Putting it plain, I'm going to blow the whistle on you unless you care to pay my very, very reasonable price for keeping it under my bonnet. The price being, as you've no doubt guessed, a joyous return to our relationship of old, and us both living happily ever after. How does that sound to you, Graham, old fruit?" The jealousy, resentment and bitterness were coming out in gouts now, the contempt, almost hatred in his face and voice naked and ugly. "Well?" he said harshly, all the mock-irony discarded. "Give me your answer, do. You've got one minute", he added cruelly, looking across at the kitchen clock.

Graham stood leaning on the wall with his head hung low, his expression hidden from Tyldesley. He remained like it for some time, doing some very hard thinking and making no response at all. Tyldesley watched him with gleeful malice, taking his attitude to indicate an utterly confounded and broken spirit.

At last Graham raised his head. "May I ask how you came by this...information?" he said. Watching Tyldesley's face he had no difficulty in reading the conflicting emotions there. Natural prudence vied with the desire to flaunt superiority and appear clever.

Vanity won. "I was eavesdropping on some chat in the pub the other evening, and happened to overhear someone mention your friend — Wedgwood? No, *West*wood, that was the old girl's name. Very ill, so they said. Well, one of these people had paid him a visit, it seems. And while he was there Westwood slipped off into a delirium, and apparently, *your* name was mentioned. Well, of course, the old ears pricked up at that, and I got the rest the same way. Easy, you see. All you need is a teeny-weeny bit of luck. By the way, there's no doubt about it being true. The person doing the talking was one of *your* friends — that stuck-up lecturer or professor or whatever he was, at Imperial College. Not a friend of mine at all, as he was kind enough to point out when I asked him to tell me more. There I was, all solicitous concern for your old friend, and he was like an oyster."

During this account Graham had slumped back into his former posture against the wall, with his chin on his chest and his eyes cast down. After another long pause, during which he hardly moved, his head came slowly up once more. "And your price for not exposing an unprofessional and illegal sexual affair with a pupil here is that I resume our relationship as before?"

If Tyldesley had been a little less puffed up with his own cleverness and the apparent runaway success of his stratagem, he might have taken some warning from the ominously quiet voice and the emotionless demeanour. But he was puffed up and detected nothing. "Just so", he said, preening.

"All right", continued Graham, in the same quiet, dangerous tones. "But surely you wouldn't get a lot of pleasure out of such a relationship, knowing it was only held together by duress? Wouldn't even you find it a bit false, knowing that I wouldn't be with you if you weren't blackmailing me?"

"I think you're forgetting how very good I can be at certain wicked accomplishments, darling. No, you leave me to worry about whether I'm enjoying life or not. I'll soon tell you if I'm not. But I'd see *you* all right, and you'll have forgotten this preposterous affair with this poor boy in no time, dear. By the way, Gray, I'm not *altogether* sure I liked that 'even you' very much. I can see you haven't had that tongue of yours filed down. We must do something about that; but all in good time."

"One more thing", Graham said, still speaking very quietly, and standing in the same slumped position. "What guarantee have I got that if I resume our old relationship, you won't tire of me in six months this time, and decide to blow the gaff about me and this boy after all?"

"You clever girl!" squealed Tyldesley fatuously. The high, queenish voice was affected to irritate Graham. Underneath the tasteful and restrained make-up the beautiful limpid eyes were hard and bright with intelligence; but he was too sure of his victory to be alert. "No guarantee at all, dear! I may decide I'm fed up with you. I may indeed. That may depend, in part, on you, dear Graham. It will be nice to feel that this time it will be *you* who has to behave, or risk the unthinkable. You're going to know how it felt for me, Graham, *dear*, knowing if I kicked over the traces too hard I might lose you. Well this time the boot's on the other foot, isn't it, just a teensy-weensy bit; and *you're* going to have to watch your step, or I may just possibly let a choice little titbit of information drop into the wrong ears.

"Of course, I may get tired of you and decide to let it drop anyway — just for a little bit of fun, you know; or an experiment — that's it, it would be an *experiment*. Just to see what happened next, in the true spirit of enquiry." The false, brittle banter ceased and his voice came out hard and merciless as machinery. "You'll have to take your chance, as I took mine, and rely on my good nature, won't you, Miss Curtis?"

"One thing I don't understand at all", muttered Graham into the third button of his shirt, "is why the hell you want me, feeling as you do. I mean, listening to you here it's as clear as daylight that you hate me for whatever it is you fancy I did to you. So what the hell do you want me for?"

"I want you, my sweet little chicken, because you're a very nice, succulent little piece of crumpet, which I want for myself, to amuse myself with for as long as it pleases me, and then to discard if it suits me, as you discarded me. But, like I said earlier, I still do want you, and I still do need you, you or someone like you, and I'm genuine as far as that goes. I'd like to get back to the old relationship. We really could have fun, Graham, you know, if you'd come down off that high horse you were always so fond of mounting."

To his utter amazement, Graham saw that the further change in the man was also genuine. He really had become serious in the passing of a couple of sentences, and was speaking without the cruel hardness that had come out over the preceding ten minutes. The voice was all smooth, contemptuous and confident. He cast his mind back to the long talk he had had with Reggie Westwood, striving to recall as much of the exact conversation as he could. He remembered clearly that he had at no point mentioned Stephen's name or anything by which he could be identified. He kept his head down for a further few moments and made his decisions. Then he looked up.

"You know the one thing I wish was different about you?" he asked tonelessly. Tyldesley raised an eyebrow contemptuously. "You couldn't be expected to know this", said Graham, pouring a far more than equal volume of contempt into his own voice, "but way back in — oh, the twenties, I should think — there were several very fine cricketers called Tyldesley. Spelt your way, too. Played for Lancashire, and one of them for England. And do you know, I really wish to God you didn't share their name." He paused for a moment to let that sink in, then, while Tyldesley was still registering amazement at the inconsequentiality of the remark, he went on, "still, that's by the way. As far as your — er — proposition is concerned, you've been given false information, I'm afraid. Not that I'd have a moment's truck with you even if you'd got it right. But as it is, you've wasted your time, your petrol, and all that venom you had stored up. You can go to hell, but for the moment, you can get out of here. I trust I'm not expected to soil my hands on you?"

Tyldesley stood open-mouthed. This defiance was the last thing he had expected, and he wondered where the easy-going, complaisant young man had gone in the past year or so, the restless, anxious young man who had his moods and tantrums but mainly worried in case he had upset his friend. This cold-eyed, raw-voiced man who had materialized out of the slumped, abject figure against the wall, was a stranger to him.

The stranger spoke. "You're over your time. I'll give you ten more seconds to start moving."

And at last Tyldesley moved. "You bastard", he breathed. "You insolent, arrogant bastard! You stood there and took all that — you...you *let* me hand you all that, knowing you were going to..." There was only one answer. "I'll have your blood for that", he cried furiously, clenching his fists. Graham raised an eyebrow in surprise. Tyldesley was no fighting man, as far as he knew. However, he tensed himself in readiness.

Tyldesley was quite a big man, a good two inches clear in height and reach of Graham's compact five feet nine. But he was out of condition, whereas Graham was in full training, hard-muscled, lithe and fast. Tyldesley saw what he thought was an opening. "Here I come!" he roared.

"And there you go", commented Graham, stepping aside and driving a fist home against Tyldesley's ear so hard that he keeled over sideways and crashed to the floor of the kitchen, bowling over a chair as he fell. Graham heard wood snapping, and made a mental note to examine the chair for damage, while the enraged Tyldesley struggled to his feet, with tears of pain squirting from his eyes, and made another bull-like charge.

The fight, such as it was, was over in seconds. Tyldesley's left ear was already angry and swelling; his right eye, which also got in the way of one of Graham's paralyzing straight right jabs, was purple and swollen, and there was a lot of blood from his nose all over his face and shirt. He had no stomach for any more punishment of this order. Graham had not raised a sweat.

He hauled Tyldesley to his feet by his collar and hustled him roughly out of the flat. Then he retreated behind his front door to recover his breath and his composure. He watched through a window as the beaten Tyldesley barged down the path to his opulent car and roared off.

He was conscious of a feeling of suprise at his own calm and equanimity in the wake of a severe shock; but the cheerful mood had returned as Tyldesley had disappeared in a puff of exhaust round the corner of the road. It persisted while he examined the damaged chair, and while he deftly touched up the whitening on the pad and finished off the boot he had been working on when the doorbell had rung. That seemed like a lifetime ago, though it had been little more than half an hour.

When he finished he rang Stephen's number and apologized for being late. At ten-fifteen, delayed by no more than a quarter of an hour, he picked up his cricket bag and went out to his car.

***

There was no logic in it at all, but somehow telling Stephen about the incident as he drove the sixty miles to the opening match brought a luxurious lessening of the tension that had existed between them for most of the last two terms.

Stephen's eyes had opened wide when he had told him of the visit. When he came to the brief fight at the end the boy slewed in his seat and gazed at him in wonder and admiration. "Wow!" he said, and repeated it. "I've never had a master who'd thumped anyone", he said, as proudly as if he had laid out the blackmailing intruder himself. Graham laughed. "You have", he said. "I'm sure some of our bods have had their moments. Law of averages alone. But I see what you mean. It's not a profession that sets a great deal of store by street-brawling competence."

"But he can't actually do you any harm, Graham, can he?" asked Stephen next, the sparkle leaving his eyes as he considered the serious aspects of the matter.

"No, I don't think so. Knowing where he came by the information is a comfort. I'm glad he couldn't resist crowing about it, as if he'd been clever in some way. I never told Reggie anything about you or who you were, or gave anything away that you could be identified by. Of course", he added, "it's just conceivable that if someone knew about that idiot Colin Preston and his antics last season, and then heard this little titbit, he might put two and two together. But really, the chances of

Andrew coming back here to make trouble after the reception he got this morning are — well, thin, to say the least.

"I must say, that's the part that I find the most puzzling", he mused. "I couldn't reconcile the two things at all. I mean, you only had to get a quick look at his face, or hear the loathing and contempt in his voice, to know that he hated me like the very devil. And yet when he was talking about wanting me back, and still wanting and needing me, I was just as sure he meant it. I suppose he wanted to humiliate me, and thought he had me in his power to do it." He shrugged.

"What would you have done if he really had had the goods on you, Graham?" asked Stephen curiously.

"To tell you the truth, I wondered that myself, because for quite a while before he told me where he'd got his information I was thinking he actually might have. I made my decision then, and I'm sure it's what I'd do if it happened that way."

"Yes?"

"I'd go to the old m...the headmaster and — up to a point — throw myself on his mercy", said Graham, keeping his eyes on the road. "I'd have to resign on the spot, of course — there'd be no choice about that whatsoever. Schoolmaster in a boys' school having an affair with one of the boys — the papers'd fry me, let alone the courts. So I'd be gone, there and then. But then I'd ask him, nicely at first, to leave it at that. He'd have to have you in and interview you, of course. But I'd trust that you'd back me up..."

"Of course I would", cried Stephen, passionately. "Just give me the chance!"

"Well, I can think of less disruptive ways of demonstrating your loyalty", Graham said, laughing. "But I know what you mean, and I love you for it." Stephen's heart performed minor gymnastic feats. "Assuming your story corroborated mine, and was believed — that would be the biggest hurdle, being believed, for both of us — then I'd planned to say to him, 'look, you don't want a scandal for the school. I don't want more trouble than I'm in already' — police trouble, I'd mean, of course — 'and there's no real harm been done.' Then I'd ask him to accept my resignation and leave it at that, which I'm pretty sure he would — no headmaster wants it all over the tabloids that he can't control his school. And then, assuming he agreed, I'd simply get out of the country as fast as I could, just in case the bastard decided I hadn't had enough punishment and went to the papers anyway."

"Where would you go?"

"France", said Graham without hesitation. "It's a civilized country, including about this sort of thing. And of course, I'm very familiar with it, and speak the language as well as most Frenchmen, so I'd be able to get work over there easily enough."

They talked easily and happily throughout the journey. By the end of it they had become so relaxed that they had unconsciously slipped back into the habit of using endearments; so it was something of a shock, and a sad one, to have to slip right back out of it again the moment they got out of the car, stretching and flexing stiff limbs, at the ground.

The weather had been bright, with a drying wind, for some time before the match, so the conditions were ideal for cricket. There was nothing in the wicket for the seam bowlers, and the heavy going was very hard on their legs, so Stephen was called into the attack unusually early, and though it wasn't turning a lot he was able to make it bite, and the wind aided his flight. He had to bowl his first over to the opposition's minor-county opener, who usually took a lot of runs off them. This time he got nicely set early on and was coasting through the forties, looking ominously assured, by the time Stephen was brought on.

Stephen got him with the third ball he bowled him. Tossed high and beautifully flighted, it pitched just short of a length, a foot outside off stump. But he contrived to make it dip late in the flight and turn the perfect amount from the off. It beat the batsman's forward defensive stroke, screwed itself between his inside edge and his front pad and took a coat of varnish off the outer edge of the off stump, just tipping the bail. The wicket-keeper was already yelping "Beauty, Stevie!" and beginning his war-dance of triumph as he gathered this peach of a ball in his right hand and the bail in his left as it fell.

After this he took no more wickets, but he bowled inventively and economically to finish with the outstanding figures of one for thirty-seven off twenty-one overs, and he frustrated the batsmen to such an extent that they took risks with the toiling seamers at the other end, and were all out for an uncharacteristically meagre score of 134.

Don Parker was absent, so Graham was promoted opener for

the day, and scored a brisk twenty-seven, scampering the lot in singles and twos, and laying a sound basis for a seven-wicket win. Everyone was jubilant in the pavilion afterwards, since this was a fixture that had had only two kinds of result in the last thirty years — defeat for Elderton Park or no play because of the usual April monsoons. After a fairly quick drink Graham and Stephen set off in high spirits, delighted to have started the season with a completed match, even more delighted to have started it in such fine style, but, mostly, simply delighted to have started it at all, and to have been together as they did so.

***

The new phase of their relationship continued over the next few weeks. The weather, though not especially pleasant, was at least merciful enough to take them through April and into the school holidays without a single match affected by rain, and they both made impressive starts to the season. Stephen quickly established himself as a genuine all-rounder, and Graham was widely toasted for his foresight in capturing him for the club. Graham himself went off at a great rate, with three scores in the fifties, a seventy and a ninety-eight not out when he ran out of partners. Graham drove Stephen to the matches and usually gave him a lift home as well, and they remained relaxed and free from tension together. When they were alone in the car they were able to be as affectionate as the circumstances made possible.

Meanwhile Stephen slept with Richard almost every night. They kept up a pretence, for the form of the thing, that he occupied the spare bed which Richard had installed in his room, and it was ritually made up every week. They put a hollow in it of the appropriate shape each night, for public relations purposes, by the simple expedient of making love in that bed once a night before migrating to Richard's — he had a double, the spare was a single. As the days passed more and more of Stephen's possessions found their way to Richard's house. When he offered to pay something towards the cost of being treated as more or less a member of the Fitzjohn family ("sort of a son-in-law, really, aren't you?" as Richard put it) Richard's father laughed and refused to discuss it.

Occasionally he felt twinges of guilt about his own parents, but the tension between him and them was constantly becoming more and more electric whenever they spent a great deal of time in each other's company, and his move to virtually living at Richard's home was received with almost undisguised relief by his parents, as well as by Stephen himself. And, once the new arrangement had been established, almost by default, he was agreeably surprised to find by subtle hints and questions that, having once satisfied themselves that he was still carrying on a normal existence and not neglecting his schoolwork, they were rather revelling in their own unexpected freedom, and seemed to have got accustomed very quickly to being able to devote themselves to their own interests without the necessity of taking him into consideration; so it was a very satisfactory arrangement on all sides. He never mentioned Richard to Graham, and Graham asked no questions.

A few days into the Easter vacation Richard's parents told him, to the delight of both boys, that they were planning to go for a break on the Continent. They invited both boys to accompany them; but, without being indecent about it, they contrived to give the strong impression that they would not be broken-hearted if the offer were to be declined. They discussed it that night, bouncing up and down in each other's arms, and the desired answer was conveyed at breakfast, giving satisfaction all round.

Then, on the last Saturday of the blissful vacation, Stephen went back to his own home to wait for Graham to pick him up and take him to the match. It was an away match against one of the most distant opponents in the fixture list, on the south coast near Brighton.

It was a thoroughly enjoyable day. They took the usual pleasure in being alone together in the cocoon of the car, and the day was bright but cool and fresh, perfect for cricket. The ground was beautiful, with the sea murmuring at the foot of a low cliff thirty yards beyond the longest boundary. The outfield was like a bowling green, the wicket more like a billiard table.

In the end the match itself was the only minor let-down. The opposition batted first and deplorably to be dismissed for a miserable 162, nowhere near enough on their beautiful batting shirtfront. The quick men ran through them so effectively that

Stephen didn't get a bowl, though he made up for it to a limited extent by taking a blinder in the gulley. And since Don Parker was back in the side and on the top of his form, which was somewhere on the bright side of County standard, Graham failed to get to the crease. The openers made 165 in less than even time, Don getting, magnificently, no fewer than 114 of them. As they came off Stephen saw something he had never seen before in a club match, when the entire fielding side rushed Don and carried him off. There was serious drinking in the bar, and several of the team made an impromptu, but very wise, decision to spend the night in the pavilion, leaving their cars in the club car park and driving straight to the Sunday fixture early the following morning. Graham and Stephen, though, after a private conference, decided to drive home that evening.

They had reason to bless the early finish of the game before they had travelled twenty of the seventy-five miles home. The car hiccupped and spluttered asthmatically a few times, and finally died on them as they entered the outskirts of one of the myriads of little picture-postcard towns dotting the Sussex Downs. Graham got it restarted with considerable difficulty, and they limped into the middle, where he got it under an ivy-covered archway and into the car park of an ancient coaching inn.

"Shouldn't've fancied trying to find anywhere to get it off the road in the dark", he muttered as they got out and craned ineffectually under the bonnet. "Not much good me peering under here and trying to look knowledgeable", said Graham. "It's too near dark to try and do anything with it now. Have to look at it in the morning."

"What'll we do?" asked Stephen, trembling as he guessed.

"Have to take a room somewhere", Graham said. "Here looks as if it might do."

He led the way through a side door, pausing to look at a menu in a brass surround. "Hmm. They're not cheap", he grunted. "Still, I've got my cards, and a fair amount of cash." He marched up to the reception desk.

***

There was only one room available, fortunately a double, which neatly avoided any awkwardness. Graham booked it and signed in, then they set off for a tour of inspection of the little town. They wandered into several pubs, looking round and enjoying the change of scenery over halves of lager, and Graham bought them a pleasant, unpretentious dinner at the last of them.

Stephen managed to slip off on the pretext of using the lavatory for long enough to telephone Richard to explain the predicament. Richard chattered for a minute or two, and wished him an affectionate good-night, accompanied by a series of lurid sexual penalties he proposed to exact from Stephen the following night to make up for his missing a night. Then he blew kisses at Stephen down the line before breaking the connection. Stephen noticed that he carefully omitted to ask if it was with Graham that he was stranded — he had tactfully said simply that "the" car had broken down. But he made it clear that he knew the score, in a small but typical piece of Richardish kindness. It was characteristic of him in that its generosity was matched only by its delicacy. After blowing the kisses, he murmured, very softly, "Enjoy tonight, sweet; and come back to me tomorrow." Then he hung up.

The castaways were both thinking about what was to happen later, and it was still early when they returned to their inn and, after a last drink in the bar, they were in their room before ten. There the unusual lack of tension of the day made them gay and abandoned. All the frustration, jealousy and loneliness of recent months erupted and escaped like pus from a lanced boil.

Afterwards Graham slept, his head cradled on Stephen's forearm. Stephen lay propped on one elbow looking down at him. He looked peaceful, relaxed and, he thought, very beautiful. The moonlight coming through the open window lit up half his face in silver, so bright that Stephen could see the small movements of his eyes under their lids. I wonder what he's dreaming about, he thought, feeling that he could have made a good guess. Soon he slid down beside Graham and, taking care not to disturb him, slid an arm round him. Graham moved slightly in his sleep, making some small murmuring noise, and Stephen felt an arm slip round his neck. Soon he too was asleep.

They awoke early. They were stiff and cramped from huddling together in a bed made for one, but in the pleasure of each other's nearness they hardly noticed it.

"God, it's fine to wake up and see you beside me", said Graham, stretching luxuriously and smiling beatifically at Stephen. "I wonder how many ways I could bring a smile of pleasure to your pretty face", he said, rolling over and grabbing him.

More than an hour later they showered and dressed, grimacing comically as they put on yesterday's clothes. "Hmph! They'll do, I suppose", grunted Graham, sniffing his socks tentatively. "They'll have to, for now. D'you want me to drop you at yours? I could lend you some socks and underwear if you like. We've got a match today, don't forget. If we wear these in the dressing room they'll be giving us forced baths. Remember what happened to poor Hoody that time he came wearing yesterday's feet?" Stephen shivered and grinned. "I'll borrow some of yours, if it's all right", he said.

When they were ready to go down to breakfast Graham put his hands on Stephen's shoulders. "This can't make much difference to anything, you know", he said. "You do understand that, don't you?"

Stephen nodded, the sparkle fading from his eyes as he thought ahead. "Still", he said, trying to recover the brightness of a minute before, "there's not long to wait now, is there?"

"Not long", Graham assented. "Just as long as you realize — it's got to go back to the old regime again. You do understand, don't you? That it's for the best?" Stephen held him tightly. "I understand", he murmured. "I don't like it, but I can put up with it, just as long as I know you'll give me that chance in July."

"Don't worry", said Graham, freeing himself reluctantly. He kept his own doubts to himself.

They left the room quietly and went along the corridor to the stairs. Neither of them noticed the open window onto the fire escape at the end of the corridor, from which they had come. Outside, the man perched uncomfortably on the iron fire escape platform pricked up his ears as he heard the sound of their door opening. He hunkered down until he could just see over the sill of the window, checking that his pocket-sized Minolta was ready. He secured a good shot of the two of them emerging from the room and a better one as Graham briefly ruffled Stephen's hair, while they were still almost halfway inside the room; but his real *coup* came when the two paused in the corridor for a quick kiss. With that momentary but damning embrace safely on film he ducked quickly out of sight in case the tiny sound of the shutter had been heard.

When their voices had faded he clambered nimbly through the window and cat-footed to the door of their room. As he had expected, they had left it unlocked for the chambermaid. He peeked round the door, snapped off a couple of wide-angle shots of the room, and scribbled rapidly in a notebook. Less than thirty seconds after slipping in through the window he was leaping swiftly down the fire escape, making no sound in his rubber-soled shoes. He dived into his car, shot under the ivy-covered arch and was swallowed up in the morning traffic.

***

It had been an exhausting weekend for Graham. After the long drive and the emotional lightshow of Saturday they had had a nerve-racking hunt on Sunday morning for a garage mechanic to see to the car. Starting at the inn when Graham paid their bill, they were sent from one person who might help to another. None of the possibly-helpful people could actually do anything for them, but they all knew someone else who might, with the result that they spent two hours chasing a series of wild geese all over the little town before finding a surly and taciturn mechanic who spent ninety seconds making a microscopic adjustment and then demanded twenty pounds for it. All this time they were getting more and more frantic at the prospect of missing that day's match, so when the car started up without trouble Graham was so relieved that he paid the outrageous charge without protest, almost throwing the notes at the man as he put the car in gear and shot away.

However, the car performed perfectly, and once they realized that they still had plenty of time to get home and change their slightly sticky clothes comfortably in time for the match, their nerves settled down.

It was a lively game, culminating in a maniacal and wicket-peppered run-chase. It ended with the Elderton no. 11 making a titanic slog at the last ball at ten to eight and scuttling through for a bye in near-darkness for a desperate triumph, with the other nine batsmen pacing up and down and biting their nails in the enclosure, unable to see anything and many, in any case, unable to watch.

After all these excitements, Graham woke late on Monday. With the summer term starting on Wednesday he had preparations to make at school. He left in a hurry, still slipping his jacket on and swallowing a last mouthful of toast. The mail was on the mat. He scooped it up on his way out, thrust it into his briefcase and promptly forgot about it until he found time to snatch a quick break in mid-afternoon.

He flicked through it as he sipped his coffee in his empty form-room, dropping circulars into the overflowing waste-paper basket and swearing over a couple of bills. He was left with a large board-backed manila envelope with his name and address printed in heavy black felt-tipped capitals, and the name of a motor-cycle courier company in red. He slit it open carefully, wondering what it could be, and tipped it up over his desk. Three ten-by-eight-inch photographs slithered out and lay face-down on the desk-top.

He turned them over curiously, and was promptly engulfed by a wave of dizzying nausea which made him gag. He had to swallow desperately to prevent himself from vomiting up his breakfast right then. His eyes bulged from his head as he gazed at the three glossy black-and-white photographs, and he had to grip the sides of the desk-top hard to steady himself as another sickening shock-wave of giddiness hit him, leaving him feeling sick and faint.

The first picture that met his horrified gaze was of himself and Stephen in an anonymous-looking corridor. They were half-turned towards each other, smiling into each other's eyes, and their lips were touching in a passionless but palpably affectionate kiss. The photograph had obviously been taken by a highly competent photographer: the resolution was brilliant; the features unmistakable. He stared at it for a minute or more, picking out finer details: his right hand was resting on Stephen's left shoulder-blade, in a gesture that could not have suggested with greater clarity an easy, casual familiarity. Stephen's left arm was curled round his hip, the hand resting lightly on his own buttock. He could even see the crease in the fabric of his light slacks where

Stephen's fingertips were curled into the soft part of his buttock, so perfect was the definition of the shot.

Aghast, almost in a daze, he examined the next one. It was a less damning shot, of the two of them coming together through a doorway, equally anonymous, into the same corridor — a picture on the wall identified it as the same one. Not that he needed the clue. Stephen was in the lead, smiling and clearly blissfully happy. Behind him, just fractionally less sharp, but devastatingly, damningly sharp enough, was Graham himself. He was laughing, and saying something to Stephen. At the same time his right hand was raised, and his fingers were clearly visible, curled among Stephen's luxuriant mop of heavy dusty-blond hair.

Beginning to feel less ill as numbness set in, he shuffled the pictures to see the third. The corridor was the same, the door from which they were seen coming now closed, with its big brassy number plate, 7, prominently visible. They were a little farther from the lens in this final shot, their backs to the camera. Their hands were swinging level with their hips, slightly blurred in the picture from the movement; the fingers were firmly interlaced.

Graham sat back in his round-backed chair and breathed deeply, trying to quell the panic that persistently tried to rise up and engulf him. He became suddenly conscious that he was running with sweat, snatched his handkerchief from his trouser pocket and pulled it fiercely across his forehead. He felt sweat break out in prickles even as he mopped himself. He sat forward over the photographs, and a droplet fell heavily from his hair and splashed onto the glossy surface of the topmost one. Instinctively he blotted it carefully with his handkerchief, not even aware that he had done so.

After a lengthy interval in which he sat in a state of semi-paralysis, he sat back, his movements jerky and unco-ordinated for the moment. He picked up the big envelope and peered inside it to see if there was anything else.

There was. He worked a couple of fingers inside and drew out a sheet of plain white bond paper. On it was a single side of black type. He read it quickly, his eyes widening. It was clearly an extract from a report, written in staccato, stilted prose, suggesting a police report or some other such official document. It described the movements of the unidentified writer as he followed two men, identified as "Subjects" in the stilted manner of the document. His eyes caught the salient points as he scanned rapidly down the page.

...both subjects left cricket clubhouse at 1841 hrs and left club precincts in m/v described previously, subj CURTIS driving, subj HILL in front passenger seat...

(The writer went on to give a minutely detailed description of the route they had taken from the cricket club on Saturday to the coaching inn.)

...kept covert observation while CURTIS spoke with receptionist of hotel... Both subjects went up stairs at 1924, returning to lobby at 1936... from conversation with receptionist and surreptitious examination of register that both subjects booked into double room, no. 7 (the only room vacant)... later secured relevant page of register (enclosed)... followed subjects from inn to...

(There followed a precise itinerary of their stroll and minor pub-crawl through the little Sussex town.)

...subjects appeared to be on intimate and affectionate terms throughout...animated conversation, laughter...subjects frequently smiled at each other in an intimate and affectionate manner... in The Martlets p/h I saw HILL use pay telephone in rear lobby. Unable to observe number or hear conversation... both subjects consumed meal, seated in bar of same p/h. CURTIS paid using Barclaycard, number not ascertained...

("Dear God, he even logged what we ate for bloody dinner", thought Graham; this tiny detail seemed to him perhaps the most obscene thing of all, somehow worse than the minute details of the pursuit, the reduction of their emotions and gestures to officialese jargonisms — "smiled at each other in an affectionate and intimate manner", thought Graham with a shudder — worse than even the photographs.)

...subjects returned to Feathers p/h-hotel and entered lounge bar. CURTIS consumed ("consumed", thought Graham, with the same shudder — he makes the act of drinking sound like an indecency so obscene that it has to be described by a Latin word) *two single measures of gin, each with one split bottle of tonic, ice, lemon slice; HILL consumed one pint Tuborg lager. CURTIS paid on all occasions. Both subjects left bar at 2151. I followed and saw both subjects enter room 7 at 2154. Neither subject left room during night...*

The characterless, inhuman prose ran on and on, charting their movements in a welter of details, indiscriminately, every detail given equal weight, whether it recorded the price of a pint of lager bought in a pub or a passionate kiss exchanged in a deserted back-street of a small Sussex town. Jesus Christ, thought Graham, it's the kind of prose you might imagine an insect writing if insects could write — fussy, buzzing, infuriating in its tone, its relentlessness, its utter alienness. Insects are the most alien of all the other things that walk or creep, Graham suddenly found himself thinking, with a kind of dislocated inconsequentiality. He shook himself, physically, and tried to pull himself together.

He thought about the police. But what could he allege? He took it for granted, even at this early moment, that blackmail must be the object of the sender of the report and the pictures. And with that thought his mind turned instantly to Tyldesley. But there was nothing whatever to connect Tyldesley, or anyone else, with the matter.

In the end he concluded that the only thing to do was to do nothing — with one exception. He must, he knew, tell Stephen, and as quickly as possible. He shuffled the items together and slid them back into their envelope, pausing for a moment to gaze once more at the photographs. He sat musing to himself for a moment, reflecting how the mere circumstances of their taking could contrive to turn something as innocent as a ruffle of a friend's hair or the touch of a friend's hand into pornography. "It's worse than pornography", he muttered to himself. "Pornography's clean..."

The feelings of shock, revulsion and illness which had threatened to unman him had gone, and he felt a cold, practical resolve settling over him. There was a problem to be dealt with. He locked the envelope in his briefcase and went to use the telephone.

There was no answer when he dialled Stephen's home number. He tried the cricket club next, but after a pause the steward returned to say that Stephen was not in the bar and that no-one had seen him that day. He hesitated before testing his third guess, but realized that the matter was too urgent to permit personal reservations. He resolutely dismissed all emotional considerations from his mind, consulted the local directory and dialled Richard Fitzjohn's number. "Richard Fitzjohn?" he asked calmly when a youthful voice answered.

"Yes, speaking."

"I wonder if you can help me. Is Stephen Hill with you, please?"

There was a moment's silence. Then the voice said "Er... who is it?"

"It's Graham Curtis, Fitzjohn, and I'd like to speak to Stephen, if he's there, please. It's very urgent, or I wouldn't have disturbed you. Is he there?"

"I...er..." the boy faltered, clearly playing for time. Graham could imagine the consternation at the other end. He cut across the hesitation, barking brusquely into the receiver. "Please, Fitzjohn, tell me. This is more important than you know. Hurry."

"Oh. Er...hold on, will you, sir." There was a sound of the receiver being set down at the other end, and a few moments later Stephen's voice came on the line. He sounded unsure of himself, and a little scared, Graham thought in the few fractions of a second before he took the initiative. "Stephen? It's me, Graham. Look, I'm very sorry to call you there like this — very sorry indeed — but I've got to talk to you. I mean, *got to.* Something's happened, and we've got to discuss it, as soon as possible. Can you see me now?"

Stephen stood by the telephone table in silence for a moment, thrown into turmoil by the unexpectedness of the call and the unpleasant sensation of menace that had somehow insinuated itself into Graham's voice. However, to his credit, he wasted no time asking questions, but said simply "Yes. Of course. Where are you?"

"I'm at school", he said, "but we can't discuss it here. How soon can you be at my flat?"

"Ten minutes", said Stephen without hesitation.

"Right. Be there, will you, Stephen. It's rather important, or I wouldn't have disturbed you."

"It's quite all right", said Stephen, anxiously. And then, with the scared note edging back into his voice, "is there something wrong, Graham? Are you all right?" There was a serious, adult note of concern in his voice which Graham had time to find deeply affecting. "Nothing that can't be sorted out, my..." he said, biting off the spontaneous endearment as he remembered where he was. "I'm perfectly all right, just got a bit of a problem to sort out. I'll see you soon, okay?"

"All right", said Stephen. "I'm on my way."

***

"So there it is", Graham said. "You had to know about this at the earliest possible moment, simply in case whoever it is tries putting the pressure on you. I don't see that it's likely, seeing that he's sent the material to me, but it's a possibility. The question is, what do we do about it? We'll have to deal with him somehow or other."

"Deal with who?" demanded Stephen unexpectedly. "We don't know who it is, yet, do we? We haven't a clue. We don't even know for sure that it's a blackmailer. We're assuming that."

Graham looked at him with some respect. He had been impressed and surprised by the boy's reaction to his account and to the materials he eventually let him see. There had been no hysterics, no helpless revulsion, just a mature, almost scholarly interest in the report, and, most surprising, a fond smile, as of pleasant memories, when he looked at the photographs.

"You're taking this very well", he said.

Stephen grinned at him. "No point in getting upset and losing control", he said, sounding very self-assured. "You taught me that, you know. Remember that time I got practically hysterical about losing you? Well, you showed me the value of staying calm. Once you lose your cool you lose control, that's how I look at it. Besides, they're nice pictures, aren't they?"

Graham shook his head, reflecting for the thousandth time since he had been a schoolmaster that there was no known method in the world of predicting boys' responses to any given stimulus.

"I don't think there's much doubt about its being blackmail", he said pensively. "And there's very little doubt in my own mind about who's doing it. I'm expecting to hear from him any time."

"This Tyldesley?"

"That's my guess", he said grimly. "The question is, as I said, what do we do about him?"

"Tell him to get fucked", suggested Stephen, surprising Graham yet again. He hadn't expected either the calm

187

acceptance of the horror that had, for the first few minutes, demoralized him to the point of paralysis; neither had he expected the robust response that Stephen was demonstrating.

"That's one way, certainly", he said thoughtfully. "The most attractive, in some ways. But it would have certain very undesirable effects, for me particularly."

"That's the only thing that bothers me", said Stephen crisply. "He can't do a thing to me. I couldn't care fucking less if the whole world knows I'm in love with you. I'm proud of it. If it was only me involved I'd tell him to stuff his silly pictures and his snooper's report up his arse. But you're different. You've got something to lose. What can we do?"

"Let's assume it's blackmail", said Graham, feeling encouraged as he would never have dared to hope. "I don't think there's any doubt of that, anyway. And let's assume it's Tyldesley, as well. He's the only person I can think of who it could be.

"The first thing we don't know is what he's going to demand. Money? Doubtful. He's loaded. I couldn't pay him enough to make any difference to his finances if I gave him half my salary, and he knows it. Could he possibly still think I might go back to the old relationship if I'm put under enough pressure? I doubt that, too. He's suggested that once before, and got a black eye. He's no Einstein, but he's no fool either — he's shrewd, in a nasty, malicious, calculating sort of way. He's certainly adept at calculating his own best interests. No, I don't believe that. But what else?"

"Humiliation?" suggested Stephen. "Maybe he just wants to get revenge. Maybe he's not going to blackmail you after all", he said, his voice rising in sudden alarm for the first time. "Perhaps he's just going to blow the gaff, but he wants you to suffer first, and worry about it."

Graham pondered the possibility, and nodded. "You could be right", he conceded. "that would be a whole new ballgame, wouldn't it?"

"What would he do then?"

"Well, he could go to the police, and try to get me prosecuted for having sex with you while you're under age", he said slowly. "But I rather doubt if he'd be very keen on that idea."

"Why?" asked Stephen. "It's what I'd do, if I really had it in for somebody.

"No", said Graham, absent-mindedly running his fingers through Stephen's hair. "No, he'd be very reluctant to do that, because once he'd got the law involved I'd no longer have anything to lose, so there'd be nothing to stop me from bringing a cross-prosecution for blackmail."

"But he wouldn't be blackmailing you, if he just wanted to expose you and get you into trouble", Stephen pointed out.

"No", Graham said with an unpleasant, meaning smile. "But the police wouldn't know that he hadn't tried blackmail first, would they? I think they'd rather tend to assume it, don't you? Especially if one told them he had."

Stephen stared blankly at him for a moment. Then a mischievous grin spread slowly across his features. "Graham!" he said reprovingly. "That is a very wicked idea. And you in charge of young minds... formative years... undoubted influence for evil... go to prison for forty-six years..."

"Pack it up, you young idiot", said Graham, laughing despite himself. "No, I don't think he'll be anxious to try that line of attack. I still think it'll be blackmail. I simply can't think of anything else that makes sense. Possibly he does want revenge for my reception he got the other day, and thinks bleeding me is a good way of hurting me, since he can't have what he really seems to want — though I'm buggered if I can work out what possible satisfaction he thought he'd get from that."

"Like I said, humiliation", said Stephen. "Anyway, what are we going to do?"

"Well, I'm no expert about these things", said Graham, "but I've been thinking about it, and it seems to me that we're — I'm — in a pretty bad box whichever way I jump."

"*We*, not *I*", said Stephen earnestly.

Graham gave him a grateful look. "Well, you didn't think I'd take everything you've given me, only to rat on you when things turned nasty, did you?" asked Stephen. "I've known for yonks that it would come to light some time or other. Richard said it would ages...". He broke off in dismay, his hand flying to his mouth in a schoolboyish motion that Graham found irresistibly touching.

"You don't have to keep up a pretence that Richard doesn't exist", he said gently. "I rang you there, and spoke to him, if you remember."

"So you did", agreed Stephen. "But I've tried not to talk about him, because I thought it would be painful for you to be reminded. Richard said that too, actually."

Graham gave him a keen, thoughtful look. "He's quite a boy, this Richard, by the sound of him." He gazed wistfully at Stephen for a moment longer, then dropped his head and jotted a few lines on the back of the stiffened envelope. Then he jumped up and paced about the room, thinking aloud.

"Okay", he said, glancing down at the notes he had made on the board-backed envelope as if it was a clipboard and he was delivering a lecture to a class. "As I see it, there are five options open to us. One: pay. Two: go to the police and make an accusation of blackmail — assuming that's what it turns out to be. Three: tell him to go to hell. Four: try and deal with him ourselves. And five: do nothing — just totally ignore him. Agreed?"

"I can't think of any other way you can deal with it", said Stephen, thinking hard.

"Okay", resumed Graham. "Let's go through the five choices we have and see what we might do." He glanced at his notes again. "Number one — we pay him whatever he demands. What do you think?"

"Never!" said Stephen belligerently.

"Quite right. No blackmailer should ever be paid, out of the simple rightness of things. It isn't right that some blood-sucking bastard like this should be rewarded. No. No payment, whatever happens." Stephen gazed up at him, with immense affection and respect in his expression. He felt for a moment like a starry-eyed kid, he thought to himself, gazing raptly on some hero-worshipped idol.

"Number two", said Graham, raising an eyebrow interrogatively at Stephen. "The police, and a charge of blackmail against whoever this is."

"I don't like it", said Stephen. "It would be very nice to see this bastard get his comeuppance, but..."

"Yes, quite. But... But they'd almost certainly feel obliged to bring charges against me, as well, for illicit sex — you're under age, of course."

"I've heard the police don't like to charge blackmailers' victims", said Stephen, chewing Graham's ballpoint. "It deters people from coming forward, and allows the blackmailers to get away with it."

"Yes, you've got a point", said Graham. "Or rather, you would have, if only I was being blackmailed for anything other than this. Unfortunately, homosexuality is the great *bête noire* of the British. Also, the British absolutely love to work themselves up into a storm of righteous outrage over mistreatment of the young — especially by schoolteachers.

"Right. Number three", he went on, looking at his notes again. "Tell him to go to hell. How do you feel about that one, love?"

Stephen gazed into space, wrinkling his brow in thought. "As far as I can see, that's the best one", he said slowly, after a pause. "Mostly because I can't see what else we can do."

"Maybe", said Graham. "Let's have a look at the others, then. Number four was dealing with him ourselves. Well, I shouldn't think we're likely to be able to get much of a crack at him. Blackmailers know they're playing a dangerous game and tend to cover their tracks pretty well.

"In any case, I'm not quite sure what I could do if I tried to tackle him myself. If it's just Tyldesley, I can handle him, no sweat. But if he's got himself organized, well, I might be running into a mob of thugs, or something. Besides, I'm a schoolmaster, not a gangster. I think we give that one a miss.

"Number five, simply ignoring him. The risk there, I think, is that he'd get upset and perhaps expose me out of simple malice. I'm not too worried about his going to the police, because there would always be the risk of his getting caught himself — and he'd do a damn sight longer in stir for blackmail than I would for sleeping with you, since you're consenting, even if you are under age. No, what I think he'd do would be to expose me to the headmaster. He might not get whatever it may be that he's planning to demand, but he'd at least have the satisfaction of knowing that he'd lost me my job. I remember I told you before, my job wouldn't be worth a sprazi if they found out we'd slept together.

"So we come back to telling him to go to hell. But what occurs to me there is that it's running exactly the same risk as completely ignoring him, isn't it?"

"Mmm...yes", said Stephen. "But at least we'd have the

satisfaction of letting him know he's not going to get away with it, wouldn't we?"

"Maybe. But we'd also be giving him information, wouldn't we? He'd know, for certain, what we were going to do. At least if we simply ignore him he won't know what we're planning."

"Nor will we know what he's up to", objected Stephen.

"Hmmm. You've got a point", mused Graham, dropping onto the sofa beside him. "But I'm blessed if I can see any way round it so we'd be completely safe. It's too difficult for ordinary mortals, this. I wish there was someone I could go to for advice. Still, there isn't, so we'll just have to do the best we can, and hope. Have I missed anything, d'you think?"

Stephen racked his brains to think of alternatives, and drew a blank. "Well, that's about as far as we can go for the time being", said Graham, tossing the envelope aside. "We've got to wait for him to make his next move now."

He sat back on the sofa with his hands behind his head. "There is one thing that occurs to me", he said after a while, turning his head towards Stephen with a faint, ironical smile.

"What's that?" asked Stephen.

"Well, if we're known about, by someone with the worst possible will, and are likely to become known about by one and all — which I must say I think is the most likely outcome of all this — there doesn't really seem to be a lot of point in denying ourselves an occasional treat, does there?" He relaxed completely as he said it, sprawling lazily back on the sofa and switching the ironical half-smile onto full beam. His eyes shone with a deep love and compassion, mixed with a powerful sense of gratitude towards the boy for his strength and support and the generosity of his spirit. He wondered, in passing, how much of Stephen's fast-growing maturity and strength he owed to the influence of Richard. He felt glad that he could contemplate Richard without envy or resentment, but there was no answering the speculation; besides, he had other things on his mind.

Stephen too was smiling, the same sort of broad, lazy smile, as Graham's meaning dawned on him. He stood up and held out his arms.

***

Term started uneventfully. It was chaotic as usual on the first day, by lunch-time on the second it was resuming the rather less than even tenor of its way, and on Friday it was almost as if the holidays had never happened. At seven-thirty on Saturday morning Graham was woken early by the doorbell.

He went to the door in his dressing gown, still half asleep and cursing the early caller, hoping it would be something easily dealt with so he could snatch another hour or so's sleep. He opened the door, blinking.

"Rise and shine", said Andrew Tyldesley.

"You again?" said Graham, instantly wide awake.

"Little me. Can I come in?"

"No. You can go to hell."

"I think you want to talk to me this time, dear. I believe your mail has been rather spectacularly interesting lately", grinned Tyldesley.

Graham thought for a moment, wondering whether to risk providing the neighbours with a topic of conversation by laying him out on the path, regretfully rejected the idea, and stood back to allow his visitor to enter.

Tyldesley sat on the sofa without waiting to be asked, picked up Graham's bat, which was propped against the arm, and stroked it in the middle, a red-stained, slightly concave area where most of the balls bowled at Graham made contact. "Mmmm", he said appreciatively. "Not many marks on the edges, I perceive. Very good."

"Put it down", said Graham quietly, and the menace in his voice was heightened by the pleasant, conversational manner in which he said it. Tyldesley saw at once that the man he was dealing with was the formidable stranger he had seen on his previous visit.

"You're not at all pleasant to talk to these days", he said, with an attempt at a light laugh.

"Tyldesley, I'd like you to listen very carefully to what I'm going to say to you", said Graham in measured tones. "Because I'm only going to say it the once. I'm sure you remember what happened last time you came here to make a nuisance of yourself. I see the bruises have faded." Tyldesley gave him an ugly look. "You can glare as much as you like, as long as you keep your mouth shut", went on Graham. "You can have your say when I've finished, not before. Is that understood?" Tyldesley considered him, decided that his mood was ugly enough to result in serious trouble, and signalled to him to continue.

"All right, then, my friend", said Graham. "All I've got to say will take two minutes, not more. You can have the same time to say your piece, and then you can go. None of that's negotiable. If you give me any trouble, I'll serve you as I did before, with one difference: if I have to lay hands on you again, I'll make what I did to you last time look like shadow boxing. They'll need a sewing machine to put in the stitches. Understand?" Tyldesley nodded.

"All right, then. From what you said just now, I know it was you who sent me those photographs and that report. A private detective, I take it. All right, then. When I finish talking, you can speak to the extent of answering one question, perhaps two. First, what do you want? Second, I'm interested to know why you're doing this. I don't suppose you'll be willing to gratify my curiosity, but I'd rather like to know, because I'm curious. But mainly, as I say, I want to know what you're going to demand. When you've told me, I'll either give you my answer, or I'll tell you when I'll give it. Then you'll go.

"I expect you're thinking this wasn't in the script, and that you were going to be in control of this interview, dictating the terms on the strength of your nice little line of blackmail. Well you're not. If I suddenly decide, at any point, that I don't like the way this little chat's going, I'll close it. If I do that, I take it you'll reveal the evidence you're holding on me to whoever you plan to reveal it to. In that case, I shall have nothing to lose — and you know what you can expect then.

"Don't make any mistakes this time, Tyldesley. You can't afford to make even one, because you know how much chance you stand if we get physical, you and I. I don't underestimate your intelligence: I know you're no fool, so I credit you with enough perception to know whether I'm bluffing or not. Think about it; and when you've thought, answer my question: what do you want? Then, if you care to satisfy my curiosity, tell me why the hell you're doing this, what good you think you're doing yourself by it. Answer that one or not, as you please, it's all the same to me. But if you've got as much sense as I think you have you'll take the rest of what I've said very seriously. Okay. Your turn."

Tyldesley sat and thought in silence for some time. Then he looked up at Graham and nodded. "All right", he said, seriously, all the affectations dropped. "I think you mean what you say, and I've no wish to get myself hurt. Not that you've done yourself any good. Quite the contrary. Last time I remember calling you insolent and arrogant. I also remember accusing you of putting on all these macho airs. Well, I underestimated you. You've come out in your real colours now, haven't you, Graham? You've shown your real self — a common thug. You've also, you'll be interested to hear, just doubled the price.

"So, what do I want? You knew what I really wanted. I told you that last time. I had to accept that I wasn't going to get my own way. You were quite convincing. Well, I don't like not getting my own way. I was dreadfully spoilt as a child, and got used to the idea of expecting to get what I go after. If I don't get it, or if I'm told I can't have it, I get very cross, and very unpleasant.

"Now you've balked me, Graham, and you haven't done it just once, or even twice. You've made a habit of it. You not only walked out on me, you were the only lover I ever had that I planned to stay with — you were the only real love I ever had. So when you gave me the elbow you wounded me. You *hurt* me, Graham. And that's something that doesn't happen.

"But that, as if it wasn't enough, wasn't all. You went on to rub all this in — contemptuously, conspicuously, and often. I wonder if you ever thought how I felt when we used to see you in the bars and the clubs, with you swanning around being the life and soul of the party, and treating me as if I was just another empty-headed little bit of fluff, while all the time every other bitchy bastard in sight was nudging his affair and saying 'See that one there? Well, *she's* the one who put that supercilious, superior Andrew Tyldesley in his place. That's the sort of thing they were saying about me, you know. I had to stay at home for a month, I was so conscious of the whispers behind the hands. I'll *never* forgive you for that.

"And then there was last time. After all that, I was actually so besotted with you, I actually came up here and grovelled to you to try and get you back, and what did you do? More humiliation, you see.

"And so, at last, at the end of my tether, I decided that a little retribution was in order. And that's what I'm going to have. I chartered a little man that someone had recommended to me over something else, and hasn't he got the goods on you? You and your high-and-mighty, self-righteous talk. I'd got false information, had I? And all the time you were having the almighty gall to look down your long nose at me, there you were fornicating with your little fancy piece of cricketing rump, you stinking fucking hypocritical bastard, you."

His voice had grown progressively harder, louder and shriller as the eruption of bitter antipathy drew to its conclusion, and Tyldesley himself came closer and closer to hysteria. By the end he was literally spitting out the words in a passion of hatred and fury; Graham had to retreat a pace to get out of range of the fine spray of saliva that burst from his lips as he raged on. With the end of the tirade, though, the passion died in a moment, all its force spent, and Tyldesley sat glaring up at Graham through a sheen of tears.

Graham looked down at him, his face calm and expressionless. "You've answered the optional question", he said eventually, "but not the important one. Tell me what you want. And try not to take quite as long answering this one, if you will", he added.

Tyldesley stared at him with a baffled expression. "Haven't you got any mercy?" he asked, seriously, and quietly as if he was talking to himself. Then he pulled himself together with a visible effort, and continued.

"Well, I decided that if I couldn't have what I really wanted. I'd have something else. But something that would irritate you, something that I could look at like a miser and comfort myself with the thought, 'That bastard Curtis has *suffered* to give me this'. I want you to suffer, suffer for a long time — and pay — until you're a hundred, and maybe you'll one day feel sorry for what you did."

He fell silent for a while, eyeing Graham with vast distaste, and then spat out his last few words. "I want money. Not because I need it, but for the reasons I've just given. Money now, and then regularly, to keep my memory fresh in your mind."

"How much?" asked Graham unemotionally.

Tyldesley stared at him again, trying to fathom the calm, remote manner. Then he gave a small shrug. "A hundred — a week", he said baldly, watching Graham closely.

Graham didn't move, or react in any way at all. His expression remained as it had been all the time Tyldesley had been speaking: neutral and impassive. "I'll give you your answer in a day or so", he said evenly. "You can leave now."

"There's another thing", Tyldesley said. "I want it delivered by you, in person. I want you to bring the money to the pub, every week, on a day to be decided over the telephone, and hand it to me there, at a time not earlier than ten o'clock in the evening. That's all. Those are the conditions. If you don't like them, or rather, if you refuse to accept them, the detective's evidence, including the photographs, goes to the police. Then we'll see who's the high and mighty one. I'd come to your trial — for a gloat."

"And shortly after that", commented Graham, "you'd go to your own, for a prison sentence for blackmail. Really, you crass ass, do you think I'd let the police charge me with illicit sex without laying charges of blackmail against you? I can tell you, incidentally, that after I got out from my three months, I certainly would *not* come and visit you while you finished your seven years for blackmail."

"I may well conclude that it's worth that", said Tyldesley, sounding weary. "But even if that threat works, I can still expose you to your headmaster, and I wonder how long your feet would remain touching the ground then. Think it over, dear Graham. You can let me know by ringing the bar, or leave a message with one of my clubs."

"Goodbye, Tyldesley", said Graham. "Now get up. It's time for you to go."

Much to his surprise, Tyldesley did get up and indicated that he was ready to leave. Graham escorted him to the door, watching him carefully and wondering if he might make a revenge attack. When they got there, Graham put his hand on the knob and said "I don't know whether to despise you for being a stupid, vainglorious ass, or pity you for suffering from egomania, or megalomania or galloping paranoia, or all three. What I do know is that you'll get your answer when I said you would, in a day or two. In the meantime, don't come here again. If I see you again before I'm ready I'll rearrange your face so a blind man won't even fancy you."

"A hundred quid a *week*?" exclaimed Stephen, on the way to the match later that day. "That's money. But why all this business about you having to go to this place in London to pay it personally? And why after ten at night, for Christ's sake? I don't get it."

"Oh, I understand that all right. It's quite clever, quite inventive, in a malicious sort of way. He wants to hurt me, remember. He wants that very badly. But he can't do what he'd really like to do, because it would run his own head into a noose at the same time. So he can't expose me to the papers, or to the police, because he knows full well that I'd immediately hit back by telling the police about the blackmail. So he's left with a simple demand for money, which he reckons I just might pay up. Then he'll extort it for as long as he feels like it, and when he's had enough fun, and caused me what he reckons is a fair amount of misery, he'll do as he let slip this morning, and send his pictures to the head. That can only end one way — I'd have to go. So he loses me my job, which he'd regard as a reasonable compensation for his grievances, plus he's had the satisfaction of making my life a misery giving me the run-around for a fair time before he finally strikes, and he's quids in for several months, I'd imagine, into the bargain. Making me deliver the money after ten means that I have to trek to London every week. He'd make it a weekend, I dare say, hoping it would mess up the cricket, and, more important, he'll be hoping that it will prevent me from seeing you. And making it after ten at night means that I'll have to stay in London overnight. More trouble, and maybe the Sunday match fucked up as well, you see? As I said, it's quite inventive."

"What are you going to do? Not pay it?"

"No, no, of course not", said Graham, nipping past two lorries. "No, I shall do what we agreed was the best plan — ignore him altogether, and do nothing. Except one thing, of course."

"What's that?"

"Start making preparations for a fast move."

"Oh, God", said Stephen. His voice was filled with pain. "You're going away?".

"Well, it's quite likely, isn't it? You remember we discussed all this? If it comes out I'll have to go, and go I shall. It will avoid a scandal, and it will protect you. I'll get myself a job somewhere in France, if need be. Meanwhile, I shall be getting myself used to the idea, getting mentally attuned to the idea of being somewhere else, without you. You'd better start doing the same thing, I'm afraid, Steve. There's another thing, too."

"What's that?"

"There is a chance that this may fizzle out. He may be bluffing, hoping we'll be so terrified that he'll get what he wants without a fight. I doubt it — I shouldn't think he can have been under many illusions after the way I dealt with him this morning. But there's always laziness. After all, he's got a life to lead. He can't be willing to devote his entire existence to pursuing this insane vendetta against me. I may survive here. So it means you and me keeping our heads well below the parapet for a while, Stevie, sweetheart. I'm as sorry about it as you are, but I think it's only common sense." Stephen nodded gloomily. But he reached across the car and ran his fingertips gently through the short hairs on the nape of Graham's neck, offering what reassurance and comfort he could.

And so they went on their way, discussing it pointlessly from every angle and running every time into a brick wall.

***

Two unexciting draws did nothing to alleviate their gloom, and Stephen was irritable and uncommunicative in bed with Richard that weekend. On Monday morning Richard sat in the library, ostensibly revising but actually debating in his mind whether to ask Stephen to confide in him.

At lunchtime he went in search of him, and found him mooching moodily round the cricket field, hands in pockets and head down. He came up behind him and, heedless of the eyes of the few other boys walking round, put an arm firmly round his shoulders. "Why don't you tell me about it, Stevie?" he said. Coming out of his brown study with a start, Stephen looked up into Richard's face, and was touched by the anxious concern he saw there. "I... I'd like to", he said. "I'd like to tell someone, just to get it off my chest. It's awful knowing something like this and not being able to do a thing about it. You feel so bloody helpless. But..."

"But me no buts, love", said Richard. "I might be able to think of something to help. I'm fucking clever, you know." Stephen laughed, as Richard had planned. "Come on, love", he urged. "Tell uncle Dick all about it. Problem shared is a problem halved, and all that."

Stephen looked gratefully at him. "I wonder if anyone, anywhere, ever had a better friend than you, Richard", he said, feeling inclined to burst into tears.

Richard saw his eyes moisten, and squeezed his shoulders. "Don't blub, old chap", he murmured. "Much more sense to tell me all about it. I am the clever half of this partnership. Come on", he added, adopting a businesslike tone. "Let's have it."

So Stephen told him, making his eyebrows climb. He was only halfway through the tale when the bell shrilled in the distance, summoning them to the afternoon's bout of revision. "Better get back, I suppose", muttered Stephen.

"No", said Richard sharply, realising that if the flow stopped he might never prize Stephen's confidences out of him as easily again.

"The bell's gone", said Stephen, not very firmly.

"Stuff the bell", said Richard very firmly indeed. "Bugger, sod and fornicate the bell."

Stephen tried not to laugh, but failed. "All right, then", he said, with a grudging chuckle. "You win."

"I always do" said Richard jauntily. "Come on, now."

Stephen went on with his story, until Richard was abreast of developments right up to Saturday morning. He watched Stephen steadily out of the corner of his eye, and his heart throbbed with compassion and a fierce protectiveness. They continued walking in a friendly, companionable silence for some time before Richard spoke again.

"I'll give it my best", he murmured. "If I can't think of a way to set this bastard back on his heels I'm not the man I think I am. You trust me, Stevie, baby. He won't be worth a plugged nickel by the time I'm through with him. I'm into westerns at the moment", he grinned, as Stephen turned and stared at him.

Stephen laughed again, unable to help it. "Christ, you're

good for me", he said. "I say, d'you know what I fancy?"

"No, but you could always try telling me. My mind-reading's a bit rusty these days."

"I could murder a pint", said Stephen. "Come on, Richard", he went on, becoming animated as he thought about it. "Let's skive off into town and have a drink. Christ, that's the first good idea I've had since I started thinking about this business."

Richard looked at him sternly. "What about revision?" he asked. "Have you forgotten that the bell has rung?" Stephen stared at him for a split second before the penny dropped. Then he fell on him, and they wrestled playfully for a minute before heading briskly for a strictly out-of-bounds but popular, unofficial exit from the school grounds.

At that moment it seemed like nothing more than a minor piece of schoolboy naughtiness. But, unknown to them as yet, they were about to fall victims to the colossal, earth-moving power of coincidence. Their illicit visit to a pub was to have fateful consequences for several people, not least for themselves.

***

They wandered about aimlessly for a while when they got to the town centre, enjoying the unplanned freedom, and the mild tang of rebellion more. Eventually they found a large, smart-looking pub that stayed open throughout the day, and pushed happily through the doors.

One minute later they were back on the street. The barman had taken one glance at their school blazers, pointed to the door and said "Out!"

They had better luck with the next pub they tried, however. It was a large, shabby establishment in a side-street. They bought pints and carried them off to the table farthest from the bar to continue discussing Graham's problem. There were only three or four other customers in the big bar, all with newspapers open at the racing pages, and nobody took the slightest notice of the boys.

They had been there about ten minutes, and Stephen, who was thirsty, had almost finished his lager, when the door flew open with a force that almost took it off its hinges. A tall, slim, dark-haired boy of about seventeen burst in and shot across to the bar. The landlord dropped his own copy of *The Sporting Life* and glared at him. "No need to knock the..." he started to say, when the door was hurled open again, this time admitting two grinning youths in half-mast jeans, heavy working boots and skinhead haircuts. They were about the same age as the dark-haired boy, but a great deal bigger. They stared arrogantly round the room, and spotted him immediately at the bar. They barged tables and an old man out of their way and made a bee-line for the boy, who looked desperately about for an escape route. Their grins grew broader.

Before anyone could intervene the first and bigger of the two of them had cuffed the dark boy heavily round the side of his head, knocking him spinning along the bar. As he reeled under the force of the blow and flailed his arm in an attempt to keep his balance, he struck a group of about a dozen dirty glasses which the landlord had put on the bar for washing. They went flying, smashing in a minor explosion and showering glass in all directions. The boy's efforts to stay on his feet failed, and he went headlong into the jagged fragments on the floor. The other customers goggled at the sudden violence in their midst. Stephen and Richard looked at each other, and began to rise from their chairs; but someone was quicker.

One of the other drinkers lowered his paper and got slowly out of his seat. He was a stockily-built man of medium height, about forty-five, wearing casual clothes and thick, black-framed glasses. He threaded his way between the tables and came finally to rest between the sprawling dark-haired boy and the two youths. As he went he made a negative motion with his hand to the landlord, who was heading fast for the telephone. "Don't trouble, Bill", he said. Stephen and Richard sank back onto their chairs, still ready to help but watching the other man curiously.

So were the two skinheads, who had faltered in their charge towards their fallen victim and halted, eyeing the newcomer warily. "Mind yer own business, mate?" suggested the leader amiably. "We ain't got no quarrel with you."

"Making it my business", he said, equally politely. He stepped half a pace closer to them, casually placed a large palm in each chest and, without appearing to use any great effort, shoved. The two boys, big though they were, flew backwards, their feet slipped from under them and they landed on their backsides, glaring up at the man with identical, flabbergasted looks of surprise.

"Tut!" the man said, clicking his tongue. "Two onto one. Not cricket. Not cricket at all. So why are we beating the kid up?"

They glanced at each other, beginning to rise to their feet. "E's a poofter", said the leader eventually, deciding that conciliation was sensible policy until they had gauged the likely quality of this unexpected opposition. "E's a fuckin poofter, like. We don't like is kind, so we was givin im a lesson, stay away from round ere, narmean?"

"Ah", said the man softly. He half-turned to look down at the dark-haired boy, who was picking himself up out of the debris of broken glass. "Queer-bashin, are we?" He turned back to the two of them and wagged a finger at them. "Don't go away now, will you?" he said gently, and went over to the other boy. "That right?" he asked. "You gay?"

The boy stared at him, colouring up like a traffic light and looking uncertainly into his eyes. After a moment he nodded. "Y-yes", he stammered.

"Okay", said the man. "Look after them for me." He took off his glasses and laid them on the table, on which the winded boy was now leaning. Then he stepped without hurry back towards the two youths, by now back on their feet and eyeing him in mingled hostility and uncertainty. "Well lads", he said conversationally, "your luck's changed." They looked at him, not understanding.

"Come on then. Don't stand there gapin at me as if you just been goosed. I said, your luck's changed."

"Dunno whatcher mean", said the one who was spokesman, sullenly.

"What I mean, son", he said, as if humouring a backward child, "is that there you were, two big, brave, strapping lads, out for a little queer-bashin, and all you could raise was one frightened kid. An then, out of the blue, where there was one, suddenly there's two." They still stood motionless, trying to assess him. He saw that they still didn't understand his meaning.

He took two paces towards them, halted a few feet away, standing easily with his feet apart, and hooked his thumbs in the belt of his jeans. "I'm gay", he said, pleasantly. His voice was soft, but it sounded like a loud noise in the dead silence. He took two further paces towards them. "Try me", he said, more softly still.

The two had by now made their assessment, and began backing towards the door, eyeing him wolfishly but clearly not willing to take their chance against someone so evidently confident and, therefore, almost certainly dangerous.

"No?" he said, with apparent regret. "Well, you're not a bad judge, son. I'da put both of you in traction before you'd got a hand on me. As it happens, you see, I'm a sadist, as well as bein gay. I'm actually gonna enjoy breakin your fingers", he went on, walking unhurriedly towards them as they crowded in the doorway. He halted a few inches from them as they fought and tangled in their efforts to get the heavy door open without taking their eyes off him.

"Before you go", he remarked after watching the performance for a moment, "let me tell you something. I use this pub often. And all the others in this area, too. Not regularly, but often. Not at any particular time. So you'll never know if I'm around or not. But if I ever catch you two at this sort of game again, I'll put both of you in intensive care, for a good long time. Now you can get out." He turned his back on them and walked away, taking no notice of them whatsoever. They at last managed to get out of the door and escaped. The man ambled back to the dark-haired boy, who was sitting at the table he had been leaning on, and sat down opposite him.

"You all right, son?" he asked.

The boy nodded nervously, and Stephen and Richard could see his hands shaking from across the room. "Y-yes, th-thank you", he said, offering a slightly tearful smile from under his dark brown fringe. "Th-thank you very m-m-much."

"Don't you thank me", he said, dismissing the matter. "Our sort gotta look after each other. Nobody else will." He saw the boy's trembling hands, got up and sauntered across to where the landlord was watching, looking slightly bemused by events. "Gimme a brandy for the kid", he said. "Large."

The landlord came to with a small start and hastened to the optic. He gave the glass to the man, and waved his money away. "On the house", he said. "You done noble there. Saved the kid a nasty hiding. I'm too old to handle young roughs like that.

Have one yourself."

The man nodded his thanks, accepted a pint of Guinness, and went back to the boy, who was trying to compose himself. "Here y'are, son", he said. "Drink it down quick, it'll steady you down."

The boy thanked him shyly, and ventured to ask a question. "Are you... er... are you really...?"

"You just heard me tell the whole room I am, in a loud voice", he replied, with a faint smile.

"Well, y-yes", said the boy, taking a gulp of his brandy and gasping. "But I thought that was maybe just a blind — a cover to give you an excuse to... well, sort them out", he said.

The man laughed. "Nah! Nothing so complicated", he said cheerfully. "No, I'm gay. An like I said, we gotta look after each other. We can't all be fightin men, so it's up to the ones of us who are to take care of the ones who aren't. Wannanother?"

"Well, er yes, but please let me... And thank you again for... for what you did."

"Forget it, son", the man said. He leaned easily back in his chair and drained the remaining half-pint of his Guinness in a single long draught, and allowed the boy to get him another.

The drama over, the boys became aware that their glasses were empty. Stephen went and got refills from the bar. On the way he had to pass close by the dark-haired boy and his rescuer. He looked curiously at the man as he passed, and received a frank stare of appraisal in return.

When he got back to their table with the drinks he found Richard beaming with self-satisfaction. He seized Stephen's arm the moment he had set the glasses down. "I told you I'd think of something", he whispered excitedly in Stephen's ear. "Well, I have. It's sure to work."

"What are you talking about?"

"Graham's problem. I told you I was going to think of a way to get this bastard off his back, and I have. I'm brilliant, aren't I, Stevie?"

"I dunno till I hear what you've thought of", said Stephen. But he said it with a grin in which he managed to combine amusement and fondness with expectation, for he had an enormous respect for his friend's fertile mind, and he suspected that if Richard thought he had found a solution that might work, he was very likely to prove correct. "Go on, then", he said.

Richard told him. When he had finished hurriedly sketching the idea Stephen stared into space, thinking. "Hmm. It might work", he said doubtfully.

"Don't be so pessimistic. I know it'll work", hissed Richard. "But let's ask him, anyway, why don't we?" Stephen nodded slowly, and they waited.

A little while later the dark-haired boy rose and went out, thanking his rescuer profusely. Stephen and Richard got up and, taking their drinks with them, went over to the man. "I...er, I wonder if we might have a word with you", said Richard politely. He looked up enquiringly at the two of them; then waved at the empty chairs round the table. "Siddown", he said.

"All right", the man said when they had ranged themselves across the table from him. "What can I do for you?"

"Well", said Richard, "it was what happened just now that gave us the idea of speaking to you. It must have been pure coincidence, of course, but it might have been some sort of...of providence, almost. As if there's some sort of fate... Anyway, the way you dealt with those two thugs, we thought maybe you could tell us what to do. We've got a problem, you see."

"I rather thought you might", he said gravely. "Well, I never set myself up as an agony uncle, but I'll hear your problem, if you like."

"I...er...I suppose you're not a... a policeman, or anything, by any chance, are you?" asked Richard.

"Not by any chance whatsoever", said the man, grinning. "Perhaps we better introduce ourselves. I'm Terry Garrard. I suppose I'm best described as an ageing hippy — sorta dinosaur that's somehow managed to survive intact since the Sixties. How about you boys? And what's the problem?"

They introduced themselves shyly then carried on, Richard providing the beginning and Stephen finishing with the full story. They offered nothing to identify Graham, and Terry didn't ask.

"Okay", he said then. "What's your idea, Richard?"

"How did you know it was my idea?" asked Richard, curiously.

"Because I'm not blind", said Terry, and his expression did not encourage further questioning.

Richard explained his idea quickly. "Would it work, do you

think?" he asked anxiously.

"It might", said Terry. "It might not. Whatever, you got nothing to lose. Shit, if the guy still goes ahead, your man sounds as if he's got his head screwed on. He's sized up the odds, and he's already said he's preparing for a quick out. If you try your idea and it works, well, so much the better. What part have you written for me in this script?" he said abruptly, shooting the question at Richard in one of his lightning changes of direction.

"Well, none, really", said Richard, almost taken by surprise again but covering fast. "When I saw how you dealt with those two just now, I thought you might be the sort of person to get some advice from, but I didn't think much further than that, really."

"When d'you wanna do it?"

Once again he succeeded in taking them unawares. "Well", said Richard, "I suppose the sooner the better, really. That's something we haven't had a chance to discuss — we haven't discussed any of it yet. I only had the idea while we were watching you do your stuff there."

"Fair enough. You haven't said a lot", Terry said, swinging round on Stephen. "What do you think?"

"I'd like to see this bastard fried", said Stephen. "The only thing that would stop me is if I thought the other man might get in trouble because of anything I did. I wouldn't do anything to put him at risk — any more than he is already, that is."

"Good", said Terry. "And you're planning to go and do it yourselves, are you?"

"Yes", said Richard.

"I think I'll come along and oversee, if it's all right with you", said Terry. "If you'd like that, that is. When can you get away to do it?"

The jubilation with which they greeted this announcement made him smile. "When?" he repeated.

"How about next weekend?" suggested Stephen. "No problem with getting out of school that way. I can cancel my cricket for the weekend — I'll say my parents want to take me to see someone in London or something. Will you really come with us?" he asked excitedly.

Terry nodded, draining his glass. "Can you be sure of finding where this geezer hangs out?" he asked Stephen.

"I think so", he said.

"Okay. We'll meet in here at eight, Saturday night", Terry said. "Now you boys get outa here. I gotta find some horses." He picked up the paper he had fetched from the table at which he had been sitting when they had arrived, and ostentatiously stuck his nose in the racing page. The boys crept silently away, feeling slightly light-headed from a combination of elation, excitement, trepidation and too much lager, almost whispered their goodbyes as they went off to Richard's house and each other.

***

"Sure you'll recognize him?" asked Terry. Two seriously scared but determined faces turned whitely towards him and nodded in the faint glow from the nearest streetlamp.

"I've seen him in a photograph, and I don't think I could forget that face", muttered Stephen, fighting to suppress the fear that continuously made him want to leap out of the van and run into the nearest pub to drink a pint of lager, go to the lavatory, talk about cricket, do anything normal, mundane and unthreatening. He could feel his own heartbeat, racing wildly where his breast was pressed up against Richard in the passenger seat of Terry's old Ford van. Richard was in a similar state, and he could feel him, too, trembling slightly — though whether it was from excitement or the same horrible, unmanning fear he didn't know, and was afraid to ask.

"You kids all right?" asked Terry, sounding calm, almost bored. Two slightly tremulous voices assured him that they were fine. "Scared?" he asked casually.

"Y-yes, I am, a bit", confessed Stephen, trying unsuccessfully not to let the chattering of his teeth be heard. "N-no", said Richard at the same moment, making the same attempt, equally unsuccessfully. There was a chuckle in the darkness.

"That's how I had it sorted", he said. A match flared and fizzed suddenly. In the darkness and the silence and the heavy, crawling atmosphere in the van, pregnant with their combined fear, it sounded like an explosion, and both boys jumped out of their skins. Stephen felt his sphincter almost give way, and only just managed to repress a faint moan. Christ, he thought, that's all I need. That'd really impress Terry boy, wouldn't it now? What a way to win a reputation as a fighting man, shitting myself all over his front seat the first time I'm faced with action — and us three to one, at that.

"Well, you pass the first test", said Terry quietly, and they could clearly detect the undercurrent of suppressed laughter in his tone. "If you'd both said you were scared, I'da called the whole thing off right then." Stephen shrivelled internally at this public broadcasting of his cravenness. "And, by the same token", went on Terry cheerfully, "if you'd both been too stubborn to admit it, I'da called the whole thing off right then, and there you have it. It panned out as I expected. You'll be all right once it starts", he added after a pause. "It's always worse by far when you're waiting for the action to start. Once you get moving you'll find you're too busy to think about more than one thing at a time. Don't worry. And don't worry about being scared. If you weren't there'd be something wrong with you—and it's the worst thing you can have wrong with you. I wouldn't fight with someone who wasn't scared."

"You looked awfully scared in the pub with those two yobbos", ventured Richard, a little piqued to realize how transparent a failure his attempts to conceal his fear had been.

Terry gave a short bark of a laugh, filling the cabin with the exhalation of smoke that accompanied it. "Those two? That wasn't a fight, nor ever was gonna be one", he said quietly. "First rule a fighting is, don't. Second rule a fighting is, you gotta be able to tell the difference between people who're gonna put up a real fight and those who're nothing but wind and piss. Those two kids in the boozer were just small-time low-life slag, good at beatin the crap outa frightened kids half their size like the poor little sod they were after that day. Shit-fire! My friggin sister coulda taken them out without workin on it. No, you never wanna take a crap over someone that ain't worth a wet fart. Save the loosening bowels for the one who's worth crappin yourself over. I'd guess from what you've told me this guy tonight's worth a coupla strains over the can, an maybe you wipe it with one sheet a toilet paper, just to make sure. I don't think he's gonna prove dangerous. Hush now — somebody's comin."

The atmosphere instantly became more highly charged. They were parked in the darkest point in a very expensive mews in South Kensington, about twenty yards from Andrew Tyld-esley's address, which Stephen, feeling rather despicable, had managed to worm out of Graham. They heard steps ap-proaching, and a moment later a man, above middle height, a little flabby but nonetheless quite formidably built, came into sight round the slight bend in the mews that concealed them from the main road it led off. As he came closer his features became clearly visible in the light from the street-lamp. "That's him", muttered Stephen, feeling the churning of his innards approach crisis point. "Shall we go?" asked Richard in a strangled voice.

"Wait", said Terry calmly. Still they sat tight, until the man was so close that the boys would have sworn that he could see them inside the old van.

When he was twenty paces short of his own front door, Terry gave the order. "All right, lads. Put your gloves and the hoods on. As he gets to the door, rush him. But stay calm, and don't run, just jog up to him. He'll never know a thing. And let me do the talking", he added, slipping a hand to his mouth.

The three of them put gloves and black balaclava helmets on. By the time they had completed this the man was almost at his door. "Come on", murmured Terry, and slid out of the van, pushing the door gently to behind him. The boys piled out on the other side.

The first Andrew Tyldesley knew of the attack on him was when, as he arrived at his front door, three figures materialized as if out of the fabric of the building, or out of the darkness itself. One moment he was alone, fishing for his key. The next he was surrounded by the three men, all enormous and heavily muscled, as it seemed to him, and all utterly terrifying in jeans, dark shirts or sweaters and, most appalling of all, black balaclavas, such as he had seen the IRA and other terrorists wearing on television. He froze to the spot, his hand clenching into a claw in his pocket. A dank, rank sweat suddenly broke from him in every single part of his body, the parts that normally sweated and the parts that didn't alike. The sweat was so cold it felt almost as if it was freezing. His breath stuck in his throat, and he didn't even notice that he wasn't breathing. And if the boys had come close to evacuating themselves as they waited in the van, he came even closer. A thin dribble of thick, hot fluid did actually squirt into his pants before his bodily reflexes, taking over from his para-lyzed conscious, could slam his sphincter closed. Not that he noticed that, either, until later.

"Open your door, quietly and calmly", said a soft voice from the largest and most terrifying of the assailants. There was something strange about the voice: afterwards he thought that perhaps the man had suffered from a cleft palate, or a hare lip or some such disorder. For the moment he was too stricken by the most abject terror to think at all.

"Come on", said the same voice, still very soft but taking on a terrible cutting edge of menace. "Open the door and go in. If you try to slam it, I'll cut your throat." Tyldesley managed to pull himself together to the extent of doing as his terrifying assailant ordered, and opened the door. They filed silently into the large and luxurious mews house. "Lights", said the voice. Tydlesley flicked a switch, and the long main room was suffused with soft light.

The three menacing figures wasted no more than a second or two on a swift glance round the beautifully and expensively furnished apartment. "Draw those curtains", ordered the spokes-man", and the other two, who looked, now, quite a lot younger, ran to the windows and obeyed.

"What's the most valuable object in this room?" asked the spokesman, still speaking very quietly through his impediment, whatever it was. "Don't even think about deceiving me." The menace was back in the voice, rippling and coiling sinuously into Tyldesley's imagination. He pointed to a picture on the far wall, of a Roman goddess in armour. It glowed and pulsed and danced with subtle lights, and none of the three needed Tydlesley's quavering information that it was by Rembrandt. "Genuine?" grated the spokesman. Tydlesley nodded. "Get it", said the spokesman tersely to the taller of his henchmen. The man ran noiselessly to the wall, fiddled behind the picture and brought it to the leader. "Hold him", ordered the leader to the other henchman. Tyldesley felt strong arms pinion him from behind.

"Gimme", said the leader, and the taller henchman passed the picture over. The leader grasped it firmly halfway up each side of the frame, and held it out at arm's length. He nodded to his assistant.

Stephen, hating what he was going to do, walked round to a

position in front of Terry and the picture. He drew back his fist.

"NO!" screamed Tyldesley. The leader glanced his way, handed the picture back to his assistant, and stepped up to Tyldesley, who was now struggling wildly in his captor's pinioning arms. He stopped struggling smartly enough, though, when the leader hit him very hard in the solar plexus. Then he simply flopped over, doubled in the other man's arms, and if Richard hadn't held onto him firmly he would have flopped to the floor, every morsel of breath cruelly expelled from his body by that terrible, paralyzing blow. The leader paid him no further attention, but motioned the other assistant to set the picture down against a chair. He did so. Then all three waited, one holding Tyldesley up, the others ranged in front of him.

"Door. Check" ordered the leader, and the taller acolyte scampered to the front door, opened it a crack and peeped out. He closed it silently, came quickly back, and shook his head.

The leader looked at Tyldesley and assessed that he was recovered enough to pay him attention. "Can you concentrate on what I say?" he asked. Tyldesley nodded, his eyes bugging out of his head to an extent that genuinely alarmed Stephen, watching from the security of his black anonymity. He wondered if they might actually bulge right out of his head. He imagined them popping out of their sockets and hanging bouncily down his cheeks on the ends of the thick, twisted cables of their optic nerves, boing, boinnngg, boinnnngggg.

"We're not here to rob you", said the leader in the thick, soft voice that he had used throughout. "We're here to warn you. First I'm going to give you a choice. We're here to teach you a lesson. You can have it yourself, or we'll take it out on that picture there that you're so obviously attached to. Which would you prefer?"

"Hit me, do anything", cried Tyldesley. He was howling now, tears almost spurting from his eyes, and there was a long tendril of yellowy-grey snot running out of one nostril and squirming down his upper lip. "Do anything, but don't hurt the painting. It's a Rembrandt. Please, I beg you, have mercy on the picture. Do what you like to me, but Rembrandt never hurt you, whatever you're doing this for. You can't destroy something as beautiful as that because of something I've..." He broke off, overwhelmed and convulsed with hysterical tears.

Richard and Stephen were both feeling sick to their stomachs with disgust and revulsion at the spectacle, and both would gladly have ended it there and then. Not so the leader. He touched Stephen on the arm. "Hit him", he said. He saw Stephen blench, saw the fastidious revulsion in his eyes, and his own glinted dangerously. "You've started this. Now you finish it", he hissed into Stephen's ear, so quietly that neither of the other two heard a word of it, but so ferociously that Stephen had no more idea of disobeying. He hardened his heart, aiding the process by thinking consciously of the misery Graham had suffered of late, and stepped in front of Tyldesley, still held firmly from behind by Richard. He signed to Richard to release him. As Richard did so he aimed a heavy, swinging punch at the point of Tyldesley's jaw, hoping to finish the matter in one blow. Unfortunately the moment Richard let Tyldesley go he stumbled forward, and Stephen's fierce right cross, instead of laying him out on the spot, made a fearsome mess of his left eye. He still went down as if pole-axed, however.

"Door", said the leader. This time Richard cat-footed to the door, peeped out and came back putting a thumb up. The leader motioned him to the front and to Stephen to pick Tyldesley up. Richard had seen how much effect Stephen's reluctance had had, so he didn't even bother to offer any resistance. When Tyldesley was set on his feet again Richard hit him efficiently, as a man with an unpleasant task to get done, and Tyldesley's lips were smashed and mangled against his teeth. There was a sharp cracking sound, astonishingly loud in the room, as one of his front teeth broke under Richard's heavy blow.

"Hold him up", said the leader. Both boys helped Tyldesley to his feet and held him up as Terry stepped up in front of him. Tyldesley's terror and pain were so huge, beyond any imagination of fear and pain in his direst nightmares, that he had ceased to make any sounds of pain or protest above a terrible, piteous whimpering that wrung the boys' hearts. Neither of them would have had the stomach to go on with it then.

"We want you to know that this is a common reward for blackmail", said the fearsome leader, whom Tyldesley would see in nightmares for long afterwards, and associate for the remainder of his life with the true meaning of the word *terror*. "There's only one more thing to say. If you make any further attempt to commit blackmail, of anyone at all, you'll get the same again, but a hundred times harder. You think you've been hurt now. Well, you've been given a mild reprimand, which we hope and trust will teach you the lesson you need. If you try again, we'll show you what pain really feels like. You and Rembrandt there. We're sparing the picture — this time. Not next time; so you'd better make sure there isn't a next time, hadn't you? Do you understand what I'm saying to you?" Tyldesley nodded.

"Okay", said the leader. "We're going now. If you call the police, we'll be back, though you'll never know when or where we're going to pop out from round a corner, or be waiting for you when you walk back in here. If there's any more blackmail, we'll be back for you and Rembrandt. If you behave yourself, on the other hand, you'll never see us again. Your choice." He turned away, and Tyldesley's face crumpled in relief. As he was beginning the long, agonizing process of relaxing, the leader turned with a fast, economical movement and hit him again in the same place as before, a deadly, killing blow which might indeed have killed if he had not pulled it slightly at the last moment to rob it of the last crucial fraction of its power. Tyldesley crumpled under it like a sheet of thin cardboard, and dropped almost without a sound into a broken, heaving tangle of loose limbs on the beautiful deep carpet. His bowels had opened in full by now, and a rank, noisome stench polluted the room.

The leader squatted beside him and shook and slapped him lightly with a black-gloved hand until he came to and raised his head. "Are we going to have any more trouble with you?" he asked gently.

Tyldesley, who was not without courage of a sort, was nowhere close to being able to cope with such treatment. He looked up at Terry's empty, pitiless, expressionless eyes through blinding tears of agony, indignity and terror, and shook his head. "N-n-no more t-t-tuh-tuh-rouble", he said in an almost inaudible, gargling moan. His bloodied, badly torn tongue flicked in and out to moisten his lips, leaving bubbles of blood, fragments of tooth and bloody scraps of flesh from his smashed lips and tongue on his mouth. "Nuh-nuh-no m-m-more t-t-t..." His right eye rolled up, the left now completely closed and swollen like a tennis ball, and he slumped into a faint.

Terry shook him ruthlessly until he came to again, gazing at the terrifying form from his one eye in a despair that was almost palpable. "Tell me the name of a friend, and his telephone number", Terry said, shaking him again.

"T-t-tuh-tuh-Trevor V-v-Vick-Vickers", croaked Tyldesley, and managed to stammer a number. "Check it", ordered Terry. One of the boys ran to the telephone, found the directories and checked the number. He stuck a thumb up.

"We're going now", said Terry. "Don't forget what I've told you."

He led the way quickly to the door, peeped out to see that there was no-one about, and left, a black shadow into black shadow, into the night, followed by the other two. They were in the van in ten seconds. In ten more they were under way, easing the van out into the deserted road into which the mews ran. "Gloves and hoods", said Terry, once they had put a quarter of a mile between themselves and the mews. They handed them over. "I'll get rid a these", he said. "By Christ, it's a relief to get rid of this, too", he added, spitting a large pebble into his hand and dropping it into one of the balaclavas. Thirty seconds later he pulled up beside a telephone call-box, slipped out, leaving the engine running, and made a call.

"He didn't want to get out of bed at first", Terry said, grinning as he got back in and pulled away. "But I managed to convince him, I think, so our friend back there should be getting some sort of assistance shortly." He drove on in silence for a while. Then he said "You boys wouldna gone on with it back there, would you?"

"No", they said in chorus, both remembering the appalling, undreamed-of sights they had been forced to witness, and both feeling slightly sick at the memory.

"I thought you'd get cold feet", he said, laughing. "Another lesson a fightin — it's just as nasty hurtin other people as bein hurt yourself — well, no, it isn't, but it's not pleasant. But you had to go through with that business back there. Wanna tell me why? Any offers?"

"So we were implicated in it?" suggested Richard. "So that we couldn't get bad consciences about it and confess, without incriminating ourselves as well?"

Terry laughed again. "You got a mind like Machiavelli, son,

ain't you?" he said. "But you could be right, in part at least. But that's not the main reason why you had to finish it."

They waited. "Okay, I'll tell you. It's because you started it. You finish what you start. Otherwise you become just another typical specimen of Mr Average, twentieth century man — in other words, just another four-flusher whose word's worth as much as a promise in an election manifesto and who's got as much integrity as he's got courage, which is none at all. You start something, you finish it, not drop out when it starts offendin your delicate sensibilities. That's the way to survive in this miserable world, and survival's the name a this game — an it's gonna be increasingly as the grub runs out. You remember that. You might be grateful to old Terry one a these days."

Three quarters of an hour later he drew into the kerb just outside the centre of the town. They had half a mile to walk to Richard's house. He relaxed and looked steadily at them. "Tell me", he said, speaking softly as usual, in a manner chillingly reminiscent of his voice in Tyldesley's home. "Are you glad we did what we did tonight?"

They looked unhappily at each other for a moment, thinking about it. Stephen broke the silence. "Yes", he said, and his voice sounded firm and decided for the first time since they had entered the house in the mews. "Yes, I am", he repeated. "It made me feel ill when we were there. I've never hit anyone before — well, I mean, not — not like that, in cold blood like that. It made me want to throw up, and I very nearly did. But yes, I am glad we did it, now I've had time to think about it. He was a cruel, vicious, calculating bastard, and he deserved a lesson. I expect I'd feel the same again if we had to do anything like that again, feel sick, I mean, and I hope I never have to do anything like that again in my life. But when you ask, I can't say I'm not glad, because I am."

"Richard?"

"It's not as easy as that for me", Richard said slowly, "because I'm not as personally involved as Steve. I see what he means, but I can't feel it, inside me, if you know what I mean. I feel as if I'm dirty, somehow. Making a man howl and cry, and that awful whimpering, and scaring someone like that, so he... so he shits himself — well, it makes me feel... I don't know... it's indecent, somehow."

"You're learnin good", said Terry. "You just learned that there's no victors in fightin. Ain't such a thing as a just war, or a clean fight. Fightin's nothin more than winnin, an the winner more often than not feels as soiled as the loser. If he's human, an a decent specimen a the species, that is. Trouble is, most people aren't. Just have a thought as you go home now. If our friend back there'd been in your position tonight, an you'd been in his, would he have had your delicate scruples? I'm sayin nothin, because I know the answer. So do you, or I'm very much mistaken, which is why I'm leavin it to you to come up with it yourselves.

"Now I'll say goodnight to you, with one last thought, an it's the most important a the lot. If you'd a gone there to do him over without me, you'da bottled out just about when I got you involved — i.e., with the firin a the first shot, right? An that woulda handed the advantage over to him on a ceremonial plate. He'da been given a breather before he was properly hurt, an he'da taken that chance with both hands and both feet. Your squeamishness woulda got you right in the nick, my little friends. That's why you needed me there tonight, an that's why I made sure I was there. I didn't give a shit about your private problem with the man. I still don't. I don't even know your man who's got the problem. But I liked the look a you two, an I knew if you went strollin down there to beat the crap outa him on your own you'd never get beyond the first hit. I didn't wanna see your two pretty little asses in the slam, an there you have it. I'll see you boys around, right?" And he put the van into gear and shot off before either of them could say a word.

"He's right, you know", said Stephen.

"Yes", muttered Richard as they started to walk in the direction of his home. "I suppose he is. I just hope it works. I'd hate to have to go through that again."

***

For a long time it seemed that their unpleasant night's work had worked indeed. Graham followed his original intention of totally ignoring Tyldesley's threats. He paid nothing, never went near the gay scene in London where Tyldesley and his cronies hung out, and carried on with his life at the school and the cricket club as if nothing had happened. The weeks passed and he heard nothing, until the mid-point of the summer term was close by. Richard and Stephen continued to enjoy each other and their own lives. They never consciously thought about the raid on the mews, and in time it faded away, leaving only a thin, nightmarish under-memory of horrors endured. As for Terry Garrard, he followed his own mysterious paths. They never saw him again.

And then, one morning just before the mid-point of the term, the headmaster touched Graham on the shoulder as the masters were dispersing from the common room after morning assembly. "Will you come to my study in half an hour, please, Graham", he said, his face grave and unsmiling.

At the same moment the deputy headmaster, acting on orders that had not been explained to him, was detaining Stephen Hill as he left the school hall, and taking him to an empty classroom, where, following the same orders, he sat with the boy, chatting generally and frankly admitting his ignorance of what was behind the puzzling procedure, until they were called for.

Graham went off to arrange for the form monitor to take charge of his first class, assuming it must be some routine school matter. It never crossed his mind that the summons could have anything to do with the problem at the beginning of that term. When he entered the study and closed the door silently behind him the headmaster gestured to him to be seated. He slid a brown folder across the desk.

"I'd like you to open that and look at what it contains", he said. "And then, I'd be grateful to hear your explanation. If you can explain them." His face was grim and stern, and, worse, there was a cutting, contemptuous disgust in his expression which flayed Graham like a lash. He opened the folder curiously, and jerked back as if he had been thumped heavily in the chest. Staring up at him was a familiar picture, of himself and Stephen gazing lovingly into each other's eyes as they exchanged that single kiss, utterly innocuous yet utterly damning, in the hotel corridor in a small Sussex town.

***

218

"It gave me a very nasty jolt, I can tell you", said Graham that evening.

His interview with the headmaster had taken up almost two hours. When Graham had gone Stephen had been called in, and he had been there for considerably less. When he had emerged, shaky but defiant, obstinately denying that any impropriety had ever taken place between himself and Graham, it had been lunch-time. He had gone in search of Graham, and found him, as he had expected, strolling round the cricket field on his own. They had compared notes briefly, and agreed that they were both feeling too drained to want to discuss matters then, so they had arranged that Stephen would go to Graham's flat that evening, early. "Get there at five, if you like", said Graham. "We'll go over it then, and then I'll take you out to dinner, if you'd like that. Sort of celebration, only a bit double-edged, eh?" Stephen had smiled. "Not for me, except in the short term, maybe", he had said, and sensing that Graham wanted to be left alone with his own thoughts for a while, he looked round, saw that there was no-one in sight, and gave him a brief, hard kiss on the mouth. Then he tactfully slipped off in search of Richard.

"So what did he say?" Stephen now said, sinking comfortably into the cushions on Graham's sofa and hoping the smile he couldn't get off his face didn't look too much like a cat that had succeeded in upsetting a jug of cream.

"Well, of course he began by taking it as an open and shut case", said Graham. I just stonewalled to begin with. I didn't really see what else I could do. He felt that the picture more or less convicted and condemned me. The other two didn't really matter, but the one of you giving me that quick peck in the corridor, or me giving you one, whichever the hell it was, that one was deadly. I started by suggesting that the whole thing was a storm in a teacup, and had been blown up out of all proportion. Just a gesture of affection between a schoolmaster and a favourite pupil, who also happened to be very close friends outside school, I said. But of course, I knew that all the time there was that bloody private detective's report in the background, so I reckoned I was pretty well up against it.

"So did he, and yet, if I'd but known it, I was on far firmer ground than I realized, because actually Tyldesley hadn't included the statement at all. If only I'd known that I could most likely have bluffed the whole thing out and got away with it on lack of real evidence. But there it is — I didn't know, so there I was, assuming he'd got me snookered, while all the time he'd got nothing else up his sleeve at all. It would have been quite funny, really, if it had been happening to someone else, or in a film. There I was, not using all kinds of arguments I would have used if I hadn't thought he'd got the murder weapon up his sleeve to confound me with if I told any lies, and him sitting there wondering what the hell this 'other evidence' I kept referring to might be.

"Anyway, as I say, all I thought I could do was stonewall, so I did. I refused to admit that there had ever been sexual intimacy between us — he kept using words like 'misconduct', of course. But I didn't actually deny it, either, which I think was getting him pretty frustrated.

"But in the end he got down to the serious horse-trading. He said that these days an eighteen-year-old was pretty well an adult, so that maybe it need not be regarded as being as serious as it would have been thirty years ago. Well, I said, for openers, that I couldn't really see what thirty years ago had got to do with anything. Not in so many words, of course: you don't talk to headmasters like that, even if they're out to give you your cards — which, of course at that point I thought he was.

"Look, if I go through the whole rigmarole we'll be here till midnight. Let me cut a very long story very short indeed, and give you the result, shall I? Then we can go and have a nice dinner somewhere."

"Yes, please", said Stephen, still wearing the same rather smug smile.

"Well, he felt that whatever the truth of the matter, and he accepted that he might never get to that, I had been at the very best grossly unprofessional, indiscreet, and a whole string of other adjectives, mostly beginning with 'un' and none of them very complimentary. At worst, I'd been guilty of the foulest and most despicable form of professional misconduct, etcetera, etcetera, etcetera. I tried to point out that if we took the worst possible case, for argument's sake, even then the worst I'd been guilty of was having a love affair — I emphasized that, because he seemed to think like so many people, that heterosexuals fall in love with other people while homosexuals just have sex — yes, a love affair with a fully consenting man who was fully sexually, physically and emotionally mature.

"Well, none of that cut much ice, as you can imagine. However, he said that you *were* eighteen, and the evidence was pretty flimsy — I'll leave you to supply my interjections there from your own imagination — so they had decided that the police and the law need not be bothered with the matter. Well, you can imagine the size of the sigh of relief I let go there. But, he said, the most important influencing factor of all in that decision was the fact that if he called in the law it would do the school a terrible amount of harm, and also the boys, at a critical stage in the academic year. So would I be willing to consider the following proposal: I quietly resign, with effect from the end of this academic year, they pay me to the end of the year, in other words, to the end of the summer holiday, but I go more or less immediately?

"Well, honestly, Stevie, it sounded too good not to jump at it — especially compared with what I *thought* he was in a position to do to me. Of course, once again, if I'd only known what he hadn't got, as well as what he had, it might have been a different matter. But frankly, I reckon my goose was cooked whatever he had or hadn't got, and whatever I did or didn't say. Whatever the rights and wrongs, whatever the truth of the matter, he was convinced that I'd been carrying on with you — 'misconduct' — and nothing short of positive proof was going to change his mind.

"Still, I got a couple of extra concessions. He would have liked me to clear my desk right then — you know, wait till my formroom was empty, then collect any personal possessions of mine from it, and be off the premises by lunchtime. On the other hand he didn't want a scandal, and he realized that if he went about it that way he'd be assuring himself of a scandal in spades. If I was whizzed off the premises with nobody even knowing I'd gone, he'd be starting enough hares to keep him chasing them for the next two terms. I pointed that out to him, of course, but he'd got there already. So we agreed that I would come in for the next few days, and spread a story that I'd been offered some position I couldn't refuse, and that he, having begged me with tears in his eyes not to desert him, had magnanimously, generously and with tremendous regret, acceded to my urgent request for immediate release. That way my going is accounted for, and even if there are a few doubters who don't think it sounds very plausible, there's no other obvious reason. If I give such a story and he backs it up, why should anyone not believe it? There's no reason not to, so people will. I also pointed out another reason why I wanted a couple of days' grace — and I meant it — was that I'd like to have the opportunity to say my farewells to a lot of the boys. I said that there were some I wouldn't be sorry to see the last of, but there were many more I very much wanted to say goodbye to.

"He accepted that — not with especially good grace, I'm afraid, but he saw the sense of the arrangement. Then I asked him what he'd do about a reference. He asked me where I was intending to go, and I told him my idea about France, and he liked that — puts a decent distance between him and the source of likely contagion. So, he said, provided that he was never asked to give a reference for me for a position entailing my being in a position of trust over children, he'd give me a belter. He would prepare it immediately, and show it to me tomorrow, if that would suit. Well, it did suit. It was the best bargain I reckoned I was going to get, so I took it.

"And that's about it, love. I'm more or less finished here. I shall actually be saying my goodbyes over the next couple of days, and I think I should travel to France early next week, to find a position, and look round for a place to live. It will give us a few evenings to get used to the idea, and I don't want to drop out of the cricket this weekend at such short notice."

"There's one thing puzzling me about the head having those photographs", said Stephen.

"What's that?"

"Why didn't he include the detective's report, as well as the photos? That would have put it beyond doubt: it was much more incriminating than the photos, wasn't it?"

"I don't think there's much doubt about it", said Graham. "The photographs on their own wouldn't have been enough for a successful prosecution. The head would probably know that, and if he didn't the school's lawyer would. That meant that with the photos but not the statement the school wasn't likely to drag in the police — it would be kept within the school. And that meant that I'd lose my job, and most likely all prospect of employability in future, but it wouldn't get to such proportions that I'd feel I'd got no more to lose and so hit back with allegations of blackmail. Tyldesley's no fool."

They discussed the affair round in circles until they were sick of it, then went out to dinner, feeling a heady sense of liberation, despite their anxieties, at being able to go where they pleased and not give a damn who saw them together. When they got back to Graham's flat they went back to their discussions for a while, but Stephen was playful and flirtatious, and a little bit tarty, a mood in which Graham was wholly incapable of resisting. He was intending to put in an appearance at the school on each of his final few days, but there was no longer any impulsion to keep regular hours; as for Stephen, the A-levels were so close that he was more or less left to his own devices. So after a last coffee they went joyously to bed together, savouring every second and every small act of love in their first coupling free from the shackling restraints of propriety and official disapproval.

They made love again, luxuriantly and languorously, when they woke in the morning. It was tinged with sadness, because the fruit of all their talk was a firm decision by Graham to travel to France at the beginning of the following week to find a position for himself in some congenial region, where he could get settled in advance and wait for Stephen to join him — as he had made an undeviating resolve to do immediately after the exminations.

With this decision made, with what they both regarded as their first true night together, in the sense of its being unconstrained, and most of all with plans firmly made to spend that evening together, they both felt a lot brighter and more cheerful than they would have dreamed possible.

There were two difficulties that would have to be dealt with, and soon. One was the question of Richard. Stephen loved him, not, admittedly, with the same devotional love he bore for Graham — that was close to worship — but with a very deep, unshakable trust and affection; and they had grown very used to each other. He knew that Richard, brave though he would undoubtedly be about losing his beloved friend, was shortly going to be desolate, unhappy and alone. He would require a lot of love and help.

Graham, for his part, had long ago got over his intense spasm of jealousy; though he was happily ignorant of the raid on

Tyldesley and Richard's instigating part in it, he was fully aware of Stephen's immense debt to the other boy. He had a shrewd idea, too, of how much he himself owed Richard, for keeping Stephen sane and balanced — for keeping him there for him; even more, they both felt an awed sense of the quite extraordinary selflessness with which Richard had given of himself and his support, as solid and dependable as the earth itself. There was an ocean of gratitude to be discharged there, and another of guilt that would have to be coped with later on.

Of the second difficulty they knew nothing as yet. The blackmailer, too, had his plans.

***

Graham drove Stephen almost to the school next morning, dropping him round the corner. "Better not take you right in", he said, giving him a peck on the lips as he reached across him to open the passenger door. "That would be tantamount to a two-fingered salute. There's no point in provoking antipathy for the sake of it. Now, I'm here for an hour or so, but I shan't be here at lunchtime, or in the afternoon. Why don't you spend some time with Richard, love? I don't reckon to be back till about seven tonight, so I'll see you...where? How about the cricket club? I'm going to be missing cricket a great deal, and so are you, I imagine."

"Okay", said Stephen, who was indestructibly cheerful. "What are you up to today — if it's any of my business? Only being nosey."

"My business is your business now, I guess", said Graham. "And today's little bit of business concerns you anyway. I'm going to see Andrew Tyldesley."

Stephen's eyes widened. "Really? Wow. Why?"

"Time to balance the accounts. I've got nothing more to lose now — nothing he can touch, anyway. I've got a hankering to punch his eyes out."

Stephen grinned. He wondered whether to tell Graham that someone had got there before him, but decided it would be judicious to let that wait. "Don't get arrested for assault and battery", he said, and the youthful concern in his voice and face made Graham's heart throb painfully for a moment. "I won't", he said softly. "He's never going to want to say too much to the law about me. Where I'm concerned he'll always have a big illuminated sign saying 'SEVEN YEARS' prominently in his mind, because of what I might say to the police myself, if I was so minded. But thanks for worrying about me. Now we'd best get on, or it'll be this afternoon." He waved a hand as he drove off.

Stephen was especially gentle and affectionate with Richard that day. He took him off to a semi-disused book store-room, full of the dry smell of out-of-date textbooks, and told him the full story. Richard was his usual bright and irrepressible self, but Stephen noticed that there were odd moments when he seemed not to hear what was said. He racked his brains for ways to soften the blow, and failed to come up with a single idea. All he could do was to radiate tenderness and make a point of enjoying and appreciating Richard's company to the last degree possible. When Richard was completely up to date they slipped off early and walked to Richard's house, stopping on the way for a pint at the pub where they had met Terry. When he left him at the door of his house, where Stephen had more or less lived for a long and happy interlude, Richard smiled, a little sadly but with no jealousy visible at all, and said goodbye to him with all his usual brilliance. As a performance it was first class; but Stephen remembered the trace of sadness in the smile, and it wrung his heart. He walked ten yards, then turned back, calling to Richard.

"What's up?" asked Richard, brightening visibly. "Do you want me to clear all my things out?" Stephen asked him, deeply troubled. He wandered distractedly off the pavement and into Richard's front garden. "Oh, God, I feel so bloody guilty about you", he cried, and turning to Richard he threw his arms round him and clasped him as if he never wanted to let him go.

They stood there, in full view of the road, holding each other fiercely, desperately, in each other's arms, for some minutes on end. Stephen kissed him on his cheek and ruffled his thick golden hair with his fingers, and Richard responded as he always did to Stephen's touch of any kind. "Let me come in for a bit", said Stephen when a third motorist gave them a fanfare on the horn from the road. There was no way of telling whether the musical signals represented encouragement or not, but they sounded more like derision.

Richard, delighted at having Stephen unexpectedly to himself for a time, hurried him in up the stairs to the bedroom that Stephen knew so well. He had only been away for a single night, yet it felt like the return of the prodigal son, to both of them.

"What am I going to do about you?" asked Stephen. "Tell me, Richard. Come up with an idea. Can't you have one of your brainwaves? You told me once, you're fucking clever. Well, I know you are. You never let me down when I needed some extra brainpower. Not once. Well, use it for yourself, can't you?"

Richard hugged him and rolled with him on the familiar double bed, ending up lying on top of him with his distinctive light brown eyes looking down into Stephen's deep ash-grey ones. "I also told you once, Stevie, that I knew one day Mr somebody else, as I used to call him, would come back for you, because he'd be insane if he didn't. I said, if you remember, that I knew that my little lease would be up then, and that I'd have to reconcile myself to losing you. So okay, it's happened. Well, we had a lot of very good times, and I've enjoyed loving you. I dare say I'll always love you — you were the first, and I think you're very special. I think I was very lucky to find someone like you to be my first. But it had to end, and I'm glad it's ended calmly, and well for you, with you happy."

"Does it have to end, though?" groaned Stephen, the new-found effervescent mood of the last thirty-six hours went to shreds in seconds, and a vast, racking emptiness of guilt moved inexorably in to take its place.

"Of course it's got to end, sweetheart", said Richard gently. "And if you ever dare to pity me, I'll go and put a contract out on you with Terry Garrard. We'll still have a piece of each other, a piece that belongs to the other for ever. But this part of it" — he gestured round the bedroom — "and this part" — he put a hand between Stephen's legs and rubbed him gently — "will have to come to an end, of course. Not quite yet. I think I'll still have you to myself for a little while yet. But not for much longer."

Stephen groaned loudly in pain.

"Don't be silly, Stevie, sweetheart. I took you on those terms, and I took you with my eyes open. I knew — at least, I felt pretty sure — that one day I'd have to lose you, so I can't complain when my own prediction comes true. And if you come to that, I'm not complaining, am I? It's you doing all this moaning. Now stop worrying. Just do one thing for me, that's all I want."

"Anything I can do, it's yours", said Stephen, aching with love and guilt. "You know that."

"Yes, I do", said Richard with a spark of his buoyant cockiness. "Just give me all the time you can spare before you finally go away with him." This was altogether more than Stephen could bear. He rolled onto his face, pulling Richard with him, and sobbed great, retching howls of anguish into Richard's duvet.

***

Richard knew his way around Stephen, and used every way he knew to comfort him and help him down from his pinnacle of grief. He managed to get him calmed down and on his way to the cricket club on time for his appointment with Graham. He got there, in fact, a quarter of an hour early, and sat with a pint of lager, waiting in mingled impatience, anxiety and a residue of the troubled, tormented feelings of guilt and sorrow left over from earlier.

Graham saw the smudges left over from his earlier grief as soon as he walked into the pavilion, and felt thankful that the place was still almost empty, with just a group of four elderly members playing bridge in a corner. He waggled his fingers at Stephen, glanced at his glass, and brought him a new pint from the bar. "How was it?" he asked gently as he dropped into the chair beside Stephen's.

"What happened?" asked Stephen at the same moment, and managed a shaky grin.

"You first", said Graham.

"I told him everything", said Stephen. "I don't know what we're going to do about him, Graham. It nearly broke my heart, telling him I was soon going to just walk out on him. And I kept on thinking of little details, things we'd never even considered — like, I thought of how I'd have to tell his parents, for instance. They've been wonderful to me, you know. They've treated me just like a member of the family. They've let me live there, they've never once asked awkward questions, they've fed me, made me a part of the family. They must've spent a lot of money keeping me like that, apart from anything else — and the one time I tried to say something about it — you know, offer them a bit of money, his... his father laughed at me, and wouldn't let me get a word in.

"And then we went up to his room, and I looked round, and it was only then that I realized how many of my things there are there. It was like looking round my own room for the last time, Graham." His lip was trembling, and he was very close to tears. Graham wisely stayed silent, waiting for it all to work its way out of his system.

"And then I thought of him, still using the room", Stephen went on in a kind of suppressed wail that moved Graham greatly. Stephen's bare recital of his imaginings conjured up a vivid image of Richard's feelings of forsakenness, and the fine hairs on Graham's forearms and the nape of his neck prickled. "I thought of him, still going up to it every day, every night, and me not being there, and him knowing I was with you..." He stopped, and for the moment he couldn't speak.

Graham sat staring gloomily into space, knowing what he had to do, only wondering if he had the strength to do it. After all that had happened in so comparatively brief a span of time, after the lurching switchback ride of his own emotions, his hopes and fears from extreme to extreme, when it looked as if he might have secured a degree of fulfilment, even the prospect of serenity, it seemed an especially bitter fate to have to utter himself the words of release and then stand back to watch as it all dissolved and died, like the last of the light bleeding out of the sky.

He pulled himself together and stood up, picking up his glass. "Come with me, Stevie", he said, speaking very gently. Stephen looked mutely at him, but obeyed after a second or two. Graham led him outside, and set off round the ground.

They walked halfway round the ground before Graham spoke. Then he halted and took a long swig from his pint. When he turned to Stephen his face was full of sadness and pain, and Stephen suddenly realized what was coming. "N..." he began, but Graham moved quickly to his side, put an arm round his shoulders, and tenderly, almost lovingly, clamped a hand over his mouth. Stephen's eyes moved to look at him. "Better let me have my say", said Graham, knowing he was doing the only thing that was right, and somehow finding himself strong enough to do it.

"I'm offering you your release, Stevie", he said, and removed his hand. It was the supreme act of love and devotion since Stephen had known him, and Stephen knew it. He was a highly imaginative boy, and knew well how much the offer had cost Graham, and he felt his own love for the man ascending new heights as the magnitude of what he was offering assumed its full proportions in his mind. "Don't answer yet, please, Stevie", said Graham softly. "Finish walking round and think about it. I'm going back for a drink. I'll need one for when you get back. When you know your answer come back in the clubhouse and tell me. I shall know, I think, from your face, but you'd better tell me, just to be sure. Go on." He put a hand on Stephen's shoulder and pushed him gently in the direction they had been taking. He himself set off back the way they had come, striding fast back to the pavilion.

There he went to the bar, drained his lager, and bought another pint, and one for Stephen for when he returned. He also bought a treble brandy, and carried all three drinks over to the table they had been seated at, leaving the steward looking after him and wondering what the special occasion was.

As he had expected, he knew the verdict the moment Stephen appeared in the doorway, and he felt a terrible shadow of fear that had settled over him flap briefly and vanish, like a smothering tarpaulin being lifted off him and flung far away out of sight by a howling, cleansing gale.

Stephen approached the table and Graham as if he was picking his way bare-footed across a beach of sharp flints, and slid into the same seat as before. He looked steadily at Graham. "I can't leave you", he said very quietly. "But, oh, God, why can you never love two people? Why isn't there room?" The pain in his voice was magnified by the quiet, even tone in which he said it.

"There's a poem by Ted Hughes", said Graham slowly. "I can't remember much of it, just two lines: 'Crying, You will never know/ What a cruel bastard God is'." He drew in a long, deep breath and let it out. He held the brandy up to the light and swirled it in the glass, watching the light behind it sparking coppery glints in the liquid, then put the glass to his lips and drank it in a single, steady draught. Then he picked up his untouched pint of lager, raised it to Stephen, gesturing with a motion of his head to Stephen to take his. "To us", he said. "I think it deserves a bit of a commemoration." He drank the beer down in a series of long, slow swallows, without taking the glass from his lips. Stephen watched, then copied him.

"What are you two celebrating?" asked Bill McKechnie, who had walked in the door in time to see the whole performance, and come straight over to see what was afoot.

"I've just passed an exam", said Stephen.

"Oh, yeah, course, it's your A's, isn't it?" said Bill. "Congratulations, mate. Lemme get you a refill." He tramped over to the bar, good-natured as ever, pleased at hearing a member of his team's good news, and wondering why the two of them were suddenly seized by a fit of wild, slightly hysterical laughter. He never did know what it was that he had said.

They sat and chatted with Bill for some time, until a few others drifted in and took him away, and Stephen was at last able to ask about Graham's call on Tyldesley. "What happened?" he said.

"Nothing happened at all", said Graham, frowning. "It's a bit of a mystery. I went to all his old haunts, and nobody had seen him, or had any idea where he was. Apparently he hasn't been seen or heard of for weeks. So I went to his home. He's got a lovely place, down near the Albert Hall — he's as rich as Croesus, you know — and that was even odder. I rang the bell, and a young woman answered. Arabic, I think. So, of course, I asked if he was there, and she'd never heard of him, didn't know who I was talking about. Then her husband appeared, and he said they'd rented the place for a couple of months, through an agency, while he was in England on business.

"Well, you can imagine, I was pretty curious, so I asked if I could take the name of the agency, and they invited me in. I couldn't believe it. That place used to be like a cross between Aladdin's cave and a miniature art gallery. He had all sorts of stuff there — I don't know much about art, but I do know he had at least one original Rembrandt — some goddess or other — and a Rubens, and various others, plus all manner of Ming and Meissen porcelain, and I don't know what else. Well, it was all gone. The place was furnished, after a fashion, but it was all new, modern, functional stuff, with as much personality or individuality as an office — admittedly, the managing director of an oil company's office — which is probably what this Arab was. He'd have to be something like that to be able to afford the rent round there.

"Anyway, this couple gave me the address of the agency, and I rang them from a pub. And it seems that Tyldesley's put the place in their hands for a year, and they're in sole charge of it. He's just vanished — disappeared. Blowed if I can understand it. I mean, why would anyone with a beautiful place like that leave it at the mercy of an agency and the tenants? Doesn't make much sense, does it?"

It made plenty of sense to Stephen, but he decided it was the wrong time and place to say so. A little spasm of pleasure ran through him, though, to hear the far-reaching effect Richard's idea had had. It was instantly cancelled out, however, by the reminder of Richard that it brought in its train, and his face crumpled a little. Graham saw, and divined the cause, without suspecting any of the train of thought that had led there. "Shall we go home?" he suggested quietly.

"Yes, please, let's", said Stephen.

"I'll get Bill a drink before we go, though", said Graham. "It was a very kind intention. He can't be blamed for mistaking the kind of exam you meant." They both laughed, and Graham went off, chuckling, to find out what Bill was drinking. Then they went home to Graham's flat, cooked spaghetti, watched some cricket on the television, and went with very mixed emotions to bed.

***

"I've got to go to London again today, dear", said Graham over breakfast the next morning. "I've got to get my green card — car insurance for driving abroad", he elaborated, seeing Stephen's raised eyebrows, "and there are one or two other bits of business I must get done before I go off to France. I want to go and visit poor old Reggie, too. He's been very ill, and I've only been to see him once. He'll be wondering what he's done to offend me. I'll most likely sleep at his place tonight — he's gone home from hospital now, I know.

"Don't look so worried, you ass", he said, smiling at the anxious expression that had instantly come over Stephen's countenance. "The poor old chap's over seventy, and still very frail after hospital. Also we haven't been lovers for years, so there's no need to get jealous, young man. There's nothing to be jealous of. In fact, I hope you'll be meeting Reggie very soon. If we can find a decent place in a nice part of France, fairly quickly, I'd like to invite him over to convalesce, with us to look after him, once we're settled down. You'll like him, of that I'm certain. Anyway, all that's in the future. The long and the short of it is that I reckon I'm going to be in London for the rest of this week. Pity, actually. I'd hoped to go into school every day this week and say my farewells in small batches. But it can't be helped, and I've said goodbye to everyone who matters.

"What I was going to say was", he went on, grinning at Stephen, "that this is an ideal opportunity for you to spend some time with Richard, and try to give him what comfort and peace you can. Don't worry about me", he added, seeing Stephen's expression falter. "I'm not stupid. I know what you've been doing together for the last however long it is. And I'm not the kind who regards an act of sexual intercourse as the be all and end all of a partnership. If I can accept and tolerate your being in love with Richard, which I do — in fact, I've found it a great source of comfort and reassurance, because I know how much it's done to keep you on an even keel while you had to wait for me — if I can cope with that I'm not likely to crack up at the idea of your going to bed with him, am I? Comfort him in every way you know how. He deserves that much, at least, along with a lot more that we can't offer him."

He dropped Stephen at the same place as before, round the corner from the school, and kissed him softly. "I'll see you on Saturday, at the club", he said as Stephen got out of the car. "You'd better make your own way there, because I can't say for certain whether I'll be back on Friday night or whether I'll drive straight there from London. You take care of your sweet self, now, and take care of Richard too. Bye, love." Stephen stood on the kerb and watched him drive out of sight, raising a hand, and seeing Graham do the same as he disappeared round a bend in the road. Then he walked, feeling a little disconsolate, round the corner and into school.

He found Richard toying with revision work on the sixth form balcony in the library. Richard was overjoyed to discover that he had Stephen to himself for three whole days, and they spent the day together, doing a little perfunctory revising, then slipping off to their back-street pub at lunch-time. When it was time for them to return to school they looked at each other enquiringly, and agreed without a debate that they had better things to do. "I'm pretty well finished with my revision", said Richard, justifying the unspoken decision they had just seen in each other's face. "If I'm not ready now I'm never going to be."

"Same here", said Stephen, emptying his glass. "Shall we have another, or shall we go home?"

He saw the answer in Richard's face, and stood up.

**

Over the next three days they hardly slept at all. The hours and days dissolved into one another in a continuous blur of talking, sex, occasional visits to their scruffy pub and even more occasional flying visits to school, to show their faces. Stephen smothered Richard in affection, and Richard, appreciating his motive and loving him for it, responded for all he was worth. They spent untold hours in Richard's room, which began to reek so strongly of sexual activity that on the third day they left it with the windows wide open for the whole of the day to air, and spent the morning in the school library and the afternoon in the pub.

Between their prolonged and inventive sexual bouts they talked endlessly, analyzing what they felt about each other, as the young will, about how they were situated, about everything under the sun. It was Saturday morning before they had stopped to draw breath. "I'll go to the cricket", said Stephen as they stood in the shower washing the traces of their night's activities off each other, "but it's a home match today, so I shan't need to be out very late. I'll ring you as usual, twenty minutes before I'm going to leave, and see you in the usual place."

"But Graham..." began Richard, putting his finger on the flaw in this suggestion.

"Yes, I know, he'll be back", said Stephen, "but I've decided I'm going to spend all my time with you until... until I have to go and join him in France. We owe you that much, Richard, and much more. Graham'll agree with me, I guarantee. He'd have suggested it if he'd thought of it, I know. So I'll tell him after the game, and have a drink. If there's anything I need to know about I may go back to his flat for a short while. But I'll be back here with you before it's late. Oooh! Do that some more", he added with a shiver as Richard began pleasuring him inventively with one soapy hand and one soapy finger.

Graham was already in the pavilion when Stephen got there, changed into whites and propping up the bar with a pint of lager in his hand. As Stephen had predicted, he supported his idea of giving Richard as much time as possible. "Yes, love", he said, not bothering to suppress the endearment, and causing a number of heads to turn in surprise. "You do that. It's a generous thought, and nothing less than he deserves. In any case, I'm going to be up to my eyebrows in odd jobs — you know, tidying up my affairs, loose ends, that sort of stuff. I'll be snowed under next week, as well. I've got to make arrangements with an agent to sell the flat, and fix up an accommodation address, make arrangements with the post office to forward mail, all kinds of things. I'm off on Friday, and I want to take you down to London on Thursday if it's at all possible.

"Yes, things are moving very fast, aren't they?" he said, answering Stephen's expression. "Hovercraft's booked for Friday afternoon. And on Thursday I want to take you to dinner with Reggie. He's fit enough to go out for a short distance, and for a short time, and he was very anxious to meet you. I spent the entire afternoon and evening with him, and I told him the lot. You'll be glad to know we've got his blessing — not that I doubted it, but his opinion always matters to me. I think when you've met him you'll see why, and you'll be glad to have his favourable opinion, too.

"So we'll take him somewhere for dinner — I haven't decided where yet, but I'd like to take him somewhere decent, within reason. Anyway, leave that to me. Then I'll have time to whizz you back here and hand you over to Richard — and I want to make his acquaintance, by the way, once we've got ourselves settled down. And then it's down to Dover and anchors aweigh — or is it chocks away for a hovercraft? I don't know, but whichever. I'm booked in at the Sauvage in Calais for Friday night — I always stay there on my first night, and then I've got the whole weekend to drive to Strasbourg — that's where I'm heading first off. There could well be a job there for me, I think, and I want to get myself fixed up as soon as possible. I've got some money, enough to keep us for a few months, actually, so I don't have to take the first post I'm offered; but I want to feel that we're secure for the first year, which is going to be the tough part, as far as getting used to a completely new lifestyle's concerned. Now, you leave all the arranging and the worrying to me, and have a quick drink with me. Bill's won the toss, and I'll have to pad up in ten minutes."

Graham scored a good twenty against strong opposition that day, and bettered it on the Sunday, when he flayed a fair bowling attack murderously, scoring almost at will in an arc from fine third man to the finest of fine legs for a magnificent seventy-six, in which there was not one chance to score runs from which he did not actually score. "Well", he said sadly as he emerged from the dressing room after stripping off his pads, "if that's my last game I couldn't have wanted a much better one to go out on, could I?" It was undeniable. He received numerous reminders of the jug that it would now be his pleasure to buy after the game, and a lot of generous congratulation, mixed with inquisitive, and barely-suppressed, interest in why it was his last game. As he had decided long ago, when the idea was first conceived, he said nothing to give away their plans.

After that game, Stephen saw little of him for some time. He compensated by seeing Richard for every moment of every minute of the day and night that they could contrive to be together.

He met Reggie Westwood over a sybaritic dinner, and they liked each other enormously, to Graham's proud gratification. After the dinner Westwood dispensed wisdom effortlessly, Stephen drank it in like sand soaking up moisture, and Graham looked on, proud of the impression his two closest friends made on each other.

They got home late, and Stephen felt that he did not dare to ring Richard at such an hour, so he slept in Graham's arms instead. He saw Graham off in the morning, waving till the car was a speck in the distance. Then he went in search of Richard, and devoted the weekend to a two-boy orgy with him. The exhausting rapture was broken by periods of recuperation in which he scored a bright fifty-five not out in an otherwise sluggish draw, and a fizzing little innings of twenty-seven to win a thriller on the Sunday. The following day he began taking his A-level papers; and halfway through the ten day period of his exams, the blow fell.

***

Andrew Tyldesley, although he was not a coward, was not notably braver than most people either. Terry Garrard's methods had frightened him to an extent that shocked him and shook him to the roots. He had prudently vacated his beautiful house within days of the horrifying raid on him, and then he sat down to decide what to do next. He thought seriously about going to the police, but found his courage wanting. He had heard a good deal about the kind of conditions that could be expected in prison, and he suspected that for someone with his looks there would be other horrors in store, of a kind not spoken of in even the more lurid newspapers. He also had a very unpleasant suspicion that blackmail might not be a particularly good offence to be inside for. Knowing that Graham would unquestionably retaliate if he put the thing on an official level, he decided instead to snipe from cover, so to speak.

His investigator required only a single morning, using detective work of the most elementary kind, to establish (1) that Graham had resigned from the staff of the school and left the country (though his destination was not known) and (2) the address and other personal details of the boy he had photographed with him in the Sussex hotel. Tyldesley had this information in his possession the same afternoon, and sat considering two questions. The first was what exactly he could get out of the information he had acquired. In the end he decided that simple revenge was what he desired most, as well as being the only kind of satisfaction obviously available. He sat in his borrowed apartment, thinking how best to turn the information he had acquired to the downfall of his one-time lover, now the target of his obsessive, maniacal hatred.

***

They had woken, deep in one another's arms, and the first thought that came, joyously, to both of them was that neither had a paper to sit that day. They went down for breakfast and said goodbye to Richard's parents, who were both going out for the day. As soon as they had the house to themselves they promptly went back to bed and stayed there until lunchtime.

They got themselves a scratch meal in the kitchen, leaving a large pile of washing-up and a dirty hob where something boiled over, and they were just on their way back upstairs when the telephone rang.

Richard happened to be nearest. "Hallo", he said, giving the number. "Oh. Yes, just a moment."

"It's for you", he said, passing the receiver to Stephen. "It's your dad." Stephen raised his eyebrows. "Oh", he said. "Wonder what he wants. Hallo, Dad?" he said into the telephone.

"Hmph!" he said in disgust when he put the receiver back in its cradle. "They want me to go back. Right now, apparently. Said it's very urgent. He wouldn't say what it was, though. Something to do with UCCA, maybe. I suppose I'd better go, hadn't I?" he said hesitantly, clearly hoping for advice to the contrary.

"Yes, you go", Richard said, disappointingly confirming his own feeling. "I'll just mess about here, and I'll see you when you get back. Hurry back, won't you, though." He put his arms round Stephen and hugged him tightly for a minute, then let him go and followed him to the front door.

"See you in an hour, I should think", said Stephen, setting off. "I can't think it'll take more than that, whatever it is. Bye love."

Richard watched him out of sight then shut the door and went to see what was on television.

**

His parents had evidently been watching while they waited for him, because the door opened as he turned in at the gate, and both of them stood in the doorway, as if to greet a favourite relative returning after ten years in Australia. They were both wearing looks of stupendous seriousness and concern, and parted to allow Stephen into the house like footmen sweeping apart to admit guests to a ballroom. Impatient and irritated as always by them in their more presbyterian moods, Stephen strolled breezily in with a casual "Hi", guessing that this would annoy them more than any other entrance. They closed the door and followed him into the dining room, closing the door of that room too.

"Please sit down, Stephen", said his father gravely. Stephen turned and looked at them, a little puzzled by the portentous expressions on their faces, but not yet anxious. He followed his father's wave and drew out one of the heavy mahogany dining chairs that they had inherited with the vast square table from his grandfather. He rested his elbows on the mirror-like surface of the great table and waited.

His parents took seats at the mid-points of the two opposite sides of the table, so that the three of them formed a triangle with Stephen at the apex, farthest from the door. "Now, Stephen", began his father. "I've summoned you here because we have received some very disturbing — er — information, which requires an explanation. I believe that we have taken an altogether too lax attitude towards the ideas of independence that you have been entertaining of late, and the notion you've recently had that you can just go out and make friends with anyone you please. It seems that you've been associating with some very unsavoury people, who appear to have led you into... into what I must confess I can find no other word for but sin."

Stephen gazed at him, temporarily at a loss for words. He was quite busily occupied by his efforts not to laugh, the impulse which always came most readily in the wake of irritation when his father was being pompous, but his mind was also racing as he tried to think what they could have discovered, and how. He couldn't think of any answers to either, so he waited.

"We should like, please, an explanation of these from you, Stephen", his father went on. He reached across from his seat to a large sideboard, and brought down from it copies of the three photographs of himself and Graham. He slid them over the polished surface, and Stephen looked at them with interest.

Stephen riffled through them, studying each one intently before moving on to the next. When he had given all three an intensive scrutiny he pushed them away, sat back and stared at his father. "Well, what do you want to know?" he asked, softening the blunt words with a quiet voice and a half-smile.

Both parents bridled and looked surprised simultaneously. "What do we want to know?" echoed his father. "I should have thought it was self-evident what we'd like to know. What does this mean, that's what we want to know?" He sorted the photograph of the kiss in the corridor from the other two and held it up, tapping the two in the centre of it with a forefinger to emphasize what he said.

"Christ!" ejaculated Stephen, irritation finally gaining a narrow points win over amusement. "I'm getting sick to death of people taking one glance at that sodding picture and having an instant fit of the vapours. What does it mean? I'll tell you what it means. It means exactly what it says — it's a picture of a man kissing another, younger man. To wit, me. What does it *look* as if it means, for Christ's sake?"

His parents had sat through the brief explosion impassively, with only their tight-compressed lips betraying the depth of the scandalized shock with which they had heard it. "I wanted, and still want, Stephen", his father now said, "to know not what the picture portrays, but what it signifies — a rather different matter. Kindly answer that for us, and if you have learned the language of costermongers from your new acquaintances, please reserve it for use among them. In this house you'll keep a civil tongue in your head, please."

Stephen cocked his head on one side, wondering whether to be brutal or whether to try to soften the blow which, he felt sure, it would be, either way. He decided to soften it. "What does it signify? Right, well, I'll tell you then. It signifies that somebody from the cricket club gave somebody else from the cricket club a lift to an away match, his car broke down on the way back, so the two of them had to spend the night in a hotel, where there was only one room free, and this is them on their way down to breakfast the following morning. That's what it signifies." He fell silent, and waited once more.

His father grunted expressively. "You'll have to do better then that. I think you're being deliberately disingenuous. What's the kiss in aid of?" he pressed.

Stephen considered, and decided that there was nothing for it but to let them have it. He sighed. "The kiss. Well, it's a gesture of affection", he ventured.

"Are you trying to be deliberately insolent?" said his father.

239

"No, I'm not. But I find it a little difficult to be asked to explain a kiss. I'd have thought everybody knew what a kiss was — what it signified."

"Stephen! You will kindly do me the elementary courtesy of not trying to appear dense, and answer my question."

"Okay", snapped Stephen grimly, "if you will have it. He's kissing me because it's an elementary gesture of affection. He feels a lot of affection for me. In fact, he loves me. As a matter of fact", he added spitefully, "he'd just finished screwing me in this room here" — he indicated the door of no. 7 on the photograph — "a few minutes before this was taken. There. You've got it out of me. I hope it's what you wanted, and that it's made you feel better."

His parents goggled at him. He didn't feel very proud of the feeling, but he couldn't help it: the more they radiated horror and dismay, the more powerfully he felt a current of exhilaration thrumming through him. He waited, trying to keep the grin off his face.

"But...but this is frightful", groaned his father eventually, in genuine dismay. "This man is a master in charge of you and other boys at school, isn't he? He's been picking you up and transporting you to the cricket matches all this time", he went on, his expression becoming more and more aghast as further implications of his son's admission struck him. "Are you telling us that all that time he has been seducing you?...."

"Most of the time he didn't need to", said Stephen in mock gravity. "I was hooked within a few weeks. After that it was me who did most of the pushing. He was hanging back because of his position. It took me a hell of a long time to get him into bed, but I managed it in the end." He could hardly contain the laughter bubbling up inside him now.

His father gazed at him, his expression skittering back and forth between horror, disgust, anger and concern. Anger won. "But this is appalling", he said, flushing. "This man must be prosecuted. Molesting boys in his care. I don't know what next. The police must be informed. I shall have to speak with the headmaster immediately."

"No!" snapped Stephen sharply. "He won't be prosecuted", he went on quickly, instantly serious. "He's no longer a master at the school. The headmaster let him resign, and agreed not to take any action, because of my age and the fact that I consented to the affair. And he's not in this country any more — he's left the country for good. I'm joining him as soon as I finish my A-levels."

"He must be prosecuted", said his father decisively. "Not only has he grossly abused his position of trust with regard to you and the other boys, he has also committed a terrible sin, for which he must be punished. Your own views in the matter, and those of the headmaster, are irrelevant. What he has done — and it applies to you also — is against the will of God Himself." Stephen could hear the capital letters.

"Oh, please", he groaned, "you're not going to start dragging in the bloody bible, are you?"

"Be silent", ordered his father, appalled. His mother, who had not yet said a word, let out a soft hiss of fright at the blasphemy.

"There's another reason why you won't be calling in the law", said Stephen, feeling calm and implacable.

"And what may that be?"

"Because it won't do a lot for your image if you're seen conspiring with a blackmailer to persecute someone for being in love, and dragging your own son's name through the same dirt in the process", he said nastily.

"Blackmailer? What blackmailer?" snapped his father.

"Where did those come from?" asked Stephen, gesturing at the photographs.

"They were sent anonymously, presumably by someone concerned about your well-being", said his father. At least he had the grace to look a little shifty as he said it, thought Stephen.

"What was that about being disingenuous?" jeered Stephen, openly hostile now. "Concerned? About my *well*-being? Just who does he wish well to in this case, would you say?" He waited for a moment, then went on, the jeer in his voice more pronounced. "I know who sent those pictures. He's already tried to use them to blackmail us, only we told him to go to hell. Then he tried to use them to get Graham sacked from his job, but Graham was too quick for him. Now he's obviously just trying to do as much damage as he can. And you're mug enough to let him use you as his dupe", he snorted disgustedly.

His parents looked at each other in some perplexity. "We

shall have to talk about this at length", said his father eventually. "In the meantime, you will consider yourself confined to this house. You have further A-level papers to attend. You will be driven to school to sit those, and collected and brought back here afterwards. I don't think otherwise you can be trusted to your own devices."

He sat back and watched the expression of almost amused disbelief on Stephen's face. "I think we must accept our share of responsibility for this outbreak", he said after a pause. "We allowed you a very great deal more freedom than we ought to have done, and I suppose we should have realized that it was possible that that freedom would be abused and turned into licence. We could not possibly have expected it to deteriorate into outright licentiousness as it has. I must confess that I'm utterly shocked – stunned – as well as appalled, to find the path you have been seduced into following. I cannot believe that you found such a path of vice voluntarily. Therefore, you must have been directed into it by a wicked and sinful man, older in years and practised in the ways of vice. For the moment, you will go to your room, and remain there until we call you to discuss the matter with you. I think it had better wait for a while, to allow the very unpleasant attitude of defiance and rebellion to fall from you."

"You're not seriously thinking about trying to send me to my room like a little boy, are you?" gasped Stephen in amazement, staring at his father as if he had grown a second head.

"I'm not thinking about it at all", said his father grimly. "I've decided, and there will be no argument about it." He got up, advanced on Stephen, and dropped a hand on his shoulder.

"You're fucking right there won't be any argument about it", yelled Stephen. "I'm eighteen, which means I'm an adult, and if you think you can treat me like a child you've got another thing coming, as you'll find out before too long." He knocked his father's hand off his shoulder, darted round the table, and shot out of the room.

They caught up with him at the front door. It stuck a little, and he had to wrestle with it for an all-important second or two. He managed to scramble it open as they caught at him, and got halfway through it before they dragged him back into the house. Then, in a turmoil of confusion, disbelief that such things could still happen, and most of all, boiling, incoherent rage, he was lugged upstairs by main force, and locked in his bedroom.

It took him some time to convince himself that it had all actually happened. He sat on the bed and went over it in his mind, working himself up into a passion of bitter rage as he reflected how they must have planned it all before their carefully non-committal request to him to come there from Richard's. He went to the window and looked out, wondering if he might climb down by drainpipes or other aids, but there was nothing to give the slightest handhold. He supposed grimly that if there had been he would have been incarcerated in another room. He sat down again and considered various ways of escape, from subterfuge to outright violence.

After three-quarters of an hour the key turned in the lock, the door opened, and his father, grim-faced, ordered him to accompany him downstairs. When they entered the dining room he saw instantly that they had called in reinforcements, in the shape of the minister from their church. His lips curled in a bitter sneer.

He dropped into a seat close to the door, without being asked, and bestowed a ferocious glare of contempt on all three of them. He decided to open the batting himself. "If you think trundling out the God Squad's going to do your cause any good", he said acidly, "that's just one of the many things you're going to have to think again about." Having delivered this opening salvo, he sat back and glared defiance while he waited to see what they might possibly have to say to him.

"You see, rector", said Mr Hill. "See how he persists in his defiance. You hear how he speaks. This is not the son we had until a few months ago. He seems to rejoice in speaking disrespectfully, almost violently, and in disparaging and insulting everything that was once a part of his own life, and is still a part of ours. I don't know what to do, but I felt that you might be able to bring the boy back to some sense of reason."

"Well, Stephen", said the minister, cheerfully. "What have you been getting up to, to bring your parents round to me in a panic? They seem to think you've been going to the devil. I'm here to see if you can be reasoned with... Can you?"

Stephen had not expected this pleasant, friendly approach, and it took some of the wind out of his sails. But he quickly suppressed the smile that had been on the point of appearing, and resumed his earlier defensive frame of mind, suspicious of everything. "I may be reasoned with", he said, watching the clergyman alertly, "but I'm not to be bullied, or threatened, or imprisoned either. I'm old enough to know my own mind, and to go my own way, and I won't allow anyone to get in my way. I was caught last time, because I wasn't expecting them to resort to downright violence, but you don't catch the same fish twice on the same fly..."

The argument went on for some time, and as it proceeded Stephen watched his father and the clergyman covertly, from under his eyelashes, but alertly, waiting for them to relax in the reassurance of each other's presence.

At length the clergyman sat back and said judicially, as if Stephen himself was not there in the room with them, "Well, we don't seem to be making any headway. The boy seems set on pursuing his new ways, on spurning his parents and dismissing the guidance of his church and the bible with contempt. It's as bad a case as I've come across. I think, perhaps, the police ought to be asked to come into the matter. Stephen appears to be associating with some of the lowest forms of life — not merely perverts, which would be bad enough, but blackmailers and common ruffians as well."

"Tell me", said Stephen, speaking in a soft, deadly voice. Three pairs of eyes turned on him. "Is it an especially serious kind of assault to hit a priest?" he asked. "Because if you" — he turned and addressed the clergyman directly — "ever dare to call certain people perverts again in my hearing, I'll hit you right between your fucking eyes. And if I can't do it, I know people who will."

He had said it calculatingly, guessing that it would cause such shock and consternation that the chance he had been waiting for might offer itself. It did. They turned to look at each other, appalled, and for a split second he was unwatched. He stood up, unobtrusively and fast, and was through the door and into the front hall before anyone had moved. This time he was ready for the sticking of the front door, and he was out in the street before they had reached it. Once free he took to his heels and ran as if the devil himself was after him.

***

"Richard? Thank Christ for that!" he panted when the much-loved voice came on the line. "It's me."

"Where are you?" asked Richard, surprised to hear his friend on the telephone.

"Look, there's no time to explain on the phone. You've got to get out of there, quick. My people will be there any moment, and they're after me. Can you get out and meet me somewhere?" He thought for a moment. "Can you get to that pub we use? I can be there in twenty minutes or less. I've got a fair bit of cash on me, but can you bring my building society book with you? It's in the drawer of the dresser where my stuff is. Just grab that, and then get out. They're in a nasty mood, I can tell you."

"Okay", said Richard, easily. "Though what they can do to me I can't..."

"I'll explain everything", said Stephen hastily. "But get away quick, while you can, and for Christ's sake don't let anyone see where you go."

"I'm on my way", said Richard, and the line went dead.

***

"Golly!" said Richard. His eyes opened wide as he listened to Stephen's account of the scene at his home.

They were sitting at their usual table in the pub. Stephen had swallowed a pint almost in one draught, and was well advanced on his second, watched a little anxiously by Richard. As he described what had happened Richard's expression changed from disbelief to astonishment to indignation and finally to cold anger. "They can't do that, can they?" he queried. "Christ, this is the twentieth century. Don't they live in the real world?"

"No", said Stephen bitterly. "They don't, and I should have known it. I should never have let them con me into going back there like that. But I did, and it's too late now. I've got to get away. I'll have to get away to France as soon as possible. The trouble is, I don't know where Graham is. And another thing — I've got to warn him. He'd just come back thinking everything

245

was perfectly all right and normal, and they're talking about having him arrested. I've got to get word to him not to come back at all." He sat and pondered for a while, then brightened as an idea struck him.

"Look", he said, "he's going to phone me at your place as soon as he's found what he's looking for. Can you stay there, wait for him to call, and tell him to ring me? I know where I can hole up for a couple of days, and he can ring me there. Then I can tell him to stay put where he is, and join him as soon as I've taken my last few..." He broke off in dismay. "Jesus", he groaned. "Of course, that's where they can catch me. They know I've got more papers to sit. They'll just tell the school, and I'll get run in as soon as I show my face there. Oh, Christ! That tears it. I'll have to skip the other papers, won't I?"

Richard stared at him, anxious and alarmed, and ready to help him in any way possible, but not clear what he was talking about. "Calm down", he urged him, "and tell me what you're on about."

Eventually he got it out of him, and sat considering the impasse they appeared to have reached. "What's this plan you've got? Where can you lay up?" he asked.

"That's no problem, in itself", said Stephen. "I could stay in Graham's flat. I've got a key — he gave me one ages ago — and he said I could use the flat any time I liked, to revise in, if I needed somewhere quiet, or if I needed to borrow any of his books. But the point is, they want to catch me, and then they'll find some way of keeping me. I don't know how, or even if it's legal, but that's what they'll try and do. And they know I've got more A-levels to take, so all they've got to do is wait for me at school, and nab me when I turn up there."

"But what'll you do about the exams, then?" asked Richard. "You can't take them anywhere else, can you? And you can't just not take them."

"Of course I can", said Stephen. "I can't afford to take them. It's just too bad. Anyway, what do A-levels matter? Especially as I'll be in France. No", he said incisively, "I'll just have to give the rest of them a miss. It'll only mean missing the last two papers in the English, and who needs an A-level in that? I speak it all right, don't I? I'll have got the French and German, and they're the ones that matter."

"I shouldn't've thought Graham's flat was a very good idea, either", ruminated Richard. "I'd've thought that would be one of the first places they'd look, especially if they get the police involved. No, I don't think that's safe for you. Crikey, I can't think of anywhere that is safe. You can't come to mine, that's obvious." He sat staring into space as he pummelled his brains to think of somewhere. "You could stay at a hotel, I suppose", he muttered to himself, "but that'd cost a lot of money... I know! What about the cricket club? Couldn't you doss down in the clubhouse there?"

"No good", said Stephen, with regret. "That's another of the first places they'd look." They both fell silent, thinking furiously.

"I wonder if I could go to Reggie Westwood's" Stephen ruminated. But he dismissed the idea as quickly as he had thought of it. "No, it wouldn't be fair on the poor old sod", he muttered. "An old friend of Graham's", he elaborated for Richard's benefit. "He lives in London, and Graham took me to see him the other day. But he's ever so old, and he's been very ill. I couldn't go there dragging the police and Christ knows who else with me. It just wouldn't be fair."

"I've got an idea", said Richard, tentatively. Stephen looked up hopefully. "What about that chap at the cricket club? The one who bought us a drink that time, you know, the one time I went there with you? He seemed a decent sort of bloke. Big bloke with a big moustache and a face like the back of a bus."

Stephen sat brooding on it for a few moments, then looked up at Richard with his eyes shining in admiration and gratitude. "Bill", he said to himself. "Old Bill. Yes, why not? He's a good sort — and a good sport, too. He wouldn't give me away to them. Richard, I think you've hit it." He went and got more beer, and came back with his face alight with triumph. "I really do think you've got the answer", he said. "I'll sneak round there this evening, when he'll be there. But there's another thing, too", he added.

"What's that?"

"I'm going to have to burgle my house. There's some things of mine there that I'll have to have. My passport, mainly. I can do without the other things, but I must have that, for when I have to go to France. And I'd like to collect some of my clothes and things, if possible. I don't want to go over there in just what I stand up in. It wouldn't be fair to Graham to expect him to buy me things. I'm supposed to be his lover, not his son!"

Richard's eyes widened in excitement at the idea of a burglary. "I'm on for that", he said gleefully. "You've got to let me help with the burglary. You wouldn't leave me out of that, would you?"

"No, of course I won't", said Stephen, laughing despite his anxiety. "We'll have to be bloody careful, though. Look, here's what I think we do..."

***

When they finished their drinks they went into the town, and Stephen drew the entire balance from his building society account. "There was a bit more than I thought there was in it", he said in satisfaction as he rejoined Richard, who was keeping watch outside. "I've got just over a hundred quid. That must be enough to get me to France. And I'll swipe anything I can find when we break in home tonight, as well." Richard looked a little doubtful. "Are you sure?" he asked. "I mean, I'm only thinking of you, love. Are you sure you want to steal from them, even after the way they've treated you?"

"I'll only be borrowing it", conceded Stephen, who had been wondering even as he said it whether he liked the idea of theft as one of his last actions before going into exile, as he saw it. "Soon as I get myself some sort of a job in France, I'll send it back to them. But I need as much as I can get for the time being." And having thus, with the easy casuistry of youth, satisfied the half-hearted protests of his conscience, he dismissed the matter from his mind for the moment.

They walked together as far as they dared, then split up, Richard to return to his own home to await Stephen's summons that night, and to field Graham's call if it came, and warn him to remain where he was. "And don't forget to get a phone number", Stephen reminded him, already breaking into a trot as he headed for Graham's flat. "I won't forget", called Richard. "And you keep your eyes open. Have a scout round before you go in." Stephen waved a hand in acknowledgement, and disappeared into the afternoon shoppers.

He approached Graham's flat cautiously, ready to take to his heels at the first sight of a police car or anyone who looked as though they might be watching. There was nothing at the front of the flat to alarm him, but he nosed suspiciously round the back, poised for instant flight, and satisfied himself that the flat was not being watched. "Probably never thought I'd have a key", he muttered, letting himself in. The flat was deserted, and he relaxed. He made himself a mug of tea in the kitchen, then curled up on the sofa with a book to wait for six o'clock.

***

"Mrs McKechnie? Hallo. Is Bill in, please? Oh, good. Could I have a word with him, please? It's Steve. Steve Hill. From the cricket club. Thank you very much", he said politely.

After a short wait Bill's Derbyshire accent came on the line. "Hi, Steve. What's up?"

"Bill, I'm in trouble, and you were the only person I could think of to talk to", he said.

Bill was instantly concerned. "What's the trouble?"

"I can't talk about it on the phone, Bill. Can you meet me somewhere, please?"

"Course I can", said Bill without hesitation. "Where?"

"Do you know a pub called the Golden Harp? It's just off..."

"I know it", said Bill. "Surprised to hear you do, though, I must admit. Bit of a rough-house, as far as I know. But yes, I'll see you there. When? Soon as possible? Oh, well, I can be there in half an hour. That all right?"

Stephen blew his cheeks out in relief, glad the waiting was over. He padded through the flat, sparing a moment here and there to look fondly at something that reminded him especially poignantly of Graham, and peering cautiously out of all the windows looking for anything that did not seem to fit the locality. Satisfied, he slipped out and trotted rapidly through the streets, glancing about and tensing himself ready to break into a sprint at the first sign of pursuit. He soon lost himself in a maze of small residential streets, and relaxed into a walk. He reached the pub in a quarter of an hour. Ten minutes later, Bill walked in, spotted him, and came straight over. He saw that Stephen's glass was almost empty, picked it up and shoved it at him. "Knock that back", he said, and took it with him to the bar.

"Now then, what's the problem?" he said, seating himself across the table from Stephen and looking very curious. Stephen took a deep breath. "You know Graham Curtis?"

"Yes, of course I do."

"Well, you know he's... gay?"

"Yes, I know that. He told me about it that time that idiot Colin was talking out of turn. What about it?"

"Well, you remember those rumours Colin was spreading, about Graham and me having something going between us?"

"I certainly do. I bollocked Colin up hill and down dale over it."

"Well, they're true."

"WHAT?"

"Yes, it was true then, and still is. But we couldn't say anything at the time, because we'd have both got into trouble. We had to keep it very quiet, but we've been going together for over a year", said Stephen.

"Well I'm buggered!" ejaculated Bill, staring at him. He thought about it for a minute, and the initial astonishment ebbed out of his face. "Hmmm. I suppose there were signs, if we'd known how to read 'em", he said. He directed a shrewd glance at Stephen, and saw that he was watching him anxiously. "Well, you're both old enough to know what you're doing, I imagine", he said. "Anyway, what's this trouble you're in?"

Stephen breathed a sigh of relief, and relaxed. He suppressed a momentary qualm of doubt about taking yet another person into his confidence, and started at the beginning.

"...so you see, Bill, I've got no choice", he concluded. "I've got to run for it the moment Graham phones to say where he is. But until he does I don't know where to go, so I've got to hide out somewhere. Richard's house is no good, they know I've been living there for months. I thought about Graham's flat — I've got a key. But Richard doesn't think I'd be safe there. There was no-one there today, but they'll think of it in the end. I thought about the club, you know, sleeping in the dressing room. But of course, that's one of the first places they'd think of. I can't think of anywhere else, so I thought of you. I didn't want to drag you into this, and I expect Graham'll be a bit... well, I don't suppose he'll like it much, but I really couldn't think what else to do." He stopped speaking and waited, in an agony of suspense, to see what Bill said.

"Let me get this straight", said Bill, struggling to make sense of the confused narrative. "Your parents are trying to lock you up, with this priest of theirs egging them on. You're going to break in and nick your passport tonight, then you want somewhere to lie low until Graham phones from France to tell you he's on his way home. Then you, or somebody working for you, tells Graham to stay where he is. Whoever it is gets his address and phone number off Graham, passes it to you, and you do a moonlight flit in what you stand up in, and shack up with Graham somewhere in la belle France... Have I got it right so far?"

"Yes, that's it", agreed Stephen, nodding earnestly.

"Well, I must say, I've heard of some hare-brained ideas in my time", said Bill, "but I reckon this one wins the trophy." He looked at Stephen's tense, anxious face and realized that it was not the moment to do what he felt a powerful urge to do, which was to laugh long and hard. He had enough intuition to see that the absurd state of affairs could very easily and swiftly turn into tragedy. He sat for a while, looking curiously at Stephen, and thinking quickly.

"You are over eighteen, aren't you?" he said. Stephen nodded.

"Hmm. Well, as far as I know there's no law against going abroad if you're of age; but somehow I can't help thinking the best I'm likely to get out of this is the worst of it. You're not supposed to be sleeping with Graham, are you? Aren't you too young?"

"I'm not supposed to do it until I'm twenty-one", assented Stephen. "But then, I'm *not* sleeping with him, am I, Bill? They can't do anything to you about that, when he's in France and I'm in England, that stands to reason, doesn't it?"

"Huh", Bill snorted. "Be the bloody day when anything to do with the law ever had any connection with reason. Bloody hell, Steve, I wish you'd asked someone else. I don't know whether I'd be breaking any laws or not, but I wouldn't mind betting they'll bloody soon find one if they find I've helped you out, and it probably carries thirty years in the fucking Tower, or castration,

251

or beheading or something."

Stephen tried to say something, but Bill shut him up. "This business just smells bad. And if it smells bad to *me*, you can bet your life it'll smell a damn sight worse to the goddam police, or the Church Commissioners, or the Committee for Public fucking Morals, or whichever crackpot medieval body I end up being tried", he said. "Christ! Everybody knows if you cross a mean, vicious bastard with a psychopath you end up with a religious maniac who'll string you up by your bollocks for thinking for yourself, and thoroughly enjoy watching you twitch while he claims it was a sad but necessary measure required to save your soul from yourself.

"That's it", he went on lugubriously. "It'll be the stake for me. That's what'll happen to me, you can bet. You really wanna see poor old Bill burnt to the fucking ground?" Stephen shook his head, smothering a giggle despite his anxiety. Bill scratched his head, trying to decide what he should do. "Honestly, Steve, I don't know. I'd like to help you out of a hole. I can sympathize with how you feel and all that, but..." He lit a cigarette and drew on it heavily, sat back and watched the smoke he blew out curling slowly up towards the ceiling. Then he caught sight of Stephen's face. He looked very young and vulnerable, desperately anxious — and yet there was a sort of dignity there, as well. Bill sighed faintly under his breath and made up his mind.

"Okay", he said. "As far as I can see, the only thing I know I'll be doing wrong is aiding and abetting Graham in breaking the law about sleeping with you. Well, I shan't lose much sleep over that. Strikes me as a pretty half-arsed law in the first place. You're old enough to know what you want, or how you're made, or whatever it is that makes you the way you are. And your parents seem to be going off at half-cock in the most extraordinary fashion. Never heard anything like it. I'll do what I can."

He had his reward in the look on Stephen's face, and the heartfelt gratitude in his voice. "Thanks, Bill", he breathed. "I really am grateful, honestly. I'll never forget it. Thanks."

Bill smiled across at him, wondering if he was doing the right thing, but feeling glad he had agreed to help. "Don't worry", he said. "Can't see an off-spinner in trouble and not try and help him out of it. I must say, though, I'd have thought Graham Curtis had more sense than to get himself embroiled in something like

252

this. Christ, he's a schoolmaster, he ought to have seen from the outset that having an affair with one of his own kids was gonna end in tears. Anyway, that's not my problem. I don't want to see you in bother, kid, so I'll do my bit. I'm probably only helping you to make a silly young ass of yourself, but that ain't my problem, either. When you see Graham — if you ever get that far, which I should think is pretty bloody iffy — you can tell him from me that I think he's a pain in the arse, and ought to have been old enough to know better."

"It was my fault", confessed Stephen, miserably. "I pushed and pushed, and wouldn't let him go when he tried to stop it. He kept away from me for two whole terms, but I wouldn't take no for an answer. And then it was just bad luck — well, circumstances. We got put in a situation, and he let his guard slip. If anyone seduced anyone, it was me, Bill. Please don't blame him."

"Hmph! I don't think it's for me to blame anyone", retorted Bill, getting up to go to the bar. "The thing I mind is, I'm about to lose two good batsmen — one of them very good indeed — and my regular off-spinner. Why couldn't you have waited till the end of the season, at least, before going off on this ridiculous adventure?" Stephen stared at his kind, ugly face with its bristly red hair and its big Zapata moustache, and dissolved into an uncontrollable attack of giggles, and then into a series of choking gusts of laughter that made his ribs ache. Bill watched him in surprise for a moment, and then the laugh that he had been trying to bottle up became too insistent to be resisted, and he cracked up over the table.

When they had calmed down Bill bought drinks and sat down again. "Look here, young Steve", he said, trying to keep his laughter from breaking out afresh. "I'll do as you ask, that and no more. I don't want my wife and kids exposed to all kinds of aggravation from the law, let alone bloody parsons. And I don't want your parents coming round with a hatchet claiming I've aided and abetted you in fleeing the country. But I don't like seeing anyone persecuted for their private morals. They're your own affair and no-one else's if you ask me. Yes, all right, you can kip down in our spare room. Not for very long, mind — just a day or so, till Graham rings up and takes you off my hands. Okay?"

Stephen was so moved that he could hardly stammer out his thanks. Bill waved them down in any case. "Now you've got to go and liberate your passport tonight, you say? And some clothes? So you'll be up in the middle of the night, right? Okay, well, I'll leave the back door of my house unlocked, and prime Christine so she doesn't have a fit if she hears you coming in with the milk in the morning, or yell the house down thinking it's burglars — though that sounds like just what it is, by the sound of it, young Steve. That good enough?" Stephen nodded, too grateful to speak. "Okay, then. You know how to find us? You do? Good. Right, well, I'll finish this, and then I'll have to be getting back. Pity about this. I'll have to scratch your name for this weekend, I suppose."

A few minutes later he left Stephen in the pub and went home, wondering how to tell his wife the news.

Stephen immediately telephoned Richard from the payphone in the bar. "Oh, good", said Richard when he heard Stephen's voice. "There's been no word from Graham, but your people have been round, with that sky pilot in tow. They asked my people all sorts of questions, including some about me, which Dad had enough spirit to tell them to mind their own business about, bless him. Fancy, though. As if it wasn't bloody cheek enough to try and dictate to you about your sexuality, they even think they've got some sort of right to poke their noses into mine. It'll be a pleasure doing this burglary tonight, Stevie, sweet."

Stephen told him where he had secured a billet for himself, and gave him Bill's number to pass on to Graham if he should ring, and they agreed to meet in an alleyway at a point between their houses at two that morning. "They're bound to be in bed by then", said Stephen. "See you then", promised Richard, and he blew him a kiss and rang off.

***

Fortune was, for once, on their side. "Graham's rung", said Richard excitedly as soon as Stephen loomed up in the intense darkness of the alleyway. They fell into each other's arms and wasted five minutes on a passionate kiss, as if they had been a continent apart for a year. Then Stephen became businesslike. "What did he say?" he asked, breathlessly.

"He's found a job and a place to live", said Richard. "I've got the address written down, and the number. I told him you were at Bill's, and what had happened — I couldn't go into detail, it would have taken too long, but I got the main things in. And I told him not to come back on any account. He sounded a bit puzzled, but he said he was going to wait there until he got a phone call from you. I said I thought you'd be able to ring him tomorrow, and he'll be expecting a call any time. He said he'd stay in and wait by the phone."

"Great!" said Stephen, vastly relieved. "You did marvellously, Richard." He hugged him, and kissed him with great tenderness. "Now, we'd better get this bit over with", he said, breaking the hold reluctantly. They padded through the streets, making no sound in their trainers.

To their great surprise, the burglary went off without a hitch. Stephen slid his key into the lock, hardly daring to believe that there would be no-one up waiting for him, but the house was silent and in darkness. After a few moments he could just hear a faint rumble of his father's snore from above. He gave himself a few moments to accustom himself to the darkness and get his bearings, knowing that his first sound would signal the end of the mission. Then, taking immense care and moving at a snail's pace, he crept up the stairs, keeping his feet to the outside edges of the treads and lowering them with infinite caution.

He reached his bedroom without mishap, while Richard stood in the garden, straining his ears for the first sound, and conscious of his heart, racing so hard that he felt that it must be audible.

Stephen was so certain that his passport was the first thing his parents would have confiscated that his relief as he found it in its usual place in his dresser came with the force of a physical blow. He slipped it into the back pocket of his trousers. Knowing that he had the only thing that was absolutely vital, he began the riskiest part of the exercise, groping in his drawers and wardrobe for the clothes he regarded as essential. He found jeans, T-shirts, a few more formal clothes, and a lot of socks and underwear. There was more of the same at Richard's house, which he could get at his leisure, but he took as much as he could cram into a big holdall that he got from the top compartment of the wardrobe, his heart coming into his mouth as it scraped and jammed against something. He had to fetch a chair, quivering from tension, and ease it past the obstruction, but he managed it without making a noise.

He crept downstairs, taking even longer than on the way up because of the bulky, clumsy form of the holdall. Once down, he crept across the hall and put the holdall down outside the door. Richard saw, and came over immediately, grabbed the holdall and, following their detailed battle plan, ran silently out into the road and away back towards the alleyway with it. Stephen crept back into the house and, in even greater stealth, went round every place he could think of where he had ever known cash to be left. Once again his luck was good. To his immeasurable elation, he found a thick pile of banknotes in his father's bureau, where he sometimes stowed money if he had more than he felt comfortable carrying about with him. Stephen almost crowed in triumph, and immediately almost died from the realization of what he had almost done.

He carefully scooped up the money and slid it as far down into his trousers pocket as it would go. Then, resisting an almost irresistible urge to cut and run while his incredible luck held, he made himself go round all the other likely places. He was rewarded with a small additional amount of cash. At last he was satisfied that he had cleaned the house out of all the money there was. He made his stealthy way back to the door, slipped out, and took great pains over closing it, using the key to ease the tongue silently into its socket. Then, unable to restrain himself a moment longer, he gave vent to his feelings in a great, joyous bound of triumph down the path, skipped jubilantly into the street, and ran, capering in his triumph, all the way back to the alleyway where Richard was waiting.

They celebrated their triumph with a brief war-dance in each other's arms. Then they set off for Richard's house, where Richard had stowed Stephen's clothes in a holdall of his own — "keep it", he said, "it'll be something to remind you of me."

"I'll never need anything to remind me of you, my darling", said Stephen, meaning it. "No-one ever had a better friend than you."

Richard shot back inside and emerged with Stephen's cricket bag, with the bat that Graham had given him protruding at each end, tucked under the flap. Stephen had forgotten it. "Oh,

Richard", he breathed, trying not to cry, and failing. On second thoughts, however, they decided that it would be an unnecessary burden, so Richard agreed, more than willingly, to take care of it for him, against his return one day.

They set off to Bill's house, each carrying one of the heavy, over-full holdalls. When they reached the house they clung together in the back garden, saying their farewells as best they could. "I've got an exam in the morning", said Richard sadly, "and I must take it..."

"Of course you must", hissed Stephen fiercely. "But I'll be seeing you again soon, don't worry. This is only goodbye for a while, you know. And as soon as we're settled in France, you'll have to come and stay with us. You really must. But I'd better go in now. Goodbye, my darling, and thanks for everything. I couldn't have done it without you, couldn't even have started. You deserve someone better than me, with the amount you give."

But Richard had other ideas. He began fondling Stephen in one of the numerous ways he knew that Stephen was quite unable to resist, and a short while later they made love, oblivious of the discomfort of the situation, on Bill's lawn, hidden from the blind eyes of the house by a large clump of flowering shrubs. Then at last Richard had to go, and Stephen went out into the road to say goodbye. They embraced and kissed, a last, frenzied, desperate kiss that threatened to go on for the rest of the night. They were both crying silently, big, racking sobs like hiccups, that came in spasms and made breathing difficult. Then Richard worked himself out of Stephen's arms, and fled silently into the night. Stephen turned, feeling more desolate than he had ever felt in his life, and feeling also a deep, reproachful glow of remorse, almost of treachery, within himself, and crept in through the back door, left unlocked as Bill had promised.

He groped for a light switch, flicked it, and found himself in the kitchen. The first thing his eye lit on was a note, in Bill's heavy handwriting, propped prominently on the table. *Steve*, it ran, *Help yourself to tea/coffee – things left out for you by kettle. S'wiches in fridge if you want them. Your room's up stairs, second door on right. Hope all's well. Do you want waking? If so put time on this note. Good luck. Bill.* After Bill's name, Stephen was touched to see *and Christine*, added in a neat feminine hand. It was clearly done positively, a small but unequivocal gesture of support, and it touched him more than he could have said. He made himself a mug of coffee and found that he was ravenously hungry, so he ate the sandwiches. Then he used the felt-tipped pen left with the note to write "7.00 a.m. Thanks for everything" on the bottom of the piece of card, and went silently up to his room.

***

Stephen sat looking happily out of the windows of the train as it rocketed through Kent, hardly able to believe that the adventure was proceeding so smoothly.

He had woken with a start that morning, still fully dressed as he had dropped onto the bed a few hours before. There was a fleeting moment of dislocation as he stared round the unfamilar room and wondered where he was. Then he saw Bill looming above him, shaking him briskly, and remembered. "You're a champion snorer, son", said Bill, grinning. "I thought I was never gonna wake you. That were a coma, not just asleep."

"Didn't get to sleep till late", he said, grinning sleepily up at him. "What time is it?"

"Ten past seven. How's the enterprising burglar?"

"All right", said Stephen, sitting up with the instant wakefulness of youth.

"Wish I could still do that", commented Bill. "Takes me half an hour to wake up after a late one."

"I got everything I wanted", Stephen said. "And Graham's phoned, so I'm off this morning."

"Where'll you go?"

"I dunno which station the boat train leaves from. But I'll have to get a train to London. I'll ask at the station here."

"Hmmm", said Bill. "Might be a bit dodgy. They might realize you're doing a bunk, and if they do they're bound to keep a watch on the station. First place they'd look, isn't it?" He stood in thought for a moment. "Look, I'll be going to work in ten minutes. If you can be ready I'll run you in. You can get your ticket when you get there."

And that had been that. He chattered animatedly to Bill as he fought his way through the dense traffic, and thanked him profusely when he got out of the car at Victoria, which Bill thought was where the boat train for France left from. After that it had been easy. It had been the work of five minutes to ascertain that Bill had been right about the station, and that the boat train left in half an hour, at nine o'clock. The clerk had hardly glanced at him as he had sold him his one-way ticket to Strasbourg and taken sixty-two pounds out of the money he had drawn out the previous day. He had fidgeted nervously while he sat on the train waiting for it to pull out of the platform, his eyes darting this way and that in search of familiar faces or police uniforms. But as soon as it eased itself silently away he relaxed, and was almost instantly asleep.

It was only when he woke, halfway through the sunny Kent countryside, that he remembered the money he had "borrowed" in the burglary the night before — though it now seemed as if it had happened in some distant epoch, almost a previous life. He counted the remaining thirty-odd pounds of the money he had drawn out of the building society the day before, and zipped it up again in the breast pocket of his light windcheater. Then he dug deep in his trouser pocket, where he had thrust the burgled money, and brought it out in a crumpled wad. His eyes opened wide as he saw big fifty-pound notes. He dropped his hands beneath the table and counted four fifties, six twenties, eleven tens. Four hundred and thirty pounds. It was a sum beyond his wildest expectations, far more money than he had ever possessed or imagined possessing. He dug in the other trouser pocket, and brought out the oddments he had found elsewhere in the house. There was another fifteen pounds in five-pound notes. He put the fifteen, and the tens and twenties from the big wad, with his own money. The fifties he zipped up in the other breast pocket, making a mental resolution to put them in an envelope and return them to his father before leaving Dover.

His conscience salved to some extent by this resolution, he devoted half an eye to the paper he had bought on the station, while he watched England flying past outside the hurrying train with most of his attention.

Almost before he knew it the train was slowing down on the approach to Dover West Dock. He stood up and got his bag down from the rack. He had spent a few minutes before Bill hurried him out to the car carefully emptying and repacking his belongings, and had found with satisfaction that when his clothes had been neatly folded and compressed they all fitted into Richard's big holdall, so he had left his own behind, and asked Bill's wife if she would telephone Richard and give it to him. Christine, a pretty, down-to-earth young woman from Sheffield, who had mothered him in an unobjectionable manner during the few minutes of their acquaintance, and who was quite clearly entirely on his side in his adventure, had agreed cheerfully.

He got off the train and sauntered out of Dover West Dock station feeling confident and exhilarated. It was the first real adventure he had ever had, and the first time he had travelled alone, and he was determined to savour every moment. He followed complicated signs, looking everywhere with interest, and was soon within sight of the big P&O ferryboat. Following crowds of other travellers, he tagged on the end of a queue passing before some desks with uniformed men in shirtsleeves checking passports. He craned his neck to see what was happening, and saw that a few passports were being inspected and stamped, the great majority simply given a cursory glance before their owners were waved on.

***

"This looks like your boy", said the immigration officer. The Special Branch detective constable on duty at the immigration desk reluctantly took his eyes off the bosomy young woman traveller he had been ogling and followed the immigration officer's casual wave. "Bout five back", murmured the man. He saw a tall, well-made boy with a shaggy mop of dusty-blond hair. He was in his late teens, casually dressed, wearing sunglasses and carrying a bulging holdall. "That's him, for a pound", said the policeman, brightening up at the prospect of something to do to relieve the interminable boredom of watching the movements of undesirables that made up his duties "on ports". "Slow 'em down a bit, Dave", he said. The immigration man nodded, and began to read every passport as if it held a deep fascination.

The Special Branch officer slipped into an office behind the desk, picked up the telephone there and rang the local police.

"Hi. Roger Atherton, Special Branch", he said when the station officer answered. "I think we've got your runaway here." He spoke for a few moments, then returned to the desk. The willowy boy was next but one in the line, looking about him apparently unconcernedly as he held his passport ready to show it. "Okay Dave, thanks", murmured Atherton.

Dave handed back the passport he was affecting to scrutinize and waved the next on without a glance. The boy proffered his passport. Dave opened it and looked up over his shoulder at Atherton. "Stephen Francis Hill?" Atherton nodded.

"Will you go with this officer, please", said Dave, shifting to allow Atherton to open a flap beside the desk. "Just routine", lied Dave, noting the instant tightening of the boy's mouth and the bunching of his muscles. The boy relaxed a little, and went through the door indicated by Atherton, who followed, taking the passport from Dave on the way.

"You're Stephen Hill?" said Atherton, closing the door of the small, stifling office. "Yes", said Stephen. "Is anything wrong?"

"Is your address..." went on Atherton, reading Stephen's address from a small gold-clasped notebook. "Yes, it is", said Stephen. "But what..."

"I'm a police officer", Atherton interrupted him. "We've had a message from the Dover police about you. I gather you've run away from home?"

Stephen took his sunglasses off, feeling that they were faintly ridiculous in the dusty, sunless cubbyhole of an office. Atherton looked shrewdly at him. The deep fear in the boy's large grey eyes was plainly visible. He had even started trembling, Atherton noted. Poor little sod, he thought dispassionately. "Sit down", he invited, waving at a hard chair with a broken strut that stood against the far wall. The boy crossed to it and sat on the edge of the seat, keeping his holdall beside him, Atherton noticed, instantly preparing himself for a possible attempt to make a break for it.

"I'm eighteen", said the boy. Atherton logged the deep, pleasant voice and the well-spoken accent in his mental file on the boy.

"I said, I'm eighteen", repeated the boy. "I'm officially an adult. Have you got the right to stop me for leaving home?"

"Nope", said Atherton. "Not if you're eighteen as you say.

But don't ask me what this is about. I'm only doing the Dover police a favour. They're the people who want you, so you'd better save any questions you've got till they get here. They should be here soon. They're sending a car." He lit a cigarette and leaned against the wall, bored.

A few minutes later, as he had forecast, the door opened and two uniformed constables walked in. "This him?" asked the older of the two. Atherton nodded. "Okay, mate. Thanks very much", said the uniformed man. Atherton nodded, handing Stephen's passport over. "We aim to please", he said, and went back to scanning the crowds of Continental-bound tourists for terrorists, known drug-runners, undesirable aliens and women without bras.

"You're Stephen Francis Hill?" asked the older of the two PCs. Stephen nodded sullenly, glaring at him in mingled fear, despair and anger.

"I gather you've run away from home", the PC said, extracting a ballpoint and a notebook in a dark-blue leather case from the breast pocket of his jacket.

"I'm eighteen, as I've already told your CID man outside", snapped Stephen.

"Him? He's nothing to do with us", chuckled the PC. "Special Branch, he is, watching for terrorists. You've had the honour and privilege of being detained by Her Majesty's Brylcreem Boys, son. Anyway, you say you're eighteen. Got anything to prove it?"

Stephen pointed to his passport in the PC's hand. "If you look in the back of that you'll find my birth certificate", he said. The PC looked, and unfolded a long official form, printed in red. "Hmmm. So you are", he murmured. "Oh, well, you don't count as a runaway then."

"Good", said Stephen, brightening immediately. "I can go, then?" He stood up and picked up his holdall.

"Not so fast, son", said the PC, laying a restraining hand on his shoulder. "There's more to it than that. Will you turn out your pockets, please."

Stephen stared at him. "No, I won't! Not unless you tell me what this is all about. You've seen for yourself that I'm old enough to travel on my own. I'm not some silly kid running away from school or something. What right have you got to..."

"Sonny", said the PC in an ominously quiet voice, "when I ask someone to turn out their pockets, I'm not actually *asking* them at all. It's more like a kinda royal invitation — it's in the nature of a command, see? I mean, what I'm actually doing is *telling* you to empty your pockets, right now, or I'll arrest you and you can do it for the station officer at the nick. Take your pick. Only it just *might* save us a lot of time if you co-operate and do it here, right?" He was watching the boy keenly, and noted a shifty, hunted expression gradually creeping into his face to join the baffled incomprehension there. "I can tell you this much, son", he said. "We have reason to think you may be in possession of a substantial sum of money. Stolen money", he said with an ominous note.

Stephen saw that there was no help for it. He turned out his pockets, laying the contents on the chair. Last of all, very reluctantly, he unzipped the top pockets of his windcheater. The PCs exchanged meaningful glances as the pile of ten- and twenty-pound notes was added to the small pile of belongings, and again when Stephen produced the fifty-pound notes from the other pocket. "I think we'll take care of those for you for the moment, Stephen", said the PC, picking up the money. He counted it quickly, recorded it in his notebook, then turned to the back of the book and wrote again. He handed the book to his colleague, who had so far watched in silence. "Here y'are, Tim. Just countersign it for me, mate", he said. Stephen watched uncomprehendingly as the younger officer signed the book and handed it back.

"Ta", said the older man. He tore out the page and handed it to Stephen. "Look after it", he said. "It's a receipt, signed by me, PC Stanley Hubbard, and countersigned by my friend and constant companion, PC Timothy Metcalfe, for four hundred and seventy-nine pounds in notes, and two pounds and eighty-four pence in change. You'll get it all back against that receipt if we find you're in legitimate possession of it. If you are, which, frankly, sonny, I fear is somewhat unlikely.

"And now, Stephen Hill, I'm arresting you for the theft of money, suspected to be the property of Mr Anthony Charles Hill. I should advise you that you're not obliged to say anything unless you wish to do so, but what you say will be taken down and may be given in evidence. In other words, son, button it and keep it buttoned till we get to the station and get this thing sorted out. You can put the rest of your bits and pieces back in your pockets for now. And as soon as you're ready, your carriage awaits."

It had taken a minute or two for his brain to assimilate properly the subterfuge that his parents had employed to stop him in his tracks. When it finally penetrated, he swung round on the PC who had done the talking and gave him a hard, concentrated stare. "So that's how they did it, is it?" he said in a quiet, cold voice. "My father went to the police and reported the theft of his money, and named me as the thief, did he? The bastard. I knew all sorts of things he was, but I never thought he'd turn out to be a police informer, let alone that he'd grass on his own son. Well, well, well. We live and learn, don't we? Well, it's lucky he's not here with you. Because if he was, officer, you'd be arresting me for breaking his fucking neck."

The PC had been working things out for himself, and thought he saw roughly how things stood. He looked away from the boiling rage and contempt in the grey eyes in some embarrassment. "I must say", he remarked later on to his partner, "if a son of mine looked like that when he spoke about me, I don't think I'd be trying to stop him from leaving the country, even if he had nicked a monkey of my money. I'd say it was cheap at the price!"

What he said for the moment was "Well, I must say, it seems a bit sneaky", he said, "using us to stop you from leaving home. But the complaint has been made, and we're obliged to follow it up. Come on, now. We'd better get back and sort it out. We don't have to hook you up, do we son? Handcuff you, that is?"

Stephen looked at him in horrified anger, then slowly shook his head. "Good boy. Now, if you'll carry the gentleman's bag, Mr Timothy, I'll assist him to his conveyance." He took hold of Stephen's wrist, not roughly but firmly enough, and opened the door.

The crush of passengers for the ferry had dispersed by this time, so Stephen was at least spared the indignity of being goggled at by hundreds of inquisitive eyes as he was led across the concourse and outside, put firmly into the back seat of a police car with PC Timothy Metcalfe for company and driven, in a state of almost incandescent fury, to Dover police station.

BOOK THREE

THE FOLLOW-ON

At Dover police station he was sat in a grimy room and left for some time with only the younger PC, Metcalfe, who was detailed to keep an eye on him. The officer, who was barely three years older than Stephen himself, made several attempts to engage him in conversation, but after meeting with a sullen, scowling silence for the fifth time, he gave it up, unbuttoned his jacket and took off his tie, took a paperback from his pocket and ignored Stephen altogether.

After twenty minutes a lumbering, grey-haired sergeant came in with PC Hubbard, and took a lot of details of Stephen. They went through the entire incident of his arrest. Entries were made in assorted forms, heavy books with numbers on the covers, and more forms. The sergeant, a kindly, slow-spoken Lancastrian, tried to make conversation with Stephen, and got the same reception as Metcalfe until at length he asked Stephen if he was hungry or if he would like a drink. "I'd sell my soul for a pint of lager", said Stephen, hoping to provoke the Sergeant to anger.

The Sergeant, needless to say, was far too old and wise to fall into that. "So would we all, sonny", he said sorrowfully, "so would we all. But I'm afraid the Prisoners' Drinks Kitty's run a teeny-weeny bit low, just for the moment, y'understand. Must be the hot weather we're having. Still, I think the funds'd stretch to a cuppa tea, or coffee, if you prefer it. Actually", he confided, leaning across the battered table and lowering his voice to a conspiratorial whisper, "you wouldn't be able to tell the difference, but we like to give our guests the choice. It makes 'em feel that we're concerned about them, their tastes and preferences, y'know."

This, delivered without a trace of a smile, worked a small chink in the ramparts of righteous rage, wounded dignity and prolonged sulkiness behind which Stephen had taken refuge. He fought a losing battle against the smile that wanted to come up to the surface, and it popped out onto his face, a little lopsided, but visible.

"There", said the Sergeant. "I knew you had it in you there somewhere. You're really very nice-looking when you want to be, lad", he went on. "Much better than glaring at all and sundry. We're only doin our job, y'know..."

In ten minutes he had Stephen chattering almost as if to a friend, in twenty he had succeeded in prising a laugh out of him, and in forty he was telling him stories of prisoners, lunatics both in uniform and out of it, prostitutes golden-hearted and otherwise, thieves he had arrested years before, "when the job was a much more gentlemanly affair than it is now, lad. It wasn't that they weren't just as villainous, or that we were any softer on 'em, but when we hit 'em the boogers never used to complain like they do now..." He had him so spellbound that Stephen felt disappointed and resentful when a sudden commotion from beyond the room caused the Sergeant to jump up with surprising agility for a man of his bulk and go quickly out.

"I'll get you that cuppa when he comes back", said young Metcalfe, who had been edging closer and closer so he could hear the unending fund of anecdotes, and so emollient had the elderly Sergeant's effect on Stephen been that he forgot his refuge of sulks and smiled at Metcalfe before he could stop himself.

After a while Hubbard returned, however, with the unwelcome news that he would have to be locked up for a while. "Not long, son", he said, "the Herts boys should be here in an hour to take you home."

"Home?" queried Stephen, surprised.

"Well, your home town", said Hubbard. "Your local nick. That's where you'll be charged — if you're charged at all. If you want my opinion, you won't be charged. I got a strong suspicion your old man's using us as cut-price truant-catchers. It would never surprise me if he decided he wanted you stopped, called the local law in and found you were of age and couldn't be legally stopped from going where you wanted, and then had a brain-wave. Oh, thinks Dad, so the little bugger can go swanning off to gay Paree, can he? Well, not with my loot, he can't. So he makes a complaint to the local boys, who have to act on it, theft of a lot of cash and a stone-bonk suspect. We nick you, Hertfordshire come toiling and sweating down here to give you a nice taxi-ride home courtesy of the taxpayer, and then, when you get home, all Dad's gotta do is withdraw his complaint and there's one nice conviction for the crime figures gone for a shit.

"So you and your ideas of independence get it where the chicken got the chopper, Dad's got you home where he can keep a fatherly eye on you, and he's got you there free of charge, he's got his money back, and all in all, Dad wins all round. Does he care about our clear-up rate sufferin to the extent a one desperate master-burglar goin scot-free instead a languishin in a dungeon as he ought to, or about all that valuable diesel Herts are burnin at this very moment, floggin their motor round the M25? Does he buggery!"

And so, by the time he had to endure an hour's claustrophobia in a dingy, rather smelly cell, Stephen's animosity towards the police had largely been dispelled.

It was not by any means the same where his parents were concerned. Towards them, and especially his father, his feelings were still the bitterest possible.

On the drive home he managed to remain calm, and even retell a few of the kindly Sergeant's tall stories to the two young Hertfordshire officers in charge of him, and had the satisfaction of an absorbed and appreciative audience.

When they reached his local police station it turned out to be exactly as Hubbard had sardonically forecast. The complaint of the theft of the money was withdrawn, and he was allowed, at last, to go, under lynx-like watchfulness and a heavy hand on his shoulder from his father. By the time they arrived home, it was late in the afternoon. Stephen had had very little sleep after the late night adventures of the night before, followed by a long journey; all this, together with the accumulated strain on his nerves of all the events of the last few days, had finally brought him to a pitch of exhaustion approaching collapse. He wolfed a light meal, while his parents stood over him watching for signs of rebellion, and when he was then banished to his room he had not even enough spirit to protest. He flung himself down fully clothed on his bed, not even troubling to kick off his trainers, and was asleep so quickly that he never even heard the key turned in the lock.

He slept for thirteen and a half hours, waking at seven-thirty the next morning. He discovered the locked door quickly enough then, when he tried to get out to empty his bursting bladder.

"Hey", he bawled at the top of his voice, kicking savagely at the panels of the door with the flat of his foot. "Lemme out, d'you hear? Lemme out! Or shall I piss out of the window, you bastards?"

As he stood there in fast-mounting discomfort which he was powerless to relieve, his feelings for his parents were altered by a seething fit of passionate temper; from fallen illusions and a kind of vague, generalized awareness of incompatibility, for a few moments they mutated into something very like hatred. The events of the day before felt as if they had taken place in a different age or another life, and already seemed to have taken on the distorted, surreal character of nightmare, almost as if they had been happening to someone else, with him as an impersonal, disembodied observer.

There was nothing surreal or disembodied about the state of his bladder, however: it was rapidly becoming an emergency. He thumped and kicked and yelled again, and redoubled his efforts when he heard footsteps coming up the stairs. The key turned in the lock and the door opened to disclose his father, grim and forbidding. Stephen's discomfort was too desperate for him to worry about, or even notice, how his father looked, however. He shot through the door like a greyhound bursting from its trap, almost bowling his father over, squirmed past him, and flew in a single bound into the bathroom, fumbling to get his zip down as he flew. With one of the odd little quirks the mind plays sometimes, he remembered quite clearly afterwards the thought coming cleanly into his mind, even in the frantic desperation of the moment, that if his mother was on the lavatory when he got there he would piss in the basin, if not in the bath. He even remembered his quick flash of amused surprise that his mind

should be capable of thinking such a thing, with such delibera-
tion, in such a moment of panic.

His father took a couple of furious paces after him and stood
at the bathroom door, ready to hurl it open and administer an
angry reproof. But hearing the powerful stream hitting the water
in the bowl, under great pressure and seeming to go on and on
for ever, he acknowledged that perhaps the urgency had been
desperate, and relented. He waited, silent and still deeply
incensed at what he had heard, on the landing.

When Stephen came out, enormously relieved, his face still
flushed from the terrible strain of holding himself in, his father
made the second instant change of plan in the space of those few
minutes. It had been his intention to take Stephen by the collar
and march him downstairs to the tribunal awaiting him; but even
as he stepped forward he dropped his hand to his side and
merely motioned Stephen to follow him. He could not have said
precisely what he had seen, but there was something in his son's
demeanour, or perhaps in the way he carried himself, which,
though he would have cut a hand off rather than admit it, caused
him to flinch slightly inside, and to back away half a pace.

Stephen did follow him downstairs, though it was for his own
reasons. He knew that there was certain to be some sort of
reckoning before the day was out, and he had already decided in
general terms how he intended to handle it. His father went
from the foot of the stairs and stationed himself in front of the
front door, standing with his legs apart and braced and his arms
hanging by his sides, ready for instant action if Stephen was
thinking about making a break as he had before. Stephen glared
at him as he swung round and entered the dining room.

He threw the door back with a crash as it hit the heavy
doorstop and rebounded. He stamped into the room, still
feeling mortified by the indignity of his enforced dash to the
bathroom under his father's eye, and in the foulest of tempers.
He barely glanced at his mother, sitting at the far side of the big
table, and dropped into a chair at the farthest point from her.
His father came in, pulled the door to, locked it and pocketed
the key. This at last elicited some response from Stephen. He
laughed, a short, unpleasant, sneering yap of a laugh. Then he
sat back and looked round at the two of them, one after the
other, meeting then holding their eyes and enjoying watching

them colour under his baleful stare.

"Well, Stephen", began his father after a long, awkward pause. He had succeeded in suppressing his anger. "It's rather difficult to know quite where to start. I suppose, first of all, I'd like to apologize."

This wasn't at all the beginning Stephen had been expecting, and it took a good deal of the wind out of his sails. He simmered down a little, and waited.

"For two things, really", went on his father. "First of all for locking your door last night. I don't imagine you were even aware of it then, because you were snoring almost before I'd got the door shut. You must have been quite exhausted, of course, I realize that. I'm sorry you had to wait to get to the bathroom just now. It looked as if the case was rather urgent." He grinned faintly, somewhat to Stephen's surprise, for he was normally a little prim about anything to do with bodily functions.

"I'd like to explain about that in a moment", his father continued. "Before I do, I think I also owe you an apology, and a rather bigger one, for what happened yesterday. It didn't need a mind reader to see how you felt about it, and I must admit, it was hitting well below the belt. I'd like a chance to explain that too, if you'll allow me to, Stephen."

Stephen stared from him to his mother, who gave him a rather strained smile. He had been expecting almost anything except this, and it took more wind from his sails. He fidgeted, the portentous frown of ill-humour that he could feel settled firmly on his face beginning to feel faintly ridiculous. His brow cleared a little, and he nodded uncertainly. "Well, I... er... well, thanks", he said, a little grumpily. He felt that it wasn't quite playing the game to disarm him in this unexpected fashion when he had come in quite obviously spoiling for war. "I, er, I rather wanted to do some apologizing myself, actually", he said awkwardly.

"All right, Stephen", said his father. "Let me get mine over with first, though, eh?" Stephen nodded. "Well, then, to begin with the locking of your door, I did that simply because I wanted to make sure I got a chance to talk to you. I think that, however the various things we've got to discuss today turn out, you owe us that much. I mean, you owe us at least the chance to talk. We may not find ourselves in agreement, we may find that we can't actually resolve anything. It may be that the talk does no good, achieves nothing. But I do think we're entitled to the chance to find that out — even if it turns out to be the hard way, don't you?" Once again he surprised Stephen with a brief half-smile. Stephen found himself hard put to it not to respond. "I... yes", he said, hesitantly.

"All right. Well, we did try to talk to you about... ah... about recent developments the other day, but you didn't give us a lot of chance then, I think you'll agree. I blame myself as much as you for that. I thought that having the rector there might help in persuading you to unbend a little. That, I now accept, was a mistake. Anyhow, feeling as I've explained, that we were owed that much, I wanted to make sure I got a chance to collar you before you decided to make another run for it.

"And that, of course, brings us to yesterday's fiasco. Well, I could see clearly enough what you thought of me for setting the police after you like that, and I suppose if I'd been in your shoes I'd probably have felt much the same. I'll tell you what happened.

"We realized very quickly that you'd gone, and from what you'd said, I thought it was pretty certain that you would try to get abroad. I did a little checking, and found that you were not in any of the places you might normally be expected to be found in. So I did the only thing I could think of, and went to the local police.

"It was faintly amusing, I suppose, in a way. I tried first of all to report you missing. Well, the first thing the policeman said was 'How old is he?' I said you were eighteen, and he said 'He's an adult, then. Nothing we can do', before the words were out of my mouth. I tried to explain that we urgently needed to discuss personal problems of a private nature. 'Mentally disordered, is he?' he said. Well, I suppose I got rather indignant at that, but then he explained that unless you were of unsound mind your being eighteen left them with no power to stop you from going where you pleased. 'Either that or if he's committed some offence', he said, just as I was turning to go. Well, Stephen, I'm afraid it rather put ideas into my head.

"'Suppose he has committed an offence?' I asked. 'Well, has he?' he said. He didn't seem to want to discuss hypothetical cases. 'Well, yes, he has', I said. 'He's stolen some money. Rather a large sum, actually.' So then he asked for details, and when I'd explained that I had no idea of making the matter official, he said 'Well, sir, if you really want him stopped, just so you can talk to him about his problems at home' — the man seemed to assume automatically that the problems concerned us, which rather nettled me, I must say, but that's by the way — 'if you really want to spike his guns, you could play dirty, hit him below the belt, like, and lay an information concerning the theft of this money', he said. And, to cut it short, that's what I did.

"I hope you'll accept my word for it, Stephen, I had no intention of having you charged with theft. It really was merely a subterfuge to stop you before you got out of the country, so that we could have this talk. I'm not altogether proud of having resorted to it, but we were, naturally, very worried, so... well, I felt that the end justified the means. I trust that you'll understand that."

Stephen sat in thought, watching his father's face covertly from under his lashes. "I understand, Dad", he said eventually. "Actually, the policeman at Dover guessed all that. He got it dead right, too", he marvelled. "It's amazing. He knew exactly what had happened. I wonder how he knew."

"I dare say it's not the first time such a ploy has been used", said his father. "I don't suppose there's much that's new, to a policeman. Anyway", he continued, "what the policeman here suggested was exactly what we did. He would contact the Kent Constabulary, who would stop you, thinking they were detaining a suspect for theft, and then, when you were brought back here, I could simply quietly withdraw my complaint over the theft, and that would be that. As I say, I'm not very proud of what I did, but there it is.

"Now I'd like to move on to the next logical step, which is, of course, the money. I must confess, Stephen, when I found that money missing I could have...well, let's say I was very angry indeed. I suppose if you were setting off on this desperate venture, perhaps you needed more money than you could readily lay your hands on, but do you really feel that it justified theft — especially of such a large sum? Nearly five hundred pounds?"

Stephen looked shamefaced. "N-no, Dad. That's what I wanted to apologize for. I wouldn't have kept much of it, I promise you. I didn't know how much there was there, you see, until I was halfway to Dover on the train. I came in here in the dark, and just grabbed it and stuffed it in my pocket. When I counted it I nearly fell off the seat, when I saw those fifty-pound notes. But I would have sent most of it back straight away, Dad, honestly. I had the fifties set aside in a separate pocket, all ready to send back as soon as I could get an envelope and a stamp. And I was only intending to borrow the rest. As soon as I got to... where I was going, I was going to send back whatever I had left, then, as soon as I got a job I was going to send back whatever I'd spent. I didn't think it counted as theft. That's the truth."

"All right, I believe you. I still don't think it was in very good principle, and as far as the police are concerned it certainly does count as theft. Even taking from someone who would have given consent if they'd known can be construed as theft, according to the police. But all this is by the by. If you're willing to accept my explanation and apology over the locked door and the — ah — somewhat underhand way I employed to stop you, I'm quite happy to accept yours over the money. I'm not really very worried about the money in any case.

"The real matter for discussion is this business of this... this homosexual relationship with this schoolmaster, may God have mercy on his unfortunate soul, because I find it very difficult to find much for him in mine, I'm afraid.

"You must realize, Stephen — and I'm sure you do realize — what a terrible shock it was for us to discover this fact — if it is a fact — about our son. Especially to find out in such a brutal and shocking fashion. If you can't imagine that you're not the imaginative boy I've always believed that you were." He hesitated. "Speaking for myself, I'm more than ready to believe that it is in fact nothing more than a... a... some sort of phase that you will forget in time — very likely in no time. It's a phase many young people go through at school — they hero-worship an older boy or a master, or some figure to whom they look up, and that's what we hope is the case with you. In a short time, perhaps, you'll have forgotten this silly affection, grown up and moved on to more manly concerns. Perhaps you will come to see it as just an infatuation, and get it out of your system.

"On the other hand, well, obviously the possibility has to be considered that it's more than that. I hope not. With all my heart I hope not. If you do turn out to be...that way...well, I'm afraid

I don't think I'll ever really be able to say I like the fact. There's another thing. We've had to accept the fact, your mother and I, very reluctantly, that you no longer share our faith. I'm very sad about that, and so is your mother." He looked at his wife for support, and Stephen followed his glance. She was staring down at the table-top in front of her, and had not so far contributed a word to the discussion. Becoming conscious of the silence she looked up, and nodded, looking very unhappy. After a moment she dropped her head and resumed studying her reflection in the brilliantly polished surface of the table.

Mr Hill looked at her in some distress for a moment, then, with a visible effort, turned back to Stephen. "This is very difficult for us, Stephen. I expect you can understand that. You have, at least for the present, lapsed from the faith. Well, it's something that happens, and it's no good brooding about it. We both hope very profoundly that one day you may rediscover God. If you do, of course, you don't need me to give you a sermon about it. But if you don't, well, it's happened to many other families, and there's no need for it to become a cause of dissension, given good will on both sides. I'm sure we'd be able to come to an accord with you. But try to think, if you will, how this homosexuality business appears from our point of view.

"Maybe you are thinking of us as old-fashioned fuddy-duddies, stuffy, or strait-laced, from your new position — lapsed from the faith, finding a new independence and, by the look of it, enjoying it, growing away from us, your family. Well, we always realized that it might happen. Perhaps no parents can be expected to enjoy it when their children grow apart, but it's part of growing up and growing old. But homosexuality is something rather more than just part of growing up. It is, remember, utterly, and absolutely, forbidden by our faith. It's not just a matter of preference, one way or the other. To us, it is a sin, a mortal sin, jeopardizing your soul. I don't want to go on about this. There's no point. If you still shared the faith I wouldn't need to be saying any of this, and since you apparently don't, what I have to say about the matter is irrelevant. It just makes me very sad. But that doesn't get us very far.

"That, you now see, I hope, is why we felt that we *had* to have this opportunity for this talk before you did something irrevocable."

Stephen started to say something, but his father motioned to him to wait. "Just a little longer, Stephen, then you can say anything you like. But please let me finish what I've got to say. It's not easy for me to talk to you like this. Maybe I ought to be less reserved about these things, like the modern generation of parents are said to be. Maybe I've always been too reserved about intimate matters like this. Perhaps if I'd been able to talk about them more easily when you were younger you'd never have fallen under the influence of this man as you appear to have done. But we are as we are.

"I know you were very angry about what happened yesterday. Perhaps you still are, though I hope not. Your brow doesn't seem quite so thunderous..." Again there was the faint little smile. Stephen, who had dismissed his sulky mood as ridiculous and unworthy long ago, responded with a slightly less faint one. "Good", continued his father. "I'd like to try to explain, Stephen, how we've felt about you. It's never seemed necessary to explain it before. But lately you seem to have moved so far, and at so fast a pace, away from us and most of the things that we'd always thought bound the family together, that maybe it does need explaining. Maybe it always did, come to that. I don't suppose we've been perfect parents, any more than any other pair of parents. But this is how we've always tried to feel.

"It's quite simple, Stephen. We loved you. You may have found it hard to believe on the odd occasion — I expect most children do. But yes, we loved you.

"Everything we did, we tried to do with you and your interests in mind and at heart. We always wanted what was best for you. Often it may have seemed otherwise to you, but that's in the way of things. Children often feel that they know best what's good for them. You were, naturally, no exception. But whatever we did, we considered its effect on you, and for you, and chose as wisely as we were able. Parents often see more clearly than their children what's for the best for their children, while the children see only with the limited wisdom of youth, and the lower horizon that their children's stature gives.

"We brought you up in the church. That was partly because we wanted you to grow up and mature into wisdom in the ways of the Lord. That seemed, and still seems, to us, to be a most sensible and good thing in its own right. But it was also in the

277

belief that, when we were gone, you wouldn't be left bereft and alone, but would still have someone at your side, to guide and counsel you in times of trouble or when you were confused and afraid.

"Like all parents who bring their children up in their own faith, we recognized the possibility that you might, one day, apostasize. We hoped greatly that it would never happen, but we acknowledged that it might. If it happened, we thought, you would still be the son we brought into the world, reared and loved, and we would, we felt, be able to come to an accord, an understanding, with you. But at least, we felt, we would have done what we could to give you the chance of living and growing in the love of God. And when you made your decision a while ago that you no longer wished to communicate, well, we accepted it as best we could, because we recognized that it was a very private matter, for you and you alone. We were both hurt by the decision, but we had no alternative to accepting it, so we accepted it, with the best grace we could.

"And then we found out, to our utter horror, about your affair with this wicked man. And because we wanted, as we had always wanted, what was best for you, we decided that we had to put a stop to it. We could see, when we tried to talk about it the other day, that you saw only what you wanted, and, naturally — we didn't hold it against you — equated what you wanted with what was best for you; but we could see that what you wanted and what was best were two different things entirely — indeed, they were opposites, as we saw the matter. So you see, Stephen, we had to try to stop your relationship with that tragically misguided but nonetheless wicked man.

"People talk about seeing their child stretch out its hand to pick up a live coal. Well, what we saw was worse by far than that. We had to contemplate the terrible prospect of watching our child stretching out his hand to mortal sin, looking at it from the point of view of one in the faith; even disregarding the faith, which is not easy, of course, for us who have it, we were at least watching our child stretching out his hand to something that was illegal, socially utterly unacceptable, and, partly because of those things, almost certainly doomed to end in terrible unhappiness. What could we do, I ask you, Stephen, but what we did? What could we do but try to stop you?

"And so we got you back here, and I say again, I greatly regret the methods I had to use, so that we could at least have the talk we felt you owed us. I'm sorry to have turned it into a great monologue like this, but I've nearly finished, and then I'd like to hear anything you want to say. If it turns out that this talk, that we wanted so anxiously to have with you, doesn't actually achieve anything tangible, it still won't have been wasted in our view, because at least we may find it easier after it to come to the sort of accord, or understanding that I spoke of. The one thing I beg of you is to have no more of this affair with this man. Looked at in the very best light possible it's an absurd infatuation taken to ludicrous extremes. If by any chance it's any more than that, it's wicked and immoral looked at from one point of view, and even if you don't happen to share that point of view, it's in any case potentially desperately dangerous.

"That's just about it, Stephen. As I said, I'm sorry it turned itself into a lengthy sermon, but I wanted desperately to put your mother's and my own point of view to you, to try to explain the devastating sense of shock and horror that we were reeling under when we found out about this business. Now, please, tell me how you feel about what I've been saying."

Stephen sat back in his chair and looked at his fingernails, taking his time thinking about what he wanted to say.

"Well, first of all, Dad", he began at length, "thanks for being so reasonable. I really am sorry I took that money..." His father dismissed the matter with a gesture of his hand. "Well, I'm very glad you've been so decent about that. I really was going to repay it, but in a way I'm glad it's been sorted out the way it has.

"I'm sorry too, in a way, about doing a runner yesterday. I did it because I thought you would feel as you do about Graham and me. Admittedly, I thought — I was sure — you'd take a much harsher line, but I was pretty well right about how you'd see us. In a way, I'm even glad you managed to catch me before I got away, because this way, at least we get the chance of a clean start.

"There are several other things you said that I'd like to comment on. You're right about the church. I have lost the faith. Or rather, to be honest, Dad, I never had it. I always did think it was — well, there's no point in hurting your feelings for the sake of it. I never have believed, not really, not deep down, underneath. But even if I had believed, I should think the church's attitude to people like me would almost certainly have killed it off. Christianity ought to be tolerant and liberal if it's anything, and I'm afraid it's not, Dad, not at all. Not where gay people like me are concerned, anyway. I couldn't tolerate that in anything I belonged to. So I'm afraid I'm going to stay lapsed.

"Another point. You said an awful lot about children, and me being a child with a child's point of view. Well, I'm not a child, or anything like a child. I'm legally an adult, and I'm mature in every way — I mean, I know I'm going to get more mature, emotionally and so on. But I'm physically, sexually and emotionally mature enough to know what I am.

"So, granted that I'm mature in all those senses, I ought to know what my sexual orientation is. As it happens, I do know. I'm gay. Homosexual. And given that fact in turn, I ought further to know it when I meet someone and fall in love with him. And that's what's happened. It's not an infatuation, Dad, nothing like one. Graham told me somebody said that if you're really gay you have to be able to fall in love with another man, not just have sex with him. Well, that's me, Dad. I've known for ages, but I've never said anything, because I'd heard the odd word at the church from time to time, and I realized what view the church would take of it. There didn't really seem a lot of point.

"The point is, I do love him, and when I'm settled with him, it'll be just as much a marriage as if I'd settled down with a girl — except for the one thing, that we shan't have your blessing or approval. Well, I've got a feeling from things Graham's said that gay people get quite used to getting by without people's approval."

He fell silent, and waited, watching his father to see his reaction. He had dropped the reference to his settling with Graham deliberately into the conversation, to test the water. His father pursed his lips in concern. Eventually he looked levelly at Stephen, and said, "Look, Stephen, as far as settling down with this man is concerned, I'm simply not willing to countenance it. I've found that the law states that such a relationship is legal when you reach twenty-one. Well, possibly if you were twenty-one, I might feel otherwise. But at your age, I don't feel you should make up your mind irrevocably. No, I'm not willing to accept it. In anything else we're ready to let you have your head and go your own way. We found your growing apart from us less painful than we had expected, because it gave us much more time to develop our own lives, follow our own pursuits. We were surprised, to be honest, though not altogether disagreeably. So, if you want to spend half your life at the cricket club, fine. If you want to live at Richard's, fine, do that. But as to your running off to the Continent to live with this man, no, Stephen, I simply will not hear of it. You can do, within reason, what you like. But I expect to see a little of you from time to time. You're still our son, and we miss you, often. It would be pleasant to see something of you. And if it ever comes to my knowledge that you are having dealings with this man again, I shall immediately go to the police and tell them everything I know of this relationship — with the photographs we were sent. That will assuredly result in this man's immediate arrest in France, extradition and prosecution here for his illicit and immoral sexual relationship with you. It may even end in your being prosecuted for your part in the same relationship. I'd hate that to happen, but I'd sooner see you in court than in bed with this man, Stephen, and I owe it to you to be honest about it.

"I'm sorry to have to do that to you, Stephen, but I shall do it without a qualm of conscience, because I feel certain that he deserves nothing better." He sat and watched Stephen for his reaction. Stephen, however, had schooled his features to a careful neutrality, and he learned nothing of what the boy was thinking.

"You know those photographs came from a blackmailer, Dad", he said, without spite. "How do you feel about making use of material from a source like that?"

"Not altogether comfortable, to be honest", confessed his father, surprising Stephen yet again. "But there are occasions, you know, when one may, I think, legitimately take the view that the end justifies the means. Or one might even suspect the hand of providence in the matter: good coming out of evil. I simply cannot abide the thought of you, living and...and...of you living with that man. If you take my advice, you'll put him and his corruption out of your mind and spend more time thinking about girls."

"Girls!" exclaimed Stephen, mortified. "Dad", he went on after a pause, trying to sound patient. "I don't...er...Let me see. How should I put this? Girls are not something I think about. I'm not...I'm not made that way."

"Oh", said his father, his jaw dropping slightly. Stephen suppressed a mutter of impatience, wondering how it could still come as any sort of surprise. "Well", continued his father after a brief pause, "if you don't want to think about girls, think about cricket, instead. Now I must go. I'm going to be very late. Here, take this", he added, taking an envelope from his pocket. "It's your own money. I took the liberty of tearing up the train ticket you had, so I thought the least I could do was to reimburse you for it, and...I've added a litte extra as a top-up", he added, shyly once again. He hurried out of the room, leaving Stephen staring after him. A few minutes later he heard his father's car roar out of the drive.

He looked in the envelope, and his eyes opened wide in amazement. It contained the thirty-six pounds that had remained of his own money, and even the 84 pence in change. There were also two of the fifty-pound notes, and one of the twenties.

"He's being jolly decent about this", Stephen said, turning to his mother for the first time. "After I went and pinched it, too. Returning good for evil."

His mother looked up. "Your father's a very good man", she said simply. And then it was her turn to astonish her son. She got up from where she had sat silently throughout the lengthy conversation, walked quickly past him, taking exaggerated care not to come into contact with him, and left the room without a word, leaving him rooted to the spot, staring after her wide-eyed. After a moment, he shrugged, and walked out of the room himself, slipping the envelope into his pocket.

He went upstairs and fetched his holdall. Then he looked for his passport. He found it quickly, in his father's desk in the room he used as his study, and slipped it into his pocket with the envelope containing his entire worldly wealth. Then he picked up the holdall and went into the hall. On an impulse he went back into the study and swiped a sheet of paper, and took it into the dining room. From long indoctrination, he automatically took a heavy table mat to press on to avoid marring the albedo-like polish on the table, and wrote *Dear Dad, Thanks for being such a good sport. I'm deeply grateful. You're very good, and much kinder than I probably deserve. Love, Steve.* He propped it against the silver cruet set in the middle of the table and left the room, closing the door softly behind him. Then he left the house and started walking in the direction of Richard's. He did not say goodbye to his mother.

***

The first thing he did was to call at a corner shop and change ten pounds, asking for five pounds worth of fifty-pence pieces. Then he found a telephone box, fished out the scrap of paper on which Richard had noted Graham's address and telephone number. The police had missed it when he was searched, an irregularly torn-off fragment of grubby paper attracting no attention. He fed some of his coins into the meter and dialled carefully. When the familar voice came on the line he gasped with relief. "Oh, Graham", he almost sobbed. "I'm so glad to get you."

He gave Graham a quick summary of everything that had happened, and they had a few moments to exchange endearments before he had to put the last of his coins in. "I'll call you again in a little while, darling", he said, panicking in case the money ran out before he could get all he had to say out. "I've got to think how to work things at this end. I've got to make sure I can still stay at Richard's, too. I'll have to explain what's happened. I'll ring you later today, okay?"

Graham just had time to say "Okay. I'll be here", and then the line went dead.

He rang the bell at Richard's house and waited, but there was no-one at home. He knew Richard was sitting an examination paper that morning, so he went round the house into the back garden. There he sat on a bench and went over in his mind all that had happened to him over the past two days. And then, without any warning or preamble, he started to cry, a bitter spring of hot, painful tears. They were the last tears he ever shed as a boy, perhaps the first he ever shed as a man.

***

"Well, yes, I agree, he has been pretty decent about it in general", said Richard as they lay curled up together after the first joyous

283

celebration of their reunion. "But he was completely in the wrong when he threatened to drop you both in the shit with the police. That makes him no better than that bastard Tyldesley. Jesus! He's even willing to use Tyldesley's photos to do it. But that's beside the point. The point is, what are you going to do now? Have another go?"

"I don't know", confessed Stephen, arching his back and arousing Richard expertly with deft flicks of his tongue. "I don't think I should risk trying to leave the country for a while yet. I'll phone Graham, if it's all right — when we've finished", he went on as he felt Richard respond to his nuzzling. "He'll know what to do. I'll get there some time before too much longer, but I don't want to take unnecessary risks." He devoted his full concentration to what he was doing, and there was no more conversation for some time.

Afterwards he rang Graham. When he explained where he was Graham insisted on ringing off and calling him back to spare the Fitzjohns' phone bill, and Stephen was at last able to give him a full account of what had happened. Graham agreed with Richard that Hill senior had been pretty generous in general, but had put himself deeply into the wrong by resorting to blackmail. "That's what it amounts to", he said. "Of course, he's talking about something he knows very little. I should think it's quite possible that there's no extradition possible for the offence involved. Added to that there's the fact that France is a civilized country. The age of consent here is fifteen, for us as well as for heteros. They think we're fucking mad — not only about our imbecile hang-ups about sex, of course, but about them among other things certainly. So I should think it's more than possible that the French would refuse to extradite for what they would regard as non-criminal activity. But I don't know. Maybe I can find out. If I do I'll let you know.

"Now, I don't want you to take risks. We'll be together in the not too distant future, of that I'm as sure as you are. And we've waited and tortured ourselves for so long recently that a few more weeks won't be any great extra hardship. Much better to wait than for you to take a chance and stir up a hornets' nest with your father.

"Let's talk about other things. First of all, the news this end is good. I told you I thought there was a job for me in Strasbourg.

Well, there was, and there is, and I've got it. I came here, rather than all the other nice places in this country, because there's an old friend of mine — chap I was at Cambridge with — who runs a language school here. Well, I've talked to him, and he's offered me a post teaching English, and some French as well. The pay's lower than I was getting at the school, but the work's a bloody sight less demanding — none of the out-of-hours chores I had at school. Cost of living's a lot lower here than in England, too. I'll actually be rather better off than before. Plenty of money to keep me and toy-boy in reasonable comfort." He chuckled at Stephen's snort of mock-affront.

"So we're all fixed up on that front. Now, I wonder if you'll do something for me, love."

"I'll do anything, you know that", said Stephen earnestly.

"Right. Well, will you give old Bill a ring, then, and ask him to bung my name in the availability book for the weekend after next, please?"

"Yes, of course I..." It took a moment for what he had said to register on Stephen's mind. When it did he almost dropped the telephone. "WHAT did you say?"

"I'm going to be around, sweetie. Just for a couple of days. The agent's written to say he's got a buyer for my flat, so I've got to come back to crate up all my things. And as it's in the cricket season, and I'm missing the game desperately, I'd like to get a couple of games in. Tell him I'll even play for Paddy Hayward's bunch of cripples and lend 'em a bit of class, if there's no room for me elsewhere." He chuckled again, enjoying sharing his good news. As for Stephen, he was too delighted by the joyous surprise to be able to speak for a time. When he did he poured such a torrent of rapture and affection down the line that Graham's mood sobered immediately. "You're a good kid", he said, and his voice sounded a little choky. He also, Stephen thought, sounded a lot younger than he had ever sounded in earlier days.

"Graham, will we...will we be able to...?" He said jerkily.

"Yes, I reckon we should be all right. We'll have to be *bloody* careful, but I think I can work something. We'll sort it out before the matches, or after them, whatever. I'll be taking a trip to London while I'm over. Think about it in the meantime, and see if you can work things so you can come with me. I want to visit poor old Reggie again. I phoned him this morning after you rang, and he's not doing so well. He's had a bit of a relapse, and he's pretty poorly. I'd like to see how he is.

"Anyway, that's the news, and I think I'd better ring off now, or the profit on my flat'll all go on the phone bill here. Take care of your sweet self, love, and think of me occasionally", he added mischievously, chuckling once more at Stephen's squeak of protestation.

"Seriously, love, I'd better get off. I've got things to do. Give my love to Richard, and tell him he's invited to be our second long-stay visitor — second only to Reggie. Don't forget I love you, and I'll look forward to seeing you Saturday week. I aim to go straight to the club — be there about opening time. Okay? Right. Love you." He made a loud kissing noise into the phone, and hung up, leaving Stephen hugging himself gleefully and feeling as if he was cocooned in a warm, golden mist.

When he had finished rejoicing he went and found Richard, who, with his customary delicate tact, had left him alone in the room with the telephone, and passed on Graham's message. Richard was very pleased, though a little subdued by the realization that he was going to lose his beloved Stephen again for a while soon, and probably permanently in the fairly close future. But he cheered up quickly with his usual resilience, and when Stephen suggested going out for a drink he agreed readily. "I haven't got much money, though", he said dolefully after feeling in his pocket.

"Have it on me", said Stephen cheerfully. "I'm a wealthy man all of a sudden, remember. Do you mind if we go to the cricket club? I'd like to put Graham in the book." Richard grinned his agreement, and they set off.

Bill McKechnie's large, bristling eyebrows bristled their way up his forehead in surprise as he turned and saw who had arrived at the bar beside him. "Bloody hell", he said, digging in his pocket and bringing a fistful of change out. "You back again, like a bad penny? What happened to gay Paree? Hallo", he added, giving Richard a nod and a smile.

"It's a long story", grinned Stephen, "which I'll be delighted to tell you, if you've got half an hour to spare."

Bill bought them drinks and insisted on hearing the story of Stephen's misadventures. "Hmm", he grunted when Stephen finished. "I must say, I think your old man's treated you pretty decently. I'd've put my boot up your arse, to the fourth lace-hole, if it'd been me. Christ!" he exclaimed as a thought struck him. "You never said anything about nicking half his fortune when you were telling me about burgling your own house, did you? It was only your passport you were going back for, wasn't it, you crafty little monkey? I reckon you're a danger to respectable people, young Steve. I'm not sure you're safe for law-abiding citizens to be seen in company with." But he winked at Richard as he said it, and slapped Stephen on the back, almost knocking him out of his chair. "You'd better have another drink", he said, and pushed Stephen back into his seat when he proffered his wealth. "I'm not taking any of that", he said, making a sign of the cross with his index fingers as if warding off a vampire. "Eleven policemen'd probably appear outa the wood-work an chuck me in the fuckin Lubianka for drinkin stolen property, or livin off immoral earnins or some such." He galloped off to the bar leaving Stephen and Richard grinning.

"Can you do something for me, Bill?" said Stephen when he got back with the fresh drinks.

"No I bloody well can't", cried Bill in alarm. "You're not safe to do things for. I don't wanna be arrested."

"It's only to put a name in the availability book for someone" said Stephen, laughing. "He asked me to pass the message on to you."

"Oh", said Bill. "That sounds harmless enough. But things ain't always as innocent as they seem, are they Stevie?" he went on suspiciously. "Who is it? Ronnie Biggs? Son of Sam? Boston Strangler? The Kray brothers maybe?" He blew his cheeks out aggrievedly when they laughed. "Well it's bound to be some fuckin criminal, isn't it? I don't suppose you know anybody respectable except me."

"It's Graham Curtis", said Stephen, laughing.

"What! Is he coming back as well?" wailed Bill. "As if one bad penny's not bad enough you gotta bring your accomplice back as well. Stone me, if you can cause as much chaos and confusion as you do on your own, what the hell will the two of you do between you? Christ, we'll be murdered in our beds."

But he put Graham's name down for the two games of the weekend after next. "Will you be speaking to him again, do you know?" he asked, giving Stephen a reassuring smile.

"I don't know", said Stephen, "but I should think it's more than likely."

"Well, tell him he's playing for me, both days, if you do, would you? He's too good to waste on Pat. That's away at Teddington on Saturday and here against Enfield on Sunday, both eleven-thirty starts. Two tough ones." He turned to Richard. "Why don't you take an interest, son?" he suggested. "Put a bit a colour in your cheeks."

"I'm no good at cricket", said Richard. "I've never played it, except with the rabbits at school. Scoring's about the only thing I'm any good at, but..."

"Christ!" squawked Bill. "You're a scorer? Why the hell didn't you tell me, Steve? You move among international terrorists, master criminals and drug addicts and all the time you know a scorer. Why didn't you bring him along before?"

"I didn't know", protested Stephen.

"Well you should've known. Christ, we've been desperate for a scorer for three seasons. I'da paid cash money for a decent one, and all the time there's been one on our doorstep. Cor!" He rounded on Richard. "Will you score for us? You get a free tea, lunch on all-day games and all the beer you can drink afterwards." He got up and bounded to the bar before Richard could open his mouth, and returned with a thick scorebook in a dark-green leather loose-leaf binder. "Here, look at this. You could keep a neater book than this, couldn't you?" he said, showing Richard the most recent sheet. "This is what happens when you haven't got a scorer", he went on. "This was cobbled together by half a dozen of our blokes while they were waiting to bat. Half of 'em can't do joined-up writing yet, and the half who can are all fuckin doctors. Except Colin Preston, and I think he's a Russian spy — he seems to write in code. An illiterate Russian spy, at that, I should think. And then when we field, the opposition batsmen do it, and by the looks of this they're all Russian spies. Will you do it?"

"Well...", said Richard.

"Great!" said Bill. "Have a drink. Now, who've we got this Saturday? Let me see." He fished a fixture card out of his breast pocket. "Yeah, Bishop's Stortford away on Saturday, eleven-thirty start. They're a nice crowd. You'll like em. Can you be here at ten sharp?"

"Er, well, yes, I suppose..."

"Great. Gimme your glass. You drive?"

"Well, I haven't got a car of my own, but I might be able to borrow mother's..."

"There's always lifts available, anyway. You just turn up here at ten. We'll fix you up. Your mate here'll be playin, if Interpol haven't picked him up by then." He seized their glasses and went to the bar yet again.

Richard glanced a little quizzically at Stephen, looking a bit shell-shocked. "I think it's known as 'volunteering'", grinned Stephen. "I want three volunteers — you, you and you."

The rest of the evening went by happily and with startling rapidity. Bill eventually allowed Stephen to spend a little of his money. Then he introduced Richard to numerous other members, as proudly as if he had produced him personally like a rabbit from a top hat, and the boys went merrily and a little unsteadily home at eleven o'clock. Although Stephen had begun the day angry and dejected, he ended it happy and relaxed.

***

The days passed quickly. Richard was determined to extract the greatest possible amount of pleasure from Stephen's company as he could, against the day he dreaded when his beloved friend would walk away and not return. They were almost literally inseparable, except for the occasional evening when Stephen went to spend some time with his parents, and the intervals between such visits grew longer as Stephen's mother became less and less welcoming, more and more frigid and unsmiling. His father took him aside after the last visit before Graham was due to return. "I'm going to take her away for a weekend by the sea", he confided to Stephen. "She's taken this trouble of yours far more to heart than I ever suspected she would. I'm afraid it's cut her up very badly. I think it might be a good idea if you were to stay away, just for a while, you know. Maybe we could meet for a drink now and then, for a while, do you think?" His expression as he said it was wistful and a little sad, and Stephen felt a sharp pang of love for his father, and also a stab of remorse for earlier misunderstandings, impatience and occasional deceit.

With his parents and the dangers they represented providentially out of the way, Graham's return was a joyful reunion for them both. He made Richard's acquaintance, and the two got on well, though both were a little guarded. As if to make up for lost time, or perhaps to give himself something to look back on in his cricketless future, Graham celebrated his brief return to the cricket club by scoring a handsome, quick-fire fifty against Teddington, and capped it by making his first century for the club, scoring fluently all round the wicket and not offering a ghost of a chance, against Enfield the following day. In that match Stephen, as if galvanized by the presence of his beloved, took five wickets for the first time, and ensured a fine victory against a very strong side.

During the after-match drink-up, Bill came over to where Graham, Stephen and Richard were sitting chatting, Graham and Stephen enjoying a break from doing the rounds with the jugs they had had to buy. "Had an idea, Graham", he said. "As you're living on the Continent now, are you interested in the tour? We're going to Holland this year. You're nearer than any of us."

They all took notice, Graham and Stephen having forgotten all about the tour amid all their other excitements recently. Graham's face lit up briefly, only to fall a moment later when Bill read off the dates. "No", he groaned, "I can't make it. I've got to be in Strasbourg that whole week. It's the week before I start my new job, and I've got all sorts of induction courses and so on to get through. Blast it. What a pity."

"What about you, Biggsy?" asked Bill, turning to Stephen and using the nickname he had bestowed on him after the conversation in the pavilion. He only used it occasionally, and sportingly kept it to himself, to save Stephen from having to make difficult explanations.

"Biggsy?" queried Graham, and had to have it explained to him by Bill to an accompaniment of titters from the two boys.

Stephen looked at Richard. "Can you come?" he mouthed privately. Richard nodded quickly. He had taken to his new duties with keen enjoyment, despite his supposed and often-enunciated contempt for the game; and he had become instantly popular in the club for his choirboy looks, his friendly disposition and his quick, mischievous intelligence and wit. "Yeah, I'm in", said Stephen. "Me too", added Richard. "Good", said Bill, ticking their names on his list with satisfaction. "Pity you can't make it Graham. Still, there'll be other tours." He wandered off to ask the others.

**

The tour had been a resounding success, with two fine wins and two by no means discreditable defeats against very powerful Dutch sides and an excellent draw against Flamingoes, the strongest side of all. On the final night, in the Hague, the revels went on even later than the normal retiring hour of four in the morning. The Dutch players, including many from the other four sides they had played, accompanied them back to their hotel, stayed up to see them off in the morning and generally outdrank all but the hardest-headed few.

At a very late hour Stephen and Richard slipped away and went to bed together. It was a sad occasion, for Richard, alone among the touring party, knew what Stephen was going to do later that morning, when the sun was up, and even his sunny disposition was not proof against the depression that his knowledge had induced.

They made love violently, furiously. Then they lay curled in each other's arms for a while, then did it again, this time passionately but gently, with great tenderness, as Stephen tried to say with his strong, shapely body what he could not say in words. Every time they tried to speak to each other, lying entwined in a fierce, desperate embrace in the Dutch hotel room, they choked, unable to speak for tears.

At last they dressed again and went back downstairs to rejoin the milling throng of cricketers in the bar. Nearly everyone was drunk by this time, so neither their absence nor their return had been noticed. Bill McKechnie, who was among the hardest-headed drinkers, noticed both, put two and two together and successfully completed the sum, but Bill was a very kind man, and looked away before they could catch his eye and see that he knew. No-one else was focussing clearly enough to notice the dry streaks of tear-tracks on their faces — though if they had they would undoubtedly have ascribed them to maudlin inebriation rather than the unguessable real cause.

When the boys had consoled each other with a few more drinks than were good for them, Stephen slipped away again, leaving Richard staring unhappily into a glass of very strong beer. He went first to the room he had shared with Richard, in which he had so lately been making passionate love to him. He took his old windcheater from the wardrobe and slipped it on. He unzipped his holdall and took from it three letters that he had written on the hotel's stationery the night before. He sat on the bed, slipped them out of their envelopes and read them through quickly. Then he put them back in the envelopes, licked and sealed them. He took one of the letters, with RICHARD in heavy black felt-tip on the envelope, and propped it against the shaving mirror, beside Richard's toothbrush. The other two he slipped into his pocket. He got up, had a quick scout round the room to make sure he had forgotten nothing, picked up his holdall in one hand and his cricket bag in the other, and went quickly out into the corridor.

He went first to Bill's room and tried the door. It was locked. Taking the two letters from his windcheater pocket, he selected one, stooped and slid it under the door. Then he went quickly to the lift and went down to reception. The clerk on night duty sold him a stamp and showed him the box for outgoing mail. He put the stamp on the envelope marked with his father's name and address, and dropped it in the box.

***

Dear Bill,

This is just a note to tell you not to worry when you find that I'm not among the party when you all go back to the Hook for the ferry this morning, and to explain why — though I don't think you will need to have it explained. I am, of course, going to join Graham in Strasbourg.

I want to tell you also how greatly I have enjoyed this tour, and all my time with the club. It has been one of the pleasantest experiences of my life, and one of the happiest times. The friendship and welcome I have received from everyone has been simply wonderful, and nothing I could write in this note could begin to say a hundredth part of what I feel.

I shall miss everybody, but, apart from Richard of course, most of all I shall miss you. Your kindnesses have been so numerous and so generously given that I could spend a month trying to thank you for every one of them. Instead, just accept a blanket, once-and-for-all, and heartfelt Thank you.

I shall be writing as soon as I have arrived and settled in, and it would be very nice to hear from you with news of the club once in a while. Don't forget me for next year's tour.

Look after Richard for me. He is going to need a lot of kindness for a time. I suspect that you know why.

I am enclosing some money. Part of it is for my subscription to the club for next season — I want to have the fixture card, and I really do want to come on next year's tour. There will be ten pounds over, which I want you to spend on a jug when you all get home. Please make sure everyone has a drink on me.

Please give my regards to Christine, and thank her for being so very kind to me.

I shall see you all again, probably fairly soon, and maybe one day G and I will be able to return to England and play for you again like honest men. (What? Biggsy, honest?) In the meantime, I'm going to miss you all terribly, and I shall never forget you.

Your friend,
Steve

***

Dearest Dad,

This is one of the two most difficult letters I have
ever had to write, or ever will have to, I believe.
The cricket tour I told you about is over, and I am
not coming back.

I know that you would have no trouble guessing
why, so I won't even try to hide the fact — I'm
going to be with Graham in France. But I'd like you
to believe me when I say that I wouldn't have tried
to deceive you about this even if I had thought it
could be done. The days of my wishing to deceive
you are over.

I know what you and Mother think about my
relationship with Graham, and about my sexuality
in general. I still have a very vivid memory of those
terrible days when there was such bitter
misunderstanding between us. You were right to
say that time that I'd grown away from you and
Mother very far and very fast. But I think you will
agree that you and I at least have grown back
together at least part of the way, and a pretty long
part of it, I'd say. I can tell you that something has
happened to me between then and now: I've grown
up. I'm not a boy any longer. I think I'm a man
now, and I hope a reasonably decent one. If I am, I
owe most of it to you. A little of it is due to the
cricket club, much more of it to Graham, but most
of it I owe to you. You said that time in the dining
room that I probably thought you were a silly old
fuddy-duddy — something to that effect. Well, Dad,
what I actually think of you is that you're a kind,
generous and good man, and as good a father as
anyone could be fortunate enough to have.
Graham told me a joke, which he says is very old —
he said that when he was sixteen he thought his
father was a silly old bastard, and when he was
twenty-one he was amazed to see how much his dad
had learned in that short time.

I know you said when we had that heart-to-heart talk that if you found I was having anything to do with Graham you'd go to the police and have him arrested and extradited. Well, as a matter of fact, you can't, so Graham says. He's been making enquiries and it seems that the French would refuse to extradite someone for the technical offence he committed by having a sexual relationship with me. But, Dad, I'm not afraid that you'll do what you said, because I don't think, somehow, that you will do it, or even that you ever meant to do it, even at the time when you said it.

The first reason I think that is that I've learned a lot about you in the last few months. I think that goes for both of us — I think we've gained a much better understanding of each other. In a strange way I think Mother's violent reaction against me has fostered it to some extent. I'm very sorry about her attitude, but if it's brought us closer together it has at least had one unexpected good side-effect. I still hope that one day she will come to accept me as what I am, as you seem to me to have done lately.

The other reason why I don't believe you'd ever put your threat into effect is because I believe you have seen yourself that growing-up which I talked about just now. I think you, too, realize that I'm a grown-up man now. And I think, just as we've come to like each other a lot better than at any other time lately, we've formed a much deeper respect for each other, too. I think you would respect my judgment; or at least, I think you would respect my word, when I give it: and I give you my word that what I feel for Graham is not infatuation, not mere sexual attraction or lust, but love, real, deep and powerful. He's a good man, strong, honourable, dependable and just. And he is trustworthy as only two other people I have ever known have been trustworthy: Richard Fitzjohn and you. He loves me, and he respects me, as a person, and I owe it to him to give him the love he deserves.

That's why I'm going to him, Dad, and what I've said earlier is why I dare to ask you to give me your blessing. I'd still go to him if you refused, because I have to go to him; but I would like your blessing, if you can give it.

I'm not doing it this way — simply not coming back from abroad — to give you the slip, but for another reason. I can't go into it, because it involves another person's privacy, which must be respected, but I can tell you that it is to do with Richard. In any case, I shall be telephoning very soon, to ask you how you feel after reading this letter; and if your reaction is as I hope it will be, I'll come back to England to see you soon after that.

For now, though, Dad, this is not goodbye, but *au revoir*. I hope Mother cheers up and that you can get back to enjoying life and have some fun. Meanwhile, I think of you, and always with the greatest liking and respect. So, for now, much love, your affectionate son and, I hope, still your friend,

Stephen

***

My darling Richard,

I've just said at the beginning of a letter to my Dad that it was one of the two most difficult letters I had ever had to write or would ever have to. This one to you is, without doubt, THE most difficult.

The letter to Dad was a very long one, because I had a lot to say. This one to you is going to be very short, because I've got too much to say, and most of it is unsayable. We say what we've got to say to each other best in languages other than words.

All it amounts to, dearest Richard, is this. I love

you, and I shall always love you, more than I have
ever loved or ever could love any other living soul,
bar one — and I don't love even Graham any more
than I love you. Just in different ways. Why do I
choose him rather than you — which, by the way, is
the most terrible, impossible decision I have ever
had to make, or hope ever to have to? A single
reason: Graham loves me, and so do you. But he
NEEDS me, in a way I don't think you do. And I
need to be needed. You'll miss me, but you'll
recover. He would miss me, and I don't think he'd
love again. I think I'm his last chance, and I only
hope it isn't too immodest of me to say that. I don't
know if I'm making the right decision. I have to
hope so. If I'm making the wrong one, and you're
still there, I'll come back and ask you if you'll have
me. I don't think I deserve you, and I'm sure you
deserve better. I hope you find him, as I hope that
you are showered all your life with every blessing
you deserve.

That's it, my dearest Richard. You are the best
fun I've ever had, the sexiest companion, most
generous lover and kindest, truest, sweetest friend.
I shall love you as long as I live. I know it isn't
enough.

Bless you,
Stevie

***

He stood for a moment, looking down at the slit through which
he had dropped his letter to his father. Then he picked up his
cricket bag and holdall from the floor of the lobby and walked
quickly through the revolving door to the street.. It was light
outside, on a bright, fair morning. He had looked out the route
through the streets, and set off with a long, purposeful stride for
the station. As he turned the first corner he could still hear, very
faintly from the hotel, the sound of the cricketers, singing.

THE GAY MEN'S PRESS COLLECTION,
bringing back into print some favourite books from
The Gay Men's Press

Mike Seabrook
UNNATURAL RELATIONS

For Jamie Potten, burdened at fifteen with the bullying
father and an uncaring mother, his encounter with nineteen-year-old Chris brings solace and joy. Chris's love
for Jamie, however, leads to his prosecution for 'buggery with a minor', with the threat of a heavy prison
sentence. In this gripping yet tender story of two oung
people facing together a brutal assault on their human
rights, Mike Seabrook highlights the iniquitous position
of gay teenagers under English law.

"I loved the book" — Jilly Cooper
"Sensitive, masterful, fascinating"   Joseph Wambaugh

ISBN 0 85449 116 3
£8.95

THE GAY MEN'S PRESS COLLECTION

Christopher Bram
HOLD TIGHT

When Hank Fayette, Seaman Second Class, uses his shore leave to visit a movie house on 42nd Street, he ends up in a gay brothel near Manhattan's West Street piers, and is caught in a raid by the Shore Patrol. But it's 1942, a few months after Pearl Harbour, and the US Navy sends Hank back to the brothel to entrap Nazi agents.

"Very funny, fast moving... captures the tensions between blacks and whites and gays and non-gays in the New York of the period" — *Publishers' Weekly*

ISBN 0 85449 132 5
UK £8.95 (not for sale in North America)

Christopher Bram
SURPRISING MYSELF

Joel and Corey try to build a life together in 1980s New York, amid the challenges and pitfalls of the gay scene, and the problems of work and family. A subtle and intricate depiction of human relationships.

"An extremely impressive performance"
— *Christopher Street*

"Bram writes like an angel" — *The Advocate*

ISBN 0 85449 130 9
£9.95 (not for sale in North America)

Quality new fiction from The Gay Men's Press

Richard Zimler
UNHOLY GHOSTS

A classical guitar teacher from New York seeks a new life in Portugal after the death of so many friends. But the viral eclipse over sexuality pursues him even there, when Antonio, his talented and beloved student, tests HIV-positive and threatens to give up on life. Desperate to show the young man that he still has a future, 'the Professor' arranges a car trip to Paris, hoping to be able to convince a leading virtuoso there to begin preparing his protégé for a concert career. Antonio's father Miguel, a stonemason by trade, insists in coming along with them, and en route the three fall into a triangle of adventure, personal disclosure, violence, and at last a strange redemption.

Wittily funny and deeply moving, *Unholy Ghosts* was written with the support of the US National Endowment for the Arts.

ISBN 0 85449 233 X
£9.95

Noel Currer-Briggs
YOUNG MEN AT WAR

Anthony Arthur Kildwick, born in 1919 to a well-to-do English family, finds the love of his life in a German exchange student at his private school. When Manfred returns to Germany he is seduced by Hitler's nationalist rhetoric, while Tony meets the outbreak of war as a conscientious objector. Yet as the Nazi regime shows itself ever more demonic, Tony decides he must fight, and is parachuted into southern France to work with the Resistance. He discovers Manfred is now an officer with the occupying forces, and their paths cross again in dramatic circumstances.

Based largely on the author's own experience, this fascinating story conveys a vivid sense of the conflicts of the 1930s, and the interplay between friendship and internationalism, homosexuality and pacifism, patriotism and democracy, that was characteristic of those years.

ISBN 0 85449 236 4
£8.95

Rudi van Dantzig
FOR A LOST SOLDIER

During the winter of 1944 in occupied Amsterdam, eleven-year-old Jeroen is evacuated to a tiny fishing community on the desolate coast of Friesland, where he meets Walt, a young Canadian soldier with the liberating forces. Their relationship immerses the young boy in a tumultuous world of emotional and sexual experience, suddenly curtailed when the Allies move on and Walt goes away. Back home in Amsterdam, a city in the throes of liberation fever, Jeoren searches for the soldier he has lost. A child's fears and confused emotions have rarely been described with such penetration and openness, and seen as it is from the child's viewpoint it invites total empathy.

This novel by the artistic director of the Dutch National Ballet appeared successfully in hardback in 1991, and was made into a prize-wining film.

"A literary happening, not soon to be forgotten"
— *NRC Handelsblad*

ISBN 0 85449 237 2
£9.95

Gay Men's Press books can be ordered from any bookshop in the UK, North America, Australia and South Africa, and from specialised bookshops elsewhere.

If you prefer to order by mail, please send cheque or postal order payable to *Book Works* for the full retail price plus £2.00 postage and packing to:

Book Works (Dept. B), PO Box 3821, London N5 1UY
phone/fax: (0171) 609 3427

For payment by Access/Eurocard/Mastercard/American Express/ Visa, please give number, expiry date and signature.

Name and address in block letters please:

Name
_____

Address
_____

_____

_____